Beyond Beautiful

Jan Bornstein

back channel press
portsmouth new hampshire
www.backchannelpress.com

BACK CHANNEL PRESS
170 Mechanic Street
Portsmouth, NH 03801
www.backchannelpress.com

Printed in the United States of America

Cover artwork by Matthew Pippin
Cover design by Cecile Kaufmann
Book layout by Nancy Grossman

Library of Congress Control Number 2006933267

Dedication

To my cousin Evie. I need not say more.

Acknowledgements

First and foremost I have to extend my deepest gratitude to my editor, Nancy Grossman, who worked so very hard on this book. She saw my vision and had enough faith in both myself and the story to help me put it all together. To Back Channel Press for their guidance, patience and kindness in making this publication possible, I give sincere thanks.

I want to express my gratitude to Cecile Kaufman and Matthew Pippin for helping me make my idea for the cover a reality.

For their contributions of pictures, advice, research, assistance and friendship, special thanks go to Debbie Alexander, who has become a great friend; to Michelle Cairol, another acquired good friend; and to Tammy Carter, someone I have known for years, through good times and bad.

Finally, I cannot forget new friendships, support and encouragement from Suzanne Walsh and Scott Stunzenas from Mt. Blue, who have been there for me through this amazing time. Thank you both.

Chapter 1

JENNA BRADFORD HATED her piano lessons. She loved the beautiful baby grand piano her parents had given her for her ninth birthday, and she loved Deirdre, her teacher, who appeared regular as clockwork every Saturday at 10:15. She loved music. She didn't even mind the regimen of practice, practice, practice. Never afraid of hard work, she was ambitious from an early age. No, what she hated was the regimen of practice – on music that didn't excite her. The music that did excite her, from her earliest awareness of tune and tempo, lyrics and beat, was rock 'n roll. Having an older brother with similar inclinations, money for tickets and an extraordinary willingness to let his kid sister tag along, helped her taste in music mature faster than many of her friends.

Jenna Bradford, daughter of Robert Bradford, the actor, and Linda Huntington Bradford, the model turned socialite, narrowly avoided being subjected to a typically lax and luxuriously stultifying Beverly Hills childhood. Bob Bradford, for all his leading man suavity and swooning fans, was a down-to-earth, caring father. Linda Bradford took all her charities profoundly personally. If asked, Jenna could recount a pretty normal childhood – if you didn't count those two years when her mother left her father, for Jenna years twelve to fourteen.

BEFORE SHE'D FINISHED high school, Jenna was well along the path to becoming a beautiful woman and a professional musician. She'd never play Chopin at the Hollywood Bowl, but she enjoyed sitting at her piano by the hour, totally immersed in belting out the songs of the day and compositions of her own. By the time she was sixteen, both an acoustic and an electric guitar sat in stands by the piano. Her wardrobe was already a pastiche of black leather, metallic spandex and gaudy silks and satins, and her hair had run the gamut, from an iridescent blond to jet black, and every shade known to Clairol in between. When it came time for college, U.S.C. honed her interest in and talents for both pop music and the industry that produced it. Maggie James, her roommate freshman year, played drums for Chick Cheeks, an all-bad-girl band who performed in slinky black, lips and faces painted white, spiky hair that might be green one night, yellow the next and ultramarine the night after that. When their lead singer graduated, Jenna was quickly drafted to replace her.

To celebrate college graduation, the Cheeks cut a CD and took to the road in a beat up 22-foot motorhome. Hop-scotching across the country, calling ahead to book gigs wherever they could, they sold enough CDs to keep the gas tank full and get them to the next club, bar or grange hall, ending up with a few club dates in New York, which was how Jenna and guitarist Mark Newsom first connected. Blown away by what he'd heard one night, he invited her to sit in with his band the next day, an invitation she jumped at. Cheeks was fine for starters, but Jenna Bradford had bigger aspirations. The New York club scene was definitely a great launching pad for a career.

A couple of years and bands later, Jenna was ready to come back and tackle L.A. on her own terms. A year working back-up gave her time to put together her own band, with Mark at the helm on lead guitar and Maggie in the driver's seat on drums. Jenna left her own guitars at home. When she strode out on a stage, all legs and attitude, all she wanted to do was sing and strut what local entertainment writers were beginning to mention as particularly spectacular stuff. Brian Mason, an up-and-comer in the business, signed on as manager and quickly inked a recording deal with CGM. *Jenna B Live*, the group's first CD, made it to number 2 on the charts. The year was 1992. Jenna was 25. Hit followed hit. The industry recognized her with a Grammy in 1994 for Best New Group. As arresting as she was on stage, she was even more so on video; she was soon staple fare on MTV. Her professional life was as good as it gets.

Her personal life, Jenna would insist perhaps a bit too vehemently, was also as good as it gets. For a rock star, anyway. As she tiptoed over that invisible divide between her twenties and her thirties, she'd yet to sustain a meaningful relationship in her over-hectic, over-scheduled, over-committed life. Career came first; charity and benefit work, based on a sense of social responsibility she greatly respected in her mother, dovetailed neatly with that career. Everything else took a back seat, and that was okay. At least until Maggie, barely concealing her excitement, broke the news that she was pregnant, she was getting married and she was moving to Louisiana.

✳

SCOTT TENNY'S CAREER had been nothing short of textbook meteoric. From the earliest garage band days, success built on success as bands formed, reformed, melded and flowed into what would, one hung-over morning in Boston, finally take on the name 'Blacklace.'

"Oh man, what do we got here?" Dan snagged something silky from a trail of hastily discarded clothing and twirled it over his head. "Could this be a pair of ladies' unmentionables? I enter into evidence in the case of Sex, Drugs 'n'

Rock & Roll vs. the Puritan Empire of America, Exhibit A: one pair of black lace undies, ladies and gentlemen. Goin' once, goin' twice – Scotty, boy? Do I hear a bid? She's gonna need 'em." Dan Clark, guitar and comic relief, guaranteed to produce the first laugh of the day.

"Hey! That's it!" yelped Scott, sitting up and pushing aside the little groupie sprawled across him. "Blacklace! Yeah! That's it. Laaaaaadies and gentlemen, put 'em together for …Blacklace!" Scott Tenny – tall, skinny, rock-hard muscled, lead vocals, showman, wild-haired and wilder-dressed front man and babe-magnet – wrapped his lips around the name and savored it.

"Fits yer persona to a T," yawned Jeremy, running a hand through his own scroungy long black hair, the sum total of attention it would get that day. "But keep it down, man. You want to get me thrown outta here? I got neighbors, dude." Jeremy Sandborn. Lead guitar, vocals. Backup brain.

"Seventh name since Sunday," Tim all but whispered. "Gunna stick with this one?" Tim Knowleston, drummer. A huge guy who spoke softly – and carried a whole set of big sticks. Jeremy's find.

Scott staggered to his feet and gave the room a moment to stop spinning. "Blacklace. Hell, it works. Danny, my boy, you're a marketing genius. You just don't know it."

"He knows it," Jeff smirked. Jeff Aquino, back-up guitar. Dan's buddy from a previous band. "Name the band Blacklace and we'll never hear the last of what a marketing genius he is. Big mistake. You won't get my vote."

"Vote? Scott doesn't do democracy – or hadn't you heard? Scott's gonna call the band whatever he wants," Dan pointed out. No one contradicted him.

THAT WAS BACK in the days of heavy drugs, heavy alcohol and violently high times. Growing up Scott got a running start with booze in elementary school; by high school graduation, he was a heavy user of all manner of lethal pharmacologicals, which often posed a serious challenge to his ability to perform. Some who knew him well wondered if he harbored a death wish.

He didn't. He was just a volatile, hyperactive kid from a seemingly quiet town in the Lakes Region of New Hampshire who wanted to fuel a life lived square in the middle of the fast lane. He wasn't alone. A good-sized chunk of an entire generation ended up hanging out in this particularly dangerous lane – his entire band, just to mention a few.

A reckless electromagnet of a man with a craggy face that looked like it had been chiseled from New Hampshire granite, Scott had his pick of girls in every town or city they played. Both he and the others thought nothing of bringing a few frenetic fans backstage after the show, for a little blow and a blow job before hitting the road to their next gig. There wasn't much that escaped media attention. He incited criticism as much for his flamboyant dress and the gaudy scarves he tied on his microphone, as he did for his bad boy behavior. Local entertainment reporters always had something caustic to say about him in the wake of every performance.

His personal life spiked as high and low as his drug life. His first wife, the mother of his older daughter, Missy, found the drugs too much to deal with. A short fling with a singer he met in New York produced a second daughter, Laurel. As he and the rest of the band approached thirty, one by one they came to their senses about their drug consumption, and one by one, each cleaned up his act. Scott's second attempt at marriage was no more successful than his first, however. In spite of twelve years of sobriety, this marriage was also ending in divorce. AA had given him the courage to acknowledge the loving, compassionate man inside the bad boy, had given him faith in God, and had allowed him to express a deep caring for his daughters. It hadn't dampened his enormous appetites for either the music that fed his soul or for the women that music attracted, nor had it dampened a temper that could erupt out of nowhere like a violent summer storm. At forty-two, he could still play the spoiled brat with the best of them.

THE 'FIRST STEPS' show had gone brilliantly. The Southern California chapter of World Without Abuse held an annual benefit to fund its local spousal abuse shelters, and this being the entertainment capital of the world, had their pick of the best to headline their show. Jenna had been thrilled to be asked to perform, a star among stars, and she happily gave the select audience an over-the-top performance. The abuse of women and children moved and angered her far more than she could explain. She had cringed at the painful montage of images that opened the show; tears welled up at the closing montage of the brave and fortunate women and children who had found their way to WWA shelters, their first steps to a new life.

Looking across a sea of glittering celebrities at the black-tie dinner after the show, Jenna mused on the fact that this was all she had to pass for a social life these days. The next morning she'd be back on the road.

Turning, she found herself face to face with Oprah Winfrey, shimmering in silver lamé. "You were fabulous," Oprah gushed, reached for her and gave her a sisterly hug and air kiss.

"Thank you! Thank you *so* much!" beamed Jenna, looking old-fashioned drop-dead glamorous in a vintage '40s red silk crepe gown that clung to her tanned, toned curves like a second skin. Her long, thick mane of hair – Jenna had finally settled on its natural shade of brunette – hung loose and free and halfway down her back.

"How do you do it?" Oprah asked like a star-struck fan. On her it was endearing.

"How do *you* do what you do, day in, day out?" Jenna countered. "Actually, tell me what it's like –"

Jenna's words were cut short. One guest bumping into another created a chain reaction of mishaps, ending in a small tsunami of red wine sloshing from Jenna's glass – right onto Oprah's gown.

"Oh, no! I am so sorry!" Jenna gasped, reaching into her little red satin Kate Spade handbag for a tissue.

"Oh God, I'm sorry," echoed a deep voice behind her. "Here." Jenna turned to find the kind of man that black tie couldn't tame offering her a cocktail napkin.

"Scott Tenny!" exclaimed both women in unison. They both laughed.

"Ladies, I am *so* sorry," an endearingly red-faced Scott repeated. "Really. Oh, God, I can't believe I did that. I am such a total klutz."

"It's okay. If you'll excuse me, I'm going to get some water on this quick," said a hastily departing Oprah.

"Holy shit, that was so embarrassing!" Scott said. His mortification was genuine.

"That makes two of us," laughed Jenna. "Jenna Bradford." She put her hand out.

"You were great tonight! Don't worry, I know who *you* are. I've caught your show, several times, actually.

"Really?"

"Sure. Let's see. First time – um – I know, Greek Theatre. You were opening for – Kissamee Quick. Right?"

"Right! Wow. That was years ago."

"And the first time you saw me?" Scott asked, confident that of course she had.

"Oh, my God. Uhh…that would have to be – what was it called – Lingo? That club in Brentwood? Macon was playing – Jimmy Bondi's a friend of mine. You guys were there and they invited you up, and you like covered your own songs – it was hilarious. I'll never forget it."

"Man. I can barely remember it."

"Not surprising. You were wasted."

Scott chuckled ruefully. "I was always wasted. When was that?"

"Before I was legal to drink, I can tell you that. Fifteen, sixteen years ago?"

"Ancient history. That all had to end. I'll tell you –" He went serious. "I had to. It was straighten up or chance losing my band or my life. Or both. I finally woke up one day and realized I didn't want either to happen. Not that I was any guiding light. Hell, I was the last of us to see the light," he added ruefully.

"I gotta tell you – you do clean up good, Mr. Tenny," Jenna smiled, giving him a casual once-over.

"I'm rather proud of that, actually," Scott responded. "But don't worry. There's still plenty of wickedness in the ol' boy yet. Care to sit down?" he asked, gesturing to a nearby table.

"Don't mind a bit. These shoes are killing me," Jenna laughed. Scott pulled out a chair for her with a gallant bow. She dropped into it gratefully.

Scott's version of sitting down could qualify as an aerobic activity. No part of the man remained still for more than a few seconds at a time. The net effect on those sitting with him ran the gamut from mesmerizing to exhausting. Jenna found the man and his restless, almost feral level of energy entirely riveting. She sensed a mind that wanted to range as freely as the body did, and could only imagine the endless effort required to keep this body and soul functional and functioning.

Five minutes into conversing with him, she felt she'd way more than met her match.

AN HOUR OF shop talk would have gone on much longer if Mark hadn't stopped by to remind Jenna of her early departure the next morning.

"Yeah. Denver," Jenna explained to Scott with a sigh. "My coach is turning into a pumpkin. I gotta go."

"May I escort you to your pumpkin, Ms. Bradford?" Scott offered.

"Why, of course, Mr. Tenny," Jenna purred. This was fun.

As they approached a modest eight-passenger limo, the driver jumped out and opened the door for Jenna.

"My goodness," said Scott in mock awe. "You weren't kidding. You really do have a coach."

"Thank you, Randy," Jenna said to the chauffeur who was grinning at her. "It's Daddy's," she said by way of explanation, turning back to Scott. "I just have it for tonight."

Scott suddenly, impetuously leaned over, pulled her to him and gave her a surprisingly gentle, unrushed kiss. "I'm going to have you in my life some day, Jenna Bradford, so I'd suggest you do *not* forget that kiss." Jenna stared, her dark brown eyes wide open, smiled and stepped into the car. Scott held her gaze for a long moment, then stood back for Randy to close the door.

"Home, Randy," Scott addressed the bemused chauffeur, who snapped a salute.

Watching the car drive away, Scott suddenly realized he wasn't kidding about what he'd just said. He had been aware of Jenna Bradford for quite a while, as both a fellow musician and as a woman. Now that he'd met her, he recognized that it was nothing short of love at first sight.

"Damn. I actually meant every word!" he marveled as he turned and half walked, half moonwalked his way back inside.

JENNA AWOKE EARLY the next morning to pack before meeting up with the band. Staying at her parents' had saved her the long drive back to her own place in Santa Monica and another slog back to the airport this morning.

The door bell rang early. "Mi dios! What is thees, a whole flower shop?" Jenna heard Adella, her mother's housekeeper, exclaim.

Linda and Jenna converged on the front door simultaneously, Jenna still in a pair of silk tank-topped pajamas. "What on earth?" Linda gasped. Two uniformed delivery men stood on the doorstep, each holding two dozen roses. Each dozen, a different shade of pink, held an envelope. Linda reached for the nearest. "Why, they're for you, hon," she said, handing the envelope over to her daughter.

"Who knows I'm here?" Jenna wondered out loud, sweeping her disheveled hair back into a knot.

"Open it!" urged her mother, taking the flowers from one delivery man. Adella reached for the rest.

"Well? Who are they from, sweetie? Don't keep me guessing," Linda demanded impatiently. Jenna told her. The name Scott Tenny didn't ring a bell.

"He's a rock singer. You've heard of Blacklace? I met him last night."

"Black – lace?" Linda said tentatively.

"Blacklace. They're really big."

"And he's sending you – four dozen roses? Just like that?"

"Beats me. He knocked into me, I got wine all over Oprah Winfrey and we talked."

"You – talked."

"We talked. And, okay, he kissed me. Actually, he said I was going to be in his life, if you must know."

"Well, I'd say you have an admirer, my dear. And, judging by the look on your face – I'd have to say you seem a bit bemused yourself."

"Mother, please! I just met him, for God sakes. I've seen him perform and I've heard a heck of a lot about him, but I only just met him last night. Don't get excited. He has a reputation for grand gestures like this – and a whole lot more.."

Before Linda could respond, the doorbell rang again. "I'll get it this time, Adella," she called and answered it herself. Standing on the doorstep was a tall, spare and long-haired, handsome man who simply said, "You must be Mrs. Bradford. I'm Scott Tenny. Is Jenna still here?"

"She is – she is indeed. Come in, come in." Smiling, she gestured for him to follow her to the kitchen, where Jenna was trying to find enough vases for the flowers.

Jenna turned as Linda and Scott entered the room. "Scott?! What are you doing here?" she blurted.

Without a word, Scott crossed the kitchen, took her shoulders in his hands and kissed her for the second time.

"I just couldn't let you head out of town without seeing you again," a simple, tip-of-the-iceberg explanation that hardly addressed the depth of his feelings. Jenna stood speechless. He stared into her eyes, reached up and touched her cheek, then grinned at the sight of all the flowers he had sent. "Like 'em?"

"They're beautiful, Scott. Thank you. Can I ask – why four dozen?"

"I dunno. The guy asked me how many. I said four dozen. What can I say?" He smiled down at her, his jumpy hands clenching and releasing her shoulders.

"Excuse me, you two," Linda said tactfully and left them to talk.

"Jenna – how long are you heading out for?"

"Three weeks. Denver, Chicago…"

"I – I know this sounds – I'm going to miss you. I'd come catch up with you, spend time with you if I could, but I can't. We go back into the studio for rehearsals tomorrow. We're cutting a new CD, then we're right out on another tour. You know how it is."

"And it's really just as well. You know how hectic it's gonna be for me, too." He nodded.

"That's the beauty of it," he said. "Neither of us has to explain anything. We both – know."

"Yeah, well – yeah," she said, smiling ruefully. "But look, Scott – I've gotta say this. I loved talking to you last night. It was great, getting to know you a bit and all. But – you're still married. For all I know, you could go back to your wife. Besides that, neither one of us needs stories about us on the front page. You know what the media do with people like us."

Scott grabbed her hands. "It doesn't change how I feel. I meant what I said last night, that you're gonna be in my life some day. I – I don't know why, but I know that's gonna happen. Trust me." Moving his hands up her arms, he slid them behind her and pulled her close again. Slowly, he bent down and kissed her, hard this time, and she kissed backed, surprised to discover how much she really did feel for him.

"I'll see you again," he said softly, then turned and was gone. Jenna stood staring at the flowers, then burst into tears just as her mother came back into the room. Linda went and took her daughter in her arms.

"You let a good man go again, didn't you," she stated, a fact, not a question.

"Mom, you don't understand. It's – he's married, Mom."

"He's – married?" Linda looked completely confused.

"He says he's in the middle of a divorce – at least, that's what he told me. Until they're divorced, over and done with, that's just asking for trouble in my book."

"Well. I see. Okay."

"Bottom line: if nothing else, I can't be seen in public with him," Jenna stated flatly.

"No, okay, I agree. Not a good idea. Doesn't mean you have to write him off, though. I may be an old fuddy-duddy, my dear, but I'm not blind. I can still see when two people have feelings for each other. Take it from Mother: you two *definitely* have feelings for each other."

LATER THAT AFTERNOON, Jenna opened the door of her Denver hotel room and smiled. Both her luggage and the four dozen roses had already arrived and been sent up.

Chapter 2

BACK HOME, SOUTH of Boston, Blacklace hunkered down in the studio on Scott's property for a week of serious rehearsal, as they always did before going into recording sessions. It wasn't long before everyone was comparing notes behind Scott's back.

"What the hell is wrong with him?" Jeff asked Jeremy during a break, nodding in Scott's direction. "The man's mind ain't on business, that's fer damned sure."

"He missed at least five good opportunities to raise holy hell with me, that's for sure," Jeff offered.

"You think so, too?" Dan chimed in.

"His mind's somewhere south of Timbuktu," Tim said.

"It's anywhere but here," Jeremy agreed. "I'll talk to him."

CORNERING SCOTT PROVED harder than Jeremy'd expected. He finally caught him in the kitchen after a quick veal and Parm sub supper Scott had scrounged together for everyone.

The rest of the band was sprawled around the living room, catching an inning of a Red Sox-Orioles game before heading back over to the studio for a few more hours of work.

"Talk to me," Jeremy said flatly.

"What?" Scott looked up innocently. His attempt at a look of puzzled bewilderment would have come across as comical had Jeremy's radar not been up for days.

"Pull up a chair and talk to me," Jeremy insisted, doing so himself. "Something's got you wicked distracted, brother. You've been somewhere else altogether today."

Scott popped a soda and joined Jeremy. "Can't hide much from you, can I," he said matter-of-factly.

"Or anybody else, for that matter. Everyone's onto you. What the hell's going on?"

Scott sat back, belched and looked Jeremy square in the eye. "What's goin' on, you ask? Why, nothin' less than love's goin' on, my friend. Love. The real deal. The genuine article. Love."

"What the fuck... No shit! You're – in love again?" Jeremy dropped his jaw for dramatic effect. It was clear Scott was serious.

"Again, but different. Wicked different." Scott started fidgeting with a couple of pencils sitting on the table, first doodling on a scrap of paper, then playing the tabletop like a drum.

"Anybody I know?"

"Yep."

"Gonna tell me?"

"If you don't laugh."

"Scout's honor," Jeremy deadpanned, raising his right hand.

Scott beat a drum roll, waited a dramatic beat, then said the two words that had become so special, so recently. "Jenna Bradford." He sighed, then sat back and looked Jeremy straight in the eye again, assessing the impact of his announcement.

"Jenna – Bradford? As in, like, *the* Jenna Bradford?" Jeremy grimaced, scratching his head as he rolled the thought around for a moment, trying to get on top of it, his concentration every bit as intense as that of a tightrope walker crossing the Grand Canyon on a windy day. He turned and looked out the window, then looked back at Scott. "Well, bro, you don't have to worry about me laughing. Jenna Bradford's a heck of a piece."

"Excuse me, she's a heck of a lot more than a heck of a piece," Scott shot back, indignant. "*You* sit and talk to her for an hour. No, on second thought, don't. You're a happily married man. You leave the sittin' – and fallin' in love – to me."

"Gee, thanks. What a guy. Is that what they mean, about what friends are for?" Jeremy threw himself back in his chair and took a long look at Scott. "So – love. Just outta curiosity, what makes it love? That is, if you don't mind my askin'?"

Scott shifted forward in his seat, laying his arms on the table. "It's gotta be," he said simply. "Or let's just say, it's nothing like anything I've ever experienced in my entire fuckin' life. So I figger it's gotta be the real thing – love."

"Never? Joanne?" Scott's first wife. Missy's mother.

"Nope."

"Nancy?" The relationship with the mother of Scott's second child, Laurel, hadn't lasted long enough for marriage.

"Karen?" Scott's second, current and soon to be ex-wife.

"Not by a mile."

"Missy? Laurel?"

"Jeeze, that's parental love. Let's not get dirty here."

Jeremy put his hands up to placate Scott's sudden rise in temper. "Sorry, bro. Just seeking clarification. Scott Tenny – in love. Cut me some slack. It's a lot to get the ol' brain around. Who'da thought... So – like, how much time have you actually spent with this bodacious babe, anyway?"

"Not a lot," Scott had to admit. "I want to, but she's just gone on the road. Denver. She's openin' that new stadium there, you know, the one that's replacing the old Mile High? And I'm here."

"Hardly, bro. You may be here, physically, but like I said, you're wicked distracted. You might as well *be* in Denver. It's driving every-one fuckin' nuts. Want my advice?"

"Sure. I'll get it anyway."

"Take a trip. Catch her between shows. Get her outta your system."

"No way, man. You know what it's like on tour. She doesn't need the distraction."

"Look. Either she's distracted or you're distracted. I for one would like to see you get undistracted. Fast."

"I dunno. It's not ideal."

"Oh, so you want ideal, take her to Maui for a month. Does anyone in this business get time to court a woman? Not likely. Get yourself the fuck out to Denver, man."

"She's not expecting me."

"Oh, I get it. Down deep, you're worried she's got herself a road jockey ridin' her between gigs? Am I right? You –"

Scott jumped to his feet, suddenly boiling. "No, *you* – you watch your mouth. *This* woman you do *not* speak of in those terms. Got it?"

Jeremy's hands were back up. "Okay, okay, I got it. Calm down. Jeeze, man, chill. She's just a –"

Scott slammed a fist on the counter, sending a plastic bowl flying. Fortunately, it was empty. "Do *not* finish that thought, bro, or I won't take responsibility for whatever happens next," he fumed and stalked out of the room.

"FOR A HOTEL restaurant, this place ain't half bad," said Tom Jacobs, Jenna's drummer, signaling the bartender for another pitcher for the table. "Good choice, Jenn."

"Hell, you know me. I'm a sucker for seafood," Jenna admitted, sitting with her back to the room, her standard approach for trying to avoid attention. "I could eat here every night."

"Lobster in Denver. Who'da thought?" mused the multi-talented Bob Roskowski, who claimed he'd never met an instrument he couldn't master. For Jenna he played bass guitar and keyboards for the most part, lent his voice as needed, and always kept a rack of brass and woodwinds close at hand for added color. "So, where from here? Anyone got any suggestions? Dane, you know Denver."

"Better believe it." Dane Sturdevant had grown up in Colorado Springs, an hour south. "Forget *Debbie Does Dallas*. *Dane Does Denver*'s more like it. If it's got a stage and a mike, I've been there."

And if it had strings and a power cord coming off it, Dane played it. When he played for Jenna, this meant, 6- and 12-string guitar and dobro. He also knew his way around electric fiddles, banjos and mandolins. Steel-stringed, nylon-stringed, plucked or bowed, they were all part of the arsenal he could draw from on cue.

"Mark told me Acey Deucy's in town," Jenna said. "But I don't want to see them till he gets here. They'll be playin' Denver through Sunday night, so there's no rush."

"Plenty we can do in the meantime," said Dane. "Anyone want to catch the Broncos game on Sunday afternoon? My dad's got a friend with excellent connections."

"Uh, I've got a sneaky suspicion we can do better than your ol' man's friend," Tom offered, dropping his voice. "Don't be obvious, but like check it out – two tables over, at six o'clock."

The guys all found reasons to turn, stretch, drop and pick up – whatever it took to get a view.

"Holy shit!" whispered Bob, coming up with the napkin he'd supposedly dropped. "That's just about the entire defensive lineup of the Denver Broncos sitting around that table."

"Yeah," said Tom, "and one of 'em can't take his eyes offa Jenna."

Jenna turned to look, locked eyes with defensive tackle Derek Nelson – and smiled. Derek Nelson broke into a broad grin, rose to his feet as if summoned by the Queen herself and picked his way over to their table. Eyes all over the room followed his progress – and noted his destination.

Reaching Jenna's side, he put out a beefy hand to shake. "Hi. I'm Derek Nelson," he stated, then smiled. "And you're Jenna Bradford," he added as an afterthought.

Jenna took his hand graciously, tipped her head to the side and took him in. "I'm Jenna Bradford – and you're Derek Nelson," she mimicked. "I sing. You run people over."

"I knock people down. You knock people out. What brings you to town?" The band had all they could do to keep from laughing. No one breathing in Denver didn't know why Jenna Bradford was in town. The first show booked into the brand new Pepsi Center had sold out in two and a half hours flat.

"Stopped by to sing a song or two. An intimate little thing tomorrow night."

"Shucks, wish I had me a ticket. And who are your friends?" he asked her politely.

"Tom, Dane, Bob – say hello to Mr. Nelson," she introduced them like she was a third-grade school teacher.

"We're pleased to meetcha," Bob stepped in as voice of the band. "Join us for a few minutes?"

Derek looked to Jenna before agreeing.

"Pull up a chair," she offered. "You need one. You guys are having a rough year."

The 6'3½ ", 280-pound, pony-tailed defensive end did as he was told, wedging a chair in right next to her. Bob emptied a water glass into a potted plant in the middle of the table and poured the football star a beer.

"So what was it with you guys and the Patriots last week, anyway?" Tom got right to the point. "I had money on that game, man."

"Yeah. You guys looked like you were running in place. Why couldn't you get any traction?" Jenna chimed in.

"You watch football?" he asked her, surprised.

"Sure I watch football," Jenna shot back. "Basketball, baseball, soccer too. What? You've never met a female sports fan?"

"Let's just put it this way. Not a beautiful, talented, female-type sports fan."

"Oh, I bet there's more of us 'beautiful, talented, female-type' sports fans out there than you'd expect. But don't think a compliment's gonna get you off the hook. Like, where was Clement on the next to last play third quarter? Third down and seven and what does he do? That was fuckin' ridiculous, and I'm not exactly the only one saying so."

"You'll get no argument from me on that. Damned straight, that was ridiculous. They're still giving it to him in the locker room on that one," Derek agreed. "That and Barnes."

"Talk about red-zone inefficiency," Bob said, and took another pull on his beer.

"Then you have to add Zabarski to the list," said Jenna.

"Nothing much gets by you if you picked up on that, little missy," said Derek, nodding appreciatively. "You hold your own."

"'Little missy,'" Tom cringed.

"You better be careful, big boy," Dane laughed. "This 'little missy' will leave you in the dust fer that one. Not to change the subject, but if no one has any objections, I'd like to get on over to Deckers. I know one of the guys in the band that's playing the 9 o'clock slot. Tom? Bob?" Dane gave a heavy-handed, obvious nod in the direction of Jenna and Derek. "Like, uh, time to exit stage left, guys? Wink, wink." Everyone laughed as they scrambled to their feet.

"And leave me with the bill," said Jenna.

"Righto," said Tom. "Ta."

"SO I HAVE you to all myself," Derek said, affecting a Transylvanian accent and rubbing his hands like a mad scientist in a horror movie.

"Not for long, actually. I've got to be going, too," Jenna said, surprised at finding herself a bit uneasy with the situation. "We have an early call tomorrow."

"Ah, the all-purpose show biz excuse," Derek chuckled. "I don't want to force myself on you, pretty lady. But – that said – how long are you in town? I'd like to see more of you."

I bet you would, Jenna found herself thinking. "We've got the two big shows, tomorrow night and Tuesday, and a run down to Colorado Springs Monday night. We leave Wednesday afternoon, for Chicago."

"How about a late dinner tomorrow night when you're finished?"

"Okay. But only if you'll be my guest at the show. Deal?"

"Good seat?"

"How about *four* good seats in the front row?" Derek was ready to respond, but Jenna held up a finger. "Wait. That's only half of it. In exchange for – four seats for the Steelers game Sunday."

"Oh my, you do drive a hard bargain. Deal. I'll have my agent call your agent and write up the contract. Enough business, so to speak – tell me about yourself, pretty lady."

Jenna laid out the basics: life at home, life on the road. "What about you?" she asked in turn.

"Not all that different, really. Well, one sort of difference. I mean, you didn't say you were in a relationship or anything – and I'm not asking, mind you – but in my case, I am – was – married. It's over, we're separated. We're in the middle of a divorce."

"What *is* it with you guys?" said Jenna, rolling her eyes. "Every guy I meet is in the middle of a divorce these days."

JEREMY WAS IN the kitchen door before the doorbell had finished chiming. Scott looked up from a steaming bowl of cappuccino.

"Grab a cup," he offered. Jeremy dumped a backpack on a chair and a duffle on the floor and helped himself.

Settling in, he calmed himself while allowing Scott to shoot the bull for a few minutes. Then with a silent sigh, he reached into his backpack and extracted a copy of the entertainment section of the morning Boston Herald.

"Uh. I take it you haven't seen the papers today." He dropped the paper in front of Scott and held his breath.

Scott picked it up and scanned the top half of the section. "Yeah? So?" Then he turned it over and took in the lower half of the page. His eyes froze on the photo of Jenna Bradford – and a man – and the headline that read, "Will Jenna change her B to N?"

"Who the fuck is that sorry son of a bitch?" he exploded. Jeremy took a gulp of his coffee, burning his mouth in the process.

"I thought it might be better if I showed it to you before we got on the bus," he said mildly. The band was due to leave in half an hour for a quick three days of shows in Connecticut and New York.

Scott went uncharacteristically quiet, while Jeremy fiddled noisily with a spoon. Finally, Scott folded the section and handed it back. "Fuck him and the whore he rode in on. What time is it?"

Chapter 3

WELCOME TO DENVER International Airport," the captain intoned over the intercom. Jenna took a deep breath. Reaching for her bag in the overhead compartment, she felt a sharp twinge of discontent. She wasn't remotely sure she should be here.

She'd seen Derek several times before the band left for Chicago. And she'd slept with him once. The man was an athlete – and a perfect gentleman. That wasn't the problem. A woman accustomed to being in total control of her own destiny, Jenna felt like Derek was calling the shots now, not the other way around, and she didn't like it.

"Come back to Denver," he'd told her the night he showed up in Chicago. And here she was. She laughed at how the scandal sheets could inflate a few dinners and a brunch into wild speculations of a serious relationship. But here she was, not back in L.A., where she should be.

SCOTT, SWEATING AND manic, came off stage after the last of the encores, grabbed a Red Bull and a clutch of groupies and headed for his dressing room.

Jeremy toweled off and sighed. "Forget rehearsals tomorrow," he said to the rest of the band. "There was another picture of Bradford and the footballer in today's paper. He'll be fuckin' useless."

JENNA ENDED UP staying in Denver for a month. "It's the only way I can give this thing half a chance," she explained to Brian, for the fiftieth time. Her manager was furious with her, but for once she didn't care. She wanted a crack at happiness and that wasn't going to be easy, given the fast-lane nature of their lives. In the month she'd spent in Denver, Derek had been on the road the better part of two weeks.

But the two weeks he was home were whirlwinds of fun. She soon learned that when you date a football player, you might as well accept the fact that you're dating his team, too. The Broncos knew good PR when they saw it. They adopted her en mass, creating as many photo ops for themselves as they possibly could. Who knew when Bronco Boy and Grammy Girl, as the Denver papers were calling them, would hit the skids.

So Jenna wasn't surprised when half the team and a swarm of reporters and cameramen turned up at the airport to wish her safe journey and a quick return when she flew back to L.A. for Thanksgiving. Derek just laughed. At least the lack of privacy they had to endure was nothing new for him. "You have a fabulous time," he told her, "but not *too* fabulous a time, right, babe?" Then he gave her a swept-off-her-feet kiss for the cameras. The kiss made the front page of the L.A. Times entertainment section – and the gossip column page of the New York Post. Scott was in New York for Thanksgiving.

JENNA FOUND RANDY waiting for her at the Delta baggage area three hours later, and in another hour was sprawled in her parents' study across the couch, assuring her father that Derek was a great guy. Really.

"But does he respect you, kiddo?" Bob asked her with a wink. She knew he didn't want to appear to be prying – she grinned and threw him a wink right back – but he was, and it didn't surprise her at all.

"So – is it – love?" he persisted.

"Yes, Daddy, it would appear to be love," Jenna teased him.

"Are you sure you know what love is?" Linda asked, standing in the doorway.

"As much as any one does," Jenna answered. "In the utilitarian sense of the word, anyway. A good working relationship."

"How romantic," her mother said dryly.

"How practical." Her father echoed her mother in tone.

"It worked for you guys," Jenna said casually, then regretted it as both of her parents winced visibly. "I mean, look at you two, about to celebrate your fortieth anniversary. That's what I call a good working relationship. I've learned it from you."

BOB AND LINDA'S relationship hadn't always "worked," and it certainly hadn't been the peaceful and predictable relationship it had evolved into in its later decades. The early years, years that Jenna remembered all too clearly, had been fraught with turbulence. Her father's career took him away from home for months at a time. Her mother buried her loneliness in a nonstop schedule of commitments that left no time for reflection. Jenna was just discovering boys when her mother discovered that her father had somehow managed to conduct an affair that had remained undiscovered for a full four years. She packed her bags and left him with three children to raise on his own.

For a man with as many family retainers as the average Old World aristocrat, Bob was able to manage the crisis reasonably well. The children's lives went on as before, only it was Randy picking Chris up at soccer practice or taking Jim and his date to his high school prom. Adella, their housekeeper, took over mothering Jenna. Gillian Burton, her mother's personal secretary, who reported to work that day with no idea that her employer had walked out, stayed on to oversee the everyday needs of a busy household. It worked, technically if not emotionally.

Bob loved his two sons, but he doted on his only daughter. She, in turn, worshipped her father, unconsciously making personal choices to please and impress him. Acting and singing came naturally, as did a love for the limelight. She was Daddy's little girl, and definitely a chip off the old block. When her mother left, he became the center of her universe.

"SO, IS IT serious?" Bob persisted.

"Daddy, I don't know what's gonna come of it. Can't I just enjoy it for what it is and see where it goes? You're as bad as Brian."

"You can't blame Brian for trying to do his job, honey," Linda said.

"I know that, Mom. I just need some time for myself for a change. Now."

"So what's this Derek really like?" Bob asked. "And do you like Denver?"

"Denver's okay. Derek – well, he's this big ol' football player kinda a guy – what can I say?" Jenna laughed. "He's sweet. He's goofy. He's fun to be with."

"Do the sparks really fly?" her mother asked pointedly.

"Sparks fly, don't worry, Mom," Jenna answered, a bit exasperated with being cross-examined. She couldn't wait for Chris to show up. She and her baby brother, as she had always insisted on introducing him to friends, always had a great time whenever they got together, which wasn't often enough these day. A rising star in the executive wing at Paramount, he'd ridden his father's coattails into the industry but was making his way up the ranks through merit, hard work and brains. Jenna had nothing but love and respect for her baby bro.

Her older bro was another story. Jim and his cold fish of a wife, Sue, were due later that night. Jim had been fun enough as a kid, but had matured into the wet blanket of the family. Serious to the point of tedium, the aura of skepticism he radiated cast a pall over the sunniest of days. He and Sue suited each other well. Jim had found his niche in political campaign management, meeting Sue along the way. In the heat of a heavy campaign season, neither would be seen at the Bradford homestead for months at a time. Jenna had to admit that suited her fine.

"Does he want to settle down, I mean when the divorce comes through?" Bob tried to ask casually.

"Dad! Please!" Jenna covered her face with her hands and shook her head. "No more questions!"

"Just one more," Linda jumped in. "These sparks – are we talking campfire sparks – or the four-alarm kind that start conflagrations."

Jenna stood up and walked over to her mother.

"Which is to say, have you heard from Scott?" said her mother, at long last getting to the point.

"No," Jenna answered, looking down at her shoes. She raised her head and looked her mother square in the eye. "No. If you have no further questions, I'll be in my room." Her mother reached out and pulled a strand of hair from behind Jenna's ear. Jenna tucked it back in place and headed down the hall.

"That was disappointment I heard in her voice," Linda said to Bob when Jenna was out of earshot. "We don't know this Derek, and he could be absolutely terrific, I know that. I'm biased and I know that too. But that was disappointment, you mark my words."

"Yes, dear," said her husband, blandly.

Scott appreciated holidays like Thanksgiving for the opportunity they presented to continue deepening his relationship with his two daughters. An absentee father for so much of their young lives, he considered making amends to each of them a lifelong commitment, not a single occurrence, once he'd gotten his life turned around. You could apologize to an old buddy for wrecking his car when you were out of your mind on a bender and get on with being buddies or not. Your children were another matter.

Laurel lived in the rent-controlled three-bedroom upper West Side apartment her mother, Nancy Cardosa, a wild gypsy of a woman, had been living and working in as an avant guard fashion designer twenty-eight years earlier, when Scott had come so briefly into her life. Two people of equally fiery temperament, their passion quickly consumed itself, leaving behind the ashes of an ill-fated relationship – and the beginnings of a child. Nancy, never telling Scott that she'd conceived, raised Laurel in this apartment as a single mother. When she finally decided to let it go and move to a farm in Pennsylvania, Laurel had jumped at the chance to take it over as her own. Her mother's parting gift: the name of her father. Already a successful model and actress by the time she and her father were reunited, Laurel soon presented her newly discovered dad with a grandson. Her husband, Mark Kalman, was a music promoter. With much in common, he and Scott enjoyed a comfortable relationship.

"Dad!" Laurel ran to the door that Mark had answered, six-month-old Luka in her arms. Scott gave them both a huge kiss, sending Luka into fits of giggles. Scott took his grandson from Laurel and spun him in the air, generating even more laughter.

"Oh, how I wish I could have done this with you!" he said, returning the boy to his mother.

"That's okay, Dad. Uncle Vinnie gave me more than enough airplane rides – I threw up on him once, which I'll never hear the end of." She put her arm around her father's waist and walked him into the living room. "Sit. Relax. What can I get you? Dinner's not till five."

"The place smells fantastic," he smiled. "A cup of coffee'd be great."

He wasn't halfway through his coffee when Missy arrived with her fiancé, Alex Calby, in tow. His older daughter, the product of the six years that constituted his first marriage, had introduced the skilled lighting engineer to her father earlier in the summer. Missy worked freelance as a set designer both for off-Broadway and out-of-town shows. She could do worse than the moody young Brit whose talentss were very much in demand on Broadway.

AFTER DINNER, LAUREL and Missy shoed the men out of the kitchen to do the dishes and catch up with each other. Conversation quickly came round to their father.

"Is it my imagination, or is dear ol' Dad just putting on a show of being in a good mood?" said Laurel, tackling the sink.

"If you ask me, he was only half here," Missy agreed, lining up to dry.

"You know what it is, don't you? He's told you, hasn't he?" Missy shook her head. "I can't believe he told me and he hasn't told you. He's pining for Jenna Bradford, of all people."

Missy cracked up. "Jenna Bradford! You gotta be shittin' me." Laurel assured her she wasn't. "He sure does know how to pick 'em!" Missy blurted out.

"Don't let him hear you say that," Laurel cautioned her. "He's got no sense of humor when it comes to this woman. I don't know – have you seen the pictures of her and –"

"– the football player? Sure. They're everywhere. Oh, my God, that explains everything. He isn't himself at all. I mean, even Luka couldn't hold his attention. When did he tell you?"

"Like the minute he came through the door," Laurel said. "He's like 'Do you know who Jenna Bradford is?' and I'm like 'Duh, do I live on planet Earth?' and he's like 'I'm gonna marry the woman.' No, really, that's what he said."

"Is she like dating him on the side or something?" Missy asked, incredulous.

"Nope. He says he's just gonna bide his time."

"COME ON BACK to Denver, baby," Derek wheedled. "You don't have anything doin' between the holidays."

Jenna had to agree. For year's she'd made a point of cooling things so that everyone could take some time off and come roaring back after the first of the year. Family time was important. She wanted all her people to know they could count on that with her. The break had always served as a fertile time for her for writing new lyrics and the tunes to carry them. She returned to Colorado with a little three-octave keyboard under her arm.

Chapter 4

THE HOLIDAYS ARE over, Jenna! What d'ya think, the holidays last from Thanksgiving to goddamn St. Patrick's Day?" Brian's voice came badgering her over the phone line. "So when? *When*? What do I *tell* people?"

"Brian! How are you?" she gushed in mock delight. "How are things in L.A.? How am I? Am I happy? You're *so* glad to hear how happy I am. *Right*?" she exploded in anger.

"Jenna, this isn't a game, you know. People count on you. You're an industry, whether you like it or not. Tell me how am I supposed to manage a no-show! People need to know…"

"People, people – that's all you ever talk about, Brian," Jenna cried. "What about *this* person, Brian? When did I become an industry, for cryin' out loud?"

"We've had this conversation, Jenna. You know precisely what I'm talking about. Look – just answer me this: is your career the fuck over? Is this what you want? For God's sake, would you just *tell* me?"

Jenna looked out the window, across the city to the beauty of the snow-covered Rockies rising to the west. Rays of the low, late afternoon sun spotlighted certain of the multitude of peaks and crags.

It was February and Jenna was still in Denver. The best of song-writing intentions had given way to football games and partying – the Broncos' season had done a major turn-around after she'd arrived on the scene, right down to trouncing Atlanta at the Super Bowl, and the team insisted on giving her every bit of the credit for it. Whether her presence had anything to do with it was neither here nor there. Jenna had let down and finally given herself permission to indulge her inner teenager, playing the kid she'd never had the time to be.

Living with Derek felt like playing house. His apartment, hastily rented mid-season when his marriage had hit the rocks, had been just as hastily furnished with a visit to a rental outfit and the Circuit City next door. The boxy black vinyl couch was soon upgraded to a burgundy leather sectional, the laminated particle board bedroom set to rich mahogany. Derek indulged Jenna's tastes across the board. He loved what she brought to his life and constantly told her so. He loved coming home to her.

"A MILE HIGH, mid-continent, and out to sea… All them out there, back in L.A., here you and me…" Jenna pounded the keyboard in frustration, tunes beginning to flow, then stopping cold, mid-thought. *Was* her career over? Was this relationship more important than a career? Derek wanted her to take some serious time off, at least until summer when he'd have to leave for training camp anyway. Maybe it would make sense to go back on the road then, tour when he was traveling. His divorce would be final in a couple of months.

  "A mile high, mid-continent, and out to sea…"

SCOTT WAS IN a writing frenzy, turning out one angry song after another, each one darker than the last. When he wasn't writing, rehearsing or recording, he was working feverishly on other projects. He was working with his stylist on a raunchy line of unisex clothes; he was working with his accountants to find some aggressive business investments; he and Jeremy were pursuing the possibility of buying into a restaurant as silent partners. He was touchy as hell, and more unpredictable than Jeremy had ever seen him. Only one thing was predictable: any mention of Jenna in the papers or on TV would cycle him even higher into the manic maelstrom that had become his daily life.

  Scott 'dated' – if you could call it dating, this way he had of punishing an endless string of groupies for the high crime of simply not being Jenna. He was rarely seen with the same woman twice. He had always been a serial monogamist, hanging with one woman until a hotter one came along, but this was ridiculous. He never spent a night alone, but now he was changing women two and three times a month. At the same time, it was clear to the band that Scott had never been so lonely.

"I WAS TALKIN' to Gary Schellz last night," Scott told Jeremy, lounging in the studio over a couple of Cohibas. Jeremy could let down his guard when Scott pulled out a cigar; it had always signaled a mellow mood. These days 'mellow' was a relative term, but he'd take whatever he could get in that department. "He's got a guy he wants me to meet. Movie producer."

  "So now you want to be in movies?" With Scott these days, anything was possible.

"Hell, no. This life's fuckin' insane enough as it is. No, he's lookin' for investors. Wants me to put some money in. Sounds interesting. Different. Think I'll go out to L.A. for a couple days."

"L.A.'s nice this time of year," Jeremy said, tipping his head back to blow a perfect smoke ring.

THE GLARE OF the California sun hit Scott full in the face as he stepped out the back door of his Beverly Hills Hotel bungalow onto his private patio. Howard Hughes knew what he was doing when he moved into this joint, he thought to himself, dropping on a chaise for a bit of sunbathing that only lasted five minutes before restlessness sent him in search of a cup of coffee. He had to laugh: the hotel's idea of a coffee shop looked a lot like the upscale bars he'd once frequented. Settling himself at the counter, it felt like he should be contemplating cognacs, not looking at a menu that featured ice cream sodas and root beer floats. The waitress brought him an espresso – and her phone number. He took a sip from the one, pocketed the other and opened the *Variety* he'd picked up at the front counter. He hadn't read two pages when a someone tapped him on the shoulder.

"Scott?" He turned and sat up straight in amazement.

"Mrs. Br-bradford?" he stammered, practically dropping the cup in his hand. He jumped to his feet.

"Oh, Scott. Call me Linda, please!" she beamed. Clearly the woman was happy to see him. "Can I join you?"

"Oh, please, yes, do," Scott burbled, feeling faintly ridiculous.

"It's so nice to see you," Linda said smoothly in her husky contralto. "How have you been?" Scott started to answer, hesitated, then sagged.

"That says it all," she said lightly. "You don't need to say another word."

"No, no. I'm doing fine, Linda. Really," he said, pulling himself together and trying for an air of indifference.

"Oh, please. You can't fool me. You say you're fine, but your face tells me something quite to the contrary, Scott. It's Jenna, isn't it." She was stating a fact, not asking a question.

Scott looked her straight in the eye. "Yes, ma'am. It's Jenna. I guess I can tell you, that woman's a spoiler. Nobody holds a candle to your daughter."

"Don't you start ma'am-ing me, Scott Tenny," Linda laughed. "I'm in a hurry, so I'm going to get straight to the point, and the point is this: I'm not blind. I could tell you had feelings for Jenna when I saw the two of you together. I'm not really sure what Jenna wants and, just between you and me, I don't think she does either."

"That's not what I read."

Linda snorted. "Scott! For God sakes, don't tell me you believe everything you read? You of all people should know better. Think about it. We've all read the gossip columns. They're pure fiction. I see the look in Jenna's eyes when your name is mentioned – that's fact. If you want my daughter, fight for her.

Show her how you feel. When I'm your mother-in-law, you can ma'am me all you want."

She stood up, planted a kiss on his forehead and walked away, leaving behind her one wild rock star staring into his espresso cup in a state of total bewilderment.

"HONEY, LET'S LOOK at houses."

"Where did that idea come from." Jenna opened her eyes in surprise. It was morning. Derek had just kissed her awake.

"You feeling better?" he asked her, brushing the hair off her sleepy face.

Jenna took a few deep breaths and stretched. "Yeah, I think so. I don't know what that was last night. I'm okay. I really thought I was coming down with something. What do you mean, look at houses?"

"Let's buy a house together."

"But I'm not gonna be here all the time, you know that. I mean, if I do go back on tour. I –"

"Nobody has to be here all the time. I have football season, you have your thing. It'd be a place to call home, to come back to."

"How sentimental," she said, smiling at him noncommittally.

"IT'S YOUR DADDY'S sixty-fifth, and it's a surprise and you'd be the best present he could have. Tell me you'll come," Linda wheedled. "March 28th. It's a Saturday."

"The 28th, eh." Jenna glanced at a calendar by the phone. "Damn. Derek's away. He's taking his kids to Jamaica. Spring break."

Linda worked to keep the delight out of her voice. "Oh. That's too bad, honey. I wish I could reschedule, but you know how hard it is, finding times when your brothers can be here. But even if Dirk – I'm sorry, Derek can't come, it certainly doesn't mean you can't. You'll be at loose ends."

"I'll be working. I don't do loose ends, Mother. No, I'll be there. It's important. So – you want to hear the latest news? We're looking at houses."

Linda didn't respond. "Mom, you still there?

"Oh, yes. Sorry. I was just writing something down." This news did *not* make her happy. "Jenna, honey, isn't it a bit of a big step, buying a house together?"

"I'll fly out the week before the party, to help." Jenna decided changing the subject was better than discussing the issue.

"YOU KNOW YOU can always come live with me," Scott said to his father.

"And listen to your racket?" His father's laugh rang hollow. Five years as a widower had taken its toll on Joe Tenny.

"You know damned well the racket's out in the studio. Which is perfectly sound-proofed. The neighbors don't complain. Neither will you. You bring your piano, I'll be the one complaining about the racket. It's your call, Dad. Oh, my God, look at this."

Scott held up a photo of himself, his sister, his mother and father. "I can't be more than, what, seven, eight, in this one?" His father came to look.

"Six. That was the year you broke your arm," said his father, taking the photo in his hands. Scott turned back to the box he was going through, not wanting to embarrass the crusty old man by being witness to his tears.

When he felt it appropriate he resumed the conversation he'd come up to Sunapee to have with his father. "I'll help you find an agent if that'd help, Dad." A grunt was the only response. "And I'll go through the attic for you."

"I'll go through the attic."

"Well, I'll go through it and box up things I want. That'll make it easier for you. I'll get Annie to come up and do the same. Then it's just up to you." Another grunt. "I found my first guitar in the basement. Can't believe it's still here." No response. "You know, you don't have to live with me permanently. I mean, we can find you your own place, nearby. Or something near Annie?"

"Annie'd just start mothering me. *That's* never gonna happen."

"Okay, south of me and way north of her. How about that? Still puts you in shootin' distance of your buddies up here, and you can always use my place at the lake, you know that."

"We'll see."

"NOT AGAIN," JENNA groaned.

"Come on. No, really, this one looks terrific. Here, look." Derek held the real estate section in front of her face. She turned to save the frying bacon from burning.

"Will you let me make breakfast?" He backed off. "Sit down." A few minutes later she put a plate in front of him.

"What? You're not eating? Again?" Derek said. "What's with you?"

"I don't know. I just don't feel like it."

"You need to see a doctor."

"I know, I know. I made an appointment. Next Tuesday."

"WELL, MY DEAR, you're pregnant, six or seven weeks worth, I'd say. I do hope this comes as good news," said Dr. Adamson. Jenna looked down. "A surprise?" She nodded.

"We weren't as careful as we should have been," she admitted.

"Freud would probably say that carelessness is really an unacknowledged desire to have a child," the doctor suggested. "At least, that's what I've gleaned from thirty years of getting to know pregnant moms and dads." She smiled. "Do a little soul searching – and come back to see me in a month."

PULLING UP IN front of the apartment complex that had become home (for now, Jenna kept reminding herself), she found herself dreading telling Derek. Not because he wouldn't be happy about the news – if anyone had an unconscious wish for a child, it was Derek. It was abundantly clear how much he missed the four children he'd fathered with his soon-to-be ex-wife, who had moved back home to Chicago to be near her family, taking the children with her. A pro football player was hardly fit material to play the single dad.

Nothing prepared Jenna for the sight that met her as she came through the door. Derek was standing in the middle of the kitchen, juggling keys, a coat and a pair of duffle bags.

"Honey, I know this is short notice, but I gotta rush. I'm catching a plane to Chicago at eleven." Jenna took in the suitcases lined up by the door, the duffles.

"What the…"

"Evelyn called. She – she wants to talk. Wait," he stopped her, taking in the look of alarm on her face. "It's not what you think. We have a lot of issues to work through still. This is for the best. It's just – it'll give us several days before me and the kids head out for the islands. Takes all the pressure off." The doorbell rang. "Fuck, that's the car. Look, I'll call you, babe." He gave her a fast peck on the cheek, juggled the duffels and opened the door. "Just those," he said to the driver, indicating the bags on the floor. The driver grabbed one in each hand, and they were gone.

Jenna sat down at the kitchen table, dumbfounded, which was when she found the scrawled note that would have been all that greeted her had she walked in five minutes later.

"Hey, babe – gone to Chicago – Evie wants to talk – <u>good</u> idea – then to Jamaica. See ya the 5th. Love ya – D."

Slowly, distractedly, she tore the note in half, then in quarters, eights, sixteenths.

After an hour of fretful pacing, Jenna changed her reservation for L.A.

"JENNA! WE DIDN'T expect you till Sunday," Linda exclaimed as her daughter let herself in the kitchen door. Adella bustled off with the suitcases that Jenna had dropped to hug her mother. Linda registered surprised at what turned into a longer embrace than the more customary, painfully abrupt and perfunctory hug that served as a lingering reminder of the two years she'd left the family.

"Honey, is something wrong?" she asked gently.

"No," said Jenna, pulling away. "I'm just tired."

Linda pulled back as well. "You look tired. Are you okay, Jenn?"

"I'm fine, Mom, fine. I – I just decided to come out a couple days early. Derek had to go to Chicago. I –"

"Great! I'm so glad you're here. There's so much to do."

Adella returned to the kitchen and gave Jenna the kind of hug Linda often found herself envying. There was a natural easiness between Adella and Jenna that no amount of years seemed to be able to return to her relationship with her daughter.

"Mom, Adella," Linda said over her shoulder as she left the room, "just one request. If Derek calls – I'm not in." Linda and Adella eyed each other, mystified. Suddenly Linda smiled.

UNPACKING IN HER old room, Jenna kept stopping and looking out the window at nothing in particular. Finally she sat down at her desk. Unconsciously fingering the edges of the worn blotter that still exhibited examples of her teenage doodling, she picked up a pen, then went into the drawer for a piece of paper.

"*Dear Derek – I was taken totally by surprise when I got home yesterday with some very important –* " She wadded up the piece of paper, threw it in the trash and reached for another.

"*Babe – You didn't give me any time this morning to –* " Again, she gave up. This time she pulled a half dozen sheets of paper from the drawer.

"*Darling –* " And again she stared off into space. What was it she really wanted to say? She put the pen down. She knew what she really wanted to say, was crying out to say. She wanted to express fear – her fear that he and Evelyn would find a way to reconcile. That he would finally come to the conclusion that his love for four children totaled more than his love for her. The fear that he would leave her.

If Jenna Bradford had one credo in life it was 'better leave than be left.' She'd walked out on a larger number of faltering relationships over the years than she liked to admit. No one had ever – *ever* – left her. Except, of course, her mother, when she was twelve. Somewhere during those two years, she'd made one promise to herself: that kind of pain she'd never experience again.

"*Dear Derek,*" she began again. "*I know this may come as a surprise…*" She didn't mention her pregnancy.

※

JOE TENNY SETTLED in at his son's house. The situation couldn't be easier; the rambling old house was more than big enough for two. The guest suite he'd moved into even had its own entrance. He'd made it clear from the minute he'd unpacked that he intended to be his usual fiercely independent self.

"Gotta admit, though," he conceded, "I'm looking forward to getting to see more of my granddaughters." Laurel and Missy had a very special place in the old man's heart. "Never could stand going into New York to see them. Neither could your mother. Awful place. 'Big Apple,' my foot. 'Big Fuckin' Road Apple,' if ya ask me."

Scott chuckled as he surveyed the living room. "That should just about do it. Nothing Luka shouldn't be getting into." Laurel and Luka were due momentarily for a long weekend's visit. Right on cue, the sound of company stomping snow off boots reached them from the mudroom.

"Hey, Dad!" Laurel cried, coming in the room with an armful of Luka wrapped in a blanket. "Gramps! Baby, say hi to Grampi!" As she hugged her grandfather, she looked over at her father. "You take him" she said, handing Luka to a more than willing Joe. She went over and gave Scott a long hug. "How are you, Daddy?"

"Good, good," he said shortly. "I'm good." Laurel shook her head. This was the same distracted version of her father she'd hoped she wouldn't find.

"I'M WORRIED ABOUT Dad," Laurel confided in her grandfather later in the kitchen.

"Whaddya mean, kiddo?" Joe asked.

"You haven't noticed? He isn't remotely himself. At least, not around us."

"Nothin' I've seen," said Joe. "Nothin' outta the ordinary. Well, out of the ordinary for us, maybe. I mean, Scott and I – we don't really talk that much. We talk – but we don't really talk talk, if ya know what I mean. Never could get much outta that boy. Not when he was a kid, getting' in trouble all the time – him and Jeremy, God, those two boys were just trouble. Not when he was a so-called adult – the drugs, the women." He stopped, realizing he was talking to the product of one of those women. "It's just been a crazy life."

"I know, Gramps," she said. "I know. But this is different. He claims he's in love."

"Rubbish," Joe dismissed the notion. "You ask me, Scott's never been in love a day in his life."

"How would you know, if you never talk?" Laurel countered. She filled her grandfather in on her father's frustrations. "Lately, he says he's more determined than ever. Whatever that means."

"He did seem a little down when he was up at the lake. I thought it was because of my decision to sell up the place. This woman must be something. Doesn't sound like your father at all."

"Try and talk to him, Gramps. He's driving himself crazy."

"I'll try. Can't imagine how I can bring it up though," the old man mused.

Chapter 5

"OKAY, IF YOU have to know, I'm thinking things over," Jenna admitted to her mother under close questioning. "Enough with the inquisition, please!"

"The last thing I want to do is pry, darling, you know that," soothed Linda. "I just worry about you, is all. It just seems strange that he hasn't called."

"Well you *are* prying, Mom," Jenna retorted. "Let's just drop it, okay?"

JENNA GOT HER mother off the subject, but it was a much taller order getting herself off it. No, she hadn't heard a word from Derek in three days, to her amazement. When separated, they'd been in the habit of speaking daily. However, if she wanted to be honest with herself, she wasn't entirely sure she wanted to hear from him – she was still undecided as to what she wanted to say to him, what she felt in her heart of hearts.

She knew what it would mean if he announced that he and Evelyn had reconciled – that was a pretty straightforward scenario. But if he came home to her – how did she really feel about that? His unexpected flight to Chicago had pulled an emotional rug out from under her. She saw herself as a decisive, self-reliant woman. She didn't like the feeling of insecurity that had been hounding her for the past three days.

Then there was the pregnancy. She felt like she was carrying a pair of completely mismatched twins – a child, and the secret that was that child. She hadn't told anyone. For one thing, she didn't want to complicate her father's birthday party – this was about him, not her. And she didn't want her mother poking her nose into this aspect of her life, either. Morning sickness hadn't forced her hand. As long as she was symptom-free, she just wanted time alone to sort everything out, without interference, privately. At heart, she was a very private person.

"WHAT A DAY! You guys," Bob Bradford marveled, joining Jenna by the fire in the study after the last guest had left. Linda was busy supervising the catering crew who were cleaning up the kitchen. "What a great party. I can't believe who all showed up. It really meant a lot to me, I mean it."

"I'm glad, Dad," Jenna told him. "Reminds me of the party you threw for my sixteenth."

"Except you got a brand new Mustang and a trip to Paris. All your mother got me was a used car and a trip to Monterey."

"Yeah, just a 1929 T46 Bugatti and tickets to everything for Car Week, you mean. Not shabby, Dad." They laughed.

"Let me tell you, I couldn't be more thrilled. God, the thought of driving up there in that beauty – wow." He sat down next to her, pulled his shoes off and patted her on the knee.

"So, how's my sweetie?" 'Sweetie' had been his pet name for Jenna for as long as she could remember.

"I'm okay, Daddy. I don't know – I just need to take some time and decide what I'm doing. I don't know if it's Derek or if it's just me. I know in my heart I need to get back to my music – my writing and my singing. I've taken way too much time off. I'm getting nervous about being able to pick up where I left off."

She sighed. "I find I'm, like, short on inspiration or something, for some reason. I feel like I'm high and dry. It's like I'm stuck and I don't have a clue where I'm headed. Do you have any words of wisdom for someone who's career is in idle?"

"Is it your career, sweetie, or is it maybe your relationship with Derek?" he father asked her pointedly.

"Dad, I don't know. I don't think I can make any decisions about Derek until I understand where *I* am, what I'm doing. Does that make any sense? But you're right – L.A. doesn't feel right, either."

"Sure it makes sense. And if it doesn't feel right, then you shouldn't be here. If that's the case, I have actually do have a suggestion. Use the place in Boston."

"What do you mean? I thought you sold it last year."

"I talked about it, but it never went any further. Since your grandmother died, we've barely used it. But you always liked Boston. It's even got a piano. You can have your privacy, time to think. You can work there. Put it to good use. You could take some friends with you if you want."

"That's not half crazy, Daddy. But I don't have to take anyone – I know a bunch of people there. It wouldn't have to be all privacy and contemplation. Damn, I could even have some fun!"

"That's my girl! I swear, that's the first spark of life I've seen in you all week. You go get to bed and we'll get it arranged in the morning."

"Daddy, thanks. Thank you so much." She gave him a heart-felt hug and headed upstairs.

If she'd turned around and come back into the room, she would have found her father with his face buried in his hands.

JENNA'S FIRST CALL the following morning was to her manager. "Brian, we're back in business," she said without preamble. "I want you to call the band and put them on stand-by. I'm going to Boston for a few weeks, to get my act back together."

"And Denver?" he asked cautiously.

"I don't know about Denver. But I do know I need to get back to work. This isn't a whim, Brian. I'm back."

She was just finishing up making plane reservations when her mother came down. Adella pressed a cup of coffee in Linda's hand. "Will you have breakfast, Missus?" she asked.

"Not yet, Adella. I'll let you know when I'm ready. I'm much more interested in finding out what our Jenna's up to."

"She's making plane reservations, Missus. She's going to Boston."

"So I hear. She needs to call Charles to have him open up the apartment."

"All taken care of, Missus. She called." Jenna walked into the kitchen, crossed over and gave her mother a kiss.

"Aren't you the early bird. Sleep well?" Linda asked, gauging her daughter's mood before deciding what tack to take with her.

"Sure did," Jenna responded enthusiastically.

"And, pray tell, when were you planning on telling me you were going to Boston?"

Jenna noted her mother's tone, but decided not to rise to the bait. Clearly, it galled Linda that this was her husband's idea, not hers, and she simply hated to be the last to know anything. "I was going to tell you when I finished making all the arrangements, Mom. You weren't around when I came down for breakfast. I take it Daddy told you?"

"He filled me in. Don't misunderstand. I definitely think it's a good idea. You need to figure out what – or who – you really want, honey."

"I know that, Mother." Jenna tried not to sound peeved. She was in too good a mood to let her mother's knee-jerk need to control bother her.

COVERAGE OF THE Bradford birthday party made the Boston paper the following morning, complete with a lavish spread of photographs; the guest list guaranteed that. Scott was staring at a large photo of Jenna and the immediate family – and wondering if he should be reading anything into the absence of Derek Nelson in any of the pictures – when his father walked into the kitchen. Glancing over his son's shoulder, Joe decided to seize the moment.

"Mornin', son," he said casually, clearing his throat. "My, my – ain't *she* the looker."

"Got that right," Scott said, noncommittally.

"Sings pretty damned good too, don't you think?"

"Yep." Scott glanced up at his father. "Laurel told you, right?"

"Well, yeah. Implied you were pretty much obsessed with the woman," Joe said, throwing caution to the winds.

"Obsessed?"

"My word, not hers. Does the shoe fit?"

"I dunno. 'Obsessed' sounds a bit creepy. I can't get her out of my mind, if that's what you mean. Okay – I only spent a few hours with her, but, man, I gotta tell you, I fell for her. Hard. And now, like I said – I just can't get her out of my head."

His father walked to the window, looked out at the ocean for a moment, then turned back to Scott. "Not unlike when I met your mother, son."

"Yeah? Maybe it's genetic?" Scott snorted at the though.

"Don't make light of it," Joe counseled. "We Tennys fall hard when we fall. One thing I do know: when you have feelings about things, you're not often wrong. Never have been. Laurel told me you're convinced this gal's going to be a part of your life some day. It *could* happen, ya know."

Scott sat shaking his head. "Not likely.."

"You want to know what the problem is? You were always too damned impatient as a kid. Where's all that faith you keep talking about? You're always sayin' 'there's a reason for everything' and 'don't give up your dreams.' Maybe, just maybe, there's a reason for this." He went to the stove and poured himself a cup of coffee, then came back and sat down across the table from Scott. "Son?" Scott looked up at him. "Don't give up."

Scott looked away, then looked back at his father. "As simple as that, Dad," Scott harumphed. "Hell, maybe you're right. I – thanks, Dad." He got up and headed for the door, then turned back. "Thanks. I really mean it."

Joe pushed back in his chair and sighed.

"BYE-BYE, DADDY," JENNA whispered in her father's ear as he folded her in his arms. She turned to hug Linda. "Don't worry, Mom, I'll keep you appraised of any late-breaking news."

"You better, young lady," Linda responded, her tone only half joking. "We love you. We just want to see you happy, baby. You know that."

"Let her get on the plane, darling, or it's going to take off without her," Bob laughed, putting an arm around his wife. A moment later, the loudspeaker echoed his thoughts.

AS THE PLANE climbed to cruising altitude, Jenna felt her mood lift with it as she realized how tense she'd been for the past week. It suddenly hit her that her greatest fear had been that Derek might simply show up at her parents' house. She wasn't remotely prepared to deal with him.

She looked down and rested a hand on her belly. As for this abstraction, this baby, she would tell Derek when she got settled and had a clearer sense of what her long-range plans might be.

For now she was simply going to rest, relax and let down until this plane delivered her across the country, from the eternal spring of Southern California to the lingering New England winter of Boston.

Chapter 6

JENNA STEPPED OFF the curb at Logan Airport to hail a cab. Inhaling the cold air deeply, she was transported to her grandmother's Boston – the Boston of Nutcracker ballets at Christmas, Symphony Hall rehearsals and lunch afterwards, and her *own* Boston – the Boston of convivial Irish pubs, trendy watering holes, live acts all over town and after-hours dance clubs to work off whatever energy still remained.

"Miss Bradford, it's so good to see you. It's been too long." Jenna took the hand the doorman offered her as she emerged from the cab.

"Charles, will you ever go back to calling me Jenna?" she said in mock sternness.

"No, ma'am. Anyone as famous as you are deserves all the respect I can give you. No, I'm afraid I'm always going to be callin' you Miss Bradford. That is, unless you decide to make it Mrs. Something-or-Other. Then I'll call you that."

"Charles, you're hopeless!" she laughed and headed in. It was a bright, sunny day but a cold, blustery wind reminded her she'd need to wear her warmer coat.

"BYE-BYE, EDDIE. OFF you go now," Scott dismissed his manager.

"Okay. But no more of this horse shit, okay, Scott? This thing's happening on schedule. Right?" Eddie Strang was clearly frustrated. "Right, Jeremy?"

"Right, boss," Scott responded. "On schedule. You've got my fuckin' word."

Jeremy raised his right hand wearily. "And I'll guarantee it. We'll be in the studio by the middle of the month. Count on it." Strang stood up.

"Why Blacklace has to make everything so goddamn difficult, I've never fuckin' understood. Relax, you guys! Make music! Be happy! Get rich! What's so damned hard about that?" He looked back down at them. "It ain't brain surgery. Have a nice lunch."

Scott and Jeremy sat back in their chairs at Strang made his way out of the restaurant. "Phew," said Scott, "thank God that's over. Where's the waitress?"

Jeremy wasn't going to let Strang's concerns go to waste. While they waited for their meal to arrive, he pursued the topic that was really on the entire band's mind as well.

"Eddie's got a point."

"I know. I know." Peeved, Scott looked around the room, only half paying attention.

"Scott. I'm serious, brother. Listen to me. This is your best friend talkin' here." Jeremy waited for Scott to return his attention to the conversation at hand. "We're way off our pace, man. We shoulda had a new album out by now, and hell, we're not even remotely ready to start recording. 'Blast Her' is comin' together okay, but 'Automa Mama' is a perfect mess and, you ask me, that other one, 'Park 'n Ride,' whatever the shit you're callin' that thing – it just doesn't work at all, man. Read my lips: you guys have gotta get serious."

"I hear you, bro," Scott said. "I hear you. Through a fog, but I hear you."

"You gotta get clear of that fog, man. You know it and I know it."

"And so does my old man. We actually had a fuckin' father-son discussion about it. A couple of 'em. Can you believe that?!"

"No shit!" Jeremy laughed. "That had to be weird." Jeremy had witnessed too many confrontations between Scott and his father over the years. Some had turned violent. "You tellin' me the old guy's fuckin' mellowing?"

"Maybe. Maybe I am too," Scott mused. 'Maybe that's my problem."

"Yeah, right," Jeremy scoffed. "That'll be the day. I can see it now – they'll headline you in Vegas as 'Scott Tenny, the Mellow Maniac.'" Lunch arrived.

"No, I'm serious," Scott continued after the interruption. "I've come to a decision after talkin' to the ol' bastard. I'm gonna take his advice. I can't let my thoughts get consumed by this woman. I'm getting back to work. I mean it."

Jeremy put down his fork and knife. "I gotta know, what did the ol' bastard say that I haven't been sayin' for the last four months?"

"How about this for the bridge?" Scott's voice went into a whispered falsetto. "*She sobers. She chills. She inspires. She thrills...*" Jeremy took a long sip on his coffee.

"Well, it's still about her, but at least it's positive for a change. What if you double-timed it?" He banged out one rhythm on the table, then another.

Scott signaled the waitress for another cup of coffee. "You want another?" he asked Jeremy, who nodded. Scott held up two fingers.

"Stay in this mode, Scott, we'll blow Eddie's mind. We may come in *ahead* of his fuckin' schedule." Jeremy kept beating percussion on the tabletop while Scott scrawled lyrics on a yellow legal pad.

Suddenly Jeremy stopped. Looking over Scott's shoulder out the front window of the restaurant to the snowy street beyond, he thought – he hoped – he was seeing things. Jenna Bradford was standing in front of the window, looking up and down the street, obviously waiting for someone. The woman was unmistakable. It had to be her. He quickly looked away and got back to playing the tabletop.

Glancing up again, he saw another woman approach her. They kissed, then turned to enter the restaurant. The drumming stopped again.

"Scott, buddy – we may have a problem. I – don't think you're going to be able to keep that promise about Jenna," Jeremy said quietly. "Believe it or not, bro – she just came through the door."

Scott's face drained of color. Then he laughed. "You're shittin' me. This is a test, right?"

"Wrong." Jeremy nodded in the direction of the hostess who was seating two beautiful women at a table nearby, Jenna with her back to them. Scott turned and looked. Even from the back, he didn't have to be told who he was looking at. He sat back in his chair and silently composed himself. Jeremy didn't take his eyes off him.

"You okay?" he asked quietly.

"I'm okay," Scott answered, taking several deep breaths. "Yep. I'm okay," he insisted. "I – I like that double-time idea. We can go with that…"

"GOD, IT'S JUST so good to see you again, Nora," Jenna said, squeezing her old friend's hand. "Tell me *every*thing."

"Well, like I said yesterday, I sold the boutique in January. I don't have a clue what's next, but I'm okay for a while. I got good money for it, it being Newbury Street and all. Hot property. But what about you, hon?"

"Oh, man, my life's a mess. Some people'd tell you I've gone off the fuckin' tracks. I took time out from my career and really got sidetracked bad – I got involved with this guy in Denver."

"Everyone knows that," Nora laughed.

"I know, and trust me, it doesn't make it any easier. I'm just not sure where that's all going. Then I was out in L.A. – Mom threw this big party for my dad's sixty-fifth – and he had this great suggestion, that I –"

Nora's attention had strayed for a moment. "Oh, my God. Do *not* look now but Scott Tenny's sitting over there!" Jenna ventured a look. She recognized Scott from the back.

"That's him all right. And his guitarist, Jeremy Sandborn."

"They both keep looking this way," Nora giggled. "Of course, everyone's looking at you anyway. God, I can't imagine what it's like to be famous."

"You don't wanna know, Nora, you do *not* wanna know," Jenna assured her. "Scott Tenny. Oh, God."

"Whaddya mean? Do you know him?"

"I guess you could say I know him — he told me a while back that we're gonna be an item some day." Jenna laughed lightly.

"You gotta be kidding!" Nora responded. "Wow! Can I be in your wedding?"

"Don't hold your breath, kiddo. That guy's certifiable."

"What do you mean — as in nuts? No way! He's *hot*. Who wouldn't absolutely *die* to be with Scott Tenny?"

"Yeah, sure. So tell me, what about *your* love life?"

"Sorry. You aren't changing the subject that easily," Nora laughed. "You could have any guy you wanted. Why *not* Scott Tenny."

"Keep your voice down," Jenna whispered. "You know the guy's history. He's been to hell and back."

"So…"

"So what *about* your love life, Nora?" Nora finally gave in and brought Jenna up to speed on the latest man in her life.

"OKAY, I GOTTA go, bro," Jeremy said, getting to his feet. "Tomorrow, then."

"Noon, at the studio," Scott stated categorically.

"I'll let everyone know. I've gotta meet Carrie. We've got a meeting with Aiden's guidance counselor. Teenagers!" He stopped and nailed Scott with a serious look. "You sure you're okay?"

"I'm *okay,* bro. Go. I don't want your wife accusing me of screwing up your kid's future because I made you late for a meeting. I'm just gonna hang for a few. Work out the last of this." Three pages of yellow legal pad were covered with scrawls. "Later."

"Just don't do anything stupid, okay? Promise me?" Jeremy begged. "Don't go driving her away. And *no* phone calls. My days of getting you outta jams are so over, my friend."

"Go!"

"WE GOTTA GET together again, Nora," Jenna told her friend who was gathering up her things to leave. "I don't know how long I'm staying, but I'll give you a call, promise."

"I hate to run," Nora said. "You be good. Or whatever." The two laughed, hugged and Nora departed. Jenna sat looking out the window, finishing her coffee.

Scott bided his time, took a deep breath, then got up and approached her. Halfway, she turned and saw him coming. He could read indecision in her eye, a yellow light. It wasn't green, but it was better than red. He sat down next to her.

"I hope I'm not intruding. I saw you before and hoped for a chance to talk with you. How have you been, Jenna? How are things going? What are you doing in Boston?" His questions poured out in a jumble. Jenna decided the last question was the safest.

"I'm here for inspiration. I've had a lot going on. I – I needed some time to think. I want to get back to my music. I'm sure you've been in that situation."

"More than a few times," he chuckled.

"My folks have an apartment here. I decided to hole up and think about things." As she stopped talking, she wondered if she shouldn't have chosen one of his other questions instead.

"Yeah, I've been there. Fuck, who hasn't. Hey – I'm glad you're here. It's nice to see you again." He took a deep breath and committed himself. "Whaddya say – lunch or dinner sometime?"

Jenna's first instinct was to say no, but another voice whispered in her head, 'what harm would it do?' Heck, the guy *was* hot. "Well, yeah, sure." Then another voice chimed in on the issue. "But – aren't you still married to …" Jenna couldn't remember his wife's name.

"Yeah, I'm still married to Karen, legally, but the divorce is moving along. The lawyers are determined to drag it out as long as possible. They're puttin' their fuckin' kids through college on me. Which is to say, it isn't an issue as far as I'm concerned."

"Okay," Jenna decided after a moment's consideration. "Let's meet somewhere. Tomorrow night?"

"Shelley's?" Scott countered, a favorite hangout for Boston musicians and anyone passing through town. "You'll know everybody there."

"Sure. That'd be fun. 7:30?"

Scott stood up, reached down and took her hand in his. Pursing his lips, he gently touched them to it, lingering only a fraction of a second longer than necessary. Looking her in the eye, he said with utter sincerity, "I can't wait."

Jenna realized she couldn't either. She wished she had some reason to trust the sudden surge of joy she felt coursing through her.

"YES! HOLY SHIT, yes! That is *it*! First time on the fuckin' planet!" Scott slammed his fist on the piano as Jeremy, Dan and Jeff finally nailed a sound they'd been pursuing for an hour, a marriage from hell of reverb and squelch. "That is so fuckin' beautiful – no, it's *beyond* beautiful. I think I may cry!"

Each of the guys had a huge grin on his face. They didn't need Scott to tell them they'd pulled off a miracle of sound. But as his words died in the air, they also simultaneously recognized that this may well have been the first positive thought out of Scott's mouth in months, and Jeremy suddenly knew exactly why. "Scott, bro! She's goin' out with you, isn't she? You asked her out and she said yes!"

Four hours later, as they all exited the session, Jeremy put a brotherly arm around Scott. "So – tell me the fuck what happened."

"Man, you'd have been fuckin' proud of me. I was a good boy. Short and sweet. Maybe a total of four, five short, *oh*-so-sweet minutes."

"Yeah?" Jeremy encouraged him to continue.

"Clearly, something's eatin' her. She said she's here to think. And she doesn't know how long she'll be here. You know what that means: good, old-fashioned trouble in River City." Scott couldn't hide the glee he felt.

"Good work, Sherlock. Now just keep the pressure off of her, bro. Situation sounds fragile. You're not famous for doing fragile well."

"Just watch," Scott said, with a confidence that reminded Jeremy of the old Scott.

THE NEXT MORNING, Jenna was up early. A cup of coffee in hand, she perused the sparse contents of the closet and decided dinner with Scott warranted a shopping spree. She chuckled at herself as she realized that she definitely wanted to look sensational. She was just about to head out to have her nails and hair done when the phone rang.

"Shit," she said out loud. She suddenly dreaded it might be Scott calling to cancel.

"What's going on? I haven't heard from you since you got there." It wasn't Scott; it was Linda, in what Jenna like to think of as her 'forensic mothering' mode. "You're so busy I have to call you?" she said, sweetness laced with accusation.

"Mom. I'm sorry. I really *have* been so busy, it slipped my mind, honest. How are you and Dad?"

"No, how are *you*? You don't call, what am I supposed to think? You know I worry about you."

Mom, you're an expert, Jenna thought to herself. Out loud, she merely said, "I'm okay, really. I'm out and about, I'm working, I'm – I'm thinking. That's what I came here for, remember."

"Are you – seeing anyone?"

"I haven't kept count. I must pass thousands every time I step out the door."

"Jenna, stop that. You know what I mean. Are you *seeing* seeing anyone?"

"I've got a date tonight, if that's what you mean," Jenna said, trying not to sound defensive. "Surely you remember the guy with the roses. Scott Tenny? I ran into him yesterday. I'm having dinner with him tonight." Silence. "Mom? You still there?"

"That's – why, Jenna honey, that's just wonderful!" Jenna, rolling her eyes, had no trouble imagining her mother's expression. "Why – you call me tomorrow and tell me all about it, will you, hon?"

"I'll call, Mom." Jenna paused. "Mom – don't go getting your hopes up on this guy, okay? No self-respecting mother would."

JENNA FOUND SCOTT leaning cross-armed against the wall just inside the entrance to Shelley's. His face lit up the moment he saw her. "You're here!" he blurted out. "God, I feel like a kid on his first date." Might as well admit it. "Come on in," he said, opening the inner door for her. She gave him a dazzling smile.

The place was jammed, as always. Heads snapped up quickly as word of who'd just come through the door spread from patron to patron. Several jumped up from seats to say personal hellos to either or both. As it turned out, Jenna and Scott had many friends in common.

Scott was chuckling when he finally sat down across from Jenna. "What's so funny?" she asked.

"Nothing. Just the reactions I was getting. You better believe there's some wicked serious envy reverberating within these four walls right this minute. *Guys*, envying *me*," he hastened to add. "I can't imagine what the women in the place are thinkin' about you. Probably that you've gotta be out of your fuckin' skull to be hangin' with me." He laughed ruefully. "I don't have the world's best reputation."

"Oh, really," Jenna answered, feigning naiveté. "You seem like a nice guy. A little shop-worn, perhaps. A little wild and crazy. A little dangerous, maybe? Under it all – a guy who's sort of – cute."

"Man, I've been called a lotta things in my life. Cute's definitely not one of them." Scott sat back and oogled the woman across from him. "Jenna Bradford. As I live and breathe." He could only shake his head in wonder. "Somebody pinch me. I've been dreaming of this dinner since October."

Everyone in the room who could see his face could tell Scott was dumb-struck with love. Jenna was another story. As much as she wanted to give in to the same emotions that had clearly gripped Scott, she couldn't shake one reality: she was carrying another man's child. She could not allow herself the luxury of thinking, even hoping, that anything positive could develop between herself and Scott.

"THIS HAS BEEN great," Jenna said as they rose to go, and she meant it. Conversation between the two had been comfortable, easy even. They picked up where they'd left off that night in L.A. as if it only six hours had elapsed, not six months, one subject leading naturally to the next. By the time the dessert dishes had been cleared away, they both knew a great many things about each other that the gossip columnists of America would kill to uncover. But one subject lay untouched: Jenna hadn't been able to bring herself to mention her pregnancy.

"Can I take you home?" Scott asked graciously. She agreed, hoping she could find the words on her own turf. When they pulled up to the building, she invited him up.

"GUESS I'M GOING to have to rethink you completely, 'Miss Bradford.' I didn't have you pegged as the Beacon Hill type," Scott laughed. Looking around, he whistled. "Wow, great place."

"My parents are the Beacon Hill type, not me," Jenna reminded him, handing him a club soda and cranberry. Taking her own, she dropped herself on one of a pair of love seats that flanked a cozy gas fireplace. With the push of a button, a small fire sprang to life. Scott, still determined not to crowd her, sat down quite deliberately on the opposite love seat. Judging by the appreciative look on Jenna's face, the gesture hadn't been lost on her.

Jenna suddenly found herself feeling amazingly comfortable with this dark-haired, dark-eyed wild man. "Scott, I have to tell you something." She chose her words carefully. "I truly admire the way you've turned your life around. It's gotta make you proud that you've been able to accomplish so much."

Scott started to speak, but she held up a hand to stop him. "No, please, let me finish. I'm just getting started." She set her glass down and sat forward. "Given your history, most people would have destroyed themselves. And, not only have you changed your own life, but you've helped countless others as well. Nobody can take that away from you. You should be so proud of yourself."

Scott practically blushed with embarrassment. "God, thank you. I'll admit it – that means a lot, I can't tell you how much. Yeah, I guess I'm sort of proud – okay, I *am* proud of where I am today. I can say that. But I didn't do it myself. The fact is, Jenna, I put my faith in God – and here I am." His smile was humble. He raised his glass to her. "Here I am, with you."

"Here we are," Jenna agreed, raising hers in response.

Scott stood up. "It's late. I'm going to go." Jenna, flustered, rose as well. She wanted to bring up the elephant in the middle of her belly, but how could she now?

She retrieved Scott's coat and walked him to the door. With one hand on the knob, he turned back to her. "Good night, amazing Jenna." He quietly kissed her on the cheek. Breathing in the smell of her, he couldn't stop. He took her in his arms and kissed her on the lips, a long, slow, hungry kiss. Jenna melted into the moment, then pulled herself back from it with greatest of efforts.

Scott quickly let go, pulled himself together and smiled shyly. "Can I call you tomorrow – Miss Bradford?"

Jenna looked down, disappearing into herself for a split second. Then she looked Scott straight in the eye. She knew she couldn't let this train of thought continue.

"Scott, that's just not a good idea," she said, shaking her head miserably. "I really enjoyed tonight, more than you'll ever know, but – I don't think we should see each other again. Come sit down again and let me really explain myself."

She took him by the hand and led him back to the fireplace. This time she sat him next to her. Continuing to hold his hand, she launched into what she'd wanted to say with every sentence, all evening long. "Scott, I left Derek because he'd gotten a call from his wife. I got the feeling he might go back to her. Damn. I haven't told anybody this, and I'm not proud of it. This is so embarrassing. I was – afraid." She stopped, then steeled herself for the hardest part.

"I had found out that very morning that I'm – pregnant." She let the thought sink in, then found herself searching his face for a reaction. He put his free hand over hers and gave it a gentle squeeze. Strengthened by the simple gesture of support, she plunged on.

"The thing is, I didn't know what I'd do if he had told me he was going back to her. So I packed my things and left. That's why I came here. I needed time – and a place – to think, to decide what I should do. I know I have to tell him. He has a right to know. But I don't know how. And I'm not at all sure *what* I should be telling him."

Letting go of his hand, Jenna rose and stood with her back to the fireplace. She was shivering. "Scott, I can't drag you into my mess. Which is why I think it best we don't see each other any further. I'm sorry. I'm *so* sorry. I should never have agreed to see you in the first place. I knew I'd have to tell you – but I have to admit, I really did want to spend the evening with you. I hope you can understand – and forgive me." She turned away from him so she wouldn't have to see the disappointment – or anger – in his face. Nor did she want him to see the tears in her eyes, either.

Scott stood still, absorbing all she'd told him. Then he went to her and held her as she tried to fight the tears. "Do you want to go back to him?" he whispered in her ear. She stood still in his arms, listening. "If you don't, then I don't care if you're pregnant. It doesn't change how I feel about you. I told you the first time we met that you were going to be in my life. I still believe that. Unless you want him, I'm not going anywhere."

Jenna wished she could say 'all right,' but life wasn't that simple and she didn't want to hurt him anymore then she had already. She raised her lips to his ear. "I don't know if I want to go back to him, but that's not the point, Scott. I cannot – I *will* not – drag you into this, taking the chance that down the road you'll regret it or, worse yet, come to hate me." Freeing herself from his embrace, she looked up at him. "Please, Scott, just go now – and don't look back, because I can't take the look on your face."

Opening the door, looking at the floor, she stood there until he complied – but not until he'd told her, "I'm not giving up on us, Jenna Bradford." Quietly, she shut the door. Quietly, she cried herself to sleep.

Chapter 7

JENNA WOKE TO the sound of the phone ringing. She didn't answer it. Four rings later, the answering machine stepped in for her. "Mornin', Jenna," Scott's voice came from the machine in the hall. "You there? Well – later." Jenna sighed, curled up in a ball and went back to sleep.

Call followed call, all day. Each time, Jenna sat staring at the answering machine as he left his messages, each laced with mounting frustration and creative attempts at persuasion. Finally, she just got up and went out.

After a week's worth of persistence, she finally answered. "Jenna!" Scott said, surprised. "Do you want to talk, or would you prefer I leave the message I just finished working up? This one's good."

"Scott, please, either you stop calling me or I'll change the number. There's nothing more to say. I told you how I feel. That's – it." She hung up the phone. He didn't call back. Perhaps she finally got through to him.

"WELL, BOB, WHY don't you tell their fans about the surprise announcement of a special Blacklace show here in Boston." A pretty, pert announcer smiled archly into the camera.

"That's right, folks," said her co-anchor, taking his cue. "What's just been announced is a short-notice, big venue show for Boston's own Blacklace, and it's going to sell out the Garden quickly, that you can count on." Jenna gasped as a recent photo of the band filled the screen.

It had been two weeks since she told Scott to stop calling her. Sitting at the counter, a spoonful of cereal en route to her mouth, she burst into tears. She turned off the television and let her tears run their course. It was all over but the sniffling when the phone rang. Still letting the answering machine pick up, she was shocked to hear her mother's voice soundly clearly panicked.

"Jenna, Jenna! It's me. Jenna, are you –" Jenna picked up.

"Mom? Is something the matter?"

"Jenna, it's your father. He's had a heart attack. They've just taken him to Cedars-Sinai."

"Oh, Mom. Oh, God. Is it bad? Of course it's bad. I'll get the first plane out."

In an hour and a half she was approaching 35,000 feet. Staring out the window as the plane climbed through heavy cloud cover, the thought of Scott – the image of Scott – appeared before her. She wished he were holding her right now. She'd never felt so alone.

"MOM, CHRIS, JIM." Jenna found her family in the intensive care waiting room and gathered all three to her. "How is he? How's Daddy"

"He's not doing well," Linda answered soberly. "Honey, they don't think he's going to make it." She choked and turned away. Jim put an arm around her and led her to a chair.

"I can't believe it, Chris," Jenna said in a daze. "It's been less than a month… He was fine. I have to see him. Where is he?"

"Hold on," Chris said. "Go sit with Mom. I'll see if they'll let us in." In a moment he returned. "It's okay."

Nothing could have prepared Jenna for the sight she walked in on, the machinery, the tubes, the grim, businesslike faces of the doctors and nurses in attendance. A nurse stepped aside so she could approach the bed.

"Dad. Daddy, its Jenna. I'm here now. Please, wake up," she said quietly, trying not to cry. He looked so helpless, so weak, so barely alive. But his eyes did open. He tried to smile.

"Jenna," he said slowly. "My sweetie. You're here."

Jenna took his hand and squeezed. "Daddy. Oh, Daddy."

"I'm so glad. Sweetie, I – need to tell you something I should have told you a long time ago." He sagged with the effort of speaking.

"Stop, Daddy. You rest. You're going to be okay. It can wait."

"No – now. I have to – apologize." He closed his eyes, then opened them again and fixed them on her fiercely. "I did what I thought – was right for you, but – I'll never know if it was the right decision. I love you. Don't you ever forget it."

"What are you talking about? You've been a wonderful father, Daddy," Jenna said softly, "to all of us. You were *always* there for me. What do you mean?"

Her father's mouth started to move but no words came out. His eyes locked on hers, he fell into unconsciousness. Death came a half hour later.

ROBERT BRADFORD'S PASSING was headline news. Joe Tenny caught it on TV and called to his son down the hall. "Your girlfriend's father died, did you know?"

Joe knew the current state of affairs between Jenna and his son, at least that she didn't want to see Scott any further, but that didn't stop him from constantly referring to her as 'your girlfriend.' Scott happened to love it.

Scott came into the room and sat down next to his father in time to see images of the family outside their Beverly Hills home as they returned from the hospital, in time to see Jenna as she stepped out of the limo. A camera zoomed in for a close up, leaving no question as to how profoundly upset she was. She'd shared with him how very close she was to her father. Given her pregnancy, he hoped there was no cause for concern.

"Dad – this may sound crazy, but I'm getting on a plane. I have to go be with her." His father didn't look the least bit surprised.

"Go pack. I'll make you a reservation."

"FOREST LAWN." LINDA said the words as if in a trance. The family sat, subdued, in the study. "He once said he looked forward to being buried in Forest Lawn. It's a beautiful plot. 'The ultimate cattle call for actors,' he called it." She sighed.

The doorbell rang. A moment later Adella, her eyes also red-rimmed from recent tears, appeared at the door. "Jenna, someone ees here to see you, dear." Jenna looked up to find Scott standing at the doorway, clearly not sure if he should enter. Without a thought, she jumped up and ran into his arms and clung to the strength of him.

"I'm so glad you came," she murmured through tears of both joy and sadness.

Linda got up and went over to the two of them. "Scott," she said, putting out her hand. "Thank you for coming." Scott gave her a long, quiet hug instead.

"I had to come pay my respects," he offered by way of explanation.

"Jim, Chris, this is Scott Tenny," she introduced him to her sons. The three shook hands somberly. "Scott, Jenna, why don't you two go for a walk. It'll give you some time alone to talk." They quietly left the room.

Jenna led Scott outside across an upper terrace, downhill through a lush landscape of bougainvillea, hibiscus, bamboo and palm. Finally emerging from the foliage, well out of sight of the house, Scott found himself on a secluded flagstone patio, at the center of which was a pristine, crystal-clear pool. To one side of the area was a small pool house, covered in jasmine vines. At the furthest end of the patio was a little grotto; a waterfall cascaded down one wall, drowning out the sounds of the city. A small stone bench partly within the grotto beckoned to them. The night was warm and still. Scott sat down and drew her to him.

"Do you want to talk about it?" Scott asked, taking her hand.

"It was so sudden. He went so fast," Jenna answered, casting about for the right words. "I'm just so – grateful that I got here in time to see him, to let him know I much I loved him. But – it was strange. He was trying to tell me something." She stopped to wipe fresh tears. "But he couldn't finish. I don't understand what he did say."

"Which was…?"

"He said, 'I did what I thought was right for you, but I'll never know if it was the right decision.'" She shook her head, sadly. "He was a wonderful father. He was always there for me. I can't remember him ever doing anything that made me really angry, or him ever saying something was for my own good, nothing like that. I guess now I'll never know what he meant. God, it's hard."

Scott pulled her close to him and tried to comfort her. She laid her head on his chest and sighed. Then she looked up at him and he kissed her and held her tight.

"Scott, I'm so sorry that I told you to leave me alone back in Boston. I never wanted to hurt you. I didn't really want you to go."

"I know," he whispered. "I know." Then, removing only what was absolutely necessary, he tenderly made love to her.

JENNA HAD NEVER felt as warm and safe as she did in Scott's his arms as the two lay together, enjoying the heat of their bodies where skin met skin. Jenna finally broke the breathless silence.

"Scott, I've been such a fool. The night you told me I'd be part of your life – I felt something too, but I was damned if I was going to admit it. And then I went and ruined everything."

"Baby! You didn't ruin anything – don't you know that?" he said, tracing the curve of her cheek. "Don't you get it? I'm madly in love with you. I've been in love with you since that first night we met. And you know what? I have no intentions of letting you get away this time." Jenna looked into his eyes. She could see how much he cared for her.

"I'm just now allowing myself to fall in love with you, Scott. And it scares me, because I don't want to screw things up again."

"Little girl, do you know how many relationships *I've* screwed up!" Scott laughed. "You'll never have a more understanding co-conspirator than me, my dear. I'm scared too – I'm scared shitless, if you have to know. All I can say is, I know in *my* heart this is different. Give it a chance and see if it isn't the same for you. Can you?"

Jenna sighed deeply as the crushing weight of her family's realities settled back down on her. "Scott, you beautiful man. Right now my first priority has to be getting through Dad's funeral. When this is over, I promise – "

Scott, drawing her into another kiss, didn't let her finish the sentence. "Just remember, I'm here for you," he whispered into her hair.

PULLING THEMSELVES TOGETHER, they returned to the house in a confused haze of love and pain. Friends were dropping in to stay for a moment or two. Introductions were constant. Between callers, Linda took them aside.

"You two dear hearts, I just want to say something." She took a hand of each in hers. "Bob has to be so happy knowing you're together here tonight, and I'm sure he's thinking it's all because of his machinations. He was so damned proud that it was his idea, you going back to Boston, honey. When I told him you two were going on your first date, why, he just cackled." She shook her head and smiled painfully. "It was his last great idea." That first date that had been their only date, Jenna thought to herself – her father hadn't known that.

Taking Jenna by the hands, she spoke to her directly. "Jenna, honey, I want you to put Scott in one of the guest rooms. See what's free – I haven't got a clue who's coming and going. Scott," she said, turning to him. "As far as I'm concerned, whenever anyone uses the word 'family,' you're included."

Scott responded with a hug that included both mother and daughter.

THE NEXT MORNING, the family, Scott included, arrayed in everything from pajamas to suit and tie, sat quietly around the breakfast table. Sue sat next to Jim; she'd arrived at five in the morning, and looked it.

The doorbell rang. Almost immediately, Adella returned with a special delivery letter for Linda. Notes and cards had been arriving all morning. Linda opened it, started reading it, then got up abruptly and left the room.

"What's that about?" Jim wondered aloud, speaking for everyone.

Jenna excused herself and went looking for her mother. She found her in the study, reading the letter. Jenna went and sat next to her. There were tears in her mother's eyes. "Maybe you should wait a bit to read condolences, Mom," she suggested, putting an arm around her. Her mother stiffened. "Mom, what's wrong?"

"Jenna, there's – oh dear. There's something I have to tell you and your brothers that your father and I should have told you years ago. Bring them in here, will you? Scott, too," she reminded her.

Jenna rose, puzzled. Going to round up the others, she wondered if perhaps it had anything to do with what her father had tried to tell her in the hospital.

As everyone filed into the study, Linda stood by the fireplace, looking at her husband's photo on the mantle. When she turned to face them all, she found herself surprisingly composed and calm.

"As you all know, I left this family when you were all young, and I know you've always wondered why. I guess you gave up asking years ago, since we weren't remotely forthcoming on the subject. Well," she said, looking around at them all, "the truth is that one day I discovered my husband had been having an affair." There was an audible gasp in the room. "That's right. Your father, not me. It had been going on for four years. When I found out, I was devastated.

"At the time I felt it would be better for you to stay here, where your lives were. I had no idea where I was going, what I was going to do. Your father pleaded with me not to go but I had to get away from him. During those two years that I was away, he and I saw and spoke with each other often, particularly about all of his children." Linda paused and let that phrase hang in the air.

"Eventually, he convinced me to come back to start over, and so I did. We decided – for better or for worse – to tell you the only story you've known all these years, about *my* having an affair. I was willing to do that. There was plenty of reason for you all to be angry with me – I'd left you. We didn't want you to be angry with both of us.

"Well, my dears, the time has come for the truth." Everyone was silent. Scott held Jenna as Linda continued. "Your father's affair produced a child, another daughter – whose name is Kristin, Kristin Yates." Again she paused to give them a moment to adjust to this even more difficult new fact in their respective lives. "She'd just turned three when I found out. Her mother was furious when Bob ended the affair. She took off with the child. He managed to find them, but she bore him only hatred. Rather than subject the child to this, he agreed to leave them alone. He sent money every month and he saw her a few times through the years, from a distance. We went and watched her graduate from high school.

"But one day she was going through old photographs and found some of your father with her as a baby, as well as some of her mother and him. She finally got the truth out of her mother. That's when she decided to look for him. When she found him, your father explained as much as he could. But he made her promise that she would not have contact with any of you. He was terrified that you'd all hate him. She understood and agreed. When I learned of it, I told him he should tell you, so you could all get to know each other. He refused. He loved her, don't misunderstand – he loved her very much. But his shame outweighed that love, which can only give you a sense of the scale of that shame.

"Kristin is just as upset as the rest of us at the news of his death. She's asking," Linda continued, holding up the letter, "permission to come to his funeral – her own father's funeral, just as simply another person there to pay her respects. She doesn't want to make trouble or hurt any one of us in any way. She just wants to be there to say goodbye to the father she hardly knew.

"I respect her for asking me directly. I've seen her a few times and she seems to be a lovely person. I want her to be able to come to say goodbye to him. But, in order to do so, I had to tell you this. I can't speak for you.

"I don't know what your thoughts are. I can only imagine. I am asking you to please respect my wishes and accept her presence." She got up and left the room.

JENNA AND HER brothers looked at one another, visibly stunned. Jenna glanced up at Scott with a blank face, trying to get her mind around the maelstrom of thoughts and emotions swirling within her. "Oh, Scott. You don't have a clue what just happened here. Welcome to the family." Her attempt at levity disappeared, replaced by a rising fury. "How could my – our – father do this to all of us? We were raised to believe that our mother had an affair. We were raised to believe that he made her go. I didn't hate *him* for it – I felt abandoned and betrayed by *her*. And, then when she came back, God, it took forever for us to reach some sort of a comfort level with each other, and for what? *He* had the affair and, on top of that, he has another daughter who he chose to keep from us. What was he thinking?"

She covered her face. "If this is what he wanted to tell me, I'm just damned glad he didn't, because I don't know what I would have said to him." Scott put his arms around her and held her close to him. Rigid with anger, she wasn't crying.

"And this is the guy who always told us to do the right thing in life," Jim said with a snort, jumping to his feet. "Look what he did, the fucking bastard. Good to *us*, there for *us*, giving *us* whatever we needed, loving *us*. And all the while, he has another kid he ignored? To cover up his *shame*? Why did she let him do that to her, for chrissakes?" He sat back down, shaking his head. Sue took his hand and tried to sooth him.

"Don't criticize Mom, Jim," Jenna said, turning to face him. "Clearly, it wasn't her decision to make. The fact that she let him go on all these years, that was her loyalty to him. But, God, Dad – why didn't he think we'd understand, once we were older? I resent the fact that he kept her from us all these years."

"That's not all he kept from you," Jim blurted out, "Not even the half of it."

"What do you mean?" Jenna asked sharply. "What *else* don't we know? Or do you really mean just *me*?"

"Sorry," Jim back-peddled quickly. "I don't know anything else. It's – I'm just thinking that anyone who could keep that kind of thing to himself – who knows what else. I didn't mean it personally." Scott's antennae went up. Something in Jim's manner didn't wash. Something told him that, whatever it was that her father had tried to tell Jenna, Jim knew something about it.

Chris stood up and started pacing, not looking at anyone in particular as he worked his thoughts out. "Whatever the story, guys, we have a sister out there, who we don't know, who doesn't know us. And she wants to come to her father's funeral. That's the issue we should be discussing. You two can argue later, all you want. I for one think we should be as understanding as we can be, and give Mom our support in her decision." Chris – the peacemaker in the family, especially between Jenna and Jim, which whenever they all got together, amounted to a fulltime job. Both finally nodded.

Scott looked down at Jenna, knowing what had to be going through her mind. Her status as Daddy's little girl, Daddy's *only* little girl, had to be completely reconfigured. Her image of her father had to be completely reconstructed. She had some hard work ahead of her. "Would you like me to go find Linda?" he asked them all. "So you can tell her where you are in your thinking?"

SCOTT WALKED JENNA upstairs to her bedroom door and kissed her quietly. "You want to come in?" she asked tentatively.

"No. It wouldn't be seemly. And you need to get yourself some rest. This has been one long fucker of a day for you, pretty lady. You need to take care of yourself – and that baby." He touched her stomach, then took her hand and held it to his lips as he had the day they ran into each other in Boston, what seemed so long ago now. With a smile, he turned and walked down the hall to his room.

Chapter 8

LINDA PHONED KRISTIN in the morning and, in a short conversation, cordially invited her to come over to meet her half-brothers and sister early that afternoon. Jim, Chris, Jenna and Linda sat in the study nervously awaiting her arrival. The doorbell rang.

"Well…" Linda said, smoothing her hair. "Let's all try to put her at her ease. She is your sister, after all." Her well-intentioned sentiments rang somewhat hollow.

"Somebody put me at *my* ease," groused Jim.

"Miss Yates ees here," Adella announced, then vanished. Standing in the door was a slightly smaller version of Jenna. No one knew what to say.

Kristin looked decidedly uncomfortable. Linda quickly got to her feet.

"Kristin," she said warmly, taking the girl by both hands, "come in, come in. This is your family. Your older brothers, Jim and Chris, and this is your sister, Jenna. Everyone, this is your sister, Kristin." Kristin couldn't have looked more uncomfortable.

Jenna was the first to speak. "Please, Kristin – come sit over here." Jenna patted a cushion beside her on the couch.

"Thank you," Kristin said gratefully. "This is almost surreal. I feel like I see myself in all your faces."

"Let me look at you, " Jenna said, pushing a loose lock of hair out of Kristin's face. "God, I feel like I'm looking in a mirror. Surreal sure is the right word. I – I have so many questions. I'm sure you must too."

"You better believe it," Kristin answered quickly. "How do you catch up on twenty-four years of other peoples' lives?"

"MOM, YOU HAVEN'T had a chance to get a word in edgewise," Chris observed after practically half an hour of nonstop exchange between the half-siblings. Conversation, which had started out a bit awkwardly, quickly flowed.

"Darlings, I am entirely gratified, watching you all get to know each other. Kristin and I will have plenty of time to get to know one another, living as close as we do." Kristin's mother's home was just over the hill in Sherman Oaks. "I just want to say, Kristin, dear – please, think of our home as your home. I mean that. I feel like you are such a part of us, already."

"Linda, that means so much to me," Kristin said, trying not to choke up. "You can't begin to know. It's been so hard. I grew up feeling like the kid with her nose pressed up against the bakery window. I so wanted a whole family to grow up with. My mom – I don't want to say anything bad about my mom, but she's a very bitter woman." Kristin looked at her hands. She knew how hard this had to be for Linda, but she also had to say it. "She never married. She's estranged from her family. I certainly could never let her know I've become a part of your family. It's not going to be easy. But – I've taken care of her for so long. It's time I take care of myself. I – I want to *be* your sister," she said, taking them all in with a longing look.

Jenna took her hand. "You are," she said simply and sincerely.

Jim got up. "Time for you to meet the in-laws – and out-laws." He went out to the garden to get Sue and Scott, who'd both felt their presence would only further complicate an already complicated situation. While he was gone, Jenna whispered to Kristin, "I've always wanted a sister." Kristin burst into her first tears of the afternoon. "Me, too," she choked.

As Sue and Scott entered and were introduced to Kristin, Linda sat watching, but also wondering. The next few days would be hard enough. What would she do when the media started asking questions about this woman – why she was with the family and such? The media was quick to pick up on such minute details. She wasn't remotely sure how to handle it. Turning to Scott, she whispered, "Could I talk to you?"

"Sure."

"Would you all excuse us for a moment?" she asked the group. Taking Scott by the hand, she exited the room.

Down the hall, she got right to the point. "What do I say to the media when they ask who she is? Why she's sitting with the family? I mean, is that the time to tell all? It's been hard enough telling my children everything, let alone the world. I have to think of them and how they'll be hounded by all of this. What should I do?"

Scott hesitated a moment before he spoke. "Linda, I know why you want my advice and I could give you my opinion, but – wouldn't it be better to talk with your children, let *them* help decide what to do? I certainly can't speak for your sons, and I haven't known Jenna long, but my guess is she'd tell you to address the media now, just as she suggested meeting Kristin before the funeral."

Jenna came down the hall, went to Scott, who put an arm around her, then faced her mother. "Sorry – I've been eavesdropping. Scott's right. Talk with all of us, Mom, then let the media know. Now."

Linda threw up her hands. "You're right – you're both right."

"Go talk to the rest of them," said Jenna, giving her mother a squeeze. Linda headed down the hall.

"Thank you," Jenna said simply to Scott. "For someone who hasn't known me very long, you seem pretty sure about what I'd say."

"You've been eavesdropping?"

"Yep." As they embraced, Scott looked down at her. "True, I haven't known you all that long – but I think I know you better then you realize." He gave her a quick kiss, then they went to join the others. By the time they returned to the study, all were in agreement on addressing the media, letting them know why Kristin would be sitting with the family at the funeral.

HUNDREDS ATTENDED SERVICES for Robert Bradford. In spite of the 'news' about his illegitimate daughter, most were cordial to Kristin.

Scott sat behind Jenna. As her shoulders started to shake, he reached forward, put his hands on them and whispered, "I'm here for you, babe." She grabbed his hand and squeezed it in acknowledgement of her gratitude.

Kristin sat beside her older sister. Jenna could see the tears in her eyes and couldn't help but feel sorry for her. Kristin had never had the opportunity of getting to know their father. She wondered if the tears were for his dying – or for herself, knowing she would never have the chance to be in his life now. Jenna took hold of Kristin's hand. Kristin held on as if to a life ring.

When the services ended, both stayed on at the cemetery. Scott stood aside, waiting for Jenna. Jenna and Kristin walked together to their father's graveside.

"You go first," Jenna said to Kristin, moving over to Scott.

Kristin stood by her father's grave, her mouth moving in prolonged conversation. Finally, she leaned down, tossed a single rose down onto her father's casket and returned to Jenna's side.

"Go wait with Scott," Jenna suggested. Kristin did.

JENNA STOOD BY her father's grave and stared for the longest time. Finally, she started talking to him. "Daddy. Daddy, how could you? I don't know why you did what you did about Kristin, but I have to tell you – it stinks. Why couldn't you tell us about her before? We were adults, Daddy. This is crazy! Why couldn't you make her a real part of your life? And our lives? How could you do that to such a wonderful woman, person – your daughter? I feel diminished as a daughter, knowing this is how you can treat your other daughter.

"I guess I didn't know you, after all. But I do love you, Dad. I know you thought you were doing the right thing by all of us. I don't know if that's what you wanted to tell me at the hospital, but if it is, I want you to know, I forgive you. I'm going to make sure Kristin knows who you were, and that she's family to me.

"Go rest in peace, Daddy. I love you." She started to leave, then turned back. "Oh, and by the way, Dad – you're going to be a grandfather. I know you would have been a fabulous grandfather, Daddy."

With tears streaming down her face, Jenna turned to Scott and her sister, and left the cemetery.

"I CAN'T TAKE anymore of this mob scene," Jenna whispered to Scott. "I needed to get out of here before I scream." The house was awash in friends of the family.

"Come on. Let's go out back," Scott suggested. "I know a nice little bench…"

Straddling the bench by the grotto, Scott pulled Jenna down in front of him, with her back turned to him, and wrapped his arms around her. The two sat drinking in the peace and quiet. Finally, he brought his lips to the back of her neck and kissed her softly. "You okay?" he whispered.

"I could be better." Jenna paused. "God, this is all so hard."

"It's gotta be. You've been a trooper." He started massaging her shoulders, then proceeded slowly down her back. Jenna groaned with a combination of pleasure and complete exhaustion. "Sweet Jenna, I know things have been hectic – but have you given any thought to what's next?"

"You're kidding, right?" Jenna answered ruefully. "Nothing but. I had morning sickness this morning. I can't cover it up much longer. I have to get back to Boston if I'm going to have any privacy while I decide what to do."

"I can't stay much longer. I have to get back for rehearsals. Come back to Boston with me."

"I can't, not that quickly. I need to make sure Mom's going to be all right." Sitting up, she swung her leg over the bench. "And there's Kristin. I want to help her figure out what she's going to do. Her mother's furious with her, now that it's all been in the news. They aren't speaking. She doesn't want to go back there anyway."

Reaching down, Jenna picked up a pebble, tossed it gently into the little pond at the foot of the waterfall and watched the ripples till they faded away. "All the ripples," she mused. "I get pregnant. I leave. I go to Boston. You. Dad dies. You again! Kristin comes into our lives… Life is just so – so overwhelming, sometimes."

Scott ran a soothing hand through her long hair. "It sure can be."

"The last thing I want my mother to have to think about right now is this baby. I'll tell her once she's through the worst of this." Jenna leaned against him again, put a hand on his shoulder and closed her eyes. "I'd love to go back with you, Scott, but it's just a little to early. I'll get back as soon as I can. That's a promise. When do you have to go?"

"I can stay another day, maybe two," Scott said. "Let me help, anything so you can come back sooner." He leaned down and kissed the hand on his shoulder.

✳

"YOU ALL HAVE my deepest condolences." Jack Maloney looked around the dining room table where the family, Kristin, Sue and Scott included, sat assembled. "I've been Bob's friend since college. He had enough blind confidence in me to sign on as one of my first clients. We've lived a lifetime together, him and me." The attorney shook his head. "I never imagined – I'd always hoped the reading of this will would be years in the future."

"I want you to know, in everything we ever did together, I always tried to advise Bob as best as I could, but he was his own man. His decisions were always his own, including the contents of this will." Sitting down, he began reading. "I, Robert Bradford, being of sound mind…"

Linda received the largest inheritance, the house and half of her husband's estate. Jim and Chris were left equal shares of money, as well as personal items meaningful to each. To Jenna went a third more cash than either of her brothers and the apartment in Boston. Jack stopped, set down the will and went into his briefcase. Pulling out an envelope, he handed it across the table to her. "This is also for you, Jenna, with the stipulation that you not open it unless and until you are pregnant."

Jenna stifled a gasp. Scott, sitting next to her, put an unseen, steadying hand on her thigh. She barely heard Jack's further, lighter comments. "That, of course, is up to you – you keep the envelope. You don't have to come to me with a doctor's note." Chris chuckled.

"How odd," Linda commented dryly.

With everyone's eyes on the envelope in Jenna's hand, no one noticed how Jim had blanched at hearing the instructions written across its front. "Dad could be an odd bird," Jim said flatly, finally. "An extremely odd bird."

Jenna took the envelope and sat staring at it as the attorney proceeded.

"And for Kristin, $500,000 in cash and securities, and –" Again, he went into his briefcase. "Another envelope. This is like the Oscars. This one comes with no stipulations about opening it, Kristin," he said as he put it in her hands.

AFTER JACK HAD left, Kristin opened the envelope. "I'd like to read it to you all. I think it's best if there aren't any more secrets," she said before unfolding the page within. Around the room, everyone nodded. As she pulled out the letter, two pictures fell to the table for all to see. A much younger Bob, holding Kristin as an infant. The same younger Bob at a first birthday party.

"My dear Kristin," the letter began. "First and foremost, I have to apologize for not having played more of a role in your life. Your mother would never permit it. I want you to know that I thought of you constantly. Even if I couldn't be a part of your life, I want you to know that I loved you every bit as much as my other children, which is why you deserve as much consideration in my will as the rest. I hope you will accept the money and make a good life for yourself." Kristin stopped as tears began to flow. Jenna moved over behind her and put a comforting arm around her. Kristin calmed herself and continued.

"Jenna will undoubtedly be the one to tell you the most about me." Kristin looked up and smiled through her tears. "You can feel comfortable with her. I hope you'll get to know each other as sisters. She will need you almost as much as you will need her. With much love, Your father."

Jenna's eyes returned to the envelope which she'd set gingerly in front of her on the table. "Jenna Bradford – not to be opened until pregnant" was typed across the front of it.

"GO BACK TO Boston with Scott," Linda insisted. "I'll be okay. Chris is close, Jim's here if I need him, and Kristin will be with me." Surprising everyone by referring to Kristin as her "step-daughter" after the reading of the will, Linda had invited their new sibling to move in for as long as she wanted. Kristin, struck dumb with amazement, had eagerly accepted her invitation.

"No, Jenna, you go," Linda persisted. "You need to get on with things back there. I know Scott has to leave. You should go with him."

"My work can wait, Mom," Jenna said.

"Go," her mother stated flatly.

"I'll call every day." Jenna gave her mother a rare, long hug.

Chapter 9

JENNA SLEPT ALMOST the entire flight back to Boston. Scott played mother hen, making sure she wasn't disturbed.

"I can only imagine what's going through your head at this point," he said, looking at her intently as they rode into the city in a cab. "Anything you want, or need, to share with me?"

Jenna leaned over and whispered in his ear, "Just my bed. Would you stay with me and just hold me? I don't think I can be –" Her voice cracked, "– alone." Scott held her close.

Arriving at her apartment, Charles was waiting by the curb. "I was so sorry to hear about your dad, Miss Bradford," he said, helping her out of the car. "You go ahead. I'll have your bags up in a few minutes."

"You hungry?" Scott asked her. "Want to get something to eat first?"

"God, I'm sleepwalking but I *am* hungry."

"How about a little dinner? Some quiet conversation?" Scott suggested.

"Only if it's not about family or problems. I'm exhausted with all that. There's a little Italian place around the corner. You'll love it."

The place was called Rosie's, and Rosie herself, a cheerful, solid woman in her fifties, greeted them at the door. "Jenna, it's been forever. How are you? I'm so sorry about you father. I know how close you were to him," she said, embracing Jenna while flashing a winning smile at Scott. "This handsome guy looks just a little bit familiar. Introduce me! I'm a great fan."

Rosie bustled them to a table. "So sit. Eat. We'll take good care of you. I just have to tell you – you two make a good looking couple. Now let me shut up and get you something to drink," she laughed. "What'll it be?"

"Club soda for me, Rosie," Jenna said.

"Same here, hon," Scott said to her with a wink.

"You got it, you two," Rosie said, returning his wink. "Back in a shake."

SCOTT DETAILED THE next several months over coffee. "So we do these odd shows now – Worcester, Farmington, Meadowbrook, pull the new album together and then Eddie and Big Bob have one hell of a schedule cooked up for us for the summer. It's relentless." Big Bob O'Halligan was Blacklace's road manager.

"Hey," Scott interrupted. "I have an idea. How about you come to a rehearsal with me. No, wait – this is one heck of an exclusive invite here. You get to listen to us fart around, argue, screw up, probably attempt murder a couple times, get manic and with any luck actually come up with something good. It's really quite the process. And – if you're a good girl – maybe I'd even let you sing with me."

Jenna tipped her head to one side, appraisingly. "Whaddya gonna do if I sing better then you?"

"Deal with it," he answered her coolly. "You'd be amazed at what I can deal with."

JENNA TURNED THE key in the lock and opened the door of the apartment – her apartment, now – and she and Scott walked in. For some reason, it seemed so natural, so comfortable – as if they'd been walking through this door together forever. "It's never felt so much like home," she said softly, laying a hand on the hall table as if to ground herself. Scott laid his hand over hers and smiled at her in the mirror hanging above it. While she watched in the mirror, he kissed the nape of her neck. Then he helped her out of her jacket and hung it in the hallway closet.

"Such a gentleman," Jenna purred.

Turning back to her, he just as graciously helped her out of her sweater, which he dropped on the floor, and the blouse she wore beneath it. And the bra beneath that. Jenna's and Scott's eyes remained locked on each other's in the mirror.

"Nobody accuses me of being a gentlemen and gets away with it," he whispered in her ear as he nuzzled it. Then he picked her up and carried her to the bedroom, laying her down on the bed where he continued removing her clothes piece by piece until there was nothing left to remove. She lay there, naked and resplendent, as he stripped off his shirt, kicked off shoes and tight jeans, shed boxers and socks and approached her across the bed on all fours, like a sleek, sinewy snow leopard stalking its prey. Like a wild animal, he smelled her first, from behind her neck under her hair, across her breasts and on down her body, lingering to drink in her most womanly aromas and back up. Then he tasted her.

JENNA AWOKE THE next morning to an empty bed and the rich smell of coffee brewing. Slipping on a see-through chiffon wrapper, she followed the smell to the kitchen, where she found him, naked but for an incongruous apron, cutting a batch of scones and arranging them on a baking sheet. "Aren't you the sight," she laughed sleepily, coming up behind him and running her hands down his lank and firmly muscled body.

"The oven's all preheated for you, baby," he said suggestively. Opening the stove door to pop the scones in, he felt his apron strings loosen and fall, and a pair of hands slide maddeningly slowly towards his now throbbing manhood.

"Holy shit, it sure is, bakerman," Jenna laughed throatily. Turning, he slowly, deliberately, untied the belt of Jenna's slight excuse for a robe, pushed it off her shoulders and let it fall to the floor.

"I love a man who knows his way around a kitchen," she murmured huskily, rubbing her ample bosom against his rugged frame. His hands slipped down and pulled her hard against him. With a moan, she arched her back, offering her breasts to his seeking mouth. Leaning her back against the kitchen counter, he put the fifteen minutes it would take the scones to bake to excellent use. They spent the morning in bed. "Getting to know you better," was how Scott described it.

"WELL, HERE WE are," Scott said simply but with obvious pride, "and we've got the whole place to ourselves." He'd come a long way in his life, and this home was the embodiment of that journey. The rambling, five-bedroom shingled house and outbuildings, with their panoramic view of the Atlantic, rivaled any of the opulent summer cottages of the wealthy that dotted the shores of Massachusetts. "Dad's up at the lake for the week. The barn over there, that's our studio. Wait'll you see it, babe." Unlocking the front door, he turned and scooped her up in his arms. "Get used to it. I intend to make a regular practice of this," he grinned down at her.

Setting her on her feet, she turned and gasped at the scale – and casual comfort – of the richly paneled, two-story living room. A balcony above, walled with floor-to-ceiling bookshelves, bracketed two sides of the room.

"WE'LL TAKE THE Maserati," Scott decided as the sun prepared to set. Jenna expected to find a sleek, new sports car – black, she guessed – as Scott opened the garage door. Instead, the vehicle that was revealed resembled something that might have raced at LeMans – and might have been designed by a cartoonist. "Like her?" Scott asked. "One of the rare '62 151s." It was white. A pair of red racing stripes bisected her front to back.

Scott put Jenna in his car and drove her to a secluded beach nearby. Grabbing her by the hand, he took them running down to the water line. They had the beach to themselves. The air was crisp, clear and bright.

"That's Cape Cod," Scott said pointing across miles of dark blue water to a faint tracery against the horizon.

Jenna turned her collar up against the wind. "This is so beautiful," she beamed. Scott pulled her close as they tracked the shoreline.

"I love coming here late in the day, after everyone's gone. The salt air, the wind. Sometimes I just sit and watch the birds."

Scott dropped to the white sand and pulled Jenna down to sit in his lap in front of him and wrapped her in his arms. Snuggling into the warmth of him, she threw her head back, eyes closed, drinking in the salt sea air. Scott moved his hands down and laid them gently on her stomach.

"You know you have to deal with this pretty soon," he said quietly. "It won't be long before you'll start to show." Jenna sighed.

"I know. I guess I'm afraid of what he'll say. What if he wants to be part of everything, the rest of the pregnancy, the delivery? I know he has a right –"

"You've gotta tell him now. You have to give everybody time to deal with it, well before the baby's born. I could be with you when you tell him, if it'd help..."

Jenna considered his offer for a moment. "No, I need to do this on my own. As much I'd love you to be with me. No, I'll fly out and see him as soon as I can. Scott," she said, then felt herself begin to tremble at what she wanted to say. She hesitated, then plunged forward. "I was – can I ask you to be there with me, when the baby's born?"

There was no hesitation in Scott's answer. "Jenna! Oh, Jenna, baby – I was so fuckin' hoping you'd ask me. I'd be honored. I mean it. You *know* I'm there for you." Elated, Scott wrapped his arms tight around her and rocked the both of them until they tipped over on their sides, laughing. Laughter soon gave way to kisses, kisses to caresses, caresses to passion.

SITTING SIPPING ESPRESSO on the porch looking at the moon, Scott hummed a few bars of "The Hard Way," one of Blacklace's early songs. Jenna hummed a bar with him, then started singing the first verse. *"Workin' hard, playin' hard, lovin' hard –"* Scott rose to his feet, came over to her and sang close harmony with her on the last line, *"Livin' life the hard way.* My, aren't we pretty together, you all honey and backbone, me all filthy dirty grit," he laughed. "So – will you stay the night? And sit in on rehearsal with us tomorrow?"

"What about your reputation, young man!" Jenna exclaimed in mock horror. "What will the boys in the band think, when I come stumbling across the grass in my negligee, green around the gills from morning sickness, nibbling nauseously on a breakfast roll?"

"That I've finally developed taste, that's what they'll think. Will you sing with us, just for fun?"

"You sure they'd be cool with that?" Jenna asked in all seriousness.

"I've already asked them. They're totally cool with it. Jeremy's always saying, 'when Scott ain't happy, ain't nobody happy' – and it's pretty true. Anything that makes me wicked happy, makes them *waaay* wicked happy."

Settling himself on the arm of the chair she was sitting in, Scott ran his hands through Jenna's hair, then planted a kiss on the top of her head, squeezed her shoulders and then her breasts. "Hey, baby – how's about making Scott even more than waaay wicked happy." Jenna looked up at him, suddenly wary. "You know," he said with a smirk, and started to unbutton the fly of his jeans. His crotch, she abruptly realized, was practically on a level with her mouth.

"Button them back up, lover boy," Jenna said, jumping to her feet, in a steely cold tone of voice that Scott barely recognized. "I'm sorry, but that's one service I do *not* provide."

Scott quickly followed directions, then threw his hands up in surrender. "Sorry. Sorrrry, lady." His words were placating; his voice said otherwise. His final words cut Jenna to the quick. "Too good for that, eh?"

"Fuck you," she spat out angrily. Turning her back on him, she walked to the edge of the porch, looked out to sea, then turned, arms crossed tightly, and faced him. "Let's just say it ain't in my repertoire, that's all. Just get used to it. And if you can't, just say so."

Scott stared at her. She was serious. This wasn't a joke. "You mean it, don't you?"

"Yes. I mean it." She waited a beat, then softened slightly "Do you want me to leave?"

Scott gaped at her, then suddenly laughed. "Are you crazy? Throw *you* outta my bed? I'd have to be deaf, dumb, blind and stupid to boot. Come back here, beautiful. I love you."

AS JENNA FINALLY started to drift off to sleep, the room bathed in moonlight, she felt Scott's hand caress her once more. "One more thing I gotta say before you fall asleep," he whispered in her ear, "and do *not* interrupt me." Jenna reached up and stroked his face.

"Blow jobs or not," he started, but stopped when Jenna quickly retracted her hand. Reaching for it, he brought it back up to his face, and held it there. "Jenna, baby – blow jobs or not, I love you. I'm so deep in love with you it scares me shitless. You're the best thing that's happened to me in years. No – make that the best thing that's *ever* happened to me, period." Jenna started to open her mouth. Scott put a shushing finger to his lips. She settled back and listened.

"I've never felt this way about any other woman – and God knows I've sampled more way more than my share. I don't know what it is about you. I just want to be with you and love you, every minute of every day. I want to be father to the child you're carrying."

After a moment's silence, Jenna asked quietly, "Can a lady get a word in edgewise here?"

Scott kissed her. "Sure. Your turn. Go."

"You're the best thing that's happened to me, too, you beautiful man – and that's what scares *me*." She suddenly found herself fighting tears. "This whole thing, Derek and everything. It could blow up into one motherfucker of a scandal, Scott. You could get hurt." She stopped, then turned to look him in the eye. "And that could ruin things between us. I couldn't take it if that happened because – we're in the same boat here. God help me, but I'm falling in love with you too. I've never felt like this, either."

"Jenna," Scott said firmly, "*nothing* is going to come between us, not Derek, not the fuckin' gossip whores. Not your nutty sexual hang-ups." He made a comic, lunatic face at her, then went serious again. "Not nothin'. You gotta believe me. Everything's gonna be all right, babe," he murmured. "Everything's gonna be so all right." Jenna fell asleep in his arms.

THE NEXT MORNING, Jenna awoke in Scott's arms, just as she'd fallen asleep. Looking up at him, she found he was wide awake. "I've been vatching you," he admitted, doing his best impression of an Interpol spy.

"What time is it? What time does everyone get here?" she asked sleepily. Scott looked at the clock.

"It's almost eight. They'll be here by ten. Plenty of time for coffee." With a groan, Jenna suddenly bolted from the bed and into the bathroom. Scott came and held her until the retching ended. As she pulled herself together, he started the shower. The master bath was fitted out with both a deep Jacuzzi tub and a spacious steam shower with double shower heads. The pulsing hot water felt luxurious on Jenna's skin. Scott lathered first her back and then her hair.

"I can't remember when I last felt so indulged," she murmured, tipping her head back to let the shower rinse the last of the shampoo from her hair. Turning to him and stepping into his embrace, their lips met under a cascade that shimmered in the morning sun.

SCOTT AND JENNA'S voices rose and merged over a crashing piano chord just as Tim came through the studio door. "Righteous," he yelled and flashed them a thumbs up. Jeremy, Jeff and Dan were only moments behind them. Jenna and Scott finished out the chorus, then stopped, laughing. Their miniscule audience burst into applause and cheering, doing their best to pass for a crowd of ten thousand.

"Shit, you two sound sensational together," Jeremy declared. "Wow. What a sound. You two *have* to sing together. The fans'll go fuckin' nuts. Move over, Ike 'n Tina."

"Johnny 'n June," said Tim. "Sonny and Cher."

"Paul and Paula," offered Dan. "You know, 'Hey, Paula,' right?" he said in response to the blank stares he was getting.

"Seriously," Jeremy said. The others were in complete agreement.

"Absolutely," Tim and Jeff said in unison.

"Totally, bro," Dan chimed in a half-beat later.

"Done," Scott said. "Well, then, let's get to work."

"Uh, excuse me, but haven't you forgotten something?" Jenna said sour-sweetly. Scott looked at her blankly.

"Maybe we oughta *ask* the lady," Jeremy prompted him.

"Oh, fuck, yeah. Whoa. Sorry!" Scott fell dramatically to one knee, clasped his hands and held them up to her, looking for all the world like Al Jolson singing 'Mammy.' "Jenna Bradford, will you – will you be my soprano?"

"Contralto."

"My – contralto? Will ya? Say yes, baby. Make me the happiest guy on earth."

Jenna made eye contact with each of the band members. "You're all sure you're on board with this?" Her question was met with emphatic nods all around.

"Let's work up a set, then!" she said, slammed with a rush of energy. She never realized how much she needed to be getting to work. It had been way too long.

"BACK TO THE bridge," Scott said. "Tim, blast in there this time, just for the first coupla bars – *then* cut back. Sets up the final verse."

"Can I put in my two cents on that?" Jenna asked diplomatically.

"Honey, for this set, consider yourself a full-fledged member of the band," Scott assured her. "Everyone puts in their two cents."

"Bet hers get listened to," Dan stage-whispered to Jeff. Jeremy and Tim laughed out loud. Scott shot all four a dirty look.

"Seems to me, I'd want Tim to build through the bridge and crescendo *into* the final verse. Can we try that?" Scott looked dubious, but Jeremy and Tim ran a quick version of what she was suggesting, both nodding with growing enthusiasm as they saw what it did.

"That *works*," Tim said. "Let's try it." Picking up their parts, each kept half an eye on Scott, leery of the potential for trouble in these new dynamics. Sure, Scott had brought in a bunch of different individuals at over the years, instrumentalists and singers alike, to add something special for a particular song, to try out something fresh. But this was different. This was uncharted, potentially dangerous territory, and anyone could get caught in the crossfire.

Roaring off the bridge, Scott and Jenna sang the final verse to the end. As the final chord died away, there was silence in the room while Scott considered. "Yep," he finally said, "the lady's right," and kissed her on the nose.

BREAKING FOR A late lunch, everyone was animated with fresh success. Any change or experiment that worked always had that effect. All recovering from most every addiction known to late-twentieth-century man, they fed off the one habit they'd never kick: the highs that came when the music really blazed.

"Sweet Jesus, 'Ballin' fer Dollars' was just fuckin' incredible," Jeff raved. "Who knew it needed a woman."

"Makes you rethink all sorts of songs," Dan agreed. "Wonder what 'Hell 'n Gone' would sound like…"

"We'll try it," Scott said from behind the stove, ladling out a steaming clam chowder into bowls that Dan bussed to the table. "You know the lyrics?" he asked Jenna.

"Just the chorus, really."

"I'll get 'em out for you. We'll getcha up to speed, kiddo," Jeremy said with a wink.

Grabbing a box of crackers and his own bowl of soup, Scott joined everyone at the table. "Okay, this is how I see it. We bring Jenna on as a special guest, completely unannounced, a total fuckin' surprise. Man, that'll really get things buzzing."

"No need to have the press start hounding us any sooner than necessary," Jeremy agreed. "They'll be all over this the minute they get wind. And furious as hell they didn't know to be there." Everyone laughed at the thought.

"The faithfuls will be there. This'll be their reward," Scott said with satisfaction.

"Worcester's sure gonna get their money's worth," Tim commented quietly. "And then some."

"NOW IT'S MY turn to take you to my favorite little local place," Scott said. The last of the band had pulled away just as the clock struck seven. "JT's. You're gunna love it, babe."

The sight of the two of them entering the tiny, waterfront restaurant brought a small, vivacious woman hurrying over. "God, Scott! Welcome! It's so good to see you again," she said, standing on tiptoe to receive the hug he bent down to give her.

"Joannie, baby! You're busy tonight. Can you squeeze us in?"

"Never too busy for you, silly boy – *you* know that," she chided him.

"Joan, meet Jenna Bradford. Jenna, Joan Tarlow."

"My pleasure, dear. We're honored." She whisked them to the table by the window she held back for just such unexpected celebrity drop-ins. A few strategically placed potted palms afforded at least a modicum of privacy, and the view of the harbor was picture postcard perfect. Several good sized boats were tied up to JT's dock directly below them, diners who'd sailed or motored in for a meal. A little outdoor deck, an extension of the bar, overflowed its limited capacity.

In a matter of minutes a giant bowl of muscles swimming in an aromatic bath of garlic, wine and herbs was set before them. Scott was just reaching for his second when a man with a full head of graying, intricately interwoven dreadlocks, ripped tank top, ragged cutoffs and flip flops approached the table.

"Scott? Z'at you, lad?"

"My God, Howie! How the fuck are you, man? Holy shit, I haven't seen you since – what was it, Ontario? Somewhere the hell up there. How *are* you?"

Howie eyeballed Jenna, top to bottom. "I can see *you*'re doing okay, mon," he said appreciatively, exposing a lilting Jamaican accent. "*More* than okay, mon."

Scott grinned. "Jenna Bradford, Howie Gilberto. Best man on steel drums and marimba you'll ever want to meet. Best man in the western hemisphere with a three-paper spliff, too, am I correct?"

"Ancient history, my brother. Just like you," Howie laughed. "Best kept secret in music?" He whispered the answer to both of them. "You *can't* have it all – and live. God, it's good to see you. And my blessings on you both." He held a hand over each, then backed away chuckling.

Scott reached for her hand. "And that man doesn't hand out blessings to just anyone. We've been blessed for life, my dear," he said, nodding quietly.

Howie was only the first of many who stopped by their 'secluded' table before they sat back to sip coffee. "It's all your fault, you know," Scott finally said, resting his chin in the palm of one hand and feasting on her openly. Jenna rolled her eyes like he was crazy.

"No way, babe. I know what I'm talkin' about – they're checkin' you out. You and your wild hair and your fabulous, deep, dark eyes," he said, dropping his voice, speaking now into her ear, caressing every word before letting it escape. "Your incredible body – displayed for everyone in this room to see, in that itsy bitsy little top so small it can barely contain those perfect breasts of yours." His words were hands that touched every inch of her. Her pulse raced. "Down past a stomach that's gotta be the envy of every woman in the joint." He stopped to let that much do its work, then continued.

"There isn't a man here who doesn't want to tongue your naval, baby." One hand grazed her stomach, then moved to rest on her bare thigh. "There isn't a man here who doesn't want to slide a hand up under that stretchy little hip-huggin' mini skirt you've got on. They're takin' mental bets as to whether you're wearing panties – it sure doesn't look it to me. They're wondering what your legs feel like." His hand squeezed her thigh. She moaned. "They're wondering what makes you hot. They're dying to know if you're wet. They're dying to know what you feel like, inside…"

Jenna could barely get words out. "Tell me – more," she gasped, breathing heavily.

"Un-uh. That's all you get here. You wanna hear more, you gotta come down to the beach. I got a *lot* more to tell you." Sitting back, he called to the waiter, "Check, please!"

THE MOON ILLUMINATED mica in the sand and the glittering tops of breakers as they rose in one final crescendo before collapsing on the shore. Pulling off their shoes, Jenna and Scott meandered hand-in-hand in and out of the frothy surf along the water's edge in an overpowering, silent sexual haze. Jenna slid an arm tightly around Scott's waist. He bound her in his arms.

"So? You promised me you'd tell me more," she said, her voice again husky with suggestion.

"I did," Scott agreed, turning her to him. "What I was gonna to tell you was – how they all wanted to tickle you." He started to tickle her with both hands. Jenna yelped, pulled free and make a slogging dash for the dunes, Scott in slow motion pursuit. Reaching the top, she threw herself down on her back on the sand, gasping and laughing. Scott dropped beside her and threw his arms around her. "Then they imagined just this. You, them, the sand, the moon, the stars, universe upon universe, and them, and you." He reared up, looked up and down the beach and across the dunes, then, gracefully straddling her, moved to openly caress her breasts while holding her gaze locked on his. Her nipples quickly hardened. Pushing the tiny excuse for a top up a few inches, he exposed Jenna's white breasts to the night breeze, leaving her struggling for breath. He went silent in admiration, then dropped down on her and just held her to him, his groin hard against her. A few minor adjustments and he was in her.

For a few moments they simply clung to each other for dear life, rapturous in their heat, then all exploded to the sound to the surf and their own hard-drumming heartbeats. Finally, Scott pushed her to her back as they parted and he rolled onto his. As their breathing slowed, they looked up to survey the heavens.

"Think anyone'll ever do a show on the moon?" Scott mused, changing gears radically, giving her a chance to catch her breath for the moment. "How'd you like to be booked in as the opening act at Lunar Stadium?"

"Crater Coliseum," Jenna countered.

"God, with the moon's lower gravity and all, think about how you could cover the stage, bounding all the shit over the place!"

"The moon's bright enough as it is," Jenna whispered. "Just imagine how much more *you*'d light it up."

"No, how much *we*'d light it up…" Scott said, reaching for her again. As he pulled her to him, she brushed the hair away from his face and kissed him, a kiss that felt like it would never end. In one variation after another, the kiss lasted for hours. Jenna was just discovering Scott's legendary, ravenous appetite for sex. Eventually, they made their way back to the house, lingering in the shower to wash the sand off one another. With concerted effort, they made it to the bed, only to start making love to each other all over again.

Chapter 10

I CANNOT BELIEVE how unnerved I feel, singing one set with these guys," Jenna mused out loud as she paced the limited length and breadth of her dressing room. "You know I hardly ever feel nervous performing solo anymore, and in venues far larger than this joint."

"You're gonna wear out the freakin' linoleum, sweetie. Come get a rub," suggested Yumi Tagomi, Jenna's stylist, who'd changed her schedule to fly out from L.A. specially for tonight. Yumi pulled out a chair, turned it around in front of her and motioned for Jenna to come sit. Finally nodding, Jenna straddled the chair, crossed her forearms over its back, laid her forehead on them and gratefully closed her eyes. Yumi parted Jenna's hair, rendered even fuller than usual tonight with the addition of long, golden-highlighted extensions, to expose Jenna's creamy neck and shoulders. Her strong hands soon started easing the tension that had been building all evening.

"You know what I worry about, Yumi?" Jenna said between sighs of relief. "Scott's got fans. I don't mean just fan fans, I mean —" Jenna's train of thought was interrupted by a knock on the door, just meant as a formality. Dressing rooms were about as private as Grand Central Terminal. Scott stepped in without waiting for an invitation, a towel over his sweating shoulders. A torrent of sound followed him in, returning to its previous level as the door closed. Seeing Jenna in the middle of a massage, he winked in the mirror to Yumi and put his finger to his lips.

"Five minutes, Ms. Bradford," he said in a high, squeaky voice.

"Thanks," Jenna mumbled. He opened and shut the door as if he'd left, then moved in beside Yumi, substituting his hands for hers.

"No, really, Yumi, this guy's got a shitload of crazy serious fans. His wannabe-groupie-to-everyone-else-in-the-audience ratio is like fuckin' off the charts. They aren't gonna like me, not one little bit. They all want to *be* me."

"They're gonna *love* you, hon. Don't make yourself crazy," Yumi said. Scott nodded to her reflection in the mirror, encouraging her to continue. "Once you get out there, you'll forget all this. You know you always do, Jenn."

"Uh-un, this is different. This is their gig. I'm the interloper. I'm gonna blow this whole thing, the relationship, everything. Oh God, why did I ever let him talk me into this? What do I think I'm doing?" Jenna wailed.

Scott bent down and kissed the nape of her neck. Jenna jumped, her eyes bolting open to see her lover in the mirror. "You're making me love you even more than I already do, that's what your doing, Ms. Bradford," he said to her reflection. "You just remember you're here tonight because we *want* you to be. You're gonna hear plenty, both positive and negative – you know that. Stand up. Lemme see how you look."

Jenna rose, Yumi stepping in behind her to make sure the headset she was wearing was still hidden and to restore disorderly order to her hairdo.

"Fabulous. You look just fabulous, baby," Scott said, licking his lips. Jenna was wearing a thin, tight almost skin-colored tank top that came nowhere near meeting a pair of low-slung, form-fitting red cargo pantsm laced with half a dozen zippers snaking off in every direction. "You okay with the mike?"

"Sure."

"I gotta get back. I'll cue you just as we finish up 'Blasted.' I love you." He gave her a quick kiss and hurried out. Jenna activated her mike and sat down to vocalize.

A few songs later, during an instrumental interlude, she heard Scott in her headset. "Have I mentioned lately that I love you?"

"Not in the last three minutes anyway," she said to him.

"Well, this is gonna have to hold you for a few minutes more, then, babe." He signed off with an electronic kiss. The song ended and the roar of the crowd rocked the building. A few minutes into the next song, he came on again. "Okay, babe, come on 'n get it!"

Jenna jumped to her feet, threw her hair forward, flung it back and gave it a shake. With a few minor adjustments from Yumi, she headed for the stage.

"Ladies and gentlemen, boys and girls, do we have one fuck of a surprise for you this evening!" came Jeremy's voice as she stepped into the wings. The crowd roared its approval. He waited them out. "You fans don't know it. The FBI and the CIA don't know it. The fuckin' *press* don't know it. Scott Tenny's got himself a brand new girl, you are the first humanoids on the planet to hear about it – *and* she's agreed to join us for a few numbers. Put 'em together for nothin' less than – Jenna B herself! Jennaaaaa Bradford!" The house went wild. If there was any disappointment in the building, it sure couldn't be seen in the horde of gyrating fans pressed up against the stage as Scott and Jenna moved from song to song like they'd been performing together for a couple of years, not a couple of weeks. As she took her last bow, he pulled her to him and kissed her deeply while 14,000 fans screamed their approval.

JENNA LINGERED IN the wings watching Scott and the band continue without her, hyper from the adrenaline rush of singing with them, not to mention the ovation she'd received as she left the stage.

As Jeremy took over with a solo halfway through the next song, Scott jogged into the wings, wrapped her in a sweaty hug and rocked her side to side. "You were fuckin' incredible, baby," he yelled to be heard over the amplification. "We never got close to anything like *that* in rehearsal. Totally fuckin' awesomely fabulous. More?"

"No way," Jenna hollered back. "This is your show. They paid to see *you*."

"One more," he pushed her. "I'm beggin' you here. Just one. At the end, how about?"

"With the encores," Jenna said.

"Perfect," he said. "How about 'Time of My Life?'"

"Oooo. You got it, babe," Jenna smiled broadly. "'Cuz it has been."

"And this is just the beginning" Scott assured her with a kiss.

Jenna's return to the stage was met with a roar. They'd worked up the song most often associated with *Dirty Dancing* after curling up with the DVD earlier in the week, and working it up had worked them up to the point that they'd been grinding out many of the film-inspired dance moves as they sang. It hadn't crossed Jenna's mind to go that far with this crowd, but as they reached the first chorus Scott ripped off his shirt, tossed it into the audience and moved in on her.

Groin to groin, torso to torso Scott and Jenna pivoted around the invisible axis of their growing obsession with each other. Moving behind him, Jenna ran her hands, splay-fingered and for all to see, across his chest, down his trunk and a few inches into the waistband of his skin-tight pants. The crowd howled. Not to be outdone, Scott moved her in front of him until she now faced the audience, then ran his hands down the sides of her body and back up to cross her chest, and locked her there in front of him as he ground into her from behind. Still in that position as song's end, they both went into a single bow and his hands surreptitiously cupped her breasts. Jenna's legs could barely carry her off the stage.

IN THE WINGS, Scott grabbed her as the band finally exited the stage for good. The crowd would continue to clap, howl and pound the floor in frustration for another ten minutes. Jeremy grabbed a towel for himself and tossed one to Scott. The others went on back to the band's dressing room to towel down. A moment later, Carrie came looking for them. "Jeremy told me to come tell you, the press is coming. He says they look like a horde of hyenas who've just picked the lock at a meat packin' plant – his words."

Jenna took Scott aside quickly. "Shit, I was afraid of this," she said urgently. "Whatever happens, you let me answer for myself. You don't speak for me, right?"

"No problem, baby."

"You promise me?"

"Absolutely," he assured her. They turned to face the lucky reporters, photographers and film crew who'd happened to be there that night. Photos from a night like this could make a photographer's career.

Amid non-stop flashes, Scott and Jeremy started taking questions. Yes, they'd been planning this for weeks. No, they'd decided to make it a surprise. Yes, they loved the synergy between Jenna and Scott. No, Scott hadn't had any of his legendary meltdowns in Jenna's presence – yet.

Janice Long pushed to the front of the pack. "Scott!" she called, waiting for her Entertainment Nine cameraman to position himself.

"Janice. Good to see you, hon. Guess we have to wait till tomorrow night to find out what you thought of us tonight," Scott kidded with her to fill in till she had her cue. The cameraman quickly gave her the nod.

"Scott, tonight was one of those touchstone events, like Woodstock and Watkins Glen. Blacklace fans will be asking each other for years to come, 'were you at the Worcester Centrum?' Did you know it was going to be *so* important a night?" She turned her microphone to him for his answer.

"Oh, yeah, Janice, no question, not in my mind anyway."

"And the rest of the band, were they as – ahem – excited as you clearly are to be performing with Jenna?" Dan, Tim and Jeff stood to one side of Scott and Jenna; Jeremy and Carrie stood hand-in-hand on the other side.

Jeremy stepped in to answer for the band. "No question whatsoever. Thrilled," he said, started to step back, then added, "in a hands-off sorta way, that is." Everyone laughed.

"And – the question that's on everyone's minds – will you two continue to perform together, Scott? Or was this just a one night stand?" Janice asked with a good-natured wink. Scott laughed as he looked over at Jenna.

"Better ask Jenna that," he said with a grin, stepping back. Jenna moved in.

"Hi," she said directly to Janice. "I have a number of things I want to say. This was a great concert and I especially want to thank the fans. I am so, so grateful. This is without a doubt, the best band in the world. Any performer would jump at the chance to share a stage – let alone a mike – with Blacklace.

"As for future performances, we've had a number of discussions about it. I'll be joining them from time to time – and we'll be announcing those shows well in advance from now on, but Blacklace is Blacklace – they are who they are, and I have no intention of becoming a permanent addition."

"Will you be continuing your solo act as well, then, Jenna?" Janice asked. "You've been absent from the stage for quite some time now."

"Thanks for noticing," Jenna joked. "Seriously, yes, I do plan to go back on the road with my band, soon. Scott and I both have our separate careers and we intend to keep it that way. Thank you, and thank you, Worcester!" she finished, then turned things back over to Scott. Carrie gave her a hug. She and Jenna had quickly grown close.

Janice turned to her cameraman. "Boston's new Cinderella couple, Jenna Bradford and Scott Tenny. This is Janice Long, for Entertainment Nine at the Worcester Centrum," she said into the camera and held her smile until the tape stopped rolling.

SCOTT WAS THE first to wake the next morning. Turning quietly, he lay there marveling at the beautiful woman sprawled naked and asleep beside him. Her slightest movement gave him pleasure – the rise and fall of her breathing, the twitch of an eyelid as she dreamed. Where did her dreams take her, he wondered.

His reverie, and her sleep, came to a jarring end with the ringing of the phone. He grabbed for it as Jenna half rose in sleepy confusion.

"Turn on The Morning Show. Quick," Jeremy added, then hung up. Scott reached for the remote. Clicking rapid fire through a half dozen channels, he knew he was there when a close-up of himself and Jenna filled the screen. "...*This could be love because...I've had the time of my life...*" they sang in tight harmony to one another, the fire of passion clearly burning in their eyes.

"And what will be next for perhaps the hottest duo to ever hit a stage together?" asked the female announcer rhetorically. The camera cut to Jenna speaking into Janice's microphone. The announcer continued, "In Jenna's own words, 'I'll be joining them from time to time – and we'll be announcing those shows well in advance.' That's it from Worcester, Dave. Back to you." As Dave moved on to the next subject of the morning, Scott rolled over and wrapped his arms around Jenna.

"Ha! 'The hottest duo to ever hit a stage together.' They don't know the half of it," he chortled. "You think last night was hot. I'll show you hot."

They'd barely finished making love when the phone again jolted them out of their reverie. Again, Scott reached for it. Jenna could hear a man's voice blaring before Scott could get out a still breathless 'hello.' He handed the phone over to her.

"So what ever happened to 'I'll have my people call your people?' For chrissakes, Jenna, am I your manager or what these days? Why am I always, every time, absolutely consistently the last one to know anything? Can you tell me that? Explain it to me. Put me in the know here." Brian finally took a breath.

"Mornin', Bry," Jenna said congenially. "You're up early."

"Up," Brian snorted. "For your information, I never *got* to bed. The phone started ringing last night, oh, just about eight, and it didn't let up for hours. The whole world wants to book you two. And me, I'm caught fuckin' flat-footed, totally blind-sided, deer in the headlights, looking for all the world like the guy left standin' at the altar. This is how you treat me after –"

"Brian, it's called an experiment. A spontaneous appearance."

"Spontaneous, my ass. That was rehearsed, down to the last bump and grind, the way I heard it."

"Okay, so we rehearsed. We got to fooling around –"

"I don't want to hear about your sex life," Brian cut it.

"– in the studio –"

"And I don't want to know the fuck where."

"We were *singing,* you dirty old man."

"I'm younger than you are, you dirty old woman," he countered. "Which is neither here nor there. So, what do I do?"

"Come to Boston. Talk to his people," Jenna said wearily. "Oh, and Bry, just so's you're not the last person to hear – I'm pregnant. Bye." Jenna handed the phone back over to Scott and threw herself on him. "Let's do that again," she suggested huskily.

THEY STAYED IN bed all morning, fueled by a quick run for coffee, rolls and all the morning papers. Headlines blared across every entertainment section. Photo after photo attested to how great they'd been the night before. Scott gave Jenna a dramatic reading of the *Globe* review; she attacked him before he could quite finish. Eventually, she reciprocated with a review from the Worcester *Telegram*, somehow making it to the final word while Scott quietly explored her every square inch.

"Okay," Scott said, still panting from making love yet again, "seriously, I got something to say."

"Get it off your chest, babe. I'm all ears, you incredible man, you." Jenna lay across his chest and played with the tangles of his long hair.

"Baby, I – I love you so much. God, those words – I love you – they're so trite, so fuckin' puny. They don't begin to say what I feel. If you didn't know before last night, you gotta know it now." His hands trailed lightly over her as he struggled to find words worthy of his thoughts. "We belong together. We belong to each other." He looked deep into her eyes, then brought his mouth down to hers and kissed her passionately.

Jenna pulled back from him so she could look him in the eye as she bared her soul. "Okay, now *you* listen, Scott," she started, paused for a moment, then continued. "I'm a very private person. I keep close guard on my feelings, on my heart. I've been even more cautious with you because I don't have a clue what's going to happen when I finally face Derek." She stopped and gently kissed him.

"I can't do that any more, especially after last night. When we were singing together, when I saw how you looked at me, I realized it's no longer in my power to control how I feel about you. When we make love, I know I can't go slow or be careful. I love you, too. And yes, we do belong together." Moving into each other's arms, smiling, they drifted fearlessly into dreamless sleep.

"OKAY, SUZANNE, THAT works," Jenna told Brian's administrative assistant, looking up and winking at Joe as he meandered into the kitchen. "Go ahead and book the later flight on Thursday, with the Friday one o'clock return. That'll give me enough time. And would you tell Brian I've got several new songs in the works? That should make him happy.

Hanging up, she came over and poured Scott's father a mug of coffee. "Morning, Joe," she smiled and gave him a peck on the cheek.

"So you've decided on quick and dirty?" he said congenially.

"Yeah. I thought about what you said last night – and thanks for listening. I really appreciated it. I've decided dragging it out isn't going to make it any better. I'd meet him in the airport lounge if it fit Derek's schedule, dammit." Pouring herself a cup, she sat down across the breakfast table from Joe. She'd quickly come to enjoy the irascible old man's company.

"Actually, I decided on a modified quick and dirty. If I have to stay over, I might as well at least get to enjoy the next morning before I hop a plane back. I've always wanted to drive out to Red Rocks before dawn. It's this like huge, natural amphitheatre they use for concerts – it seats ten thousand, maybe more. I've always wanted to sing on that stage as the sun rises. I'm gonna do it."

"I'll call a press conference," Joe chuckled.

Jenna shot him a look. "Don't even tell Scott. He's getting more protective by the day."

"Can't say as I blame him," said the old man wistfully.

JENNA SAT AT the piano in the studio, noodling around, waiting for a melody line to emerge from a random jumble of notes. She had words for a first verse, but the tune was eluding her. She tried the opening lines with one set of notes, then another. *"Ya wanna raise his baby? Get outta here. You'll take me as I am? Get outta here."*

It had been too long since she'd felt the unadulterated pleasure of the creative process, those extraordinary 'where the fuck did *that* come from?' moments, the unscheduled arrival of the Muse.

Just as something was beginning to work, her cell phone rang. Glancing at the calling number, she smiled.

"Get outta here," she said by way of greeting.

"Just try 'n make me," Scott replied. "Hey, babe, you still coming into town?"

"Yeah. Later."

"Can you make it sooner, like for lunch? Strang's got a shitload of ideas, some good, some not so, but he's looking for decisions. I wanna chew it over with you before I commit to anything." Scott laughed. "We can write it off as a business lunch."

"Sure, I'll take a meeting with you, mister. Where do we do this thing?"

"I know this place in the North End, Brandoni's – you'll love it. You can get to Salem Street, right? "

"Yeah."

"Salem and Hull, big neon Tower of Pisa sign hangin' off the building. On the right, you can't miss it. Just past it, there's a garage on the left. Dump the car there. I'll be there by noon. I'll try to get us a table on the sidewalk. You get there as soon as you can. Traffic's a bitch today."

"Traffic's a bitch every day. Noon. I love you."

"Love you, babe. Later."

"AT 12:23, THE only good news is that nobody's gonna get a speeding ticket today in Boston," the Eye in the Sky reporter announced cheerfully. Disgusted, Jenna switched back to a Tom Petty album she'd been listening to as she made her way into Boston. Between the so-called Big Dig – the tunnel that had been burrowing its way into and through the heart of Boston for the past nine years – and an afternoon Red Sox-Mets game, the city was tied in knots. Tapping the wheel in time to the song that was playing, she'd wished she hadn't decided to put the top down on the little red Miata she'd leased. Summer had hit with a vengeance today, after a cool, wet spring. It had felt great as she left the South Shore, but now she was just baking in fumes and the top wasn't the kind you could put up or down with the touch of a button. Having inched her way along I-93 for the best part of a mile, Jenna relished a deep breath of cleaner air as she exited onto the surface streets of the North End.

Turning onto Salem Street, she started looking for the neon sign, which she saw as soon as she crossed Prince, still a good two blocks ahead of her. Scott was right, you couldn't miss it – it was two stories high. Approaching Brandoni's, she spotted him sitting out front, his back to her, hiding the best he could behind a large menu and big sunglasses. She beeped. Cautiously, he looked up, realized it was her just as she passed and gave her a quick one-fingered wave.

Half a block further on, just as she spotted the garage, just as the car in front of her turned left onto Sheafe without signaling, dammit, just as Tom Petty was singing "...*nothin's really funny,*" a giant black Jeep Grand Cheroke ran a stop sign on Tileston and plowed her sideways, slow motion, into an equally huge black Lincoln Navigator parked on the opposite curb. Scott was out of his seat and halfway up the block before a hubcap rolling down the street completed its circling death throes and fell to its side.

Chapter 11

JENNA DRIFTED TO the shores of consciousness. Like a castaway clinging to a fragile raft in a turbulent, angry sea, she was parched, exhausted, hallucinating, confused. The shoreline, sometimes tantalizingly close, more often appeared to her to be impossibly distant and indistinct, hovering on the horizon or beyond. After struggling for what seemed an eternity in a crashing surf, she came to rest upon sand, white and smooth as silk, and slept deeply.

Returning to consciousness at last, she gradually realized that something warm lay beneath her hand. As her fingers set off to explore the topography of its angular, slightly stubbled surface, the object suddenly lurched out from under her hand, which fell limply to a smooth, cool surface not far below. "Oh, my God, Jenna, baby, you're awake! Talk to me, baby, say something for me, precious Jenna," said a voice that at first seemed miles away, then abruptly seemed to be right in her ear – or maybe in her head? Trying to order her thoughts, she formed a word but could only produce an arid croak. "Jenna, baby," the voice murmured again and a hand took hers and squeezed. "Come back to me, Jenna."

Jenna's eyes opened, blinked, closed, then opened again. What was this harsh light? What were these sounds, faint noises, beeps and buzzes? Was that a public address system blaring, "Dr. Patel, extension 321," "Dr. Gold, extension 224?" And Muzak? Where *was* she? A face swam into view. A man's face. A beautiful face, framed by shaggy, long brown hair. Lips. Speaking. A disconnected voice, that first voice. "Jenna…Jenna…" Her lips moved but no sounds emerged, because she couldn't seem to remember exactly how to form them. Her eyes closed again.

THE VOICE CAME and went, but never went away. "…when you're better, we're gonna take a…" – "…are all here. Everyone's pullin' for you, pullin' for *us*, baby…" – "…and your mom's coming, with Kristin, and…" – "…and Jeremy's gonna stay with you while…"

There were other voices. "…the hemorrhaging's completely stopped…" – "…and reduce the levels of…" – "…she's showing signs of…"

Finally, a word formed in her mind and emerged from her mouth. "Scott." And then two more. "The baby?" And suddenly, bits and pieces and shards and chunks and boulders of reality came crashing down upon her.

"I COULDN'T GET to you. You were trapped, the car was smashed between them. Someone called 9-11." He held the back of his hand to her cheek, his eyes dark with sympathy and pain. "It took them forever to remove you from the wreckage. I told them you were pregnant. I let them think I was the father – hell, everyone still thinks I am." He closed his eyes and went quiet. "They let me ride with you in the ambulance."

"Stitches…" Jenna mumbled.

"Twenty-six of the fuckers," he said gently, leaning forward to lightly kiss her forehead. "Two fractured ribs. Then the hemorrhaging…" He held her as the tears came again, then again the keening, and again the slow, low animal wail. It kept coming over her in waves, the realization, the understanding, the knowledge that her arms would never hold her baby, that her baby was no longer within her. Slowly, the tears subsided and she slept again.

"MY BABY GIRL, my poor, poor baby girl," a woman's voice was whispering in her ear.

Jenna knew by smell, before she opened her eyes, that it was her mother at her bedside. "Mama," she whispered, feeling her mother's hand take hers. "Mom." Then she burst into tears again. Her mother held her and she cried, longer and harder than she had so far. How could she ever find her way to the other side of this agony, this grief? "Will this ever end, Mama? My baby…" she moaned.

"Yes – and no. Yes and no," she repeated, rocking her gently. "You'll learn to live with it, yes, but no, the pain will never leave." She whispered into her daughter's ear, "I lost two babies. I know."

Jenna started and pulled out of her mother's arms to look at her. "What do you mean? You never told me."

"Women didn't, in my day. You just went on. Nobody ever talked about 'it' again." She took a deep breath, allowing herself to revisit the pain. "But you never forget, sweetheart. You never stop wondering, you never stop thinking about lives that never happened. They'd be forty and thirty-four this year, your other sisters."

"Did you – did you name them?" Jenna asked cautiously, suddenly feeling so close to this woman she thought she knew.

"No, not really. Not name names. The first, I just always thought of her as Baby. The second, Precious."

Jenna looked down. "I'm sorry I didn't tell you, Mom."

"I understand, honey. Please, don't worry on that account. You did what you felt was right. I wish I could have helped you think your way through it all. But I know some things no one can help you with. You just have to find your own way. Life's like that," she said kindly, "and you're like that." Jenna's small smile was bleaker than March.

"HONEY, SOMEBODY WANTS to meet you," Scott said from the door. "You up for it?"

Jenna, finally released from intensive care and its attendant army of doctors, nurses, residents and orderlies, was now settled into the relative calm of a private room. A few cheerful spring landscapes on the wall hardly made a dent in the utilitarian starkness of the room. Scott brought another armful of flowers every time he passed the gift shop in the lobby to try and soften the institutional feel of what would be Jenna's world for several more difficult days.

Jenna was sitting up and feeling intensely restless. The IV to which she was tethered felt like a ball and chain. Viewed from the front, she looked fairly normal – the swelling on her face had gone down and bruising was minimal; her color was good and her fine long hair framed her face as casually as always. It was only when she turned her head that the wide white swath up the back of her head revealed the extent of her visible injuries.

"Sure," she said. It would be diverting, if nothing else, she thought. Scott ushered in a youthful beauty who appeared to be in her early twenties.

"Baby, this is my Laurel," Scott said, and Laurel smiled. "Laurel, this is my Jenna." Laurel, a warm and forthcoming young woman, stepped into Jenna's open arms as naturally as if she'd known Jenna all her life.

"Dad started telling us all about you way before you guys got together," she said while still in Jenna's embrace. "I feel like we're old friends," she added. "You make him so happy. Missy told me to tell you she'd be here too, except she's got a show opening next week and she's like totally locked."

They were interrupted by a knock on the door as Joe's head peered around the edge. "Excuse me, but is it okay for an old fart to pay a visit?"

"Oh, shit, am I ever in trouble now," Scott said. "I forgot to hang up the 'no old farts allowed' sign."

"For you, Joe, we can make an exception," Jenna smiled from the bed. "Come on in. The gang's all here."

"Hiya, hon," he said, hugging her carefully. "I got tired of watching the reruns on T.V. Decided I'd come see how you're doing in person." He turned and gave Laurel a hug as well.

"Hi, Gramps," Laurel said, giving him a quick peck on the cheek.

"Reruns?" Jenna asked.

"Oh, yeah, honey. You've been all *over* the news the last couple of days. You'd never know there's a presidential campaign on. All Jenna, all the time. Oh, yeah, and I guess they did mentioned this Scott Tenny guy a couple times too."

"They even got some of the facts right, can you imagine that?" Scott added. "The hospital held a press conference, doctors, cops, the whole nine yards."

Tearing up, Jenna quickly looked away. Scott hurried to her side and held her. "I'm sorry, baby. I am such a ham-handed idiot."

Jenna pulled herself together. "No, no, it's okay, hon. It's hormones and the steroids and God knows what all else. I barely recognize myself. Bear with me, okay?"

"Absolutely. You know that, right?" he said. Giving her a quick kiss, he put a free arm around Laurel. "Isn't she something," he said with evident pride.

"I brought you something," Laurel said, dipping into her bag to retrieve a tiny box with a big bow which she held out to Jenna. Jenna was touched. Opening it, she found a fine silver chain bearing a single silver tear drop. Laurel took it from her and fastened the chain around Jenna's neck. Unable to speak, Jenna pressed Laurel's hand to her cheek, then kissed it and smiled as best she could. The tenderness of the moment brought tears to Scott's eyes. He turned and looked out the window, then turned back just as Linda came bustling in the room.

"This is beginning to look as crowded as the ICU," Linda laughed. "And what new specialists have joined the team since I've been gone, may I ask?"

"My dad, Joe Tenny. My daughter, Laurel Kalman. This is Linda Bradford, Jenna's mom," Scott offered by way of introduction. Handshakes quickly morphed into familial hugs. For Linda, everyone was family. She gave Jenna a long, quiet hug, then stroked the hair back off her forehead.

"Hi, Mom. Where's Kristin?" Jenna asked.

"She's back at the apartment, settling in. It'll make a perfect base of operations while you're stuck here. She'll be back over shortly, sweetheart. You know, everyone, we have a number of spare beds and pull-out couches. If it'd help, save anyone a drive, whatever?Laurel? Joe? Scott, of course."

Turning to Joe, she explained, "It's the only way we can get him to leave here for even an hour." Joe nodded. No one had to tell him how stubborn his son could be.

Linda went and put an arm around Scott, then folded his weary body in a motherly embrace. "You've been here for two days straight, Scott. You need to sleep – really sleep, on a bed, in a quiet room."

Scott nodded. Exhaustion was taking its toll, and he too was in enormous pain. He too was grieving a lost child, even if it wasn't technically his own. He assured Linda he would, "later." Looking up, he acknowledged Jeremy's entrance with a "Hey, bro. And Carrie. Hey, hon. Come on in." Carrie gave Laurel and Joe a small wave as she went over to the bed and gave Jenna a big hug.

"I woulda come sooner, sweetie, but I knew I'd just be in the way. Are you okay? Turn around, lemme see." Jenna turned her head. "Oh, my God, a reverse Mohawk. It'll be all the rage by Friday, girlfriend." Jenna laughed, her first genuine laugh in what felt like ages. Carrie had that effect on her.

"We've just stopped by to see if we can be useful," Jeremy said. "Anybody need a ride anywhere? Anything we can get you, Jenn? Anything?"

"Could you give me a lift back to the apartment," Linda asked.

"Of course, hon," Jeremy answered.

"Laurel, Joe, why don't you come with me? You need lunch. We can get something sent up."

SCOTT FINALLY FOUND himself alone with Jenna. Positioning himself carefully on the bed beside her, he wrapped her in his big arms. She turned and curled up as best she could against his chest, wrapping her free arm around his neck. Holding her, they both dozed off into forgetfulness.

When Scott awoke, he looked down to find Jenna silently crying. "Baby, baby," he crooned, rocking her gently.

"It's not what you think, you dear man," Jenna managed to say, fighting for some measure of control. "These aren't tears for the baby. They're tears for you. What *you've* been through – what you've seen – what you've had to endure. You precious, precious man. I love you so much." She choked up again.

"Go ahead, baby, sweetheart. Cry. You need to let it go. You can't keep it inside." He held her while she sobbed, while her tears slowed, until she hadn't a single tear left within her. Finally, he kissed her and slipping out from under her, laid her back on the pillow.

"You've gotta be exhausted," he whispered. "Sleep. I'll be here." He started to pull a chair back up to the bedside.

"No. No, like Mom said, you need to go to the apartment and get some rest. Now," Jenna said quietly but firmly. "I know you want to be with me. I'll be all right, I promise. Do it for me. Please," she implored him.

"Okay," he said simply. "But not for long."

TWO MORNINGS LATER, Jenna was told she'd be going home before day's end. Sharing with the family some of the bin full of mail that had arrived that morning for her, get well cards and condolences sent by friends and fans, Jenna sighed with relief. She needed very much to get out of this place.

"Kristin has to get back to L.A.," Linda said, moving directly into planning mode. Kristin had enrolled at U.S.C.; summer classes started in a matter of days. "But, honey, I can stay on with you. I know Scott means well, but he can't be with you all the time. He told me he's in town a lot – he can come by whenever he's free." Jenna suddenly realized that her mother had no idea that she and Scott were living together.

Before she could figure out how to break the news, Joe jumped in. "Guess ya haven't heard, Linda," he chuckled, his usual tactful self. "These two are cohabitatin' down at the shore, at Scott's place."

"Oh, are they really now," said Linda, clearly blindsided – but not at all displeased – by this piece of information.

"More than a month now. Plenty of guest rooms for us parent types – I've got a whole guest suite myself, matter of fact. Happy to take your things down there for you, deah." Joe punctuated the offer with a wink. "I'm not there all the time, but between you and me, I think we could put together one heck of a support system for these kids. They'll need one."

"Precisely my sentiments – deah." Linda returned Joe's wink.

"Beverly Hills 90210 meets the Lakes Region of New Hampshire," Scott observed dryly.

EVERYONE HEADED FOR Scott's house as soon as plans were worked out and agreed upon; Linda would indeed move down to Scott's.

Scott stayed on with Jenna to wait for the doctor's final blessing, and when it finally came, they felt like a pair of jailbirds who'd been given their walking papers. "We're free!" Jenna smiled. Enforced bed rest had improved her mood and outlook. Scott pushed her wheelchair to the side entrance of the hospital, where Georgie Del Guercio, the band's big, burly driver, was waiting for them with the limo. Georgie doubled on security when needed.

Scott bent down, whispered in her ear, "Nothing too good for my baby," and squeezed her shoulder. Georgie helped her in.

"God's watchin' out for you, dear," he said with sincerity. "Glad to see you on your feet."

"Thank you, Georgie," Jenna responded quietly. "God bless you."

"Your folks told me to tell you dinner'll be waiting when you get there."

Jenna slept most of the way down.

JOE HEARD THE car pull up. "They're here," he called to Linda and went to open the door.

Scott helped Jenna slowly make her way up the walk, while Georgie followed with her things. Joe took her hand at the door and walked her over to a chair to sit down.

Linda was shocked that a walk of such short distance could leave Jenna so winded. "Are you all right, sweetie?" she asked her anxiously.

"I'm okay, Mom. All I've done for a week is crawl the halls with that confounded IV for company. I guess I'm not quite ready for sprints. I just need to sit for a minute."

"Supper's ready," Linda told her, "just as soon as you are."

"Thanks, Mom. I really appreciate it."

Jenna barely made it through the meal before Scott had to help her to bed. "Lie down with me," she asked him. "Just for a little while."

Pulling her close, he sighed. "It feels so good being back home," he said softly, holding her gently as she found her weary way to sleep. "You, me and the memory we'll always have of the baby we might have had…" Jenna took comfort in his words.

In no time, Jenna had fallen asleep. Scott disentangled himself and tiptoed out of the room. Coming down to the kitchen, he walked in on Joe and Linda toasting the successful completion of cleaning up the kitchen. "And to you, Joe Tenny," Linda was saying grandly, a glass of wine held aloft. "I've always said, there's nothing quite so impressive as a man who can butterfly his own veal loin." They clinked glasses.

"Oh my heavens, the mouth on you, ma'am!" Joe said in mock embarrassment. "And in front of my boy, to boot."

"He was trained by the best," Scott said, joining them. "My grandmother, Nona Stasio. She raised six sons to be great cooks."

"Half of them ended up with restaurants of their own at one time or another," Joe concurred. "Not me. I played in Johnny's a lot as a kid, though. Those were the days…"

"I do want to hear you play," Linda urged him, which was all Joe needed. Moments later, Scott could smell cigar smoke as his father hit the keys and started singing, quietly for Jenna's sake, *"I love a piano, I love a piano, I love to hear somebody play…"* A few bars later, Linda had joined him. *"I know a fine way to treat a Steinway. I love to run my fingers o'er the keys, the i-i-i-i-ivories…"* Lyrics had turned to laughter as Scott headed out to the barn.

SCOTT SAT DOWN to the studio keyboard synthesizer and let his fingers start wandering. Writing music for him was like using a Ouija board, he often thought. Let the lyrics find the keys, let the keys find the tune, let the tune find the instruments, let the instruments embrace the lyrics. Snatches of lyrics for a song for Jenna had been floating in his head since March. He'd started to write it even before he knew she was in Boston, back in the long-ago winter of his despair.

"She sobers, she chills, she inspires, she thrills…Girl of green, lady lilac, baby blue…"

He'd tried to put the song out of his head when she'd told him she didn't want to see him again. When he brought her back to Boston after her father's funeral, he'd gone right back to work on it. Jeremy and he had spent a few long sessions bringing it along.

The tune was riveting. Now he found himself buffeted from major keys to minor and back again. The song was about the relationship, and the relationship had taken on astoundingly new proportions, a staggering new scale. The relationship was exploring all the dimensions of life, not just its riotous ups, gratifications and sumptuous pleasures, but also its profound and terrifying downs, its dangers, its desperate fears. Thinking how, not ten days earlier, the woman he loved had crossed death's path, right before his eyes, he keyed in the sound of harps.

"Nice," he heard behind him and turned to find his father in the doorway.

"Dad. What's up?"

"Linda's checking in on Jenna. I thought I'd come over, see what you're up to. Sounds good, son."

"It's for Jenna," Scott said simply. "To think it almost became a requiem…" He played a few bars in a minor key.

"Yeah." Joe went quiet and sat down in front of the piano. "That girl's had one hell of an impact on you, hasn't she." Joe was making a statement, not posing a question. His fingers started to stray over the keys.

"That 'girl,' as you call her, is one hell of a *woman*, Dad. I care for her more than I've cared for literally anyone. Don't ask me to explain it, but she's definitely got one motherfucker of a hold on me." He played another line and added in a set of drum beats. Joe picked up the tune and trailed along with it. Scott tried out the melody line over the drum, nodding along with the beat, then shook his head and tried the reverse of the line he'd just played. Joe followed suit.

"I gotta tell ya," Scott continued, "when I saw that SUV come flying through that stop sign, Dad, the world stopped in its tracks. Until I saw her breathing – until I could actually *see* her chest rise and fall, I – I thought for sure she was dead. I didn't dare leave her for a moment in the hospital. At first, if I couldn't sit there and watch her breathe, I couldn't believe she was gonna make it." He reached over, turned off the synthesizer and swiveled around to face his father.

"I'll still worry about her until she's fully recovered. And that's just about Jenna – then there's the baby…"

Scott studied his folded hands. Until this past week, he couldn't recall an occasion when he'd actually talked with his father about difficult subjects. Ever, even when his mother had died. Until recently, their relationship had been all surface, with rock-solid underpinnings of tension and residual anger. Scott had been a difficult son to raise. Early on, Joe had adopted the same belt-and-hairbrush techniques his own father had liberally used on him, back in the day. It seemed to work, most of the time, at least until the boy was full-grown, but it had also formed an almost unbridgeable gulf between the two. That is, until Jenna had come into – and almost out of – both of their lives.

"I know that baby wasn't mine," Scott started, tentatively, "but – I mean it, it quickly came to feel like it – like she – *was* mine. The baby was a girl," he said quietly, looking up at his father and shaking his head sadly. "A little girl who never had a chance. I gotta tell you, losing her is just about as painful for me as it is for Jenna." Joe looked at Scott with compassion.

"May *you* have a child, one day, my boy," Joe said, putting a hand on his son's knee. "May you have a child who makes you proud. The way you make me feel right now."

"Thanks, Dad," Scott said quietly. "Thanks."

Chapter 12

"SCOTT? IS THAT you?" Jenna asked sleepily.

"Sure is, babe. I was getting concerned," Scott answered, feeling for the light switch. The curtains were drawn and the room was still as dark as night, in spite of the fact that it was almost nine in the morning.

"Have I been asleep long?" Jenna asked. "Did I hear the phone ring?"

"Just eleven hours solid," Scott told her with a kiss. "That was Carrie. She wanted to know how you're doing."

"Help me up, hon," she asked, finding herself more than a bit unsteady. Scott put an arm around her and walked her out through the living room to the porch, where Joe and Linda were sharing a cup of coffee and conversation. Scott helped her into a chair.

"Boy, get you out of the hospital with all that chaos and those blood pressure checks at five a.m. and you sure can sleep," her mother said, jumping up. "What can I get you, sweetie?"

"Some tea?" Jenna said tentatively.

"Tea and maybe some toast?" Linda countered.

"Or how about some pancakes, deah?" Joe suggested. "You know you love my pancakes. Make the doctors happy?" he wheedled.

"Make *you* happy's more like it. Okay, sweetie." Jenna smiled. She enjoyed indulging the old man.

"Back in a jiffy," Joe said as he and Linda headed for the kitchen.

"You ever seen two people so obviously in love?" Joe commented, pulling together the necessary ingredients for pancakes. "Never seen my son love anyone – two wives included – the way he loves your daughter. Nope, never looked like this. Last night he even said as much. That boy's really changed."

Standing at the window where she could see Jenna and Scott out on the porch, Linda volunteered, "It's the same with Jenna. She hasn't had that many men in her life – between you and me, I used to think she made *sure* she didn't have that many men in her life. When she did, she was nothing compared to how she is with Scott. I do hope she realizes how lucky she is, to have found someone like him."

Joe looked up from his work. Linda sounded almost wistful.

"THAT'LL PUT A pound or two on her," Joe said confidently, surveying the big breakfast tray he was carrying. Gathering up the coffee pot she'd just refilled and a pot of hot water for tea, Linda followed him out of the kitchen.

The two parents stepped out onto the porch just as Scott was taking Jenna into his arms. Both stopped in their tracks, arrested by the sweet innocence of the moment.

"Baby, I love you," Scott voice came clearly across the porch to them. Jenna's "I love you too, Scott, so, so much," was equally audible. The only difference was that Jenna happened to be facing Joe and Linda. Her eyes, fluttering open, suddenly went wide. She broke into a bashful grin.

"What? You've never seen two people kiss before?" she asked, smirking awkwardly at the two of them. Scott swiveled around to see what had prompted her words and had to laugh.

"Shit, busted!" he said, throwing his hands in the air.

Both Linda and Joe set down their loads, came over to their respective children and hugged them warmly.

As Linda poured her daughter a cup of tea she couldn't help comment on what she'd just been witness to. "Call me a busybody, but you two were just meant for each other," she said with conviction.

"My sentiments precisely, and I want you both to know it," Joe concurred. Receiving a nod when he held up the maple syrup for Jenna's approval, he poured a slow, steady stream of heavy amber until she signaled him to stop. "Every drop of maple syrup represents hard labor, righteous sweat, endless worry and the transcendence of love," he said, as if to himself.

"TAKE ME OUT to the barn, will you, babe?" Jenna asked Scott after eating the lion's share of the breakfast Joe had set before her.

"Your every wish is my command, m'lady," he said gallantly, doffing an imaginary cap. "It would be an honor and my privilege."

"God, lay it on me, Galahad," Jenna smiled, and for the first time since the accident, she realized, she hadn't had to make a deliberate effort to produce that smile. Once out the door, Scott picked her up and carried her easily down the path to the old barn. Her arms around his neck and head thrown back, Jenna let her mind play with the billowing clouds that scudded across a bright blue sky.

Taking a lungful of studio air, Jenna sighed. "Now I feel like I'm home. The blood, sweat and electicity of rock 'n roll – what a sweet perfume." She sat, then stretched out on the couch, while Scott crossed to the piano, dropped onto the bench, running a glissando from the lowest keys to the highest. Then he started playing random chords, one at a time, letting each one reverberate and die out before moving to another. "I love it in here," Jenna mused quietly.

"Me too," Scott agreed, picking out another chord, then another. "And not just for music. I do some of my best thinking over here." The chords started forming into a more orderly progression.

"Me too," Jenna said. "When you guys aren't around, I'm in here a lot. Sometimes to write, but a lot of the time I just lay here, thinking. It's gotta be the soundproofing, the complete silence. Ideas just come, straight outta nowhere. Sometimes I get this feeling it's like this really hot club that the Muses love to stop by, to jam and hang, you know what I mean?"

"Mmm…" Scott agreed with a smile. "You here to think? Would you like some privacy?"

"No, don't be silly. Can I use you for a sounding board?"

"You know you can, babe." He waited a beat. "Lemme guess…Derek?"

"Bingo," she said, smiling bleakly. "Derek. And the baby…" She paused to gather the disparate threads of her thoughts into something like order.

"I so wanted to have that child, Scott, even though it wasn't yours. I know it must have been hard for you –" Scott started to interrupt but she stopped him. "No, please, honey, let me work through this, okay?" she implored him. "I need to get this all said. I'm in such confusion."

"I'm sorry, babe. Not another word till you ask for it, I promise," he said. He mimed zipping his mouth and sealed his promise by blowing her a kiss.

Jenna smiled. "Deal. So, here I was, carrying another man's child. And you loving me anyway, in spite of that fact – and for that I am so grateful to you, *so* grateful. Your total acceptance made such a difference, I can't begin to tell you. It – he…" Jenna suddenly had to stop to fight back tears.

"She *became* our baby, biological or not," she went on. "I could see a future for us all. And then I lost her, this baby that would have been ours. That asshole, that fucking madman, in his fucking SUV, in such a fucking hurry – took our baby. That murderer killed our baby, Scott," she spat out bitterly. "I want to kill *him*. He took my baby. I never got to see my baby…"

Finally in touch with the rage that had been building unacknowledged for days, Jenna convulsed in bitter agony, hugged her empty womb and sobbed.

Scott rushed over to her, knelt before her, pulled her to him and held her close. Murmuring disconnected words of compassion and in tears himself, he rocked and soothed her as best he could. Finally, he lay down with her on the couch, holding and stroking her shaking form until the worst had passed.

Finally, Jenna looked up at him. Wiping away his tears, she pressed her wet fingertips to her lips. From the depths of her desolation, she said, "He did it to both of us." Like drowning sailors, they clung to each other amidst the wreckage in a whirlpool of mutual fury and despair. Eventually, the whirlpool subsided. At length, Jenna broke the silence.

"Help me, Scott. Do I tell Derek? What would be the point, now that there's no baby? So he can mourn a child he didn't even know about?" She paused to reflect. "Most probably he did go back to his family – I mean, he didn't even try to contact me. And if he did reconcile with his wife, I wouldn't want to cause problems." Looking up at Scott, she asked, "If it were you, how would you feel if I told you at this point?"

Scott shrugged. "I'm not Derek. I can't know how he'd feel. If it were me, though – well, we both know what I'd have done. He sure didn't have to hire a detective to find you – we've been all over the papers. He knew where you were." Looking down at her, he planted a small kiss on her forehead.

Suddenly, Scott squeezed her fiercely. Through the enormity of his emotions, he murmured, "Jenna, I love you so much."

Just as suddenly, he relaxed his grip, pulled back and looked her in the eye. "But – then again, maybe you *do* have to tell him. It's always going to bother you, on some level, if you don't. Guilt is a terrible burden to carry through life. Trust me – *this* I know what I'm talkin' about…" He stopped and looked away, revisiting painful, old memories.

Then he turned to her again. "My poor baby. I hate that you have to wrestle with these problems, my Baby Blue."

Chapter 13

"Mom, it's time for you to go home," Jenna told Linda over breakfast several days later. "Don't get me wrong – don't think we're giving you the bum's rush or anything. I love having you here, but I'm okay. I can be alone now."

"Sweetheart, I don't mind being here, not a bit. You know that!" Linda exclaimed.

"You're not listening to me, Mom. Of course I know that," Jenna responded, coming over to give Linda a warm hug. "But you've got your own life and you need to be getting back to it. You know how much I appreciate your help, but I can be on my own. And Scott and I've talked about getting a housekeeper in for a few days a week, at least for a while."

"Who's getting a housekeeper?" Joe asked, coming into the kitchen. By the looks of him, he'd been out trimming bushes, which he'd been talking about for days.

Scott looked up. "Dad, I told you, the guy who does the mowing's bringing his whole crew on Friday. You didn't need to do that."

"Well, maybe need isn't the issue, ever think about that, boy?" Joe snapped.

"Ooo, touchy touchy," Scott shot back. "I know your hairline's thinning. Skin too?"

"I was telling Mom she can start planning her trip back home," Jenna jumped in. Joe and Scott had been exchanging a lot of father-son pot shots lately. She, for one, sensed a tension growing between them just in the last few days. Privately, she wondered if their recently discovered ability to connect might not have stirred up other deep-seated, unfinished business between the two. "I'm getting back on my feet. My head still hurts like hell, but there's no reason I can't be on my own."

"Actually, I've been thinkin' it's time I found a place of *my* own, too," Joe said. "Nearby. With bushes to trim. I happen to *like* trimmin' bushes. Housekeeper," he snorted and left the room.

Jenna and Scott looked at each other in amazement. "Where did *that* come from?" Scott wondered out loud.

At supper that night, Linda announced she'd be taking a noonday flight, two days hence. Joe announced he'd been to see a very interesting little piece of property two towns over. Jenna announced that she'd lined up three interview for potential housekeepers.

JENNA AND SCOTT walked Linda out onto the front porch to say their goodbyes, Joe having volunteered to taxi her to the airport. Scott made a point of carrying the last of her bags down to the car to give the two women a moment alone.

"Now you take it easy, sweetie," Linda launched into her last parental lecture of the morning. "Don't forget to –"

"– to call you tomorrow and let you know what the surgeon said. I will." She had an appointment later in the day.

"Just get your rest, honey, that's the most important thing. Give Mother Nature time to –"

"– do her thing," Jenna finished the thought in unison with her mother. She'd heard it all her life. "Mom, you can count on that. It seems to be what I'm best at these days. That and catching up on old movies. You'll send me that footage of Daddy when the studio sends it over, as soon as you get it, right?"

The two moved into each other's arms. "I will, baby, I will. God, I'm going to miss you."

"I'm gonna miss you too, Mom. Very much," Jenna said, squeezing her. Stepping back, she still held her mother's shoulders. "Mom, really, thank you for everything. I'm sorry it had to be under these circumstances, but I'm glad we've had the time together. It's been – good."

"Logan or bust," Joe called from the driveway. "Bus is pullin' out, lady." He emphasized his point with a toot of the horn.

Scott came up the steps and gave Linda a hug. "Better hurry. He's been known to leave stragglers behind."

"Now, you take good care of my baby," Linda said emphatically, embracing him. "I'm trusting you with something very precious to me."

"You don't have to tell me that," Scott assured her.

"I know. Be good. Be happy," she said, then turned and ran for the car that Joe had just put into gear. Heading out at a leisurely pace, he managed to stay several yards ahead of her, down the long driveway to the mailbox.

"Need a lift," he called back to her when he finally chose to stop. Then he settled back in his seat and repositioned his rearview mirror for the pure pleasure of watching her come running.

But Linda ceased her pursuit, bent down and pulled up her hem to bare a stretch of leg every bit as gorgeous as anything Claudette Colbert could flash, in a move that had "goin' my way, mister?" written all over it. Joe, taken by surprise, threw the car into reverse, spewing gravel in his haste to beat it back up the driveway. Jenna and Scott doubled over in laughter as they watched their respective parents ham up the silent film playing out before them.

THE PHONE WAS ringing when they got back inside. Scott answered it.

"Be there in twenty, bro," came Jeremy's voice and the line went dead.

"Oh God, Jenn, I completely forgot to tell you. Jeremy and Carrie are coming over to see you. They're on their way. Are you up for a visit?"

Jenna sighed, then dug deep and found a smile. "I guess it's time for life to go on. Yes. I'm up for a visit."

Scott put his arms around her, held her to his heart and whispered in her ear, "It'll help. Really. At least I hope it will." She looked up at him, into the black pools of his eyes. Slowly, tenderly, their lips found each other's, touched, then formed a conduit that allowed their souls to meld into one.

By the time Jeremy and Carrie arrived, complete with enough groceries to lay out a Roman orgy of a feast, Scott and Jenna were in the mood to be entertained. "Hope you haven't eaten yet," Jeremy said at he dropped his load on the kitchen counter.

Carrie made a bee line for Jenna, gave her a quiet sisterly hug, threw an arm around her and guided her into the living room. "Come on. Let's let the guys do their thing," she said.

Dropping herself on the couch, Carrie patted the cushion beside her. "Sit and tell me how you're doing," she said directly. Jenna appreciated what she was coming to think of as Carrie's no-bullshit approach to life.

"Thanks for bringing lunch. Honestly, we hadn't even thought about it." She smiled wanly. "But I'm glad you're here. Mom just left. Having her here was good. I'm going to miss having her to talk to." Tears rose in Jenna's eyes, unbidden. She shook her head in annoyance and frustration. "God, when do you stop crying."

Carrie pulled Jenna to her. "Here's a shoulder, sweetie." Rocking Jenna, she murmured, "I remember my granny saying, 'you stop crying when you stop,' and 'crying's just a part of loving,' and 'drop by drop makes an ocean.' She never ran out of things to cry over, and she never ran out of proverbs to live by. 'Remember, Carrina, fortune turns like a wheel,' or 'Carrina, when two fight, it's the third who wins.' I can still hear her voice. In this country fifty years, she never lost her accent."

Carrie reached for a tissue from a box on the coffee table and offered it to Jenna. "Thanks, love," Jenna said, calming herself. "And thanks for the shoulder. I guess I'm going to need quite a supply of those, just like the fifty boxes of Kleenex we've got all over the house now."

"I'd have come sooner, but we though you needed your rest. Something told me it'd be hard when your mom left."

Jenna nodded. "I guess harder than I'd realized it'd be."

"You sure look a hell of a lot better than the last time I saw you," Carrie said.

"Thanks."

"I want to be there when Yumi gets a load of what they've done to the back of your head. Man, is she gonna be pissed."

Jenna smiled, then went pensive. "God, performing again's the last thing on my mind. Brian's been calling, but I haven't talked to him. Sympathy isn't one of that guy's strong points."

"Sons of bitches, managers. Of course, that's what makes them so good at what they do. X-ray a good one – X-ray Eddie Strang – and I'll betcha real money you won't find a heart."

"Same with Brian," Jenna agreed.

"I've been in and around show business in one capacity or another since high school," Carrie said. "Nothin' much surprises me. Except maybe how successfully the guys have been able to clean up, once they all put the drugs behind them. I came into Jeremy's life right about then. Those were damned scary times," Carrie reflected. "Those guys had burned so many bridges, it was fuckin' Sherman's March to the Sea. It was amazing that *any*one would agree to manage them. Eddie Strang, one thing you gotta give that guy – he may not have a heart, but he's sure got balls. The guys cleaning up was one thing. You wouldn't believe what it took to clean up their reputation."

"Come 'n get it," Scott called from the kitchen.

AFTER LUNCH, THE guys headed over to the barn, while Jenna and Carrie claimed lounge chairs on the porch so Carrie could continue her self-appointed job of bringing Jenna up to speed on more than twenty-five years of off-the-record Blacklace history.

In the studio, Scott flipped on lights while Jeremy powered up the amps. Jeremy picked up his Stratocaster and set to tuning, while Scott went over to the doorway and got in a half dozen pull-ups. After cranking a few tentative chords, Jeremy settled into an amp-blowing riff just to be sure everything was operating up to par. Satisfied, he let the instrument go silent. "Whaddya have in mind?" he asked.

"I want to finish that song for Jenna. Today, with any luck. That'd give us time to add it to a set for Manchester."

"A righteous goal, my brother," Jeremy said, then launched into what he could remember from their last session working on the song.

Scott went over the keyboard and switched it on. "Whaddya think of this?" Scott asked, demonstrating some of what he'd worked out a few days earlier. He didn't have to explain the newly-minted minor chords.

"Works," Jeremy nodded, picking up and augmenting Scott's idea.

"Kick it up, way up, a couple octaves," Scott suggested, listened critically, then tried out a line of lyrics to it. "'*A beauty like hers deserves only the best...*' Naw, drop it back down."

Jeremy tried something halfway in between. "The fuck," Scott said from between suddenly clenched teeth, turning on Jeremy angrily. "I *said* 'back down.' What part of 'back down's' too complex for you, asshole?"

Jeremy rolled his eyes. After thirty years of working together, he still never knew what in particular would set Scott off on any given day. The best you could say was that the man was predictably unpredictable. It would be an exaggeration to say Scott's routine abuse rolled off Jeremy's back – on the contrary. But it took a lot to get him to rise to Scott's bait any more, not that Scott seemed to care.

"YOU HEARD ANY more from the cops?" Carrie asked Jenna.

"The guy's still alive, if that's what you mean," Jenna said bitterly. "Just. They say if he lives he'll be a vegetable." Carrie reached over and held Jenna's hand.

"Scott's back to work. What do you have going on to take your mind off things for a while?" Carrie asked.

"Not a lot right now," Jenna acknowledged. "Maybe it *is* time to call Brian. I can't perform for a while, but I guess I could be rehearsing, or at least writing more… I can't be going to the West Coast to work with my band, though. That'd be too much."

"Why not work up some material with the guys, hon? You know they'd be happy to work with you. They love your stuff."

"I do need to write more."

"Think of it as occupational therapy," Carrie suggested. "And write what you need to write. You wouldn't be the first." Jenna nodded.

"Actually, I've been working on a song for Scott. I really do want to get back to that, now more than ever."

"Talk to Jeremy about it, Jenn. I'm sure you two could cook up something, especially if you tell him you want to surprise Scott. Hey, come on," Carrie said, getting up and pulling Jenna to her feet. "We're gonna get fat sitting around. Let's go see what those clowns are up to. "

Jenna and Carrie let themselves into the barn, then opened the inner door to the studio. Jeremy was hammering his way through a convoluted melody line. Several bars into it, Scott had to yell and gesture wildly to make himself heard. "No! No, no – Christ, no!" Jeremy pulled up mid-beat.

"Now what the hell is wrong?" he asked, frustrated.

"I'm lookin' for the harmonic minor, not the fuckin' relative minor. Come on, bro, give it to me, fer crap's sake." Emphatically, he sang each note of the minor scale he had in mind, then the line of lyrics they were working over. *"From heaven to hell, with yang and with yin, she's my woman..."* Nodding to Jeremy, they tried it again together. "Better. How about the thingie before the G#, like you did it before?"

Jeremy added a grace note. "That?"

"Yeah, that I like. Hang on to that. In fact, you could use it throughout, like both when it's in the major *and* when it's in the minor." Jeremy played the run again, Scott nodding in time enthusiastically. "Yes! Right! Okay, back up. The whole minor verse."

Jeremy picked up at an earlier point, then Scott joined in. *"Through thick 'n thin, through silence and din, she's my woman. From heaven to hell, with yang and with yin, she's my woman. My baby's blue, my baby's green, she's yellow, she's red, she's my woman."*

"A'right!" he finally yelled. "Ya nailed the sucker!"

Jeremy grinned. Complements being in short supply, he knew to enjoy it whenever one came his way.

"Good, good, good, good, good," Scott burbled happily. "It's all good." Throwing his head back, he reached up over his head, grabbed one wrist with the other hand and started to stretch – which was when he realized to his chagrin that they he and Jeremy had an audience.

"Oh. Hey, baby," Scott said lightly, trying for nonchalance as he hurried over to the door. "How long have you been here?'

"Not long," Jenna answered. "Carrie and I were just curious what you're messing with. You two putting something new together?"

"Just dickin' around with some ideas, that's all," Jeremy offered.

"We were just about to call it quits anyway," Scott said, hoping they'd believe him.

"Great," Jenna said. "Why don't we all just go back to the house and visit a bit before these two have to go home."

Exiting the studio, Scott caught Jeremy's eye and silently mouthed the words, "Thank you." Jeremy acknowledged Scott's appreciation with a wink.

As they all meandered back to the house, Carrie put an arm around Jenna, slowed down and let the guys walk on ahead. Whispering, she said, "You start writing. I'll bring Jeremy up to speed. I'll let you know what he says. You can do better than that," she giggled.

"Damned straight I can," Jenna whispered back.

"DON'T BE A stranger, Dad," Scott found himself calling to his father a week later as Joe prepared to pull out of the driveway.

With most of his belongings in storage, it had only taken Joe two trips to move everything he had at Scott's over to his new place, a simple two-bedroom bungalow located on a rustic acre of mostly scrub vegetation, bisected by a small stream. The house had been sitting vacant more than a year since its previous owner's death. Once the estate was settled, his numerous children, dispersed across the country like tumbleweed, were thrilled to find a ready buyer and were more than happy to expedite the formalities. "Gonna dam up that mighty river and stock it," Joe had said with relish.

"You be over for dinner Sunday night, Joe," Jenna called after the departing figure. Joe raised a hand in acknowledgement, climbed into his truck and drove away.

Chapter 14

Scott fidgeted as he and Jenna tried to vanish into the corner of a waiting room that was practically filled to capacity – and knew that just about every eye in the room was on them. Ten thousand pairs of eyes was one thing. This kind of public exposure was a whole other ball game.

"Dr. Williams will see you now," a pretty young nurse said from the door. Her voice registered her excitement at the tiny role in the history of rock 'n roll she was performing at that very minute. "Walk this way," she said with a choked giggle, fairly quivering with nerves as she ushered them back to an examining room. "Doctor Williams will be with you in a moment." She paused. "Can I tell you how sorry I am about what happened?"

"Of course you can, dear," Jenna answered for both of them. "Thank you. Thank you so much." She gave the young woman a thin but entirely sincere smile.

"You need to take everything off from the waist down," the nurse said, nervously gesturing to the neatly folded hospital gown on the examining table before she withdrew with a tiny wave of farewell. Jenna kicked off her sandals.

"Please, madam, may I give you a hand?" Scott offered with a lascivious grin. He came up behind her, reached around, unbuttoned and unzipped her jeans and stripped them off her. A black lace bikini followed. "I've always wanted to do that."

"What a gentleman," she replied. The loose t-shirt she was wearing provided more than sufficient coverage, so she picked up the Johnny and set it on the counter. "Those things are ridiculous things," she said in annoyance.

"The people who work in hospitals call them I-C-U's," Scott said, then picked her up and lightly set her on the examining table. "'Cuz they can *see you*," he added by way of explanation in response to Jenna's blank stare.

Jenna laughed. "Oh. Okay, I get it," she said, looking around the small room. The lightness of the moment gave way to her anxiety. "It's all so – sterile," she said quietly. "So bare."

Scott took her hand. "It won't be forever, dear woman. One day you'll see it as a bare stage, where anything can happen. We'll make big things happen, you and I. Just you watch." He took her hand to his lips and was just starting to plant a soulful kiss upon it when the Julia Williams knocked and entered. Scott took his time completely the gesture, to the amusement of both women.

"Hi, Jenna," the doctor said with warmth. "Hi, Scott. How are you both doing?" As the attending physician while Jenna was hospitalized, they shared the powerful bond that comes from getting to know one another under painful circumstances.

"Julie," Jenna said comfortably, and extended a hand. Dr. Williams was not much older than she was, which made her far easier to relate to than any ob/gyn Jenna had ever seen. "We're okay. I guess. You tell us," she added, only half joking.

"I can tell you how you are, medically speaking, Jenna," Julia responded. "But I'm just as concerned with how the two of you are coping with it all. There are enough complications with everything you've been through, but you two have to cope with the added complication of being in the public eye."

"Got that right," Scott said. "Ten to one, any six of those ladies out in the waiting room are on their cells right now, calling their friends – 'I'm at the gynecologist's and you won't believe who was just sitting not three feet from me!' And whoever they call, *they* call friends, who call *their* friends – one of which knows some muckity muck in the media, and the next thing you know, we're back on the six o'clock news. God, you better believe it gets old." Scott had long ago given up trying to disguise the bitterness that comes with loss of privacy.

"Though the flip side's just as upsetting," Jenna added. "If the media ignores you, then you're a has-been. That comes with a whole other set of baggage. My dad practically went nuts with it at one point in his career. It wasn't pretty."

"This job comes with pressures aplenty, but at least I don't have those kinds of problems," Julie said sympathetically. "I don't think there's any danger I'm going to get branded ob/gyn to the stars here in Boston. I wonder what it's like in L.A. or New York?" she mused as she parted Jenna's hair to better see how the laceration in her scalp had healed.

"Good. You've healed up beautifully," she said, carefully palpating the irregular wound than started under the hairline only an inch from Jenna's forehead, bisecting her scalp almost the entire way down the back of her head to her neck. "It looks like permanent scarring's going to be relatively minimal. Let's get these sutures out." She swabbed the area, then reached for a scalpel. Jenna only winced once or twice as Julie popped and removed each suture.

Scott kept count. "22. 23. 24. 25 and…26. Phew. God, you okay, baby?" he asked Jenna.

"No problem, except maybe for my hand," she laughed. "You can let go now. I need to get the circulation back in it." She reached over and tousled his hair. "That was way harder for you than it was for me, babe," she assured him.

"I wish it all was," he said in all seriousness. Julie smiled to herself.

"Okay, Scott," she said," how about you go wait in my office, two doors down on the right. We'll just be a couple minutes more." Scott took his cue as Julie started setting Jenna up for an internal exam. "You lie back, now, dear."

SCOTT WAS LISTENING to messages on his cell phone when the doctor walked into her office. Shutting and pocketing the phone, he looked up at her anxiously.

"Jenna will be joining us in a moment. Let me just tell you, though, things look fine, Scott," Julie assured him. "And I think she's handling it as well as can be hoped for at this point. You two are doing a good job."

"We're trying," Scott said. "I try to imagine what it's gotta be like for her. It just breaks my heart to see her in such pain. You just – I wish –"

Julie reached over and laid her hand on top of his. "Scott, she's lucky she's got you," Julie assured him in all seriousness. "She's very lucky. And Jenna knows it," she added, smiling.

"What do I know?" Jenna asked, coming through the door in time to hear her name.

"What a catch I am," Scott said immodestly.

"I do have good taste, don't I. And so do you," Jenna countered.

"You both do, most definitely," Julie laughed. "Well, now that we've got that officially established, on to more serious matters. Jenna, as I told you, you're looking really good. I know you want to get back to your normal workload as soon as possible. I'm okay with that – you're entirely ready to resume business as usual." Jenna allowed an audible sigh of relief to escape her.

"And," Julie continued, "you're ready to resume intimacy as usual, as well." Scott expelled a matching sigh of relief. "That was about as honest a response as I've ever heard!" Julie smiled.

"But – what I really want to talk to you both about is birth control. It's really best that you not get pregnant again immediately. I can't stress this strongly enough. Your reproductive organs need more time to recuperate, Jenna." Julie asked a number of probing question s concerning their daily lives and routines.

"Okay. You have a number of options," she said when she felt she had a clear enough picture to make an appropriate recommendation. "Given your schedules, the demands of travel and such, I am going to suggest you give the weekly contraceptive patch a try. It has a slightly higher rate of effectiveness than the pill does – about 98% versus 95% for the pill. You don't have to think about it daily. But it does call for being consistent on a weekly basis."

"What's involved?" Jenna asked.

"You apply the first patch within the first twenty-four hours of the onset of your period. Whatever day of the week that is, that becomes your 'patch day,' the day you change patches from then on. You go three weeks on and one week off, then start again. Once most women get the hang of it, they tell me they find it very convenient. Until you can start, you'll need to rely on backup contraception – condoms, spermicidal foam – preferably both. Or – there's always abstinence," she added with a wink.

"Yeah, right," Scott said dryly.

"The patch sounds fine to me," Jenna said.

Julie wrote out a prescription and handed it across her desk to her famous patient. "I wish you the best of luck," she said earnestly. "Both of you."

"BEAT YOU TO the bedroom!" Jenna laughed and took off running down the hall. Fortunately, it was Serena's day off. The new housekeeper had started with four days a week, but had been able to scale back to three within a week, due both to Jenna's rapid recuperation and Serena's efficiency.

They had hoped to avoid rush-hour traffic by scheduling a one o'clock appointment with Julie, but they'd forgotten to factor in the effect vacationers had on Boston on a summer Friday.

At a complete standstill in the middle of a sea of cars, Scott grinned. "Well, we might as well make the best of it," he said. "It's clear we're going nowhere fast. Weather doesn't get any better than this." It was a delicious, blue-sky afternoon; the temperature hovered just at eighty degrees. The convertible top retracted into the trunk of the little Mercedes SLK with the touch of a button.

"I was talking to the guys yesterday," Scott said, settling in to enjoy the sunshine. "The Fourth of July's next weekend."

"You told me how the guys and everyone always go up to Sunapee for the Fourth," Jenna said. "God, that was ages ago."

"I'd hoped I could take you up there, just the two of us, way before this," Scott said. "But we sorta lost a month in there." Jenna pulled her legs up under her, leaned across the console and put her head on his shoulder.

Smiling, he slipped an arm around her. "I can't wait to show you the place. You are so gonna love it, babe." Jenna closed her eyes and sighed. She could feel the restorative rays of the sun warming the blood within her as it flowed near the surface of her skin. Her mind started to let go of all its concerns and flow with it.

"Baby," Scott whispered, kissed the top of her head and ran his hand through her hair. She sighed again, more deeply this time. As his free hand slowly worked its magic, massaging tension away, inch by inch down her neck and across her shoulders, she felt her body warm to his touch as her skin had warmed to the sun's touch. By the time traffic was finally flowing, not all that far from home, she was in a state of high arousal, in spite of the fact that he hadn't so much as brushed a fingertip over any textbook erogenous zones. He didn't have to.

SCROUNGING THROUGH THE contents of both night table drawers in search of a condom, Scott came upon the envelope the Bradfords' attorney had given Jenna, the day after her father's funeral. It bore Jenna's California address, and that cryptic instruction: <u>Do Not Open Unless and Until Pregnant</u>. It was still sealed.

As Jenna emerged from the bathroom, he held it up to her. "I just found this. You never opened it?"

"Oh, my God. I stuffed it in there, back when I still wasn't ready to face telling Derek. I guess my thinking was that I'd tell Derek first, then open it. Then it not longer applied. I guess I should file it away." She took it from him.

"But not now, big boy." They made love till the sun went down.

JENNA SLEPT BUT Scott got up and went over to the studio, which was where Jenna found him at midnight, pounding the keyboard, clearly deep into experimentation. "Working?" she asked when he stopped. He turned to find her at the door.

"You been here long?" he asked.

"No," she said, smiling sleepily. "You hungry?" He nodded. "I'll go start something. You come over when you're ready."

"Babe, you're so fuckin' wonderful," he said.

"You too," she responded.

A light snack, a few minutes of *Casablanca* on T.V., and Scott followed Jenna back to bed. At the door to the bedroom, Jenna turned back to him. Taking a handful of tank top in each hand, she pulled him to her. "You drive me wild," she whispered in his ear. "Make love to me again."

A FEW HOURS later, Scott was awakened from a deep sleep by Jenna, tossing and turning restlessly beside him. Not wanting to wake her with too bright a light, he reached for the remote that ignited the small gas fireplace across the room. By the artificial firelight, it was clear that she was still asleep, but her eyes, under closed lids, darted around rapidly and her breathing was quick, agitated, shallow and erratic. Her arms flailed and her fingers were splayed as if in self-defense. Scott felt helpless as she thrashed convulsively, not knowing if he should wake her. Suddenly, she sat bolt upright, and cried hoarsely, "No. No! Please don't!" Her eyes flew open, unfocused. Her mind's eye was clearly focused elsewhere.

Scott grabbed her and held her, trembling, as she burst into tears. "Jenna, baby, you were having a bad dream. It was just a dream. It's okay. It's okay," he said over and over, rocking her down from the fearful heights she'd been scaling.

"Scott," she finally said, and clung to him. "Oh, my God, Scott." She choked the words. "I – I had this terrible dream." He continued to hold her and rock her. "It was so vivid. I was younger – a teenager, I think – and someone was trying to – hurt me." She took a ragged breath. "I – I kept saying, 'no, don't!' Oh, God, where would a dream like that come from?"

"Who knows where dreams come from," he said gently. "You need to forget this one. You're okay, baby. You're safe," he whispered, and held her until, finally, she could fall back to sleep.

SCOTT AWOKE TO the orangey glow that precedes a dazzling dawn. Glancing over at Jenna, who was still asleep, he turned silently onto his side, laid his head back down on the pillow and held his breath in astonishment as he watched the sun literally rise over the spectacular range of Jenna's naked breasts. Mesmerized, he wanted to cry out – how could anyone ever capture such perfection, such bliss, such astonishing beauty in a word, in a song? How could anyone ever capture, in any form, the intensity of a moment such as this?

Or *did* he cry out, he wondered, as he suddenly saw her stir and waken. Rising on an elbow, he bent down and kissed her, gently at first, then more deeply and hungrily as she responded with equal passion.

Finding and taking each of her hands in his, he rose up and straddled her. Pinning both hands in one of his above her head, he sent the other hand to arouse every inch of her exquisite body. She struggled to move, but he wouldn't let her. Instead, kissing his way from her naval, up and over her breasts, up the side of her neck, he brought his body down on her and held her immobilized as his lips found hers. Probing her soul with his kiss, he suddenly felt her go rigid beneath him, then twist away from him in panic. Confused, he pulled back and looked down on her. Her face was contorted with fear, her eyes wide and unseeing. "No, don't! Please, don't!" she cried out. "Let me go!"

Instantly, Scott released his hold on her and rose up on his knees. "Jenna," he said in alarm. "Baby, what's wrong? What have I done? What in the hell is going on?" But his voice was filled with anguish and concern, not anger.

"What's going on?" Jenna moaned. Spontaneously, she had pulled away, turned her back on him and rolled herself into a tight knot of a ball. Now she turned and looked up at him, suddenly seeing him as if for the first time. "Scott! Oh, Scott, what's happening to me?"

"I've never seen you like this, baby," he said. "Except last night – your voice sounded exactly the same last night. You sounded like a terrified child."

"I feel like one," Jenna said and moved into his open arms. "Oh, God. Hold me." Gently, carefully, he held her and murmured soothing words.

"Honey – has this ever happen before?" he finally whispered. She shook her head.

"Never."

"Is it me?"

"I don't think so. No. I know it's not you. I just don't know *what* it is..." She looked up at him, then reached up and stroked his face. "No, it's not you, babe. It's me. Its – God, I wish I could finish that sentence..." She kissed him. "Thank you. A lotta guys'd be out the door so fast."

He chuckled. "I can't. It's my house."

"Oh, yeah." Jenna smiled wryly.

"And I've got a band showing up in an hour for a rehearsal. Hard to come up with alternate rehearsal space on such short notice."

"Guess so."

"Hey, why don't you sit in with us? Might at least take your mind off it. I don't like the idea of you over here stewing about what happened. That's not going to help a bit. In fact, ya know what?" He looked down and kissed her on the nose. "Maybe it's your inner child begging to – hmmm…begging to get to sing with us some more?" He gave her a tentative little tickle. Jenna responded with a giggle, as he'd hoped she would.

Scott's joking mood was contagious. "'No, please' – maybe that means, 'no, really, *please*, let me sing,'" she suggested. "And, let's see – 'please, don't' – that could mean 'please don't say I *can't*.'"

"Oh, baby, I love it when you use those double negatives on me," Scott said huskily.

"And the 'let me go' could be nothing more ominous than 'let me go to the studio,' Jenna wrapped it up, wishing it *were* as simple as all that. "Maybe, on some profoundly deep level, I see you as my daddy, with the power to say yes or no, whether I can sing with you guys or not. I guess maybe I shoulda told you I always did have problems with authority figures."

Scott pulled her close and kissed her deeply. Coming up for air, he whispered, "Jenna Bradford, you can rehearse with the guys, anytime you want, baby. You've got lifetime authorization. And you can have it in writing."

Jenna kissed him back, just as deeply. Pulling him back on top of her, she said, "First we need a little more rehearsal time of our own."

"You sure?" he said, still worried about her.

"Just watch."

Chapter 15

ONE BY ONE, the boys in the band pulled up the driveway, parking their Ferraris and Porsches haphazardly around the circle in front of the house. Jenna waved down at them from the bedroom window. "God forbid anybody should park in a straight line," she laughed. "Oh, and here comes Ben." Ben Diamante, Blacklace's record producer and one of the top men in the business, roared up to the door and stepped off a perfectly restored 1945 Harley. Jenna came trotting down the stairs to greet them.

"Well, look who we have here!" Ben teased her. "You're looking bright-eyed, Ms. Sunshine." Jenna slipped one arm in his and the second in Jeremy's and personally ushered the two out to the barn.

"And what am I, chopped livah?" Dan groused, three steps behind.

"Chopped brains, is more like it," Jeff commented.

"Some people'll do anything to get to sing with Blacklace," Tim said.

"If I didn't know she had two totally un-influential slobs on her arms, I'd say she was trying to suck up to somebody," Dan said in a stage whisper. Jenna looked back at him and stuck out her tongue.

"If I didn't know better, I say the lady's high," Jeremy said back to them, "and on her I think it's perfectly adorable."

Scott watched the procession from the kitchen window and wondered just what was going on in Jenna's head.

PAULIE GATTONUCCI, THEIR sound engineer, was already in the studio and hard at work.

"Hi, guys," he said, looking up from the sound board as they all filed in. "This is Pablo," he said, introducing the kid he had with him. "He's an intern from Berklee. And he's one smart motherfucker." Pablo looked like he might be going into eighth grade, but no one was going to question Paulie's take on the kid; he'd worked with more than his share of interns. 'Smart motherfucker' was Paulie's highest rating.

With Scott's arrival a few minutes later, they all grabbed instruments and started tuning. Tim started banging away on snare drum and cymbal, working back and forth with Paulie to check sound from his quarter. Jenna warmed up at the piano, stretching her vocal chords with ascending triads of nonsense syllables, an exercise she took every bit as seriously as any opera diva. Scott hopped back and forth from pounding the keyboard in organ mode, to beating out some rhythms splay-handed on a Makonde drum sitting alongside Tim's drum set, then up to an open mike with his harmonica wailing.

"Okay, okay, okay," Ben yelled. "Everyone quiet. Whaddya want me to hear first?" he asked Scott.

"I was thinking 'Outta My Way.'" Scott looked at Jeremy. "What do you think?"

"Or 'Splittin' Hairs,' how about?" Jeremy suggested.

"We'll do 'Outta My Way,' Ben," Scott said. Jeremy, entirely used to having his input solicited and ignored, knew this would be only the first of fifty micro-insults that Scott would lob his way today. Long ago he'd decided it didn't matter. Getting this rehearsal moving was more important. Jeremy picked his fights judiciously.

So it took him by surprise when Scott said, "Yeah. 'Splittin' Hairs,' it'll be." It was only the first surprise of the morning. Scott had irritated literally no one by lunchtime.

Jenna, on the other hand, was getting on everyone's nerves, missing cues, jumping in early, slip-sliding into – and off – key, and if called on it, dragging out confusing, convoluted apologies that only wasted further time. Her mind appeared to be anywhere but in the studio.

As EVERYONE HEADED over to the house for lunch, Jeremy caught up with Scott, put an arm around him, and steered him off to the side to a couple of Adirondack chairs under a huge chestnut tree.

"Hey, buddy, I know I shouldn't ask, but what are friends for, right? What's with you two, my brother? Jenna's acting like she's high and you, you haven't torn anyone a new one all morning. You're so fuckin' quiet, it's starting to creep me out. Something's up. Spill."

Scott grimaced. "Busted as charged," he said, throwing up his hands as if under arrest. "But it's personal."

"Of course it's personal. That's why I'm asking. Otherwise, I could just wait till Friday and read about it in the Enquirer. Talk to me."

"No, I mean personal personal," Scott insisted.

"You mean more personal than you and me fuckin' half of Detroit in the same bed together personal? You mean more personal than crawlin' and vomiting our way through detox together personal? Surely it couldn't be more personal than that time we tried to share the same rubber, could it?

Scott chuckled. "Yeah, that was a pretty personal kinda moment, wasn't it. Still think it coulda worked if we'd been a little bit more sober."

"Or maybe a little bit harder," Jeremy reminded him.

"Oh, yeah. That too." The two laughed, then Scott went serious.

"We had a weird night last night."

"I thought all your nights were weird," Jeremy said.

"No, this one was out of the realm of normally weird, at least for Jenna. I'm pretty hip to what's normal for her." He stopped, then looked at Jeremy. "You can't say anything about this."

"You crazy?"

"It's like she had this wicked bad nightmare last night, okay? And then this morning, we're like gettin' a nice start on the day, if you know what I mean..."

"I can picture this," Jeremy said. "Continue, my son."

"But then she got all weirded out – and it was coming straight from the nightmare, same thing all over again. Only she wasn't asleep. It was her voice, man – you'd have to hear it. Something's going on with her, she doesn't know what. And then today. Yeah, something's wrong, and all I can think about is how in the hell do I help her?"

"Hell, Scott, with everything she's been through? She's entitled to be acting strange. Losing the baby, just for starters. The fucker that hit her lying 98% dead in the hospital. Hell, it's amazing either of you can function normally – which, of course, is a relative term where you're concerned." Scott was so preoccupied, he didn't even rise to the bait, Jeremy noted. Jeremy looked Scott up and down.

"Man, you look like shit."

"I know. Neither of us are eating right. We're just running on triple shots of caffeine. I guess it's to be expected."

"My suggestion: just focus on rehearsal. Don't let her see how worried you are or you'll just make her more anxious then she is now. Just concentrate on the next show, songs for the album. The Fourth up at Sunapee, some down time. Maybe it'll pass."

SCOTT FOUND JENNA alone in the kitchen, making a small plate for herself from the innards of one of a dozen Italian subs they'd ordered in to. "Makes a nice antipasto," he commented, coming up behind her. He gave her first a squeeze, then a kiss on the neck. "You okay?"

"I'm okay, babe." She turned, pulled him to her, kissed him sweetly, then looked up at him. "Really, I'm okay."

Scott tipped her chin up and kissed her back, then held her close. "Then relax, honey. You were a nervous wreck in there all morning."

Jenna looked away, biting her lip. Scott waited her out.

"You're right," she said finally. "I guess I *am* a wreck." As he stroked her hair, the tears started to flow once again. "Oh, shit," she said between clenched teeth.

"Can I make a suggestion?" Scott asked quietly. Jenna nodded. "Come on upstairs. Let's have us a good cry. Lunch can wait." They went upstairs hand in hand, laid down on the bed, found their way into each other's arms and let their tears mingle.

THE MANAGEMENT TEAM of Strang and O'Halligan showed up mid-afternoon, straight from a coat-and-tie meeting, to see how things were pulling together. Big Bob was ironing out the last details of a tightly planned tour of performances scheduled to start three weeks hence with two nights in Philly. Early dates on the tour were already selling out; promoters were begging for second, third and even fourth shows to be added in their venues. The one-night gig at the Boston Garden, now a week off, would serve as a dress rehearsal for the rest of the summer.

Eddie Strang suffered silently through three of Scott's signature melt-downs. As the fourth of the afternoon began to erupt, Eddie rose to his feet. Wading into the melee, this time a screaming fit between Scott and the usually mild-mannered Jeff over the seemingly simple subject of volume.

"When I say 'cut the hell back on the da-da-da,' I mean 'CUT THE HELL BACK ON THE FUCKIN' DA-DA-DA!' Scott screamed. Jeff had raised his bass guitar up over his head, looking for all the world like he was about to bring it ringing down on Scott's raging head.

"Da-da-da *this*, ya cocksuckin' dick-wad," Jeff said in quiet fury, glancing out of the corner of his eye to pace his actions with Eddie's, making sure their long-suffering manager would arrive in time to check his swing before he actually did any damage to his beloved Fender.

AS THE GROUP packed it in late in the day, Jeremy leaned over to Scott. "Guess I'm a fuckin' genius," he said.

"You?" Scott sneered.

"Well, whatever you did, bro, whether it was because of our little mano a mano chitchat at lunch or whatever the hell it was – it worked. She was as good this afternoon as she was fucked up this morning. And you, my man, you were most definitely back on your game," he said with a grimace. "For which I believe I owe you at least two 'fuck you very muches,'" he said with a pair of little girl curtsies, one for each. So – where for dinner, oh fearless leader? I need to call Carrie so she'll know where to meet us."

"Le Café," Scott said decisively. "I haven't been back there since Jenna's been on the scene. Time to get it over with. I miss the place." Indecision began to set in. "Or, Christ, I dunno. What do you think?"

"You sure that's a good idea?" Jeremy asked cautiously.

"For chrissakes, bro, how the hell am I supposed to avoid every broad I ever screwed?" Scott said. "I'd have to fuckin' stay home. Maybe she left there years ago Maybe she's happily married, a couple kids."

"It was only six, seven months ago," Jeremy pointed out. "She could be happily married – though I doubt it; she wasn't the happily married type. Forget the couple of kids."

"Maybe it's her day off. Shit, what the fuck was her name, anyway?"

IT WASN'T HER day off. Lori D'Angelito was the hostess on duty as the motley collection of rockers, techies and suits that comprised the nucleus of the Blacklace entourage came trailing through the door. A tall, tough blond with big hair, little skirt and great legs, Lori chewed her words like bubblegum. The bubbles she saved for private.

Lori was just zeroing in on Scott when Jenna and Carrie came in the door. The two women had met up in the parking lot and lingered behind the rest to catch up with each other. Jenna missed noticing that, with one glance at her, Lori's lower jaw slid forward and locked. Her demeanor turned icy as she ushered the group to a back room big enough to accommodate them all. Jenna took a seat between Scott and Dan.

When there was relative order, Lori came over and positioned herself behind Scott on the side away from Jenna. Bending down to flaunt some cleavage, she tilted her head seductively and purred, "The usual, honey?" The two innocent words were laced with innuendo. The third couldn't be clearer. Scott looked her straight in the eye and nodded. Jenna's radar went up.

Taking her time going around the table, Lori made it abundantly clear that she knew everyone, and their drink preferences, well. Prior to addressing a personal remark to each, she shot a quick, fault-finding look in Jenna's direction. She couldn't take any comfort there. Jenna had never looked better.

Lori finally arrived at Jenna's side. Icily, she simply said, "And…"

"An ice tea, please," Jenna said, her eyes locked on Scott, who put his arm around her shoulder, drew her to him and gave her a little squeeze as Lori closed her order pad and withdrew. At the door, she turned back to shoot one more venomous look in Jenna's direction, just as Scott quietly planted a kiss on Jenna's shoulder.

"So," Jenna said to Eddie, who was sitting directly across the table from her. "Are the guys ready?"

"Ready as they'll ever be," Eddie responded. "A lot readier than some tours that come to mind."

"I imagine 'Operation Smokin' Gun' heads that list?" Jeremy said with a grimace. "Will we ever finished apologizing for that forty-car pileup?"

Eddie looked over the top of his glasses at Jeremy. "First thing every promoter brings up, to this day. Doesn't matter how many years have gone by. 'This ain't gonna be another 'Smokin' Gun,' right?' Every time. One of 'em makes me include it in the fuckin' contract." Everyone laughed. To Jenna he said, "See all this gray hair? I'm actually only nineteen years old."

"Yeah, and you've been managing us since you were four," Dan said. "Somebody get this guy a case of Depends. He'll be needin' 'em before much longer." He was ready with more of the same when their waiter, a tall, lean, keen-eyed Frenchman straight from the old country, interrupted.

"Bonsoir, mesdames et messieurs. I am Pierre, your waiter," he said with Gallic sangfroid. "Are you prepared to order yet?"

"Better start with the old guy," Dan suggested. "He ain't got long to live." Pierre smiled thinly. He'd heard that one enough times, and in more languages than one.

Like every other pair of eyes in the room, Pierre's automatically gravitated to Jenna; being French, he made no secret of his appreciation for what he, a devoted connoisseur of beauty, saw before him. "Oh là là ," he said, nodding his approval, and naturally started taking his orders with her. "Bonsoir, madam. Et pour la belle femme, what would please and delight you ce soir – how you say, tonight?" His pen was poised over his order pad but his eyes continued to appraise each of Jenna's observable features.

Jenna ordered the cassoulet. Pierre kissed his fingertips. "Formidable! La spécialité de la maison." Jenna flashed him a smile, which he returned with interest. "Merci madam," he said gravely, then, with a suggestion of a bow and clearly with reluctance, tore his attention away from her to continue around the table. But as he waited for each diner to make his or her final decision, his eyes kept wandering back to Jenna.

"Something tells me this might go a little quicker if I were to nip off to the ladies' room," Jenna whispered to Scott.

"Good move. We could starve to death at the rate he's going, and it's all your fault, you gorgeous thing," he whispered in return. With a quick kiss, he added, "Have I told you I love you in the last ten minutes?"

"Nope. Hold that thought." Jenna got up, exited the back room, asked directions and headed for the restrooms, much to Pierre's disappointment.

Dan leaned across the now empty space next to him to address Scott. "So, any further thoughts on that thing I showed you this morning? On 'Run It Down'?" Dan beat a quick rhythm on the table top with his hands. "*Run it up, run it down, beat it up, beat it down...*" Repeating the riff and lyrics, he picked up the tempo. "But I was thinkin', you could do it this way," he suggested. Then he added a heavyweight counter beat. "Or like this…"

Scott started to nod his head in time with Dan's new approach. "Yeah. Yeah, good!" he said, grabbing a couple of spoons and joining in. One of his first instruments as a kid had been the drums.

"*Run it up, run it down, beat –*" Dan's drumming came to a sudden halt mid-phrase. "Uh-oh. Don't look now but – your friend Lori just went in the ladies' room…"

Scott's face froze.

"This cannot be good," Dan said quietly. "This so shouldn't happen..."

JENNA WAS STANDING in front of the mirror using her fingertips to rearrange her hair to make sure the still visible strip of scalp running through it didn't show. Narrow as it might be and now fairly well grown in, it was nonetheless a source of discomfort to her. She couldn't wait until there we no more tangible reminders of the accident.

She was fishing for a mini hairspray in her purse when Lori came through the door. Glancing up at the mirror, Jenna merely registered her presence, then went back into her bag to find the hairspray. Pulling it out, she looked back in the mirror to find Lori standing almost directly beside her. The two locked eyes in the single long mirror that transversed the wall above the row of four sinks.

Holding Jenna's eye, Lori unbuttoned the topmost of the few fastened buttons of the skimpy pink blouse that strained to accommodate her more than ample bosom. Tugging the stretchy blouse down to expose far more cleavage, she turned this way and that, assessing the results.

"So. You're Scott's new girl. Huh."

Jenna started spraying her hair, deliberately in Lori's direction. "Woman, actually."

"Don't suppose the motherfucker told you that I use to be one of his girls, too?" With one hand she pulled the neck of the blouse back and, with the other, reached in to rearrange a breast within a black lace bra. "Oh, yeah, we had somethin' pretty fuckin' hot goin', ol' Scott 'n me," she told Jenna's reflection, as she set to rearranging the other breast. Following up her manual adjustments, she gave them both a little lift, threw her shoulders back and drew in a breath.

"Very impressive," Jenna said to Lori's reflection. "Bet they set you back a few years' tips."

"Ask him," Lori taunted her, "if you're anywhere near as hot in the sack as I am. He told me 'Mouth of a Goddess' coulda been written for me. Maybe you should ask him about that, too."

With that, Lori fished a lipstick out of a back pocket of her little skirt. Taking her time, she applied an exaggerated, thick layer of blood red gloss, then ran her tongue over her full, ripe lips, first the top one and then the bottom. "Go – ask him why. I dare you," she hissed, and then she started to laugh.

Jenna snapped her bag closed, pushed past Lori without a word and slammed out the door.

SHAKING, JENNA SAT back down at the table, clenched her hands in her lap and sat there staring into space, trying to pull her thoughts back into some semblance of order.

"Jenn, honey, are you okay?" Jeremy asked from further down the table.

Jenna turned on him. "Gee, Jeremy, maybe it's none of your damned business how I am," she spat out. Jeremy's mouth fell open.

"Sor-ry," he said, sarcastically, throwing his hands in the air. "It's just –"

Carrie jumped to her feet and interrupted him before he could do any more damage. Before she could even get around to where Jenna was sitting, she said, "Honey, baby, ignore him. Men can be such total fuckin' assholes sometimes. You know he doesn't mean to be."

Scott quickly turned to her. "Baby," he said, reaching and taking hold of her hands. "Oh, God. Are you all right?"

"Of course. Why shouldn't I be?" she snapped, her tone cold as ice. Looking around the table, she beseeched them all in general, " Somebody just change the topic, okay? Please?"

"Come on, Jenna," Scott insisted. "You're coming with me." With Carrie's help, he pulled her to her feet. Carrie gave her a squeeze.

"Go with him, honey," Carrie told her soothingly. "Let him tell his side." Jenna turned and looked Carrie in the face.

"Oh, I just can't wait to hear 'his side.' This should be good," she said, her voice laced with cynicism.

Carrie shook her head. "No, hon, trust me, really," she persisted, "his version won't match hers, not one bit, I guarantee it."

"What is this? Does everybody know about this – this two-bit tramp?" Jenna cried in amazement.

"Tramp's putting it nicely," Dan volunteered.

"You *do* all know. Oh, God!" Jenna said, throwing her hands up.

"I don't know," Little Pablo commented to Paulie, down at the end of the table. "Do you know?"

"Beats me," Paulie said, baffled. "Times like this, you know you're only a peripheral player in this game, kid, but don't let it worry you – they can't make their records without us."

"You're coming with me, my love, and that's an order," Scott told her. "No more conversation." He gathered her to him, put an arm around her protectively and started to guide her out of the restaurant.

Halfway across the main room she saw Lori coming their direction, menus in hand and a pair of diners behind her. "March," he whispered in her ear as he felt her stiffen and stop. "Just keep moving. Man," he gasped, taking a firmer hold as she tried to wriggle out of his grasp, "you're harder to wrangle than a pit bull on coke. I've done that too."

"You're shittin' me, right?" Jenna said out of the corner of her mouth.

"Nope. Pit fuckin' bull 'n premium blow, I shit you not," he said, smiling genially at the curious diners they passed.

Scott managed to get her out the front door of the restaurant, propel her to a bench nearby and sit her down. Taking the seat next to her, he grabbed her shoulders and turned her towards him. The face that greeted him stopped him in his tracks. Never had he had reason to see her so angry.

"Oh God. Baby – I am so sorry. I should never have brought you here without telling you about the bitch. Honest to God, I wasn't even sure she still worked here." He stopped and hung his head. "Can you ever forgive me?"

"I don't know what I'm supposed to forgive you for," Jenna said woodenly, with virtually no emotion in her words.

"What did she say to you?"

"Not much," Jenna said tersely.

"Look, honey, please, let me just tell you how it was. We only went out a few times. I shoulda known she was crazy from the start – but I didn't. The guys had to tell me – they figured it out. When I told her it wasn't gonna go anywhere – let's just say she didn't take it too well." He let out a short, harsh laugh. "Actually, that's a bit of an understatement. She practically did a Fatal Attraction on me, stalked me, the whole nine yards. It was a long time ago. I haven't been back since. When I saw her tonight, it was too late to turn around." He took her hands. She let him kiss them.

"Tell me what she said to you," he persisted. "I'm not blind. I can see it's really got you upset."

Jenna held herself aloof, looking away into the distance, blinking hard, suddenly finding herself working not to cry.

"Honey, I am so sorry," Scott repeated. "I mean it. This you don't need." Tears finally overflowed and coursed down Jenna's cheeks. He took her into his arms and held her.

"Okay," she said through her tears. "I'll tell you what she said. She implied that the two of you had something really hot and heavy going on. She said I should ask you if – if sex with me is as good as it was with her. She – she gave me to believe that she was pretty good at – you know, going down on you." Jenna ended the sentence very quietly.

Scott opened his mouth to say something. "Let me finish," Jenna snapped. He shut his mouth.

"I know I have to expect comments from girls you've been with before. It's not like we're high school sweethearts or anything. I know it was in your past. I guess it just struck a nerve, especially after last night and – what happened this morning. I guess I'm a bit on edge. I – I reacted badly, Scott. *I'm* sorry. Let's just call it even and forget about it, and go back inside. I'll be all right." She kissed him, then jumped up and headed towards the door. Scott grabbed her arm and turned her around to face him.

"You just remember one thing, Jenna Bradford. I love you and only you." He kissed her hard, then pulled back to judge what effect the kiss was having on her. She managed a rueful smile.

"Okay. You're forgiven," she said. "But good Christ, tell me next time, will ya?" He broke out in a grin and kissed her again.

"There won't be a next time. No way, no how. Scout's honor." He held up his right hand in a peace symbol.

"Uh, honey, I don't think that's exactly an official Boy Scout salute," Jenna laughed, wiping away the last of her tears with one hand while demonstrating the proper, three-fingered Boy Scout salute with the other.

"Oh, right. Well, yeah," Scott grinned. "They closed down our local troop when they saw me coming." With another kiss, he threw an arm around Jenna and escorted her back into the restaurant.

JENNA FELT HERSELF blush as she reclaimed her place at the table. "Hey, guys," she said to everyone. "I just want to apologize for – um – well, for like overreacting a bit, shall we say?"

"You don't have to apologize," Dan said, speaking for everyone. "For what it's worth, every one of us can bear witness on Scott's behalf. He may be blind as a bat, but all us 20-20 types, we all saw it comin' a mile away."

"A planet away," Jeff corrected him.

"I stand corrected. A planet away," Dan continued his testimonial. "The minute we pointed out the mortal danger the dude was in, man, he broke it off, right then and there. Clearly, however, the broad still carries the torch. But, Jenn, please rest assured – and I hasten to tell you we came to this decision democratically, we've taken a vote on this – the next time you need to go to the ladies' room, we are all coming with you, every last one of us."

"Dan. I – I'm overwhelmed," Jenna responded in kind. "I can't thank you enough. I mean, the sacrifice you're all prepared to make on my behalf – I just don't know what to say! I am – touched."

Dropping the pose, she went serious. "Really, thank you, all of you. I mean it. I'm really sorry."

"Can we maybe eat tonight?" Eddie Strang said.

OBLIVIOUS TO PREVAILING attitudes, Lori sashayed in with the bill at the end of the meal, taking it straight down the table to deposit it with Scott. Without looking up, he handed her a credit card.

Returning a few minutes later for his signature, she positioned herself at his elbow – the one on his far side, again the side away from Jenna. Leaning over, she 'whispered' in his ear – loud enough for Little Pablo to hear at the far end of the table, "If she's not good to you, honey, you know where to find me."

Jenna turned to get her bag, stood up and faced the woman. "Lori," she said dispassionately, "Scott and I have had a chance to discuss you. He assures me I am – I think his words were 'far superior to anything you could ever be.' '*Ever.*' That was the word he used. I wouldn't be expecting him, if I were you. Ever."

The entire group piled out of the restaurant as fast as they could move. Out in the parking lot, they all exploded in laughter.

"Brilliant, Jenn. Stone brilliant!" Jeremy chuckled acidly. "Abso-fuckin'-lutely excellent. We can only hope she knows where she stands now. Pretty good, huh?" he said, elbowing Scott.

"Pretty good? Fuckin' A!" Scott threw a fist in the air, then broke into an end-zone dance. "You kicked some serious butt in there, Jenna, my love! I just wanna say, in front of God and my 'family' –" he said, indicating the entire entourage with a sweep of his hand, "Jenna Bradford, I am *wicked* proud to have you as my lover and my woman."

Jenna threw herself in his open arms. Tipping her backwards, he planted a perfect Hollywood kiss on her. Holding her dramatically in this pose for several beats, he then slowly, gently, sincerely, brought her back to her feet, never for a moment taking his eyes off hers. Still looking deep into her eyes, he said quietly, "I do love you so, my Jenna." Then he broke the mood.

"Hey, I don't want to spoil everybody's good time but I'd sorta like to take this beautiful lady home and make mad, passionate love to her all night long, so if you all could possibly excuse us, we'll see you at rehearsal." Scott took Jenna's hand and they ran for his car.

"He means it?" Little Pablo asked Paulie as they climbed into Paulie's truck. "The stuff about all night long?"

"Oh, yeah, he means it all right," Paulie assured his intern. "Didn't I guarantee you you'd get one hell of an education workin' with me, kid?"

Chapter 16

BUT AS SHE offered Scott her body that night, Jenna was practically overcome with insecurities. His every move brought a torrent of fresh fears cascading over her. The more she tried to give, the more she found herself shrinking from his touch. Finally, he pulled away from her, rolled over and lay on his back staring at the ceiling. Jenna burst into tears, the only sound in an otherwise silent room.

When she seemed to have cried herself out, Scott turned to her. "Jenna," he said in a quiet, measured tone, "what is wrong?"

Was that veiled irritation she heard in his voice, Jenna wondered to herself. She couldn't speak. Sentence after sentence formed in her head, each more unutterable than the last. All she could see in her mind's porno film house was a looped montage of lurid sex scenes, each one starring Scott, every scene involving voluptuous female bodies of all descriptions, all writhing, all moaning, all bent on devouring Scott's manhood in an endless display of sexual creativity entirely devoid of inhibition.

At length, Scott broke the silence again, and this time his words were definitely delivered in the chilling cadences of frustration. "Jenna, you've *got* to tell me what's going on. I'm not a fuckin' mind reader. What in the hell is the matter?"

Jenna sat up and wrapped her arms around her knees. Finally, she scratched her head, sighed and then launched into what would have to pass for an explanation. "Look, honey, I don't know. I believe what you said, about Lori. I just can't get past what she said about *you*. We both know I made up that stuff I said to her, about sex being better with me. She was probably ten times better then I'll ever be for you." The last sentence came out in a rush. Then she covered her face with her hands and moaned.

"You don't know how much it hurts me to say that," she went on. "Honey, I want to be every bit as good as every other woman you've ever had – but I can't. And – well, I might as well say it: I'm terrified that one day you'll go out and find somebody else who can."

Scott couldn't believe what he was hearing. Sitting up, he grabbed her, hard, and all but shook her. "Jenna! Where in *hell* would you ever get a fucked up idea like that? Good God, woman! How could you think that Lori – or anybody else, for that matter – could be better than you, or that you can't be as good as any one of them?" He stopped and pulled her into a hard embrace, waiting her out until he could feel her at last begin to relax a degree.

"You know – or in case maybe you don't know it, baby," he said, scaling back the raw emotion in his voice, "this isn't a competition for who's 'Best in Bed.' This is about me and you and the love we have for each other. You don't have to try to be better than anyone else, because you already *are* better. I love you," he said emphatically, "and that means complete with any old baggage – and any old hang-ups – you may come with. Baby, you've just got to believe me. Please. Tell me you believe me."

Jenna looked away, took a deep breath and exhaled through pursed lips. Then she turned back to him.

"Scott, I do believe you. I – I just couldn't bear loosing you. I've made a life-long practice of not letting myself get into this predicament. Loving you – is the single most frightening thing I've ever done. God help me."

They clung to each other then, each raining small kisses on the other, here, there and everywhere until their lips finally met.

SCOTT'S LAKE HOUSE sat on a heavily wooded rise, overlooking Lake Sunapee. The entry to the house sat twenty steep steps below the level of the road that fronted the property. The woods, which guaranteed privacy, barely allowed a view of the lake from the parking area above, except in winter.

"This is a spectacular spot," Jenna exclaimed. "Oh, my God, I see why you love it here. It's so beautiful, so isolated."

"You ain't seen nothin' yet, lady," Scott said as he unlocked the front door and pushed it open. A large entry hall opened into a huge, open, cathedral-ceilinged space that served as living room, dining room and kitchen, all radiating from a tremendous fireplace in the center of the room, its massive chimney rising twenty feet through heavy, hand-hewn beams to disappear into the timber ceiling above. A screened porch spanned the entire back of the structure, further fostering the feeling of privacy. It led, a few steps down, onto a vast open deck.

"The main part of the house is over a hundred years old," Scott told her, taking her by the hand. "Come on. Let me show you everything."

He took her on a whirlwind tour: five bedrooms on the main floor, two with small lofts above them; downstairs, a family room and a game room that let out onto a little gravel patio. Through the woods, back up on the road, was a large garage, once a carriage house, with rudimentary lodgings above that had accommodated the help.

"To think you don't come here that often," Jenna said in amazement. "That's gonna change!"

"I told you you'd love it," he chortled. "Let me show you the rest and the lake while it's still light out. We can unpack later." Striding down a path through the woods, Scott preceded her to brush cobwebs out of the way. Rounding a curve in the path, a fine, old, shingled two-story boathouse came into view. A deck ran along the side closest to the path, culminating in a ramp that led down to a dock floating on the serene surface of the lake.

"Three more guest rooms," he told her as they passed it and reached the little man-made beach. Standing on the sand, Jenna turned back to take in everything that lay behind her. Only from this vantage point could she see the two large boathouse doors that opened onto the water.

"The boats are in there," Scott told her. "A couple of motorboats, a nice old Chris Craft, a Sunfish, a couple of canoes. And a pair of peddle boats. Man, the kids love those things."

"Let's get unpacked, then I'm taking you out for dinner, a tiny little joint called – Tiny's. It's like maybe ten minutes from here. I practically grew up in this place. You're gonna love it. And Tom and Sue – absolute salt of the earth. Tomorrow, I'll show you the rest of town, and we can take a ride by where I grew up. I'm curious to see what the new people have done with the place."

Scott built a roaring fire when they got back from dinner, then pulled Jenna down beside him on the couch to enjoy it and each other. "Let's get naked, baby. Company arrives in the morning," he laughed.

AT THREE IN the morning, Scott came awake with a start, still on the couch. Jenna, sprawled half across him, had flung out an arm, seemingly in self-defense, given the way her hand was extended as if to say 'stop.' This time, Scott didn't hesitate. "Wake up, hon," he said, catching her arm as it started to flail again. "Come on now, wake up for me, baby," he said insistently. Her arm pulled loose. He caught it by the wrist again, but Jenna recoiled as if she'd been burned. And screamed. And seemingly woke. Her eyes were open, at any rate.

"Baby, baby, it's okay. It's me. It's only me," Scott said, but she continued to thrash and try to push him away. He repeated his words, the only words he could think to say, over and over until Jenna seemed to really wake up and recognize him.

"Scott. Oh, Scott," she whispered. "Oh, no – I did it again, didn't I? I'm so sorry."

"You didn't *do* something," Scott told her urgently. "You *dreamt* something. You have nothing to apologize for. You have no control over your dreams. No one does, babe. I just wish there was something I could do," he groaned in frustration. "I can't stand that this is happening to you. I tried to wake you. It doesn't seem to help."

She shuddered as he took her in his arms, but she'd stopped resisting him; rather, she clung to him now, with desperation born of fear.

"What can I do? How can I stop this?" she moaned.

"Do you want anything? Can I get you anything?" Scott offered, feeling a sense of powerlessness and desperation of his own.

"No, no. I'm sorry," she said again. "I – I'll be okay. Just hold me."

He did. Then he started humming, a slow, abstracted hum that wove together strands of the many versions of the song he'd been trying to write for her. Finally, she slept again. Eventually, he did too.

SCOTT ROSE EARLY and pulled on a pair of jeans quietly so not to awaken Jenna. Putting on a pot of coffee, he went out on the deck, dropped wearily into a chair and let the cool air of morning slowly work its reliable, restorative magic on him. The lake was abuzz with early morning motorboaters. Here and there he could spot a fisherman gliding through the shallows, casting optimistically for bass and trout.

This truly was one of his favorite spots. And Jenna was right: they should come more frequently. They would just have to find the time. She made him see things through an entirely new pair of eyes, he thought.

Hearing the screen door squeak open, then slap shut, he turned to find Jenna stepping down onto the deck, wearing his shirt and holding a pair of oversized coffee mugs.

"You're up early, Baby Blue," he said, shading his eyes to look up at her. "I didn't expect to see you till at least noon." He took a cup from her and set it on the table beside him.

"I woke up and you weren't there. I couldn't get back to sleep." But she wasn't awake by any means, either.

"You're sleepwalking," he said, trying not to laugh. "You could get a part in Night of the Living Dead. Come here, baby."

He sat her on his lap and held her. "This place is something else when it's just you and me, babe," he whispered in her ear, then reached up and unfastened the only button she'd bothered with.

"SO, THIS IS the house I grew up in," Scott said after driving only a few minutes, pulling up in front of a modest little clapboard bungalow sitting in the shade of a tremendous red oak. "Doesn't look much different," he added, just as a man in his late fifties or early sixties came out from behind the house hauling a ladder.

Noticing Scott, he dropped the ladder and came down the driveway. "Scott, how are you doin'?" he called before he reached them. "And how's your dad?"

"Dad's fine, and so am I. Jenna, this is Mr. Paine. Mr. Paine, Jenna Bradford."

"Nice car," he said, reaching across Scott to shake Jenna's hand. "Nice to meetcha, Ms. Bradford," he said. Judging by his demeanor, and the effect she normally had on people, it was entirely possible he didn't know who she was.

"I was just showing Jenna where I grew up. I was glad to hear you bought the place. Made any changes yet?"

"Naw, not much. Me and the wife were in Florida most of the wintuh, and it was such a late spring. Feel free to get out and show your friend the inside of the house, if you want to. Just don't mind the mess inside. We can't decide where to start first. The little woman's down at the store, so don't worry about disturbin' her none."

"Hey, thanks," Scott said and cut the engine.

"Man, he's right nothing's changed," Scott said as they looked around the kitchen. "Nothing but the stuff on the counters. It's wierd being in here and seeing other people's things." Moving into the little dining room, he said, "Dad's had his piano in here – we ate in the kitchen. He'd play for hours. We could hear him from outside." He passed through the living room without comment, taking it all in.

"This was my bedroom," he said moving down the hall. They stepped inside the tiny room. He went to the closet, pushed a few things aside and exposed a panel with a ring screwed crudely into it. "You gotta see this. This was my hidey hole for drugs. Made it myself."

They went outside and walked to a hill that overlooked a pond below. "You should see how beautiful is looks when it's covered with snow," Scott said, indicating Mount Sunapee off in the distance. "I used to love hangin' out and watching the snow cover everything in sight. And then after, it was just so majestic, the sun shining and the snow sparkling. I used to skate on that pond with some of my friends. We'd get cold and somebody'd bring out a bottle of Jack Daniels or whatever. Sometimes we'd drink it because we thought it'd warm us up. Most of the time, we did it just to get drunk. I didn't care back then."

Scott held Jenna's hand as they walked back through the yard and out to the car. The new owner had propped his ladder against the front of the house and was about to head up it. A rake and a tarp lay on the ground.

"So watcha doin', anyway?" Scott asked him.

"Cleanin' out the guttahs," said his father's old friend.

"Hey, well, thanks a lot for letting me show Jenna around, Mr. Paine," Scott said.

"My pleasure, boy," Paine said. They shook hands.

"Thanks," Jenna said with a smile and a nod.

"Say hello to your old man for me, and come back anytime."

THE NEXT STOP was the local high school. "I was kicked outta this place," Scott said as they pulled up. "Hell, I was always in trouble. Home, here, everywhere. I got off on givin' teachers a hard time, about any fuckin' thing. Fell asleep drunk more than once, too. They finally sent me to a private school, but that didn't last either. I dropped outta there senior year. I finally got a GED, a couple years later. Me and education – not a pretty picture."

Cruising slowing in front of a small coffee house, he said, "I got my first payin' gig here. It was a bar back then, none of this coffee shit. Played a bunch of places around the area, then took off to New York." Turning at the next corner, he pointed to another little place and parked. "This used to just be a summer place. They just did ice cream. It's a great little café today."

They went in and through to a small deck over the water, it being early enough to still be able to get an outside table. Once they'd made themselves comfortable and ordered, Scott turned to admire the view.

"Do you know what you're looking at?" he asked Jenna, pointing across the lake.

"That's your place, isn't it?" she said. The house itself wasn't visible, but she recognized the boathouse and dock.

"Yep."

The waitress, returning with iced coffees, looked uncomfortable. "I hate to ask you this, but are you guys Jenna Bradford and Scott Tenny? I wouldn't ask, but some people over there wanted me to. I hope you don't mind." Scott and Jenna's eyes followed her finger pointing to a table across the deck. Both Scott and Jenna gave a small, polite wave to the two couples sitting there staring at them.

"Don't worry," Jenna said, returning her attention to the waitress. "We don't mind as long as they let us eat without being interrupted. Tell them we'll give them autographs when we leave, okay?"

"Thanks, you guys. I'm really sorry," the waitress said and went to pass the word along.

Jenna sighed. "The price for fame and glory. I learned that years ago. My dad was always in the news for something, and I know he got sick of it. But he always said, if you treat your fans well, they'll treat you well."

"You're right, but sometimes they just don't know when to leave you alone," Scott observed huffily. "Hell, just cuz we're celebrities doesn't mean we don't need – and deserve – a little privacy. That's why I keep telling you, our private matters need to stay private."

"You'll get no argument from me," Jenna said, nodding, "but I gotta say, hon, one thing I've notice is that you never know when to say enough to them. You have only yourself to blame if they *continue* to hound you. I know you love them, but there's a limit and it's up to you to find it."

JENNA FELT THE peace and quiet of the lake house slip away as guest after guest poured though the door through the afternoon. "Aw, this is nothing," Scott told her as they finally did a head count. "Only twelve of us. That's like nothin'. Once we had something like twenty-seven here. Okay, a bunch were in tents, but it was a fuckin' three ring circus. The kitchen was in operation 24/7. Twelve barely registers on the radar." And after a while, Jenna had to agree.

Having vacationed together as much as they had, the Blacklace family was a copacetic crowd. According to Carrie, they'd managed to adapt to just about any new girlfriend, child, friend, in-law or whatever the fates had blow in the door any given year, for many years now.

Carrie and Jeremy arrived with their son, Aiden, who Jenna had only met a few times and just in passing. "So how old are you," she asked him when he came into the kitchen to find a soda.

"Fourteen," he said with the studied carelessness of a seasoned teenager. "How old are you?" he asked with a surprising amount of insolence and good humor.

"Thirty-three," Jenna said without hesitation.

"Damn, you look all right – for an old lady," Aiden commented casually, then turned and bolted for the porch door with a laugh.

"Cute kid you got," Jenna observed as Carrie walked past.

Jeff and Denise had their thirteen-year-old in tow. "Travis is the kind of kid who's so polite it makes you nervous," Carrie whispered to Jenna after he'd been introduced and had shaken her hand like he was being graded on his performance. "I think he gets a kick outta making Aiden look bad. Aiden, on the other hand, has made it his mission in life to get Travis to swear. He's thinks he's gonna make a breakthrough this summer."

Like Jenna, it was Dan's new girlfriend Jill's first time at the lake. For a person who generally gave the impression that she'd seen it all, she seemed more than a bit impressed once she'd had the tour. After settling in, she surprised everyone by joining the rest of the women in the kitchen who were pulling dinner together.

"So whaddya think of Jill?" Dan asked Carrie in a low voice a bit later when she'd left the room.

"You might want to hang on the her," Carrie suggested. "You have any idea what that woman can do with a pie crust? I thought you said all she could make was reservations."

"You're puttin' me on, right?" Dan asked.

"No way, Danny," Carrie said. "I mean it. She knows her way around a kitchen better than some chefs I know."

"And here I've been thinkin' I should be taking her to all the best places. Guess I can stop tryin' to impress her and let her start tryin' to impress me for a change. Who knew?! I didn't think the woman could boil water."

THE FOURTH OF July feast started before five and didn't wind down until it was almost dark. Dinner came in clearly defined courses, leisurely paced to make the most of both the meal and the camaraderie. The last of the year's black flies and the first of the year's crop of mosquitoes could only beat their wings in frustration at the mouthwatering sight of their own idea of a holiday feast, from the other side of the porch screening. All through the meal, the sound of the odd single firecracker could be heard here and there.

Afterwards, the women helped clean up while the men stoked the fire down below on the beach. As dust turned to darkness, the first rocket erupted into the air from directly across the lake. A moment later another shot up from far further down the lake. In a matter of another few minutes, the sky was alight with two official and several unofficial fireworks displays. Everyone pulled on sweaters and sweatshirts and headed out on the deck to enjoy the show.

Scott grabbed a lounge at the back of the deck, and suggested Jenna sit in front of him. "You won't be able to see," she protested. Taking her by the wrist, he tugged her down and pulled her close.

"Who says I want to," he whispered in her ear. Then, just as a huge chrysanthemum firework exploded high in the night sky and started to slide down the sky, he wrapped his arms around her and let his hands slide down her in time with the falling glitter above them.

With each new explosion, Scott's hands appeared somewhere new and unexpected on Jenna's body, until she came to expect the unexpected. He found he could time her heavy breathing and little moans of pleasure to coincide with the ooh and aahs of their assembled guests so that no one was the wiser as to the fireworks display going on right behind them.

But when he started playing little games with her, pushing the boundaries of his imagination by pinning her arms behind her and immobilizing her with one arm while exploring her with his other hand, he suddenly felt her go rigid against him and knew he'd made a mistake. Abruptly, she fought her way clear of him, jumped to her feet and fled the deck, letting the screen door slam shut behind her, but her hasty departure coincided with a particularly noisy eruption of a dozen rockets, each exploding a different colored payload across the sky, so no one but Scott was aware.

Quickly and quietly, he followed her into the house. He found her in their room, curled up in a tight ball on the bed, rocking. He sat down beside her and only touched her hair. "I'm sorry, Baby Blue. I should have known better. I love you. Can you forgive me – again?"

He wondered if she'd heard a single word he'd said. He found himself timing this episode by counting the explosions. It took more than thirty for her to finally stop rocking. When she fell asleep, he covered her, returned to the porch briefly, then went to bed with her for the night.

Their absence at such a relatively early hour raised no eyebrows.

THE FOLLOWING DAY and a half was a dizzying spectacle of over-scheduled city slickers trying to pack in as much 'relaxation' as would fit into the final two days of a three-day weekend. Following Scott's frenzied, scattershot lead, they were everywhere, doing everything, laughing riotously, living their play as large as they lived the rest of their frenetic lives. For those willing to get in a car, there was tennis, golf, a game of baseball or some pickup basketball at a nearby park; for the less adventuresome, shopping and sightseeing. Homebodies had their choice of fishing, waterskiing, motor and sail boating, canoeing and kayaking, swimming, diving and raucous games of hide-and-seek in the woods. As the temperature rose and brute energy subsided, there was pool in the game room of the main house, poker on the boathouse deck and sedate bridge, Scrabble and backgammon tournaments in simultaneous progress on the screened porch. Everyone tried their best to do it all.

Keeping up with the vacationing Joneses, Jenna managed to exhaust herself to the point that she was able to get through the rest of the weekend without another dream or flashback. The dread of either never left the forefront of her mind.

As the women packed up the kitchen for the return trip to Boston after lunch on Monday, Travis chased Aiden though the house and out onto the porch. "Aiden, that's mine!" Travis screamed. "You get the hell back here!"

Aiden stopped dead in his tracks and was well into a victory dance before Travis could knock him to the floor.

Chapter 17

THE MORNING OF the show in Boston found Jenna pacing frenetically in the studio. "I sound like shit!" she kept repeating.

"You do *not* sound like shit," Scott kept disagreeing. "You sound like Jenna. You sound fantastic. You're crazy."

"I probably *am* crazy," she agreed. "I can't get anything to sound the way I want it to sound. Nothing's coming out right. It sounds like shit."

"You're outta your mind, babe. You're getting' yourself all worked up over nothing." He stopped and laughed. "Hell, that's my turf. God, if the guys could hear this. They think *I'm* bad!"

Jenna grabbed a live microphone. *"This is the day. This is the way..."* she sang into it without accompaniment, then exploded in frustration, " Shit, pure unadulterated fuckin' grade A shit! It's gonna sound awful tonight." Scott hit the reverb on the sound board just as she went into her tirade. Jenna scowled as the eerily enhanced echo of every syllable found its way to the furthest corners of the space and back.

"Good thing this joint's soundproof," Scott said, shaking his head. "You're just plain off your rocker, lady."

"I just want it to be perfect," Jenna wailed.

"Christ, listen to yourself!" Scott said. "For starters, there ain't no such *thing* as perfection. It's just an illusion. It's like a goal, something to strive for. *Be* perfect? Sorry. Can't be done. Let it go."

"So now you're goin' all fuckin' Zen on me?" Jenna scoffed. "Mr. TNT is telling *me* to lighten up?

Scott came up behind her, put his hands on her hips and kissed her on the side of her neck. Pulling her back against him, he let his fingertips wander and caress Jenna's fine, firm belly, gently tracing pathways across the breadth of her, letting her feel his sudden desire as it kindled and grew within him.

"I know one way to get you relaxed, baby," he whispered in her ear. The small moan that escaped her lips urged him on. "Do you like that?" he said softly, as his hands slipped inside the waistband of her low-rise shorts and circled closer and closer to the center of her sexual self. "Is that calming you, my precious?" he murmured, his hands moving slower and slower with every pass, pressing her tighter against him, forcing himself against her more insistently until she threw her head back and gasped her need for him.

Slowly, her legs giving out beneath her, Jenna sank to the shag rug and rolled languidly onto her back. Scott knelt above her and slowly stripped her of the few insignificant smatterings of clothing she had on. The day breaking hot and humid, little had been needed. His lovemaking was as hot as the day outside. Before long, the two lay panting and breathless, a hopeless tangle of arms, legs and love.

"Feeling a bit calmer now, are we?" he asked her, turning her to him and kissing her once again. Euphoric, she could only laugh in response. "You really have nothing to be nervous about you know. You were great the first time and you'll be even better tonight," he whispered.

"Thank you. I guess I needed that," Jenna admitted. "My but you do know how to relax a woman."

"I dunno. You sure you're relaxed enough? Maybe you could you use a little more?" he said suggestively as his fingers began to tease her smoldering body to even greater heights of desire.

"Oh, Scott," was all she could gasp. "Oh, my God. Yes."

Burying a hand deep in her thick mane of hair, he brought her lips to his, then bent down to draw one nipple into his mouth while he excited the other with his ever-questing fingers. Returning to her lips, he kissed her passionately, then he rolled to his back, his hand still in her hair, drawing her with him, until she lay astride him. Throwing his head back, he pushed her head down, just wanting her to excite his nipples as he had hers, nothing more.

Suddenly she froze, shuddered and cried out yetagain, "No! Don't! Oh, God, please stop! Please!" Scott instantly stopped, pulled back and gasped at the look of pure horror on her ashen face. The voice was again the voice of a terrified child.

"Jenna! Jenna, baby! Now what is it? What in God's name is wrong?" Again, she didn't appear to hear him. Pulling her trembling, unresponsive body close, he repeated his mantras in her ear, "Jenna. Jenna, it's me, Baby Blue. I love you. I'm here for you. Come back to me. Let me help you."

Continuing to hold her with one arm, he did the only thing he could think of, caressing the contours of her face and keeping up a running murmur of encouragement and love. With quiet persistence, he finally managed to reach her and gently guide her back to reality. "Breathe deep," he whispered. "Breathe." She did, taking several slow, deep breaths.

"I –" she started, then closed her eyes as a shudder pass through her. When she opened her eyes again, she was finally able to focus on Scott. "I – oh, God, I feel so – disoriented," she managed to say.

"What was it this time?" he asked her with palpable concern. "Baby, I'm so worried about you."

"It was – it was like a flashback again," she said with agitation. "Not a dream. Not a memory. It was like it was happening this time."

"What was happening?" he asked her.

"Oh, God. I – I don't know. It was just terrifying, whatever it was. I don't know," she said again. "A face. I think he – he was hurting me. He was. I was begging him to stop." She buried her head in Scott's shoulder and sobbed, unable to say any more. Scott pulled a throw from the couch, wrapped her in it and held her and rocked her in his arms.

SIPPING A CUP of tea he brought her, Jenna was calmer but still just as distressed and deeply frightened by what had happened.

Scott tried to lighten the mood. "I guess maybe fucking isn't the answer to everything in life," he said and was glad to see she was able to respond with a rueful smile.

"Maybe not," she had to agree. "God, I thought I was worried about singing tonight. Now I'm just worried about all this."

"Ah, well at least we cured the first problem, then," he joked. She gave him a little shove, then snuggled back into his arms. "See, I *am* crazy," she said, then found herself pursuing that thought, reflecting how true that felt right now. "Crazy," she whispered.

"You're not crazy," Scott disagreed. "You may be a whole lotta things, young lady, but crazy ain't one of 'em. Something's wrong, that's for sure. Hey – would you mind if I talk to a friend of mine about it?" he asked her.

"Just who do you have in mind?" she asked, suddenly nervous.

"Len Ornstein, a therapist. I used to see him all the time, now just occasionally. Great guy. Would you let me run this by him? He might have some thoughts, you never know."

"I guess that's okay. He'll know who I am, of course. That feels a little weird. But I trust you, honey."

"What we're gonna do is take you back to the house and tuck you in for a bit of a nap, and then I'll see if I can get him on the phone." Jenna was more than willing to let Scott take charge. She was exhausted.

LEN RETURNED SCOTT'S call within the hour.

"Scott, man, how have you been?" he asked in his hearty, genial voice. Len was the kind of guy even the most introverted person could easily warm up to.

"Good, Len, good. You?"

"Just fine, my friend. So – should I believe what I read in the papers? You've finally met the love of your life? Or is that just the gossip mongers doing their thing."

"Nope," Scott laughed easily. He'd always gotten a kick out of how Len would cut straight to the chase. "For once, they're gettin' it right, imagine that.

We're made for each other, Len. I just wish I could find words to describe how I feel about her that haven't been used and abused for centuries – I feel like I need a whole new vocabulary to explain how I feel about her and about us."

"Phew. That says a lot. So – you called. What can I do for you?"

Scott briefly outlined the problem. "Would you be willing to give us just some direction?" he asked. "Neither of us have a clue what we're dealing with here. It's scary."

"Sure sounds like it," Len said. "Sounds like a bad relationship, maybe?"

"She says she's never had one, I mean not a frightening relationship. Everyone has bad relationships."

"Of course," Len agreed. "It could be something more serious. Something she's had to suppress…"

"Like…?" Scott fished for more information.

"Like abuse, maybe. Sexual abuse. It happens. And it can cause flashbacks. The little girl voice…"

"There is another thing. Her father died recently. He left a sealed envelope for her, with clear directions not to open it until she's pregnant, of all things."

"Fishy," was Len's one-word comment on that.

"Any suggestions?" Scott asked.

"Would you like a referral? Maybe she'd like to talk to someone."

"I'll get back to you on that. Maybe she will."

"Sure sounds like she's ripe for some answers to a lot of questions she may not even know she has. This isn't easy stuff to work through. Keep me posted, okay."

Scott stood staring out the window, the phone still in his hands. "It couldn't be. A vibrant, sexual being like Jenna – she couldn't have been abused. She would have told me. Wouldn't she? Christ, look at me. I'm talking to myself." He shook his head, hung up the phone and went back up to the bedroom. Jenna was still asleep. Looking at her, now in serene repose, he studied her, wondering if it were indeed possible she had been sexually abused as a child.

Tonight there was a show to play. Tomorrow, he intended to find out what he could about Jenna's childhood.

"DAMN, IT FEELS good being backstage again," Jenna said as she inspected her cramped but decidedly atmospheric dressing room.

"It's great being back here," Scott agreed. "Man, I love this place. And it's gonna feel so good having you back on stage with us," Scott said, giving her a hug.

"Okay, let me get dressed. God, I hate doing a show without Yumi to make me gorgeous," Jenna said, fussing with her hair as she looked at herself critically in the mirror.

"I told you to bring her out," Scott said.

"For one night – I couldn't ask her. It would have completely disrupted her schedule. It's not like I don't remember how. It's just that – having her there, her presence, is so soothing. She's so grounded. She keeps me sane." Jenna smiled at Scott's reflection in the mirror.

"We'll keep you sane, baby" he said back to her reflection, with a solemn nod. She blew his reflection a kiss. He turned her around and gave her a real one. "Woops, looks like we have an audience," he chuckled as he pulled back.

Jenna turned to look at the empty door. "What audience?" she asked, puzzled.

"Them two in the mirror," he said indicating the reflection with his thumb.

"Get outta here!" she laughed and pushed him out the door.

SCOTT FOUND THE rest of the band members drifting around on the stage, tuning all their instruments, doing sound checks, conferring back and forth both with crew and among themselves.

Historically, Scott was most demanding and peevish right before a show. Everybody gave him wide berth, knowing that nothing they could do could ever please him. Tonight was clearly different. Jeremy easily sensed Scott's preoccupation.

Hands and ears busy tuning, he wandered over to Scott who was standing in front of the keyboard, staring up into the empty rafters. Scott's fingers meandered over the keys in random fashion, occasionally stumbling accidentally onto a few bars of recognizable melody.

"Wassup, bro?" Jeremy asked casually.

"Stuff," was all Scott was willing to share.

"What kinda stuff?" Jeremy persisted.

Scott hesitated before answering. "Jenna stuff," he finally said.

"Need an ear?" Jeremy offered.

Scott looked around to see if Jenna was anywhere in sight. "You know anything about flashbacks?"

"Acid-type flashbacks?"

"Nope. Not drug-induged. Psychological-type flashbacks. Something's making her flip out. I've talked to my old therapist about it. He's suggesting she may have been abused as a kid."

"No shit."

"No shit."

"Oops, here she comes," Jeremy interrupted him. Jenna came across the stage to them, gave each a hug, then went over to a mike for her sound check. Jeremy and Scott quickly made themselves busy.

Heading back to the dressing room, Jenna gave Scott a passing squeeze. "I'm ready, babe," she said. "Knock 'em dead!"

"That's your job, beautiful," Scott grinned, blowing her a big kiss as she moved on. Turning back to Jeremy, he picked up where he'd left off.

"These flashbacks. It's wild. It happens when we're like making love."

"Jeeze..." Jeremy said. "You got somethin' new up your sleeve, technique wise, man?

"Jeremy, I'm serious. It's fuckin' scary as hell. Len thinks it could have something to do with her childhood. Her father leaves her this freakin' letter she's not supposed to open until she's like pregnant. I gotta wonder what *that*'s about. Thing is, I don't know how to ask her, or for that matter, what to ask her. I'm afraid I could do damage."

"And she can't explain it?" Jeremy asked.

"She says she doesn't have a clue. I don't know what to do, but I do know I need to find out."

"Is there a trigger, something in common each time?" Jeremy suggested.

"Beats me," Scott answered. "It's only been a few times, but she says each one's a little more vivid than the last, and definitely more frightening."

"No wonder you're preoccupied."

"Yeah. Half my mind's on her, no question. I just thought you should know, in case there's a problem?"

"Sure. God, I'd *rather* you were throwing tantrums, bro," Jeremy said. "That shit's harmless."

"We better get finished up," Scott said, changing the subject. "But, hey, thanks for listening."

"What are brothers for?" Jeremy asked rhetorically.

SCOTT STOPPED IN Jenna's dressing room just before heading out to face fifteen thousand screaming fans. Coppafeel, an up-and-coming punk/grunge band, had opened for them. The crowd was revved up and ready to rock.

"Oh, man, Scott, you look fuckin' fantastic," Jenna said, transfixed by the sight of his reflection in her mirror. Swiveling around to face him, she ran an appreciative hand down the leg of a pair of skin-tight, shiny black spandex pants that rode precariously low on his hips.

"You sure you don't need suspenders with those, babe?" she teased him. "I *love* this look! Phew, this is *beyond* hot!" Rising, she wrapped herself around him, her body tight against his, running her hands down his back. "Satin and spandex. I'm not so sure I want you goin' out there, big boy," she said in her seductive, velvet alto.

Stepping back to check out her outfit, Scott whistled. "Christ, and look who's talkin'. I should have my head examined, turnin' you loose on a stage like this." A tiny spangled tank top didn't come within eight inches of meeting a skimpy purple skirt that hugged her shapely bottom like a second skin. He ran one hand up under her top while his other hand explored the considerable amount of thigh exposed to his touch.

"Baby," she whispered. "You just better have to time to finish what you start."

"Wish I could, lady," he said, nipping at her ear, "but that's just gonna have to wait. I'm just a workin' man. Gotta go clock in. Keep me in mind, though, while you're out there struttin' your stuff, Ms. Beautiful." He kissed her deeply, then turned and left.

Several songs into the lineup, Jenna went into the tunnel that led to the stage and waited for her cue. Jeremy announced her and, as the crowd roared, Scott came and escorted her up onto the stage. Several follow spots wrapped the pair in an incandescent blue-white light as they stepped to a single mike and started right in on the first verse of "Storming the Road," the song with which she'd opened every concert for years. The audience shouted its approval. At the end of the first verse, Scott stepped back and let her have the floor. Again, the crowd let loose. He stayed in the shadows until the song ended, but his voice rejoined her on a separate mike for the last verse. Their individually distinctive voices wove together, creating an electrifying new sound. As the final notes faded away, the applause was deafening.

Lights came up on the entire band as they moved into "Sexwax and Shellac," an early hit tune for Blacklace, a sort of Beach-Boys-meets-the-Dark-Side tribute to '60s surf music. Always a showstopper, the incongruous addition of a female voice gave the tune a whole new twist that wasn't wasted on this audience.

As the set came to an end, Scott stood back to allow Jenna a solo bow, then stepped forward and pulled her into what would become their signature Hollywood kiss as the crowd roared louder than ever. Jeremy launched into his solo as Scott took Jenna's hand and walked her back off the stage to a standing ovation.

The plan was for Jenna to come out for one more number after the next two. A stool had been positioned just within the entrance to the tunnel so she could make herself comfortable. Perched on the stool, she was just within Scott's view.

With a crashing chord from Jeremy to set the tone, Scott threw everything he had into the next song, a new one he'd hashed out over the winter and into the spring with Jeff's help. Disagreeing on a title, they finally settled on a compromise with "It's Hard (It Ain't Easy)."

Two verses in, Scott crouched to the floor and wailed into the mike, looking up and projecting every ounce of energy to the fans in the top rows of the balcony. *"It's so hard bein' small, When everyone is tall... They push you all around, They push you to the ground..."*

Halfway into the chorus, he realized that Jenna was no longer standing in the tunnel. Continuing to sing, he managed to catch Jeremy's eye. During a break in the lyrics, he keyed his headset to act as an intercom between them.

"Jeremy, take the next verse for me. I think Jenna's in trouble. Do your other solo next," he said quietly and left the stage.

Chapter 18

SCOTT HURRIED DOWN the tunnel to Jenna's dressing room. Entering without knocking, he found her sitting on a small folding chair facing the wall, her knees drawn up under her chin, her arms wrapped around them. Shaking, rocking rhythmically, with tears running down her face, she was staring intently at the blank wall in front of her. She could have been a kid engrossed in a T.V. show – except for the silent tears and the shaking, Scott thought to himself.

"Jenna?" he said quietly. Once again, she didn't answer. Coming up behind her, he laid a hand gently on her shoulder. She started, panicked and the little girl voice was back. "No! Nooo! Please, no!" she screamed. She pulled away from him violently and would have fallen from the chair if he hadn't caught her. The near-fall broke her trance, however; she immediately started blinking, shaking her head and gasping for air. Quickly he wrapped his arms around her and held her tight. Her arms crossed over his and she openly sobbed. "Oh, my God, Scott. Oh, my God," she whispered again and again.

"What did you see?" he asked her carefully.

"Oh, God. No!"

"Jenna, tell me what you saw," he insisted, soothing her as best he could.

"Somebody – somebody coming towards me. Scott, I was so afraid. I tried to get away but I couldn't move. It stopped for a minute, but then it started all over again. It was like thirty seconds of film, on a loop – it just kept starting, over and over. Oh sweet Jesus, what is happening to me?" Scott held her until she could calm herself. Suddenly, she looked up at him.

"Scott, you can't be here. You're supposed to be on stage," she said, aghast, now completely aware of her surroundings and circumstances. "You've gotta get back."

"I will, baby, when I know you're okay," he said firmly. "You think you're all right now?"

"I'll be okay. I – I'm not sure I'll be able to sing again, though."

"Honey, don't even think about it. That's the least of your worries, Jenn. You just pull yourself together. Do whatever feels right, okay? Promise me?"

"Okay, I will, hon. Scott?" She took his face in her hands. "Scott, thank you. It helps that you understand."

Scott hurried back to the stage, wishing he did.

JENNA WAS ABLE to join them for the last number. No one watching the show would have ever known anything was amiss. Both the band and the tech crew had abandoned the play list they'd started with and were taking their cues directly from Scott via intercom.

Without Jenna, Blacklace came back out to finish the night with a couple of encores. By the time Scott could to make his way off stage once and for all, the tunnel had filled with crew and well-wishers. Pushing his way through as best he could, he hurried back to Jenna's dressing room. She wasn't there.

Coming out, he found Jeremy looking for him. "Don't worry about Jenna, bro. She's down the hall talking to the press."

"Oh, thank God," Scott said and went looking for her. It wasn't hard to find her, stranded in the eye of a hurricane of reporters and photographers.

As she saw him wading into the melee of journalists, she finished answering the question at hand, then said, "You've asked me enough. Here comes Scott. I'm sure he'll be happy to answer any more questions you might have." A few of the more polite reporters mumbled their thanks, but the majority simply surged towards Scott, straining to stretch their microphones as close to him as they physically could.

Reaching her, he put his arm around her. "You okay?" he asked quickly.

"Fine," she said. "I'll just go back to my dressing room."

"Stay with me," he begged. "Let's give them a show." He winked at her, then gave her a kiss. The press loved it.

AFTER A QUICK, late bite to eat at Shelley's, the bistro that catered to musicians in need of quick, late bites, everyone headed for home. As Jenna and Scott came to the first traffic light, Jenna cut back the volume on the radio and turned to Scott.

"Could we stay at my place tonight? Would you mind?" She tried to sound casual, but there was a noticeable overtone of panic in her voice.

"Not at all, babe," he said. "Not a bad idea."

"I – I just want to spend the night somewhere where I haven't had any of these godforsaken dreams. I feel like I'm still on shaky ground. That probably sounds crazy but I need to," she ended. Her few works barely conveyed the fear and confusion that gripped her completely now.

THEY FELL INTO bed just before two. Jenna quickly fell asleep in Scott's arms, and he soon followed suit.

Before long, restlessness set in, then Jenna again began to struggle and thrash, waking Scott immediately. Before he could wake her, she emitted a strangled scream and sat bolt upright. Instinctively, he reached for her, but this time she resisted, passively at first, then struggling to push him away from her. "Don't touch me again," she begged, again in the voice of a powerless child. "Please, please don't touch me!" Whatever it was that Jenna's eyes, wide open, were witnessing, what Scott saw written in them was stark naked terror.

Desperate to hold her but knowing he couldn't, he used his voice to reach out to her. Quietly but urgently, he called her back from the abyss. "Jenna, come to me. I'm here for you. Come back, Baby Blue, come back to me." And finally, she did. Trembling from head to foot, she found her way into his open, waiting arms.

Kisses, murmurs and quiet, gentling hands soothed away the shaking, time slowed the tears, but when Jenna finally spoke, the terror was still present. "There's nowhere to hide. This nightmare – it dwells within me, it's there waiting for me. It comes whenever it wants to, whether I'm asleep or awake. What am I going to do?" she said, her voice disturbingly quiet, flat, devoid of emotion, the sound of a thoroughly jet-lagged traveler.

He kept whispering to her, until she was really back, till he could hear *Jenna* in her voice. Until she could actually cling to him, not just let him hold her. Until she could say, "Oh, my God, Scott, what in hell is happening to me?"

With those words, tearing at her hair, she rolled onto her back and stared at the ceiling. "It was so godawful this time, Scott. Oh, my God, I am so afraid." She rolled back into his arms, convulsed, then let out a long sigh.

Scott sat up in bed, bringing her with him, and rocked her. Finally, he lay her back down beside him and looked at her. "Baby, tell me about the dream. Don't be afraid. I'm here. Nothing can happen." He stroked her hair, then bent over and kissed her. Jenna curled up, laying her head on his thigh.

"I was in the pool house – our house, when I was a kid. I – I *was* a kid. Somebody came in, while I was dressing. He – he came towards me and he started to grab me." Jenna went silent. Finally she made herself to continue.

"I asked him to stop but he wouldn't. Then he grabbed me again. He picked me up and threw me on the couch. Then he was coming at me again, and again I was yelling at him not to touch me, but he still wouldn't listen. I think that's when I woke up." By the time she finished forcing herself to speak, she was shaking once more.

Scott gave her plenty of time to calm down, then cautiously began to probe. "Jenna, honey, do you remember anything at all – someone trying to hurt you, or like force you to do things, when you were little? Anything?"

Searching her soul as well as her memory, she could honestly shake her head and say, "No, Scott, nobody's ever tried to hurt me. Who would have hurt me? I'd certainly remember something like that."

"I know," Scott said. "I know it seems like you would – but people don't just have dreams and flashbacks for no reason, honey. It all has to come from somewhere."

"Scott, I know you mean well – and I appreciate it, please believe me, sweetheart, I *so* appreciate it," Jenna said emphatically. "A lotta guys would be, like, see ya, I'm outta here. But, good Christ, if something had ever happened to me – trust me, I'd sure as hell remember." She was shaking her head no, firmly rejecting the possibility – but her eyes told Scott otherwise.

It took a while, but at length she fell back asleep. It took Scott far longer.

WAKING BEFORE SHE did the next morning, Scott quietly got up, went down to the kitchen and put on a pot of coffee. Reaching for the phone, his first call was to Jeremy.

"Yo, bro. You up?" he asked, when Jeremy answered.

"Three-quarters. Everything okay?"

"Could be better. Jenna had another one of those fuckin' dreams last night, three in the morning. This one was wicked bad. I got her to talk about it. Somebody coming after her. And she knew where she was this time – in her family's pool house."

"Oh, man. That's not good."

"That's what I'm thinkin'."

"Do you think you could get her family to talk about it?" Jeremy asked.

"If they know anything. My first thought's her old man, of course. And he'd dead. I only met him once. Her mother left him for a couple years at one point. Who knows. Christ. This is gonna drive me crazy."

"I'd try talkin' to the family. What's she got, a couple brothers or something?"

"Yeah. I met them at the funeral. One's married, a real prick. The other's okay. Workaholic, I think. Her mother's cool. Maybe they do know something," Scott said. "I guess I could call them."

"For this, you might be smarter getting on a plane and going out there, sitting down with them. You can't read a person on the phone," Jeremy pointed out.

"Not a bad idea."

"Why don't you suggest just taking a few days off, going out to the see the family, a few days in L.A. kinda thing?"

"I could make reservations, then tell her it's a surprise. A little time off before we have to hit the road," Scott said, warming to the idea. "Hey, thanks, man. Thanks for the use of your brain. Mine's fried."

"Any time, bro. Hope it helps, that's the main thing."

Scott then put a call in to Len Ornstein, who returned it almost immediately.

"Yeah, Scott. Talk to me."

"It happened twice more yesterday, Len, once a sort of two-episode flashback, back-to-back, the other a dream last night. She talks about being in the family pool house, somebody coming after her, throwing her around. Same little-kid voice. I'm thinking about both of us going out to L.A., where she's from, visiting her family. See if anyone can help us with it. What do you think? Should we?"

"How close are you to them?" Len asked.

"I was out there for her father's funeral. The mother, very. One of the brothers. The other's not easy to get tight with. I'm thinking about getting a hotel room so we're not right in the thick of things. Maybe talk to them myself first?"

"Sounds reasonable."

"We've got a window of opportunity for a few weeks. Then I'm back on the road. I wouldn't dare leave her here alone. I'm really worried for her. I've never seen such fear..." Scott gulped back his emotions. "Len, I really care about this woman, like nobody I've ever known."

"I hear it, Scott. Go see what you can find out. You know where to reach me. Any time. Let me know how you make out."

SCOTT MADE A brief call to speak with Linda, but she was out. Adella answered the phone.

"Oh, yes, Meester Scott!" she said warmly. "How are you, and how is Jenna?"

"We're fine, Adella," he stretched the truth. On some levels, we're fine, he reminded himself – just not on the kind of levels someone like Adella would want to know about. "We're coming out for a quick visit. I'd love to make it a surprise. Linda's home, right? Not away or anything?"

"Oh, no, Meester Scott. She'll be so glad to know you are coming."

"How about we keep it a little surprise, Adella, just between the two of us, till we get there? Jenna doesn't even know about it yet. If for some reason, she decided she can't come, I'd hate for her mother to be disappointed." Sounds credible, he thought to himself.

"Oh, yes, I see. I won't say a word. You have my promise, Meester Scott," she said, laughing. "I love secrets!"

Scott had just finished making plane and hotel reservations as Jenna came wandering into the kitchen. He folded up the paper he'd been making notes on, tucked it in his pocket and offered her a cup of coffee and a seat beside him at the table.

"How come you let me sleep so late?" she asked, sitting down and kissing him on the cheek.

"I thought you could use a little extra, given the night you had. How are you?" he asked, brushing the hair out of her face and kissing her gently.

"I'm all right. What are you doing?" she asked.

"Well, let's just say, you need to shower and get dressed, and then we need to go home and pack, all in about two hours flat. I was just about to come wake you." He had a big grin on his face.

"What are you talking about? Where are we going? What – what do you have up your sleeve, Scott Tenny," she asked, finally zeroing in on the grin.

With a hug and a kiss, he told her his plan. "I woke up thinking that, after everything that's happened since the accident, we both could use a little time away. I have some business in L.A., so I thought we could go out for a few days, deal with that, have some fun, see your family. I've made all the plans. Our plane leaves in about four hours, so we really have to get going."

"You never mentioned any business in L.A.," Jenna said.

"It's no big deal. It just came up yesterday," he said, hoping he didn't sound too vague. He hated lying to her, but accepted the necessity. "It'd just be easier to handle it in person. I'll tell you all about it later. Right now we have to hustle."

A QUICK SHOWER and they were on their way to Scott's house to pack.

Coming in the door, Jenna said, "I'll be up in a minute. I want to let Mom know we're coming."

"Why don't you hold off on that. Don't you think it'd be more fun to surprise them?" he asked, the picture of innocence.

"We're staying with her, right?" Jenna asked. "Mom'd be like totally insulted if we didn't."

"Honey, I made hotel reservations. I just want to get us out of Dodge, I wanted to get it planned before you got up, and, to tell you the truth, I just didn't feel comfortable calling her up and inviting ourselves. Who knows, she could be traveling, anyway."

"I talked to her a few days ago. She's home."

"Well, great. Then we can pull it off as a surprise. She'll love it." Coming over to her, he pulled her to him. "Plus, beautiful Jenna, it'd be more romantic. You ever stayed in a Beverly Hills Hotel bungalow?" he asked her, suggestively.

"I plead the fifth," she countered.

"Hey – no problem," he said, momentarily taken aback, then laughing. "I have my Lori's in the closet. You're entitled to some skeletons of your own."

Dropping the banter, he said, more seriously, "I did have another reason, babe. You wouldn't want to worry your mom, if you had nightmares while were there…"

Jenna, who'd been heading for the stairs, stopped and turned back to him. "You're right, hon. That's the last thing she needs," she said, then smiled at him. "You think of everything, Scott. Thank you."

Chapter 19

IT WAS A long flight, but Jenna slept much of the way, and insisted they stop by to surprise her mother before she and Scott went to check into the hotel. With the time difference, the late morning non-stop flight had put them into LAX by two on a typically Southern Californian, predictably sunny afternoon.

Riding up Coldwater Canyon in their little silver-blue BMW Z3 convertible rental, with hot, dry, eucalyptus-scented Santa Ana winds blowing through her hair, Jenna threw her head back, closed her eyes and deeply inhaled the familiar smells of the dry dessert heat, letting its mystery and magic permeate her weary bones. "Home," she whispered.

Scott couldn't hear her. He had Blacklace cranked to the max, checking out the car's 320-watt, state-of-the-art sound system. "Gotta get me one of these," he yelled over the din. "Minute we get home." Jenna couldn't hear him.

Her mother had no trouble hearing them come up the driveway. Wondering what on earth could be responsible for such rank, uncivilized noise that was definitely coming to her door, she hurried from out on the patio, through the cool of the house to the front hallway. Adella arrived, puffing, from the far end of the house at just about the same time. "Who on God's green earth could that be, Adella?" Linda exclaimed, reaching for the doorknob. Adella knew without looking.

Jenna was out of the car before the last echo of "Zippered and Zapped" faded into the gnarled branches of the giant overhanging catalpa she'd loved to climb in her tomboy childhood.

"Mom!" she cried, and ran into Linda's amazed and open arms.

"Baby!" Linda held her long and close, then held her back at arms length to survey the state of her daughter. "You look wonderful."

Jenna called her on the flat-out lie. "I look like I've been sleeping in the gutter for a month, is more like it. I'm a mess."

"Ah, but you're my blessed mess," Linda laughed and gave her another motherly, rockabye-baby hug. Opening one arm, she turned and enfolded Scott into the hug as well. "I'm so glad you're here, both of you. How long can you stay?"

"We're only in town for a few days, Mom," Jenna said. "But, oh, it's so *good* to see you!"

Linda slipped one arm each around Scott and Jenna's waists and started heading them for the door. "Well, come on in, you two!"

She propelled them several steps, then suddenly halted. "Oh, look at me, forgetting my manners! Where are your bags?" she laughed, as Jenna had correctly predicted, word for word, she would.

"You're going to have to forgive me," Scott said, quickly stepping in. He and Jenna had carefully choreographed this critical part of the opening moments of their visit on their way up from the airport, knowing it could make or break the underlying mood of the next few days.

"You're gonna absolutely hate me, Linda," Scott went on. "It's my fault entirely. The romantic in me booked us a bungalow." In Beverly-Hills-speak, everyone knew that 'a bungalow' meant a bungalow at the Beverly Hills Hotel, no explanations needed.

"It's a nostalgia thing for me, really. I have a soft spot in my heart – for their coffee shop, if you must know." Jenna missed the wink he sent Linda's way. Linda got his wink – and his drift – and beamed. 'How well I know their coffee shop!' she winked back at him.

"You're forgiven, Scott," Linda said indulgently. In her book, Scott could do no wrong. She ushered them out and down the path to the lower patio and the pool, where, within moments, Adella appeared with tall, frosty glasses of ice tea. As soon as they were comfortably ensconced, Linda launched into her favorite activity: making plans.

"Well, I hope you have nothing special arranged for dinner," she said, "because Chris called this morning. He looked at his calendar and discovered he has nothing to do tonight. Can you imagine that! So he announces that he wants to take his doddering old mother out for dinner. I informed him that he was plumb out of luck, then, as he didn't *have* a doddering old mother. He said, 'Well, if that's the case, then I guess you'll just have to do.' What a sweet boy!"

Her golden laugh rang across the rippling blue water of the tree-shaded pool, stirred up by the gusting afternoon wind. Scott noticed Jenna's glance wandering to the pool house. The water wasn't all that was being stirred up by those legendary Santa Ana winds.

"You two have to join us," Linda continued. "Toscanno's. It's a family favorite, Scott. You will absolutely *love* it. We can surprise Chris – won't that be fun!"

Jenna turned back to her mother and smiled in agreement. "That'll be –"

"And," her mother interrupted her, "Kristin will be joining us. And I'll call Jim and Sue and see if they can join us. The icing on the cake. Wouldn't that be wonderful!"

Jenna's smile thinned. "Perfectly wonderful, Mom."

ARRIVING AT THE hotel, Scott and Jenna were greeted at the front desk by an overbearing assistant manager. "I am Mr. Gustafsen. The Beverly Hills Hotel welcomes you," he said in a rich, melodious baritone and with a slight bow. "Your bags will be delivered to your bungalow. If you will follow me."

Arm-in-arm, Scott and Jenna dutifully followed in the wake of the self-important Mr. Gustafsen. "Straight out of central casting," Jenna whispered to Scott as they hustled to keep up with their guide. Room key in hand, he conducted them through jungles of dense foliage to the door of their bungalow, opened it and turned to usher them in.

Scott scooped Jenna up in his arms, gave her a quick kiss and carried her over the threshold of their secluded little luxury bungalow and straight into the bedroom where he dropped her inelegantly onto a deeply quilted, apricot satin bedspread. Returning to the front door where the assistant manager stood stiffly waiting, he slipped a twenty into the outstretched hand of the disapproving Mr. Gustafsen. "Split that with the bell-hop," he told him. "We'll be otherwise engaged when our bags arrive."

Returning to the bedroom, he closed the door behind him. "You, my dear lady," he said at the sight of Jenna, splayed enticingly across the elegant spread in a low-cut tiny black knit dress, "are the cure for jet-lag." He threw himself down beside her and reached behind her for her zipper.

TOSCANO'S WAS CASUAL, comfortable, crowded and agreeably noisy when Scott and Jenna arrived.

"Buona sera. Have you a reservation?" the host asked formally when they approached him. He represented the last vestige of formality at Toscano's, and he took his role seriously.

"We're joining the Bradfords," Jenna answered for them.

"Ah, yes, most of them are here already. Please, right this way, my dear," he said, a broader smile replacing his starched expression of simple courtesy. He ushered them to a big corner booth that could easily accommodate more guests.

"Buon apppetito," he wished them before signaling the waiter to come see to the new arrivals.

Jenna reached hugs all around before sitting down next to Chris. For Kristin, she had a kiss as well. "Thank you again for everything, when you came out with Mom," she whispered to her. Kristin gave her an extra hug in return.

Though she'd already included Chris in her round of embraces, she couldn't help turning to him and giving him another good squeeze. "How's my baby bro?" she asked happily. "Anybody reading you any good bedtime stories these days?"

"Nobody could ever be as good as you were," Chris laughed. "Heck, Jenna put on full-on, Masterpiece Theatre-worthy bedtime *performances* for me when I was a kid," he explained to Scott. "Costumes, sound effects, the whole nine."

"Gee, you don't do that for me," Scott pouted. "Actually, neither did *my* older sister, come to think of it. I had a deprived childhood without even knowing it. Damn!"

"So you're a 'baby bro' too?" Chris asked him.

"Yeah. Annie's two years older than me. Same as you two, right?"

"Right," Chris said.

"Any others in your family?" Sue asked from across the table.

"Nope, just Annie and me. She's down in Connecticut. Teaches elementary school. Husband, two kids. Five acres, two dogs, who knows how many cats." He started ticking animals off on his fingers. "A pony, three alpacas. Oh, yeah, and chickens. God only knows how many chickens."

"How nice," Sue commented. Her delivery made it perfectly clear that she'd kill herself before she'd ever find herself living that particular lifestyle.

"We're not what you'd call close," Scott volunteered, apropos of nothing. Sue looked slightly puzzled by the remark, but wasn't interested in exploring the subject, picking up her menu instead.

Jim had buried himself in his menu during the entire interchange, Scott noted.

After ordering, Scott picked up the same topic. "So Jim, were you and Jenna close as kids?"

"Sure," Jim answered noncommittally.

"What kinda stuff were you into as a kid?" Scott continued, determined to get some kind of picture of the world Jenna had grown up in.

"Stuff. Music, for a while. Politics from an early age. Tenth grade, I guess. Carter-Reagan, 1980."

"Which side?" Scott asked.

Jim shot him a look that clearly said, 'are you kidding?' It might have included 'asshole' too, but Scott wasn't sure about that. "Reagan," was all he actually said.

Kristin jumped in. "What were Dad's politics?"

"Democrat," Jim dismissed the subject sourly.

"Now, Jim, the rule is no politics at the dinner table. You know that!" Linda said brightly, hardly a challenge for a woman who had been controlling far trickier dinner table conversation for the better part of her life. Leaning across the table to take the hand Jenna had laid there, she squeezed it. "Jenna, I just have to tell you how good you look, sweetie."

Jenna smiled a bit bleakly, then looked away. Under the table, Scott took her other hand from her lap and held it.

"You've been taking good care of her, Scott," Linda said approvingly. "I knew you would. Didn't I tell you that, Kristin?"

"You sure did," Kristin agreed with a laugh. "Three thousand miles worth, give or take a mile or two."

"Coulda been worse. Coulda been by car," Scott pointed out.

"Got that right," Kristin agreed. "Shoulda hijacked us a Concorde."

"Wow. Now there's a challenge," Scott said. "Or, wait…whadda movie!"

"Done," Chris said. "It's in the can. I think they're calling it *Mach 3* or whatever the hell they travel at – I can never remember. Due out any day. Sorry."

"It's Mach 2, Chris," Jim said, condescendingly.

GENERAL CONVERSATION CARRIED them easily through to dessert. While everyone was considering – and ultimately rejecting – the truly inspired but undeniably high-calorie offerings, a band was setting up for the evening's entertainment. Everyone settled instead for some equally inspired coffees and put in their order.

Kristin turned to Linda. "So, when are you going to pop the news?" she asked her, just for her ears.

"Later, at home," Linda said. "They're about to have music. I'd rather we can all really talk about it."

"Talk about what, Mom?" Jenna asked.

"Let me explain later, okay, sweetie?" Linda countered. "Oh, my goodness, would you look at these," she exclaimed at the waitress brought a tray of further temptations for them to consider.

Kristin broke down. "I'll have a cannoli," she told the waitress.

"*Uno cannolo o due cannoli?*" the waitress asked her with a wink.

"*Uno, por favor,*" Kristin answered pertly.

"'*Uno*'s Italian, *por favor*'s Spanish," Chris pointed out.

"Heck, what do I know about Italian? I grew up in Los Angeles," Kristin laughed, pronouncing the name of the city with a perfect Spanish accent. "It's practically my second language. I should just go ahead and get a degree in that – it'd sure be easier than acting."

"How are your classes going?" Jenna asked.

"Okay. I was able to get Dramatic Analysis, Intro to Theatre and Movement I. The summer's already flying. Man, it's so much work!"

Jenna looked at her 'new' sister with genuine admiration. She had taken her new life by the handles and was giving it everything she had.

"Hey, sis, how about lunch tomorrow? Can you squeeze me in?" Jenna asked. "Man, I love the fact that I have a sister!"

Kristin smiled broadly. "That'd be great, Jenn. I just have classes in the morning."

"It's a date then," Jenna said, pleased.

"I'll pick you up at the hotel. I can be there by noon."

"Excellent. We can decide where to go from there. Maybe some shopping too – sis," Jenna suggested.

"Sure – sis," Kristin answered, a bit shyly.

Jenna reached across the table and gave Kristin's hand a squeeze. "I'm really looking forward to it," she said. As she did, she noticed a new face on the little stage at the end of the room.

"Oh my gosh, that's Neil Giovanetti!" Jenna exclaimed. "God, I haven't seen him in, what, God, four years at least. We worked together on bunches of things." Catching his eye, she waved. With a word to one of his fellow musicians, he set down his guitar and came over to their table. Reaching over Scott, he gave Jenna a big hug, then pulled back to greet Scott.

"How *are* you guys? I'd heard you two are an item. That is so goddamn great!" he beamed. "How you been, Scott? What was that thing we did? The concert after the earthquake in Afghanistan, wasn't it?"

"Yeah," Scott said. "New York? '97? '98?"

"Had to be '98," Neil agreed. Turning to Jenna, he smiled broadly. "You're looking good, girl. God, it's good to see you."

Jenna made introductions around the table, then reached over and gave Neil's hand a squeeze. "You better get to work, singerman." Blowing her a kiss, he headed back to the stage.

Jenna clapped enthusiastically as the first song came to an end. "Boy, he's better than ever," she enthused.

After a few more songs, Neil sat down on a stool and started chatting amiably with the audience. "So good to be back here at Toscano's. Everyone who's everyone's played on this stage, one time or another. Now, I've gotta tell you, tonight we've got a couple of somebodies who are *really* somebody, out there in the audience. Not only does this Angelino sing with her own band for her own fans, but these days, she's singin' with her man's band, to boot. You know the one I mean: Blacklace. Ladies and gentlemen, how about puttin'em together for Jenna Bradford and Scott Tenny!" Scott and Jenna stood up, grinning, and waved to the noisy crowd.

"I'm thinkin' about invitin' em on up here, but I'm gonna leave the decision-making up to you all," Neil told the audience, who immediately roared their approval of the idea. Jenna shrugged in acquiescence and turned to Scott, whose expression clearly said, 'why, sure!' Hand in hand, they headed for the stage.

Jenna took the mike from Neil. "My goodness! This is such a great surprise! Scott and I are in L.A. to see family and cop a few days of R&R, but I never imagined we'd run into my old pal Neil here. Thank you so much for the warm greeting you've given us. Let's see what we can sing for you."

Jenna, Scott and Neil put their heads together for a moment, then Scott and Jenna launched into a tight rendition of "Just You, Me and the Roaches," an old

Blacklace standby. Neil joined in on the chorus, and his band had no problem backing them up. The audience was elated.

After another quick consultation, Neil came and joined them at the microphone. "Okay, one more," Jenna said, in response to the prolonged applause. "Not many people know it, but Neil helped me write and produce this next number. It's called 'Kiss of Seth' and it did pretty well." The audience chuckled at the understatement.

Jenna and Scott made their way back to their table amid a standing ovation, shaking hands as they went, while Neil continued to heap on the praise from the stage. "Aren't they great! I know you all appreciated it as much as I did. Jenna Bradford and Scott Tenny!"

The enthusiasm back at their table was just as great. Kristin reached across the table to squeeze Jenna's hands. "That was fabulous!" she gushed. "You guys sound *so* good together! No wonder people are eating it up! Man, what a wicked cool way to get to hear the two of you together for the first time!"

"Well, I for one, am not a bit surprised," Linda stated simply, if proudly. "You can tell when two people singing together are in love. You two are the real McCoy."

That was the last positive thing Linda had to say, once the wrangling over the bill commenced. Linda won. She always did.

Chapter 20

BACK AT THE house, Linda shooed everyone into the study. "I'll be there in a minute. You all make yourselves to home," she said.

"Anyone want a drink?" Jim offered, heading directly for the bar, where Sue and Chris soon joined him.

"Anyone want some decaf?" Jenna proffered an alternative. Scott put his hand up, as did Kristin. Jenna headed for the kitchen.

Returning shortly with a pot and a tray of mugs, fixings and a plate of cookies, Jenna set up shop at the end of the bar. As she started to pour, Jim sidled up to her.

"Hey, sis, how come you haven't had a drink all night? When did you go on the wagon?" he asked, a bit nastily, Scott thought.

"What's it to you, Jim?" Jenna retorted. "And, come to think of it, who appointed you Lord Minister of Who's Drinking What?"

"You're not pregnant again, are you?" Jim did a quick appraisal of her exposed belly. Jenna stopped stirring the cream she'd just poured into her coffee, turned and stared at him, speechless for several seconds.

"I drink or do not drink by choice, brother dear," she finally decided to answer him. Composed now, she spoke slowly, succinctly, one word at a time. "Which is a hellova lot more than you can say." Reaching for the sugar bowl, she added quietly, "No, I am not pregnant. I believe etiquette requires that I thank you for asking." Pursing her lips, she looked down before continuing.

"No, Jim, I make a point of not using alcohol when I'm with Scott, simply out of respect for him. But of course, you wouldn't know much about respect. I doubt it's a motivation that polls well with Republicans."

Linda had just come bustling into the study. "No politics, no politics! I simply won't have it in the house. Look, you two – just stop it. Why is it you can never seem to get along? When you were younger, you were inseparable. When did you grow into mortal enemies? What ever happened between the two of you?"

Jenna turned and faced Jim as she addressed her answer to her mother. "Why don't you ask your son, Mom? He's the one who's been acting the ass, for years. What did I ever do to you, anyway?" she said, turning the question on him.

Jim preferred to address his mother than deal with Jenna. "Look, I'm sorry, Mom," he said. "Promise, I won't be an 'ass' for the rest of the evening. Truce. Now, how about you just tell us what this family confab's all about."

Jim freshened his drink, almost unconsciously, Scott thought, as everyone settled into a seat. Linda remained standing.

"Well, my dear children, it's just this. I've been thinking long and hard since your father died. You're all out on your own now – except, of course, for Kristin now. This house is far too big for Kristin and myself. We don't need the square footage and I definitely don't need the expense of maintaining it all. I've decided to sell." She paused, waiting for a reaction, a murmur, but they were all quiet. "I know you may be upset with me, but unless any of you want it, I think it's for the best."

Jim was the first to react. "Personally, I'd say it's the best damn thing you can do, Mom, so no argument from me."

Chris agreed.

Jenna found herself shaking slightly and wondering why. Scott noticed, and reached for her hand. After thinking a moment, she said, "Whatever you want to do about the house is fine with me, too, Mom. I – I don't know why, but I actually think it'll be a good thing for all of us. Do you know where you'll go?"

"Well, as you know, Jim and Sue are selling their house. I'm thinking – if they'd accept my offer – I'd buy their place. It's a fine size for Kristin and me, plus they wouldn't have to hurry about moving out." Jim and Sue looked at each other in amazement. Both nodded; this idea suited them just fine.

"I'm so glad you all agree. It'll take me a while to go through everything in this house," Linda continued, "and decide what I want to keep. Knowing Jim's house as well as I do certainly makes that chore easier. I do want all of you to go through things and take what you want."

Linda paused, then addressed Kristin in particular. "Honey, I want you to go through things with Jenna and the boys to see if there's anything you'd like to have, too. It would mean a lot to me…" She let the thought trail off.

Jim took the moment to jump in. "Mom, if you're sure you want to buy our place, that's certainly fine by us. We can put a call into the agent first thing in the morning."

Standing up, Jenna stifled a yawn. Scott noticed. "Bedtime for this one," he said. "Time to head back to the hotel." Jenna nodded, then moved over to Kristin to firm up lunch plans.

Scott took the opportunity to approach Jim. "Can I speak with you for a moment?" he asked.

"Sure," Jim said. Scott maneuvered the two of them a bit apart from the rest.

"While Jenna and Kristin are having lunch tomorrow, I'd really like it if I could talk with you and your mom. About Jenna."

Jim got a smug, so-you-want-to-ask-for-my-sister's-hand-in-marriage look on his face; Scott did nothing to disabuse him of the notion. "Ah-ha," Jim said, clearly enjoying this new role as patriarch. "Yes. I could meet you and Mom here at lunchtime tomorrow. No problemo, man."

"I'd appreciate it," Scott said cordially. His thoughts were anything but.

AS THEY WERE getting under the covers, Jenna mused. "It's going to seem strange, not having that house to come back to. A lot of memories, for all of us. But Mom's really the only one left there. I guess it's just as well she go and make her own new memories, like the rest of us have done."

"New memories," Scott echoed, pulling her close. "New's good," he murmured into her ear. His hands started traveling over her body as if for the first time, tentatively, tantalizingly approaching each erogenous zone, a pair of fearless explorers charting unknown territory, assessing the riches hidden within before journeying on to the next.

"Mmmm...let's make some more new memories for us," Jenna whispered throatily. "Oh, yes..."

IN THE MIDDLE of the night, it started again. Scott woke to another round of Jenna's thrashing.

"Jenna, honey, wake up. Wake up now," he said quietly but firmly, hoping to spare her the worst of her dream. His words only folded themselves into the terrifying dialog playing in her head. Carefully, he reached for her. The moment his hands touched her, she screamed, pulled into a tight ball and started keening like a trapped, wounded animal.

Scott reached for a light. The clock read 4:20. Jenna's eyes were open, her nostrils flaring. She was shuddering and her breathing was forced, harsh and ragged. Her mouth was moving, but the only words to emerge were "no" and "don't," often preceded by a desperate "please." Scott lay down facing her, practically eyeball to eyeball with her, but it felt like she was seeing through him to another world, not seeing him at all.

"Jenna, baby. My Baby Blue. Breathe. Deep breath. Thata girl. Come back to me, Jenna. Come on back, precious Jenna," he murmured, over and over, not touching her. Finally, her focus tightened.

Her mouth kept moving, but at last she finally whispered, "Scott." Her voice was hoarse, low and flat. "Oh, Scott." Tears started to flow. She seemed oblivious to them. This time she needed no prodding.

"Oh God, Scott. The pool house. I was in the pool house. Someone was there, hiding, watching me. I was undressing. He came out of nowhere. I had nothing on. He kept walking towards me. I was so scared. I told him to get out, but he didn't. He kept coming. Then he grabbed me. I screamed. Then I woke up, but the whole thing – it kept playing in my head, over and over and over..."

"Who?" Scott asked softly, gently laying a hand on her still trembling shoulder. "Who was it, baby?"

"I don't know," Jenna said, then moaned. "I've never seen him before in my life," she added, then moved into his embrace. "I just thank God I have you, honey," she whispered. "I couldn't survive this without you." She moved tighter into his arms, pressing herself up against him, both needy and demanding. Spasms of fear still wracked her body.

"Make love to me," she said. "Now. Hard. I need you. I need you so much."

Scott was taken aback. "Are you sure, baby? Making love won't end your fears." Touching her face, he looked deeply into her eyes. "*Are* you sure?"

"I've never needed you more than I do right now," she said fiercely. "Now, please, now."

Scott made love to her with a passion – and a compassion – he'd never experienced in his life. Jenna's ice cold tremblings of fear gave way to white hot tremblings of passion as she totally surrendered herself to him.

Finally, feeling warm and loved and safe in his arms, she drifted back into a dreamless sleep.

JENNA WOKE BEFORE Scott. Turning and propping herself up on an elbow, she played with the long tangles of his raven hair. "You beautiful man," she whispered. "You beautiful, kind, caring, loving man." She made a coil out of one long hank of hair and set it on his brow. "There was a little girl and she had a little curl, right in the middle of her forehead. And when she was good, she was very, very good, but when she was bad, she was horrid…" She quickly uncoiled his hair and tucked it back where it belonged.

She was moved, looking at him lying there, sleeping so peacefully. "Scott Tenny, I just love you so much. I never knew I could love anyone the way I love you. I never thought anyone would love me the way you do. I am so lucky – and so thankful – to be a part of your life. You mean so much to me."

Scott opened his eyes. "And you mean so much to me, too," he said with utter sincerity. "But – you're the little girl, not me."

"You've been listening!" Jenna protested. "You've been eavesdropping on my private conversation with myself. You creep!" She attacked him armed only with her ability to tickle him in his vulnerable nakedness.

Scott retaliated by getting her in a bear hug from which there was no escape. Sensing her stiffen beneath him, he quickly let go, rolled over and winked at the confused look on her face. "No way we're setting you up for another flashback," he said, then kissed her on the tip of her nose. "I don't know if you've noticed, but you definitely do *not* take well to being pinned down, my dear." He pulled her on top of him. "But you, my love, can feel perfectly free to pin *me* down all you want."

Chapter 21

KRISTIN KNOCKED ON Jenna and Scott's door at 11:45. "I know, I'm early," she greeted her sister. "It was wicked weird – there was this huge accident on the 405 going north, just before where the 10 crosses it, so there was like *no* traffic on the 405 when I got on it. It was eerie. I made great time. L.A. would be so great, without traffic. Can you imagine?" The two hugged.

"Scott just left. He told me to give you a hug." She delivered that one too. Grabbing her purse, she said, "Let's get outta here. Where are you parked?"

"We have to get the car back from valet parking. Man, I don't know my way around this place. I had to ask directions like six times."

Waiting for the car, Jenna asked, "So, what shall it be, little sis? Rodeo Drive? Westwood? Santa Monica? Or shall we be truly decadent and run up to Malibu?"

"Oh, man, that'd be fun. Let's do it," Kristin grinned.

"You don't have homework you need to be doing, right?"

"Now you do sound like a big sister. Chill – homework's covered. It's not every day I get to spend time with you," Kristin said. "Oh, here we are." A little black Miata was just pulling up to the curb.

"Cute," Jenna said appreciatively.

"I got it used. It's a '97. It had like no miles on it. I love it. I call it Stanislavsky. He's like my hero. You know, the father of method acting?"

"Don't worry, I know, I know. You don't grow up in the Bradford household and not know Stanislavsky," Jenna said. "Dad wanted me to be an actress so bad. I think I learned to say 'method acting' before I learned how to say 'Daddy.'"

As they got into the car, Kristin reached over to move a copy of the L.A. Daily News that was sitting on the passenger seat. "Oh, wait. Have you seen today's paper?"

"No. Should I?" Jenna asked. Kristin handed it to her. It was just the entertainment section.

Splashed across three columns above the fold was a close-up of Jenna and Scott, hand in hand on the path to their bungalow, both looking up at something Jenna was pointing at. The angle from which it was taken suggested that the photographer was shooting from a second or third story window. The grainy quality of the picture had telephoto lens written all over it.

"Oh, God, those fuckin' paparazzi," Jenna moaned. "You can't escape them, even at the Beverly Hills. I know exactly when they took it. The Goodyear blimp was just going over."

"The downside of fame everyone talks about?" Kristin suggested.

"Honey, you don't know the half of it. They're like getting' the crabs. You ever had the crabs?" Kristin shook her head no. "Count yourself lucky – you're obviously running with the right crowd, kid. Crabs – think head lice in your panties." She gave Kristin a moment to let the image sink in. She knew when it had. Kristin's hand rose to her mouth and her face went red.

"Oh, my God. You're like kidding, right?"

"Hardly, kiddo. Anyway – the point is, hard to get rid of. Paparazzi – impossible to get rid of. And they'll drive you every bit as insane. Hope you never get famous, little sister."

"SO LIKE, DID you ever act?" Kristin asked Jenna once they'd gotten underway.

"Oh, yeah. Until I got old enough to stand up to him. Sixth or seventh grade, I guess it was. Actually, I know exactly when it was – it was when he wanted me to audition for the first touring company of *Annie*. Actually, it was about the time Mom walked out. That probably had a lot to do with it, I suppose…"

"Can I ask – like, what *was* that about, anyway?" Kristin asked, curious to hear about it from Jenna's point of view.

"She had an affair. He threw her out. End of story. That's what they told us. However – it wasn't true."

"You're kidding, right?" Kristin was dumbfounded. "You guys had to grow up thinking that?"

"Yep. He passed himself off as this totally old-fashioned, straight-laced kinda guy. Growing up, everything was either right or wrong, black or white with him. Then, like out of the blue one day, she was back. He'd forgiven her, supposedly. She was covering up for him. The bastard had to keep his reputation squeaky clean."

"Where'd she go?" Kristin asked.

"Her parents, in New York. She was from New York, originally. Well, New York, Southampton and Palm Beach. And Paris."

"Yeah, she's told me a lot about all that. What a life."

"She's quite a person. I've been trying to get her to sit down and write about it all. It'd make a heck of a good book, if you ask me. I think she's embarrassed to. Under it all, she's a very private individual."

TRAFFIC WAS LIGHT on the 20-mile stretch Pacific Coast Highway from Santa Monica to Malibu. Breezing along in the little convertible, both women grinned like a pair of care-free school girls on holiday.

"Hey, have you ever been to Casa Pesados?" Jenna asked as the approached the outskirts of Malibu. "Great seafood, deck, on the beach – what more could you ask for?"

"Directions."

Jenna threw her head back and laughed. "Kid, you're great!" she said. "If you weren't already my sister, I'd get Mom to adopt you."

"SO, HAVE YOU decided if you want to keep on living with Mom, when she moves?" Jenna asked Kristin as she savored a salad that featured blackened mahi-mahi and plump, sweet black grapes. The breeze off the ocean was intoxicating. "I know she wants you to. It's hard for her, not having someone to mother any more."

"I'm going to stay with her while I'm in school, that much I know for sure," Kristin answered. "Your mom's been so kind to me, so understanding, and we get along great. She's done so much for me, helped me figure out things. I mean, my life's done like ten three-sixties in the last three months." She described several circles in the air with her fork. "I really appreciate it, especially given the circumstances. I'm not so sure I could be as accepting if I were in her situation."

"The sins of the fathers…"

"Yeah."

"What was it like, growing up with no dad in your life?"

"Sad," Kristin said, candidly. "Holidays, especially. I mean, I had plenty of friends without dads in the house, but they were in their kids' lives one way or another. My mother told me he'd died before I was born. But then, when I was fifteen, I found pictures of him holding me as a baby and I recognized who he was. She tried to deny it at first. But then one night, when she'd had too much to drink, man, it all came vomiting out. She hated him. She wanted me to hate him too. I met him when I was sixteen. I was so scared."

"God, I can only imagine. What on earth was *that* like?"

"Like nothing I'd ever want to live through again in my life, I'll tell you that. I talked to him on the phone and he agreed to meet me, on the fuckin' Santa Monica Pier of all places. It was like in a movie. I took a bus there." She stopped and thought for a moment.

"He was tall and handsome – well, I don't have to tell you. He was everything a kid could want for a father. Only he didn't want to be *my* father. He said I couldn't ever meet the rest of you. He made a big thing of how he'd sent money all those years, like that was supposed to make me happy or something. Like I was supposed to be grateful, like I should say thank you and disappear back into the hole I'd crawled out of." Jenna was amazed by Kristin's matter-of-fact rendition of such painful memories.

"I stayed at the Pier until two in the morning that night – I couldn't make myself go back home. I had no father and I hated my mother. A really nice old couple drove me home, finally. They were there celebrating their 50th wedding anniversary. They'd honeymooned in Santa Monica. They said they weren't going to bed that night, they were going to 'live it up 'til dawn,' even if it killed them. They were the kindest people I'd ever met. I told them what had happened. They felt so bad for me. She gave me this ring."

From the neck of her blouse, Kristin fished out a chain with a tarnished old wedding band on it and showed it to Jenna. Most of the gold plating had worn away long ago. "The old guy said it had cost him $12.95 – 'top of the line at Woolworths' he said. He'd given her a new ring for their fiftieth. She was so happy with it, and she wanted me to have this one. It was the kindest thing that ever happened to me – until the day I met you guys and your mom."

Jenna reached across the table and laid a hand on Kristin's forearm. "How do you grow up like that, and turn out to be such a strong, self-possessed, confident young woman? I have so much respect for you, Kristin. I mean that."

Kristin looked off at the ocean, then looked back at Jenna. "Thank you. You can't begin to know how much that means to me."

"I think I can," Jenna said. "We're all the products of Dad's dishonesty and deceit, one way or another. But you got the worst of it, by a long, long shot."

"I guess," Kristin said. "Anyway, that's all a long way of saying, your mom accepting me and treating me more like a daughter than my own mother, well I love her for it, very much. But – there's something you've gotta understand." Kristin put down her fork. "I don't want you thinking that I'm like trying to take your place or anything."

"Oh God, Kristin, that never crossed my mind!" Jenna exclaimed.

"I mean, you're her only daughter and she loves you very much. She's told me how much she regretted leaving you for those two years and how you felt abandoned by her, and how it took so long for the two of you to be able to have any kind of mother-daughter relationship after she came back."

"Years," Jenna said. "It wasn't bad enough just going through the regular teenage crap – I was furious at her on top of all that normal stuff."

"She told me that. She said she just held on for dear life, basically, and she's so glad that you can accept her back into your heart now. Those were her words."

Jenna smiled sadly. "It took the death of a baby to open my heart back up to her," she said quietly. "Even after I understood what had happened back then, how she'd taken the fall for him, so to speak, I still couldn't forgive her. I couldn't let go of it. Until I had a bigger frame of reference, until I came to see it in perspective. Until I was almost a mother myself." Now it was Kristin's turn to hold Jenna's hand.

"She'd do anything for you, you know."

"I know," Jenna nodded.

"And she's so happy that you and Scott are together. Her dream is to see you two get married. Soon."

"Oh, God!" Jenna laughed. "She's been dreaming of seeing me walk down the aisle since I can't remember when. I'm probably the only girl in Southern California with a hope chest."

"What's a hope chest?" Kristin asked.

"That's what I mean," Jenna laughed long and hard.

After a quick explanation that left Kristin rolling her yes, Jenna got serious. "You must have questions," she said.

"Well – tell me – everything," Kristin begged her sister. "Tell me about the childhood I missed with a less-than-perfect father and a scapegoat of a mother."

For the next three hours, Jenna did just that.

Chapter 22

JIM'S BRAND NEW Mercedes SL500 was already parked in Linda's driveway when Scott pulled up. Both Jim and Linda were sitting in the living room when he walked in. Linda rose, came over to him rather dramatically, Scott thought, took his hand in hers and offered her cheek for a kiss. Jim remained seated and nodded his greeting.

Half turning, Linda called over her shoulder to the kitchen, "Adella, Scott's here. You can go ahead and put lunch on the table, dear."

Adella appeared in the doorway. "Would you like some coffee while you wait, Meester Scott?" she offered. "Or iced coffee? Iced tea?"

"No, Adella, but thank you," Scott told her. "I can wait."

"Not for long, not to worry," Adella assured him with a smile and disappeared again.

"Now, Scott, sit down. I'm dying to hear what brings you here today, in the middle of your little L.A. getaway," Linda said. "Please, don't keep us in suspense one minute longer." Scott got the distinct impression that she'd spent half the morning amassing recommendations for wedding planners. He hated to have to burst her bubble.

Sitting, he studied his folded hands for a moment, then raised his eyes to theirs. "I have a few questions for both of you. Quite a few, actually." Linda looked confused.

"You – you aren't –" she started to say.

"No, not yet anyway, Linda. If I have my way, you better believe I will be, before you know it, but, no, not today." He stopped. Looking out to the gardens, he searched for the right words. Finally, he stood up and faced them.

"It's what's been going on with Jenna," he said, waiting to see if Linda might give any indication that she knew what he meant by this. Clearly she didn't – if anything, she looked more perplexed than ever. Jim, on the other hand, was beginning to look irritated, like someone who'd been dragged in under false pretenses.

"I had a feeling she hadn't confided in you," Scott said.

"So she *is* pregnant?" Jim said. Linda's mouth fell open.

"No!" Scott said, now confused himself. "Where did you get that idea?"

"She wasn't drinking last night," Jim said, "and she got really defensive when I mentioned it. Downright bitchy, actually. I just wrote it off to runaway mommy hormones."

"What a sensitive brother," Scott remarked acidly.

Linda jumped in. She was used to playing watchdog over her older son's ham-fisted social behavior. "Jim, enough. Scott, what's going on? Please, tell me."

"Jenna's been having nightmares. Nightmares and flashbacks. They started just after the accident. At first, that's what I thought they were about. It certainly made sense, post traumatic stress, that kinda thing. But they kept up, and she was able to start describing them. They have nothing to do with the accident."

"What do you mean, flashbacks?" Jim asked.

"Mostly when we're making love, actually. But other times too. It's happened when she's alone. Sometimes I find her, sitting and rocking, in the middle of one. She goes into these trances, these – these waking nightmares, flinching, trembling, calling out to me to stop, screaming – only it isn't me she's seeing, it isn't me she's trying to stop. All in the voice of a kid, not her own voice at all. It'd scare you to death, the sound of her voice when it's happening."

Linda's hands rose to cover her mouth. "Scott, what ever can it mean?" she asked him, frightened.

"Linda, we don't know. I wish we did."

"What does she dream? What does she see?"

"At first," he told them, "it was just somebody, somebody trying at get her. But then she started remembering details. Each time it happens, she remembers a little bit more. Anything that makes her feel trapped seems to trigger it, at least I think that's what's happening."

"Has she talked to anyone about it?" Jim asked, rather casually considering the seriousness of his sister's problems, Scott thought. He'd been watching Jim closely. He was fairly certain he was seeing a reaction more of fear than concern, but he couldn't be certain.

"She hasn't, not yet. But I've spoken to my own therapist about it. From what I've been able to tell him – well, he thinks it's possible that she was sexually abused when she was a kid."

The house – the world – seemed to go silent. Scott's words lay on the still air, slowly ballooning until they filled every corner of the room before seeping out the doorways, flowing like a noxious cloud down the hallways and into the most private spaces of a family's life.

Stunned, Linda gasped, but no words emerged. Rising slowly to her feet, her eyes focused on the far distance, almost in a trance herself, she walked to Scott and took his hands in hers. She took a deep breath, then looked him in the eyes.

"If anything happened to Jenna, I'd certainly know about it. Except –" She looked down.

"Yeah, *except*," he echoed her, nodding, having no trouble imagining the painful terrain this train of thought was crossing.

Scott pulled her into an embrace of understanding, two souls hanging on to each other, helpless to help the one they loved. Finally, she said, "I think I better sit down." She chose a chair directly opposite Jim's spot on the couch.

"She never said anything – anything like what you're talking about – when I came back," Linda said, looking up at Scott. "But we barely spoke the entire first year as it was. It was very hard. She was so angry with me. She was an angry teenager in general. She channeled it all into her music. Basically we just stayed out of each other's way for several years."

With each sentence, Scott watched as layers of composure slipped from this woman who seemingly could take anything life dealt her in stride.

Linda sat silent, then finally forced herself to form the most painful word she'd ever uttered. "Who?" This question was directed to no one in particular, and no one wanted to attempt an answer. Suddenly Linda exploded.

"Who? Who on God's green earth could do such a thing? What kind of animal could hurt a child? Could I – is it possible that I could have been married to such an animal and not know it? Could Bob have kept such a ghastly secret from me? From all of us? How could this be? And how could Jenna not know? How can she not remember?"

Scott felt he could at least tackle the final question. "Not remembering – it happens. Memories too painful to face can be suppressed, relegated to the subconscious. Not as often as people might have you think, but it definitely does happen. Whatever happened to Jenna, something's starting bringing those memories back up to the surface."

Agitated, Scott was pacing now. "Think of everything she's been through, just since I've known her," he said, ticking off one life-changing event after another. "Her father's death. The loss of her child. Me – heck, some people think dealing with me qualifies as trauma."

Linda smiled wryly at him. "Just kidding," he said, but immediately continued. "But really, a new relationship – an intense new relationship. A fairly radical change in her situation – coming out to Boston, not touring, pregnant. The accident, for God's sake."

Linda went back to the question that frightened her the most. "Who?" she almost whispered, terrified of the answer.

Scott stopped his pacing to lay a comforting hand on Linda's shoulder. "She keeps saying she doesn't know who it is. I think she'd be able to identify

Bob if that's who was coming at her in her dreams, don't you?" Linda asked, looked up at him hopefully.

"Do you think so?"

"I do.

"Oh, Scott, I do so pray you're right. How can we help her?"

"Oh, God, I wish I knew. My first thought was that one of you might have some idea, a clue, some key to what's happening. I was hoping she could take that key to a therapist and, with help and with all our support, be able to finally get to the bottom of it all – and get past it. Let her get on with her life."

"I so wish I had that clue. Oh, that I did," Linda said, sagging with dismay. Then she dropped her gaze across to Jim, who was busy studying the iron scrollwork under the glass coffee table top. "Jim?" His name in the role of a question hung in the air. He looked up, his face a blank page. "Jim, do you know anything?"

He shrugged. He didn't shake his head no, Scott noted.

"I think you do," Scott said finally, quietly. The two men locked eyes briefly, then Jim's darted away.

THE SILENCE IN the room was palpable. Scott sat down and allowed it to continue. Linda finally couldn't take it any longer.

"Jim. Say something."

Jim's eyes roamed the room – the empty chair by the fireplace where his father had habitually sat; a photo of his father at his most handsome, in his late 40s, on the desk; the small Remington bronze of a galloping Indian his father had never wearied of contemplating.

Jim's eyes came to rest on the family portrait over the fire place, for which the family had never sat. A modern oil, all five Bradfords were ranged individually about the swimming pool, all standing, rendered sharply against the perennial blues, greens and harsh sunlight of Southern California as a David Hockney might have depicted them. The composition had been worked up from photographs. The one of Jim had been taken at his graduation from Westlake, the tony prep school in North Hollywood he'd once attended, along with so many other sons and daughters of household names; in the portrait he appeared in cap and gown. The shots of his father, Chris and Jenna dated from roughly the same period. A photo of his mother was taken specifically for this painting, a few months after her return, six months after he'd graduated. The artist had produced a deft study in profound sadness and isolation. Bob had wanted to refuse it and sue the artist for the return of his deposit. Linda had hung the family portrait without a word.

Scott followed Jim's eyes to the painting. In the background was the pool house. Jenna stood in front of it. Alone.

"There's one thing I haven't told you," Scott said in a quiet, measured tone. "Her dreams, her flashbacks – it's always in the pool house." Jim's uncontrollable shudder wasn't lost on Linda.

"Jim! If you know something, this is the time to speak up," she said hotly.

Scott, still pacing, circled behind the couch. Jim's eyes swung to look out to the patio and the jungle of vegetation beyond.

"No, over here, Jimbo. Forget the view," Scott said harshly. Jim turned quickly to face him, a trapped look on his suddenly ashen face. "I don't know what you know or don't know, Jim, or what role you played, but she's your sister, for chrissakes. I'll be damned it I'm going to stand by and watch her being tortured by these nightmares. You owe it to her to spill whatever it is you know." Jim's mouth was still clamped shut. Whether he realized it or not, his hands had formed into fists.

Scott wasn't finished. "And you know what, Jimbo? I think the reason you're not close anymore, I think the reason you drink so much, is because you *do* know something, and you feel guilty as hell about it. Am I getting' warm, Jim?" Scott slammed a fist on the sofa table behind the couch. Jim gulped, looking back and forth between Linda and then Scott.

"Okay, okay. I'll tell you. But you have to understand. I was only seventeen. I tried to help, but I couldn't. There was nothing I could do. I failed. God damn it, I failed my own sister! I – I –"

Jim broke down. Wracked with sobs, he buried his face in the sofa pillows.

Chapter 23

"LUNCH IS READY, Missus," Adella brightly said from the doorway.

"Lunch will have to wait, Adella," Linda said firmly, holding her hand up like a traffic cop bringing a line of cars to a halt, but not removing her eyes from Jim.

"Oh!" Adella said, startled. "No problem, missus. You just tell me when you're ready." She quickly withdrew.

Though she couldn't see him from where she was standing, she'd heard Jim's sobs. Clearly, something dramatic was transpiring in the living room. She hurried out to the patio to retrieve glasses of ice ready for tea. She had a feeling they'd be glasses of water long before the lady of the house announced that lunch could be served – if it was served at all.

"OKAY," JIM SAID when he was finally able to speak. "Okay." He closed his eyes, heaved a sigh that he'd needed to heave for twenty years, and started in. Every word he uttered caused him physical pain.

"It was Peter Malone."

Linda gasped, buried her face in her hands and started shaking her head in disbelief. Jim addressed Scott with a monotone, begrudged explanation of just who Peter Malone was. His mother needed no reminder. Scott came around and perched on the far end of the couch.

"Peter Malone was Dad's best friend. They went to college together. He and his wife and Mom and Dad were all good friends, took trips together. They even owned a place down in Cabo together for a while. We called them 'Auntie Alice' and 'Uncle Pete.' The families got together all the time, but their kids were way younger than we were, which was a pain. Jenna babysat for them for a while."

He stopped, sighed, then plowed on. His voice turned hard and bitter.

"She started babysitting for them when she was eleven. By the time she was thirteen, she was making up all sorts of bogus excuses as to why she didn't want to anymore. She wanted to hang out with her friends, she had homework, anything. But I'm getting ahead of myself."

Jim got up and walked over to the fireplace. He stood there, studying the family portrait, hung his head, then finally turned back to face them again.

"Good ol' Uncle Pete lived on the edge. He was always putting money – big money – into risky investments. He was the guy who'd always bite when somebody's whisper to him, 'hey, buddy do I ever have a deal for you.'

"He made a shitload of money on some of them, lost a shitload on others, but somehow, he managed to keep this act afloat for a heck of a long time. But finally, the losers started outpacing the winners. He started gambling – as if he wasn't already. He became a heavy drinker, started screwing around.

"Dad tried to get him to clean up his act, which made him furious. He knew Dad had been having an affair for a couple of years, with the woman who was Kristin's mother. He started dropping hints to Mom, so she confronted Dad. What he didn't know was that Dad was no longer involved with that woman. By this time, he was having an affair with Pete's wife. 'Auntie' Alice."

As Jim had been speaking, Linda nodded silent affirmations of the facts he was stating, her face still in her hands. Now, dropping her hands to clutch the arms of the chair in which she sat, she looked at both Jim and Scott.

"Let me explain this part of it," she said quietly. "He didn't just 'drop hints' to me. He tried to seduce me, only I turned him down cold. That, too, infuriated him. Then he systematically set about to destroy us.

"First he started making all sorts of insinuations about your father, Jim. I kept brushing them aside. Then one night he out-and-out told me that Bob had been having an affair. His description was lurid – and detailed. He told me there was a child. He said, 'Don't believe me. Ask your motherfucker of a husband.' So I did." She covered her face again at the memory.

"But it was like Jim said. That was over, had been for a year. But he admitted to me that he *was* having an affair. Like Jim said, what Peter didn't know was that it was with his own wife. With Alice. My – best friend, supposedly.

"It was horrible. I confronted both of them, Alice and Peter, together. I told them what I now knew and turned around and walked out the door. He ordered her to leave, and she left all right, then turned around sued for divorce. Apparently he'd gotten totally drunk and spilled everything about all *his* little exploits.

"Next thing we know he's threatening to drag the whole thing through the press and destroy Bob's career. And it would have, believe me. He ended up blackmailing Bob, partly to shut Alice up. He made me leave, to punish Bob. *That's* why I left."

"Oh, my God, Mom," Jim said, genuinely moved. "The son of a bitch." He sat there shaking his head in disbelief. "I knew the guy was scum, but I had no idea. The cocksuckin' son of a – sorry," he said, reacting to a look from Linda. "You get my drift."

"We get your drift," she assured him, her mouth puckered with distaste. "So? You can take it from there." She handed off the duties of narrator, suddenly keenly aware of how little she really knew about so much.

"Okay. So – Mom leaves. Pete's finances were getting more and more desperate. So was his drinking. He wrecked a couple of cars. He started picking fights, doing all sorts of crazy shit. Apparently he'd even started sneaking around here at all hours of the day and night. The gardeners found him asleep under a bush one morning.

"Dad offered to pay for him to go to a rehab clinic. It was a toss up between Silver Hill and Hazelden. Pete finally hit him up for the Hazelden cure. Twenty-eight days for twenty-five big ones – no church basements for this guy. And when he comes back, he's like crazier than before. He left a drunk. He came back an angry non-drinker, which lasted all of a month and he was back on the bottle, worse than ever. And now he's blaming *everything* that ever happened to him on Dad. He was like totally obsessed.

"He started showing up when he knew Dad wouldn't be around, just come strollin' in the front door like he owned the place. I remember walking into the sunroom once and finding him sitting there reading the paper, like he was in his own house. I'd tell Dad, but he was powerless to stop him because of everything the bastard held over his head.

"Once day I caught him behind some trees, watching Jenna and a bunch of her girlfriends swimming and sunbathing. We're talking a bunch of twelve and thirteen-year-olds, for chrissakes. I told him I was calling the cops. He told me to go right ahead – if I wanted to ruin my father. I didn't know what he meant.

"I said 'You're the one who's going to get ruined, not my dad,' and he just laughed, and then he said, and I can hear it like it was yesterday, 'Hell, I ain't seein' nothin' you can't see miles of at the beach.' Then he repeated that if I said anything, it'd end up ruining Dad. So I didn't…"

Jim took a break and rubbed his temples.

"I know this isn't easy," Scott said, coming to feel something like compassion for a brother who'd obviously carried a heavy burden for years.

"No, it isn't," Jim said, "and it gets worse. A hellova lot worse."

He took a ragged breath and went on. "I couldn't do anything about it , but I started really watching for him, and one day I caught him behind the pool house, standing on a milk crate, looking in the window of the shower and changing area. It's pretty high up," he explained to Scott. "It's really just for ventilation.

"Anyway, I came up behind him and shoved him off the crate. He came back at me like a madman, grabbed me and threw me to the ground. He was a big guy, and I was pretty much of a flea-weight when I was a kid. So like he kneels over me and grabs me by the shirt and gets in my face and tells me he'll hurt Jenna if I say anything. And he says he'll know if I do. And I believed him. I didn't know what to do."

Linda got up, came over to him. Gently she touched his arm and started stroking it soothingly.

"Most of the time Jenna came out to the pool in her bathing suit, but there'd be times she'd be out there in regular clothes and then decide to swim, so she had a couple suits she kept in the pool house she could change into out there. I was so afraid she was in there changing when he was looking. After he took off, I came around fast. She was sitting inside the pool house on a lounge chair reading a magazine. I casually asked her if she'd gotten dressed out there. She had.

"No way I could know if he'd seen her, but I'm looking at her in this little bikini and I'm thinkin', man, this pervert coulda gotten a hell of an eyeful. I mean, Jenna developed pretty early. She was only thirteen, but she was already a knockout, and had a pretty sexy way about her that young, too. I was a senior that year. Let's just say, my buddies were always finding plenty of reasons to drop by.

"I figured I had to wise her up to what was going on, but I didn't want to scare her either. But I told her I'd caught him at the window. She hadn't seen him, but of course she wasn't looking, so who knows. But then she swore me to secrecy and told me why she'd stopped wanting to baby sit for them. She hated the son of a bitch.

"She'd been babysitting for them one night. This was like six months earlier. They were getting in really late, so the deal was for her to sleep over. She'd done that a couple of times, no big deal. But this time he came into the guest room and started touching her. She woke up, of course, and he tells her it was okay because he loves her. Yeah, right. I couldn't believe what she was telling me. I asked her what she said to him. She said she told him she didn't like what he was doing and begged him to stop but he wouldn't. He kept on touching her until he heard his wife calling for him. She tried to make herself forget about it.

"Then, like the next week or something, he was driving her home from babysitting and took her on a 'detour.' Into a wooded area, an old construction site."

Jim stopped, closed his eyes and took several deep breaths. "He raped her. And – and other things."

"Oh, my God," Linda whispered and dropped onto the edge of the chair beside the fireplace, the leather recliner that had always been her husband's favorite chair.

Scott interrupted. "What other things?"

"I'd really rather not –"

"I don't blame you, but I need to know, Jim. What other things?"

"He – he forced her to – I'm sorry, Mom – good ol' Uncle Pete forced her to perform oral sex on him. For quite a while." Jim closed his eyes and shook his head several times before he could finally continue.

"He told her not to say anything to anyone because they wouldn't believe her anyway – it'd be her word against his and he'd say she'd made the whole thing up. When she got home she hid in her room and wouldn't come out till the next day.

"Then she started giving Dad all these reasons why she didn't want to baby sit anymore, that she didn't want to watch the kids because they were getting to be too much for her and that she needed time to study more and stuff. She asked him if he'd tell them so he did. When Pete and Alice would come by, she'd vanish. Nobody knew why or acted much like they cared. They just wrote it off to her being a moody teenager. She told me all this. I was horrified. But I didn't dare tell Dad, either."

Jim turned back and lost himself in the family portrait again. He reached up and touched the hem of the skirt of the skimpy little red and white polka dot dress Jenna was wearing in the painting. She was posed facing square to the viewer. Her hair was worn bone straight and long. Her bangs met her eyelashes. Her posture was poor; she slumped in the knock-kneed manner of the hollow-cheeked British runway models of the '60s, the Twiggys and Jean Shrimptons. Her arms were crossed over her little girl breasts; her hands disappeared into her armpits, leaving only a pair of thumbs exposed. She stared at the viewer with eyes that smoldered with anger.

Still facing the painting, unable to turn and face his listeners, Jim shuddered once again. "Oh, Jenna," he said. "Oh, my poor, poor sister. Forgive me." The rest of what he had to say he addressed to the image of her over the fireplace. He couldn't turn back to face the inevitability of the even greater pain in his mother's eyes. What was there even now was unbearable to see.

"After that, Uncle Pete stayed away from Jenna for a month or more. I know that for a fact, because whenever Jenna was home, I was home. She didn't know it, but I was never far from her side and I was always on the lookout. Everyone was giving me a hard time because I didn't have a summer job. I had *more* than a full-time job.

"So, like after a month, I was beginning to hope that maybe we'd seen the last of that S.O.B. Maybe I'd let my guard down a little. I was on the phone, with Frankie Cantrell – he and I hung out a lot together – and Jenna went down to the pool and went into the pool house to change into a swimsuit. I knew she had some girlfriends coming over, but they weren't due for another half hour. Dad was at the studio, making *Six Day Wonder* – I'll never forget. Chris was off at camp.

"What she told me later was that there was a knock on the changing room door. She thought it was just one of her friends, early, so she just yelled for whoever it was to come in. She was half out of her clothes. She'd taken her shoes and shorts off. She just had a little halter top on, and panties.

"She said he stood there blocking the door and just talking to her like it was any normal situation, like they'd just met on a street corner or something, real even and quiet like. He said he wasn't very happy that she'd decided she didn't want to baby sit for them anymore. She tried the not having time line, but he wasn't buying it. He said they both knew why she didn't want to be alone with him anymore.

"He called her a liar, still talking in this normal, ordinary, everyday kinda voice – she said it was just like in a horror movie she and her girlfriends had watched at a sleepover the week before. He told her she had to be punished for lying.

"She tried making a dash for the door but he grabbed her and clamped a hand over her mouth so she couldn't scream. Then – he did just about anything and everything a lunatic pervert could ever do to a little girl. Every time she'd try to fight him off – and she kept trying – he'd punch her. She was fighting right up to the end, even after he'd raped her. She almost managed to land a vicious kick to the balls, bless her little heart. He beat her to a bloody pulp for that and left her laying there, splayed out on the lounge, totally exposed and practically unconscious. That's how I found her.

"I'd just gotten off the phone and went looking for her but she wasn't in the house, so I yelled out the window down to the pool. He heard me and came bookin' out of the pool house. I got a clear view of him. I got down there as fast as I could but he was gone and Jenna was – Jenna was –"

Jim finally turned to face his mother and Scott again. He seemed like a new person, Scott thought. A human being, a man with a heart – a broken man with a broken heart.

"I ran in there and found her like that. If I live to be nine hundred, I swear, it was a sight I'd still never be able to forget.

"I rushed back up to the house, screaming for help. Adella came running. I had her call 9-11. Then I got back down there with a blanket. I couldn't let anyone see her like that. The cops gave me a hard time about that – crime scene shit and like that. Like I cared. Christ.

"She was completely in shock. An ambulance came. I rode with her to the hospital. Adella called Dad. They both got there almost as fast as the ambulance. They took her to Children's Hospital. It was a nightmare – this place that's decorated like it's a daycare center and there's my little sister, raped, beaten and barely conscious.

"And then there was Dad. He went ballistic. And he was furious with me, for not keeping a closer eye on her. And then I told him who did it. And what had already happened. Everything I knew at that point. I thought he was going to throw up. He was ready to go out and find Pete and tear him limb from tree.

The cops got him calmed down. Finally, he told me to tell them everything I knew, everything Jenna's told me. They put out a warrant for his arrest. They picked him up two days later."

"And Jenna?" Linda asked, not at all wanting to hear the answer.

"She was cut up bad, bruised all over. Her face was a mess. The doctors confirmed that she'd been sexually assaulted, and not for the first time.

"She was only semi-conscious for a couple of days. When she really woke up, she wouldn't speak to anyone, and she was terrified of anyone male – even me and Dad. They assigned her only female staff. They got her a female psychiatrist and a counselor to try to help her with the trauma. And female doctors to deal with the physical trauma. It took her a couple more days before she could even let Dad hold her hand. She was a wreck. By the end of the week, though, she let Dad and me hug her.

"The shrink and the counselor both agreed that she needed intensive counseling, that she should go into a private hospital for a while, that it was going to take time for her to deal with all this. Dad refused at first. He didn't want her to bear the stigma of having been in a psychiatric hospital for the rest of her life. He finally agreed, but only that she be there for a short time.

"We went to see her almost every day. They put her in Lakeview Hospital in Thousand Oaks. It was okay. She liked it there. They treated her beautifully. She was really beginning to make progress, but after about a month and a half, she started getting sick. She was nauseated almost all the time, and she was loosing weight like crazy. She didn't have much to loose – she was a scrawny kid. She couldn't sleep. The doctors started running tests. Bingo – she comes up – pregnant."

This was too much for Linda. She sank back in the chair and covered her face again.

"God, Mom, I'm so sorry," Jim said, who moved behind her and rubbed her shoulders. "God, if I could undo all that happened – if I didn't have to tell you this. No, I do have to." He stopped as she slid a hand up to squeeze one of his. She understood, and only wished she could spare him the agony of having to finish this nightmare tale.

Jim turned to Scott. "I have to thank you," he said humbly. "This had to come out some day. It wouldn't have if it weren't for you. I wasn't man enough."

"Cut the 'man' talk. Nobody's blaming you, Jim. No way," Scott said with feeling. "You're doing it and I have nothing but respect for you, nothing but."

"Thanks." Again, he took a deep breath. "I wish I could say this gets easier or that the worst of it's over – but it isn't.

"Dad was devastated, needless to say. He had to make a decision, about what to do. There was no way he was going to let Jenna have a child at her age, especially as a result of rape. There were two alternatives, of course. Let her carry the pregnancy to term and place the child for adoption. Or abortion. Dad weighed the options and spent a long time talking with her doctors. Everyone agreed abortion was the best solution."

Tears were running down Linda's face now. Scott found a Kleenex, brought it to her and pressed it into her hands.

"Jenna had an abortion. But she never knew about it. She'd make so much progress – they were afraid that knowing would cause a terrible, maybe an irreversible set-back. They told her she needed surgery to fix something that was discovered as result of the assault. She had no idea and never had any reason to think anything different than what she'd been told.

"And then –" Jim stopped, then looked Scott straight in the eye. "And then she was hypnotized, backed up with medication. Her memory of the entire thing was eradicated."

"Good Christ," Scott muttered. "What on earth were they thinking."

"It was 1980. The mentality in the '80s, especially in California, was that your shrink could fix anything. Just be a good patient – or parent of a patient – and follow doctor's orders. I'm sure she's not the only one who's dealing with flashbacks these days."

Scott nodded.

"She came home, and kept seeing a local shrink who kept tabs on it all for a couple of years afterwards, did a little fine tuning. By the time you came back, Mom, she was down to seeing her once or twice a month."

"I remember," Linda said, recollecting. "Dr. – Dr. Allenberg. Supposedly, she was dealing with not having a mother for those two years and with my suddenly coming back into her life."

"That was the party line," Jim concurred. "Dad pretty much told me everything that was going on, since I'd been in on it from the start. He never wanted you to know. He figured you'd blame him and leave again. He also knew if he told you, you'd probably insist that Jenna know everything. He couldn't face that."

Chapter 24

"AND WHAT HAPPENED to 'good ol' Uncle Pete'?" Scott asked.

"The bastard got fifteen to twenty, and I hope he died in there, a miserable death, ideally. They said Dad'd be told if he was up for release, and he never got a call, as far as I know. Maybe he did die."

"It wasn't all over the papers?" Linda asked.

"The whole thing was kept out of the papers. Don't ask me how Dad pulled that off. The court documents and police records were sealed, partly because Jenna was a minor, but mainly because of Dad pulling strings."

"Well, I plan to pull some strings myself and find out exactly what the status of the whole thing is today," Linda said decisively, her chin raised in defiance of everything this decision would require.

"Damn Bob. Damn him for thinking he knew what was best. Damn him for listening to those doctors. Witch doctors, if you ask me! Damn him for not telling me, so we could go back and sit down with those witch doctors and let me see if I agreed. Damn him to hell," she said, her voice cold as steel.

Jim had sat back down as his mother worked through her thoughts. Now he threw himself back on the couch and covered his face again. "I was supposed to live with that for the rest of my life. Now you know why I can't be close to her – I can't be, with what I know. My father swore me to secrecy.

"Damn it, I love my sister. She should have been told, but dear ol' Dad was determined to protect her – and himself, and the hell with the cost. Well, guess who else suffered trauma and has to live with it every day? Yeah, me, and did my father think or care about what it did to me? No. But I can take care of myself," Jim hastened to add.

"Scott, I don't know what'll happen when Jenna finds out, but you've got to be there for her. You may be the only one who can help her. I mean, she loves and trusts you so much – it'd take a blind man not to see it. Mom, all I can say is – I'm so sorry. Dad should have told you what happened. I should have made him."

"Enough blame and enough mistakes," Linda said. "It's time to straighten out this mess, even if we're twenty years late doing it.'

Scott jumped in. "Jim, you were seventeen years old. You had no idea that guy was around. You couldn't know what was going on in the pool house. It's not your fault and you need to stop blaming yourself. Jenna wouldn't, if she knew what had happened."

"Jim, Scott's right," Linda agreed. She sat down beside him and pulled his hands from his face. His eyes were shut fast. "It wasn't your fault, Jim. You were just a kid yourself." She took him in her arms and held her son truly close for the first time in years.

SCOTT STOOD LOOKING out the patio doors. The roof line of the pool house was barely visible from here. Finally, he turned back to them. "We've gotta decide how to tell her. It isn't gonna be long before she remembers it all. I think we oughtta tell her before then."

"Scott, do you have any idea why this is happening now, after all this time?" Linda asked.

"My therapist said it could have been the anesthesia. Apparently it sometimes does trigger memories that have been forgotten."

Linda turned back to her son. "Jim, is this the reason you drink so much when you and Jenna are together? You really don't drink that much otherwise."

Jim hung his head. "I drink so I won't feel the guilt when I look at her. I do it to anesthetize myself, I guess."

"Do you have any idea what was in the letter your father left for her?" Linda continued.

"He never mentioned it. If I had to guess, I'd say it's probably about the abortion. A doctor would want to know about that, I should think. I doubt he'd have ever admitted about the hypnosis. He was obsessed with protecting her from knowing what happened. He probably made up some wild story to cover the abortion."

Jim got up from the couch and went back to the family portrait. "The kid in this picture is actually pregnant. We just didn't know it yet. The picture was taken at Lakeview. Oh God, what on earth is going to happen when she re-members?"

Kristin, entering the living room through the patio doors, immediately sensed that something was terribly wrong. "When who remembers what?" she asked with concern.

"Where's Jenna," Scott asked.

"Down by the pool. Some man was down there. She said she was going to find out who he was and then she'd be right in. What's wrong?"

"What man?" Jim asked. "What did he look like?"

"Um – older guy, gray hair? She didn't know who he was. Is something wrong?" Kristin's voice rose with apprehension.

Scott took over. "Kristin, you stay here with Linda. Jim, you start looking – see if he's still around. I'm getting Jenna." Kristin looked back and forth from Jim to Scott to Linda in utter confusion. "What's going on?"

Kristin moved over to Linda, who reached out to hold her hand. "We're not sure, honey, but –"

An agonized scream, coming from the direction of the pool, cut Linda's thought to ribbons. Everyone bolted for the patio door. Scott was the first one out the door, when they heard the gun shot.

JIM AND SCOTT reached the pool simultaneously. A man – Peter Malone, Scott guessed – lay on the ground in a pool of blood, barely alive. Jenna sat nearby, doubled over herself, her hair streaming down and hiding her face, her body bruised and bloodied. A gun dangled limply from her hands.

"Call for an ambulance," he yelled up at Linda and Kristin as they both arrived on the scene.

"I call," said Adella, coming puffing up behind them. "I go call. You stay with Jenna." She turned around and retraced her steps with amazing speed for a woman of her girth.

Scott knelt down beside Jenna and gently touched one arm. "Baby Blue, it's me," he murmured into her ear. "I'm here. You're okay. It's over."

"I remember you," Jenna said as if in a trance. "I remember you."

"You remember him. We know all about it now. I can help you understand. Come back to me, Baby Blue. Come back to me."

Jenna shook her head to clear the cobwebs and turned her head, only to see Peter Malone slumped over on the ground. The sight sent her into paroxysms of fear. "Oh, my God! No!" she moaned. "Not again! No!"

"He can't hurt you any more, precious. You're safe," Scott kept whispering. He started softly stroking her one arm, with great care not to frighten her further. She calmed a bit, rocking herself now as she began to weep.

"Honey, it's gonna be all right. I'm here. You're gonna be okay. Jenna, can you tell me what happened?"

Jenna looked up at him for the first time, flinging her blood-soaked hair back over her shoulder. Scott reeled at the sight of a deep, bleeding gash across her forehead, garish black and purple bruises on her face, arms and legs, her blood-splattered hands, her torn and bloodied clothing. Almost instinctively, she dropped her head again, not wanting to be seen like this, not wanting Scott to have to see her pain.

"Oh, I so wish I could hold you, hold you tight, Jenna baby," he said tenderly, embracing her with his words if not his arms. "Honey, put the gun down and talk to me. Put the gun down. It'll be okay. Try and tell me what happened."

Jenna heard his request and gingerly set the gun down in front of her on the flagstone on which she sat huddled.

Kristin knelt on Jenna's other side. "Jenna. Oh, my God, Jenna," she said quietly. With one arm she reached around and held her half-sister. With the other hand, she reached over and tenderly pushed Jenna's hair back, only to reveal even further damage to the beautiful face across from which she'd just spent the entire afternoon. She gasped. "Oh, Jenna. What kind of…" She couldn't end her thought. She squeezed her eyes shut and buried her face against Jenna's shoulder.

Jenna managed a twisted half smile of appreciation. Slowly she turned to Scott. "He hurt me. He hurt me, Scott, a long time ago, when I was – I don't know when. Those nightmares – it was him. I realized when he started to come at me. He was there waiting for me. I – I tried to get away. He grabbed me and started hitting me, just like he did before. It all came back to me."

Suddenly her eyes went wide with horror and latched onto Scott's for dear life. "He raped me, Scott!"

"Today? Oh my God, he raped you today?" Scott asked, clearly ready to finish off the man who lay not five feet away.

"He raped me – in the pool house, when I was – thirteen. He tried to do it again today, Scott, only – this time he had a gun." She was trembling all over.

Scott took her in his arms and held her tight, a powerful embrace that included Kristin as well. "It's all right, Jenna. It's all over now. He'll never hurt you again. None of us will ever let that happen again." Jenna hung onto him and just cried.

Kristin, bewildered, only knew the purest love for the sister who had so importantly, so recently come into her life and now was in such profound pain. And for the man who loved her.

"WHERE EES MY baby?" Adella cried, as she came hustling back down to the pool.

"Over here, Adella," Linda called to her. Both women loved the distraught form in Scott's arms equally. Both women suffered the pain of what they saw equally. Both women clung to each other. But it was Adella who was experiencing the recurring nightmare. It was she who'd placed the 9-11 phone calls, each time.

When Adella could speak, she asked the question that had been on everyone's tongue at one time or other this day. "Who could do this?"

Disengaging herself from Linda's arms, she forced herself to walk over to the man lying senseless, face down on the flagstone. Crouching down, she peered at the face, then covering her mouth with her hands, she screamed. "Madre santa del dios!"

Linda, who had wanted to stay as far from the inert form of Peter Malone as possible came running. "What is it, Adella?" she cried.

"Theese ees the man!" Adella babbled. "That morning. I see theese man the morning Meester Bradford he die. He come to the house. They go in Meester Bradford's office. They fight. I hear them shouting, loud. I forget teel now. I never realize eet the same man. Eet so long ago!"

"Oh, my God, Adella," Linda said, stunned, shaking her head as she struggled to absorb the importance of this belated recollection.

BY THE TIME the police arrived, Jenna was wrapped in an oversized beach towel, but Scott and Kristin were still holding her tight. Linda was holding a cup of hot tea up to her daughter's bruised and shivering lips.

"Peter Malone," a plain clothes cop said to one in uniform. "We've been keeping tabs on him since he got out. Trying to, anyway. Slippery fuck. I saw this coming years ago."

The uniformed officer squatted down by Malone's prone form, examining the blood pooling on the flagstone. "Ten, fifteen minutes ago, tops. Still breathing."

"Oh yeah? Too bad," the plain clothes cop said, nudging the body tentatively with the toe of one sneaker. Scott looked up at him.

"Lt. Caine. Detective, L.A.P.D.." He pulled a badge from an inner pocket of the scruffy maroon and white jogging suit jacket he wore with bright green pants. "Robbery/homicide, primarily. Sure wouldn't mind if this *were* a homicide. I take this one personal."

"You – huh?" Scott said.

"I was new on the force when this son of a bitch did her all those years ago. 1980. My partner and me were the first ones here. I'd seen a hellova lot of bad stuff, but this was off the charts for bad. I was all over his release. Came and saw her father. You don't know how relieved I was to hear she'd wasn't in L.A. Denver, I think he said?"

"Yeah," Scott said, "and then Boston."

"He said he was happy for her to stay as far away from L.A. as possible."

Caine stopped for a moment, scratched at his receding hairline and looked again at Scott. "Are you who I think you are?" he asked Scott.

"If you're thinkin' Scott Tenny, yeah."

Caine nodded. "Sorry, just had to check. I'd read about the two of you. Her and her career and everything – it's always in the papers out here. Couldn't help but notice. Anyway, her father told me he was happy for her to stay as far away from L.A. as possible."

"When would that've been?" Scott asked.

"He's been out since February. I saw her dad in January."

Linda stood up and turned to the detective. "I'm Linda Bradford, Jenna's mother. We've – never met. I –" She thought about how to word this. "I had left the family, for two years, back then. No one ever told me…"

"I remember," Caine said. "Your husband had some pretty harsh things to say about you."

Linda looked him in the eye. "None of what you heard was true."

Caine studied her. "I believe you," he said.

Jenna stirred in Scott's arms and painfully raised her head to stare at the detective. "You – you –" She struggled to remember. "You carried me from the pool house?" she said, more question than statement. "I remember you."

Caine squatted down in front of Jenna. "You do. That's right," he said, balanced nimbly on his heels. "I took you outta there and held you till the ambulance got here. You sure were a tiny bundle back then. You couldn't have weighed ninety pounds."

Jenna grimaced. "You – you told me you were gonna help me. You said he wouldn't hurt me anymore. You – you said you'd make sure of it. But you didn't. He did hurt me again," she said with a shudder, her voice slipping back and forth from the little girl to the woman.

"You're right, Jenna, and I'm so sorry," Caine said, hanging his head. Gulping quietly, he looked back up and straight into her eyes. "I did say that. We failed you, Jenna. We couldn't – *I* couldn't – do what I'd promised you. We tried so hard. Can you forgive me, Jenna?"

The adult in Jenna was moved by the compassion in the hardened cop's eyes. "I'm sure you did." Staring at him, a light of recognition went on. "You – you came to the hospital, too, didn't you?" she said, again amazed at the memory.

"Yeah, a couple times. And just like back then, I'm gonna tell you again what I said then. I'm here to help you, but to do that I need to ask you some questions. Do you think you can answer them for me?"

"I'll try," she said.

"Can you tell me everything that happened?" Caine asked as gently as possible.

Jenna looked down, trying to pull the chaos of the past half hour together.

"Kristin and I were coming through the back way to the house. I saw – him. I saw this guy down by the pool, but like sorta in the bushes. It didn't make sense. I told Kristin I was going to see what he was doing, who he was. I didn't have a clue."

She stopped, blinking, confused. "I didn't – but I do. I – I don't understand."

"Tell us what you know and then we'll help you make sense of it all," Scott encouraged her. "You'll understand, baby, I promise you,"

"Okay. I went down there. I called to him. I think I said something stupid like, 'can I help you?' He had his back to me. When he turned around, he held a gun, pointed straight at me." Jenna's hands came up to her mouth at the memory of the moment.

"I was – I was paralyzed by the sight of that gun. He was raving. He said I was going to pay for having him sent to prison. I didn't know what on earth he was talking about. But – I do."

Again, she started shaking her head. "This doesn't make any kind of sense, Scott. "What the hell's going on?" She started to tremble violently again.

"Lieutenant, can this wait till she's been seen at the hospital. "She so shaken up."

"Certainly." Both turned to acknowledge the screaming siren of an ambulance. "I hear your ride coming, Lady Jenna," Caine said with a pained smile. A crime scene photographer leaned down to whisper in his ear.

Caine stood up. "Yeah, get it all," he said to the photographer, "starting with him," he directed him with a nod in Malone's direction. Looking around, Caine signaled to a member of the forensic team. "As soon as Jake's through, bag the gun," he said tersely, "and lemme have it."

When the bloody weapon had been put in his hands, Caine turned back to Jenna and again squatted before her. "Jenna, I do have to ask this one last question. Did you shoot him with this gun?"

Tears streaming down her face, Jenna answered Scott rather than the detective. "He was attacking me. I tried to fight him off. He dropped the gun and I grabbed it before he could. I – I don't know what happened after that, just you all showing up down here. Oh God, what have I done?" she exclaimed in horror.

"That's enough, honey. That's okay. Nobody's blaming you for anything. You don't have to say anymore," Scott said, soothing her as she buried her head against his chest, her body wracked with sobs.

Caine turned back to the photographer. "A couple of quick shots of our friend here, so she can be on her way," he said, signaling to take pictures of Jenna.

"You need to let them take a few pictures," Scott whispered in her ear, "and then it'll be all over, baby. Look up so they can get the pictures they need," he encouraged her. She turned to face the photographer. Reaching gently, he held her hair to one side so the photo could detail the beating she'd sustained. Jenna flinched visibly as she heard each click of the camera's shutter.

A pair of paramedics came on the run, a gurney between them. One quickly staunched the flow of blood from the open wound on Jenna's forehead while the second strapped a blood pressure cuff on her. Out of the corner of her eye, she could see another pair of paramedics hovering over the unconscious form of Peter Malone.

Lowering the gurney to ground level, Jenna's paramedics quickly had her on it and on her way to the closer of two ambulances idling side by side in the driveway. All the way up the meandering path, Linda held her right hand, Scott the left. Both squeezed their support and love. Jenna squeezed back with a small smile almost lost in the swelling that was already beginning to distort her normally delicate features.

As soon as Jenna was loaded into the ambulance, Linda turned to the closest paramedic, who was quickly hooking up an IV drip. "Where are you taking her?" she asked.

"The ER at Cedars-Sinai, ma'am," he said without looking up.

"Just like her dad," Linda said half to herself. "Scott, you go with her. We'll meet you there."

Scott climbed in and the doors slammed shut behind him.

LT. CAINE FOUND Kristin and Jim standing together by the door to the pool house, looking in from beyond the crime scene tape. "You mind if I ask you two a few questions?" he said, pulling out a notebook. Both nodded their willingness to help.

Kristin went first. "I'm Kristin Yates," she volunteered. "I'm Jenna's half-sister." She proceeded to confirm what Jenna had already told him.

"And you're her brother, aren't you?" Caine turned to Jim.

"Yeah, I'm her brother." Caine's pencil remained poised over the page in his notebook. Caine nodded his head at it. "Oh, sorry. Jim Bradford."

"You live in the area?" Caine asked.

"Brentwood," Jim told him.

"You seen Malone around here since he got out in February?"

"Nope. But I didn't know he was out. Dad never said anything. I don't know if you know it, but Dad died in April."

"I was aware of that," he said. "I'm sorry, son." Jim threw him a glance at the use of the word 'son.' Caine wasn't all that much older than he was.

"Sorry," Caine said. "Habit. Comes with the badge." He tapped his pencil on his head absently. "I remember talking to you. You were still in high school, weren't you?"

"Yeah."

"That had to have been rough," Caine stated flatly.

Jim nodded. "Yeah, it was. You're not gonna believe this, but my mother didn't know about it until today. God's honest truth. I was literally in the middle of getting the whole damned thing off my chest an hour ago, for the first time in twenty years, when – when all hell broke loose. Fuckin' son of a bitch."

"Prison didn't do anything for the bastard, that's for damned sure," Caine said harshly. Somehow, Jim found comfort in his words.

Linda came looking for Caine. "Lieutenant? I need to tell you something the housekeeper just told me. Malone was here the morning my husband had the heart attack that killed him. She said there was a lot of yelling. I –" Linda suddenly burst into tears.

"Mom, what is it?" Jim said, suddenly alarmed.

"He tried to tell me about it that afternoon. I shut him up. I said 'Don't you dare ever mention that bastard's name in this house again!' I didn't let him tell me. It was turning into a fight. We never fought. Then he had the heart attack.

Now I understand. His heart just couldn't take any more..." She turned to Jim who held her until she could pull herself together.

"The housekeeper?" Caine asked Kristin.

"Adella Escabel," Kristin told him. "She went back up to the house."

"I'll talk to her before I leave." He turned and stared at the pool of blood marking the spot where Malone had laid.

"If he lives, you can at least you be assured he'll never get out again," Caine said to them all, then stopped. "Hey, you guys get over to the hospital and be with Jenna. I'll come by to check on her when I've finished up here."

Chapter 25

As the paramedics turned the gurney bearing Jenna over to the Emergency Room staff, Scott could see looks of recognition telegraphed from face to face of younger orderlies and nurses. He wondered how long it would take for the first news reporter to show up and start asking questions. Holding Jenna's hand, he hurried along as she was wheeled into an examining room.

A doctor came hurrying in a moment later. He immediately turned to Scott. "I'm Dr. Michaels. Is there anything I should know? Is she pregnant?"

"No," Scott said quickly.

"Antidepressants? Allergies to any drugs you know of?"

"Not that I know about. But she's been though a hell of a shock today, on top of the physical stuff. She remembered something that happened twenty years ago that had been repressed by hypnosis and drugs, apparently. She's very confused."

"Oh. I see. Give me a few minutes and I'll be out to talk to you. Give admissions what they need. I'll find you there."

Scott quickly took care of the paperwork, then as he started to get up, pulled out his cell phone. The admitting nurse gestured with her head that he'd have to step outside to use it. "Hospital regulations," she said with an understanding shake of the head. "Sorry."

"No problem," he said, quickly scrolling through to Jeremy's number. Jeremy answered just as he exited the building.

Quickly he brought Jeremy up to speed. "So – bottom line, it's awful but it's over. But who knows how she's going to react to it all in the coming days and weeks. We're hardly outta the woods here."

"Want me to come out, brother?" Jeremy offered. "Say the word, I'm there."

"I know you are, Jer, and it means the world to me. Thanks, but you don't have to. Just tell everyone what's happened. I'm assuming I'm here for a week at least. Keep working on the album. Work with the tracks I laid down last week

– there's a lot there. Talk to Ben and Paulie about it. And, hey, could you do me a favor?"

"Name it," Jeremy said.

"Call my dad. Tell him what happened. Have him give me a call tonight?"

"Sure, bro. It's done."

Scott could see the doctor standing in the door of the waiting room looking for him. "There's the doc. Gotta go."

"Take care, Scott," Jeremy said sincerely. "And give everyone's love to Jenna. Carrie's especially."

Scott hurried back inside.

"JENNA'S STABILIZED. CONSIDERING what she's been through, she's doing amazingly well. She keeps asking for you," Dr. Michaels said. "The cuts, abrasions and contusions, you know about. She also has a fractured left cheek bone. It took more than a hand to produce that. She's in shock. Her blood pressure's lower than I want to see it."

Scott looked up to see Linda, Kristin, Jim and Adella coming through the door. After quick introductions, the doctor repeated what he'd already told Scott.

"I'll be admitting her. We'll have to see what the next day or two brings. We'll X-ray. Depending on what we find, she may require maxillofacial surgery. She could need a plate. It's too early to tell at this point. Best case, they'll be able to reduce the fracture – bring it back into alignment – without having to operate. That's the outcome we're going to hope for.

"As soon as she's able," he continued, "we'll have her seen by both a counselor and a psychiatrist. She's suffered serious emotional trauma. Frankly, that has me more concerned then her physical injuries at the moment."

"Dr. Michaels, please tell me – was she raped?" Scott asked. Jim put an arm around his mother as she braced for the answer.

"She didn't give him the chance. I've spoken with the doctor doing the workup on the man who assaulted her. From what he told me, it's pretty clear she fought him off like a tiger. The rape exam was negative."

"Thank God," Scott and Linda both said simultaneously.

"And his status?" Jim asked.

"I was just told he's in critical condition. You can go in and see –" The doctor's suggestion was cut short by a scream from down the hall that could only belong to Jenna.

Scott didn't wait for anyone's permission to go to her. By the time Dr. Michaels had caught up with him, Scott had her hands in one of his, touching her ever so gently with the other, talking her back down, step by patient step, from the craggy heights of her greatest fears. Frantic, Jenna clung to the lifeline of his words with every ounce of her being.

"A sedative, Dr. Michaels?" an attending intern asked quietly.

"Not indicated. Hypotension," he reminded him succinctly.

"Right," the intern replied, chagrinned.

"Increase the dopamine, .35 for now." Nodding, the intern scribbled a hasty note on Jenna's chart as he turned to execute the doctor's orders.

Scott moved to hold Jenna as she slowly calmed a bit. At last, she moved into his arms of her own volition, dropped her head on his chest and clung to him.

Finally, she could speak, if only in any emotion-drained monotone. "When I closed my eyes, all I could see was what happened, over and over again. I was so afraid he was going to kill me. He kept talking about things – I had no idea what he meant. Then he started screaming that I was a liar. And then he started hitting me.

"That's when it all started to come back to me. Scott, he's the man in my nightmares, the one that abused me when I was younger."

"I know, baby. I know," Scott said. "I know all about what happened to you. I had a feeling, what with everything going on – the flashbacks, the nightmares – that something had to have happened to you. That's really why I wanted to bring you out here.

"I hoped that your family could tell me," Scott continued. "I wasn't quite prepared for what I found out, but at least it's all out in the open now. We can all deal with it, babe. The important thing I want you to know and believe is that I love you, more than anything else. That's not going to change. We'll get through all this, together, and I'll be there with you every step of the way." He kissed and hugged her, then helped her lie back on the pillow. "Now, you've got to get some rest."

"Scott, would you ask Mom to come in, please?" Jenna said quietly. "I need to talk to her for a minute and then Jim. I promise, I'll rest when I finish talking to them."

"Will do, babe. Honey, I love you so much," Scott said, kissing her on the forehead and squeezing her shoulder.

LINDA TRIED NOT to flinch when she saw how badly her daughter's face had been beaten.

"Mom, it's all right. I know it looks bad. Believe me, it looks worse than it feels," she said with a crooked smile.

"Scott told me you didn't know anything about what happened to me, back then," she continued. "I can't believe Daddy didn't tell you. I don't know why I haven't been able to remember all this time or why I started having the nightmares. I remembered enough when he came at me today."

Linda went to Jenna and enveloped her in a long hug. Jenna's strength and quiet calm brought fresh tears to her eyes. "I never should have left you and your brothers, regardless of what that man might have done to us. This whole thing might not have happened if I had been there for you. I am so sorry, my precious daughter."

"You couldn't know," Jenna murmured.

Linda shrugged. "That's one of those things we can never know. As for your father – well, it's a good thing he isn't here right now. Honestly, I don't know what I'd do or say to him. Your poor brother's been living with guilt and shame all these years, knowing all along what happened to you. He hasn't being able to say a word, to you or to anyone. It's no wonder he acts the way he does when you're around. Honey, you need to talk with him. He's hurting almost as bad as you are."

"I want to see him, Mom. It's clear to me now why he's been so hostile towards me, since I can't remember when. But what I don't understand is why I haven't been able to remember any of this."

"Jenna, sweetie, talk with Jim, then get some rest. We'll all sit down and talk about *all* of that later."

LINDA CAME OUT to the waiting room to a row of anxious faces. "Jim, she wants to talk to you. She knows about everything except the pregnancy, the abortion and the hypnosis," Linda told her son. "Be careful what you say."

Kristin's mouth fell open. She'd looked forward to a day of getting to know a lot more about her new family, but this was just too much information to process. "Wait. What are you saying, Linda?" she managed. "Jenna lost the baby in the accident…didn't she? Not an abortion…" Thoroughly confused, she looked around at everyone.

"It's a lot more complicated than that," Linda said with a sigh, then went on to explain everything. Kristin's mouth had good reason to hang open for the entire briefing.

"So – she's putting up a brave front," Linda said, turning to Jim, "but I don't know how she'd take this part of the story in the state she's in right now, so, Jim, you be careful what you tell her, okay?"

"The last thing I want to do right now is cause her any bonus pain – good Christ, she's got more than enough to get her head around. Don't worry, Mom."

"But what if she remembers that on her own, too," Kristin said in alarm, "like in the middle of the night. She's *gotta* be told."

"They're going to have all of us talk with a counselor, in just a little bit. Let's see what the counselor says, okay?" Linda suggested.

"Counselors started this whole mess, remember," Jim pointed out, bitterly. Linda had to agree.

"We'll listen, and maybe we'll get a few other opinions, if we think we should. Quickly, don't worry," Linda said, acknowledging the look of urgency on Kristin's face. Jim got up and headed down the hall.

"Over here, Lieutenant," Scott called across the waiting room, seeing the L.A.P.D. detective at the desk. Caine turned and came right over.

"How is she?" he asked directly.

"She's doing all right," Scott answered for everyone. "Her brother's in with her right now."

"I need to ask her a few more questions if I can, but it can wait till he's finished. In the meantime, if I could ask you a few questions it'll speed up things," he said specifically to Scott.

"Sure," Scott agreed.

"Maybe we should get a cup of coffee," Linda suggested to Kristin and Adella.

"You folks don't have to leave," Caine said.

"HEY, TALK ABOUT déjà vu," Jim said quietly as he came into the examining room. Jenna's face was swelling rapidly. "And it's no easier to take today than it was back then. How are you feeling, sis?"

"I'm okay," Jenna said, her voice weak but her words firm.

Jim pulled a stool up to the edge of the bed, perched on it and took her hand. "Sis, I am so sorry for what has happened to you," Jim said with a sincerity born of relief. "For this, for everything."

"Jim, it's not your fault. Scott told me what happened, and how you blame yourself. You were a kid too. You can't blame yourself. It was Dad, not you."

"When I found you in that pool house all I could think was how, if I'd been more vigilant, it wouldn't have happened. I blamed myself. Dad blamed me. The whole thing was horrible."

"Oh, Jim. It never should have been," Jenna said compassionately.

"Which is why I've felt so guilty all these years. I could only survive by ripping out my heart," Jim said bluntly. "I love you, sis. It's killed me to act like such an asshole all these years."

Jenna squeezed his hand, hard. Reaching over, he gingerly gave her a tiny hug. Sitting back on the stool, he could only shake his head.

"I wish to God I'd been strong enough to stand up and tell you what happened years ago and to hell with Dad. I don't know how he was able to live with everything that happened. I sure as hell haven't been able to forget it for a minute. I just hope that one day you'll be able to forgive me."

"*This* is the brother I've wished for all these years," Jenna managed to say through tears. "There's nothing to forgive, big brother. I love you and I don't blame you, you've got to believe me. If anyone's to blame for anything, it's Dad, for putting you in such a terrible position. He made you carry his guilt," she said fiercely. "Let's put his cruelty behind us and start being the brother and sister we use to be. Agreed?" Jenna reached up and touched him on the chest. "There. My gift to you. A new heart."

"Oh, Jenna. My dear sister. Your forgiveness, your understanding – God, what can I say?" He stood up and placed both hands a bit melodramatically where she'd just touched him and grinned at her for the first time in years. "Medical history's been made here today – a sister to brother heart transplant. Thank you, baby sister," he said, "from the bottom of my brand new heart."

The two were holding hands when an orderly came in to move Jenna to a private room. Jim kissed her hands. "See you up there," he said. "I'll tell everyone."

Jenna blew him a kiss.

Chapter 26

As soon as Jenna was settled in her own room, Lt. Caine and Scott, at Caine's invitation, appeared at the door. Jenna lay back, staring at the ceiling. Caine gently rapped on the open door. "Anybody home," he said, flashing a badge at a nurse in attendance and indicating with his head he'd like privacy. She nodded and quietly left the room.

"You speaking to me?" he said moving over to Jenna's side. Jenna looked momentarily confused, then placed him again.

"You're –" She still couldn't come up with a name.

"Lt. Caine. You can call me Matthew." Jenna mouthed the 'Matthew' as he got to it. She remembered.

"But you were pretty ticked with me, our last little chat."

"I'm sorry," Jenna said. "I –"

"Hey, don't worry, kid. I didn't come for an apology. How are you doing?"

"I hurt like hell. And I'm confused about so many things. You saw me back then. Did I look like this before?"

"Not quite so bad, physically. You had that same scared look in your eyes, though – that hasn't changed. I hope I can help make that go away. I just need to ask you a few more questions."

"Help me sit up a bit," she asked Scott. He helped make her as comfortable as circumstances could allow.

"We've talked to everyone and my people have done a pretty thorough preliminary on the crime scene. I want to get your statement and try and wrap this up as quickly and painlessly as I can for you, Jenna. Can you tell me what happened, to the best of your recollection?"

"I'll try. Should I start at the beginning again?" Jenna asked.

"Well, not the *beginning* beginning. Just what happened today. Mind if I record?" She shook her head. He pulled a small recorder from his pocket, set it on the bed beside her and activated it.

Jenna started to take a deep breath, then winced. "Right. He did say shallow breaths. Okay." She sat a bit straighter, winced again, then began.

"So. We – Kristin and I – pulled up to the house. We'd been out for lunch, up in Malibu. It was pretty close to four, I think. We came in the back way. I saw him down by the pool. I didn't know who it was. Neither did Kristin – she said she'd never laid eyes on him before. I went down to see, to find out who he was and what he was doing."

"And you said…" Caine prompted her.

"Can I help you?"

"And he said…"

"He turned around and stared at me. Then he got this disgusting, lascivious grin on his face. I think he actually licked his lips. That was the first thing I noticed. Then I saw the gun. He said something – he said 'Jenna,' that's what he said. He knew me. And he got this really pleased look on his face."

"What happened then, Jenna?"

"I wanted to run, but all I could see was that gun. Then he said something about twenty years he'd been waiting – 'waiting patiently,' those were his words – to get back at me. I said, 'What do you mean, get back at me? What did I ever do to you?' And then he went bullshit. He started yelling all this stuff, about me telling on him, that I was going to pay for that. Then he went quiet again, scary quiet, how he loved me, how I loved him but just didn't know it, how he was going to show me how he loved me – that's when I suddenly realized I did know who he was: the man in my nightmares. He said I shouldn't be afraid of him. Yeah right, like I shouldn't be afraid of this raving lunatic."

"Did you say anything or did he do all the talking?" Caine asked quietly.

"I tried to answer him, but he kept cutting me off. I kept trying to tell him I didn't know him. He said, 'You're killin' me, Jenna. You kill me, I'm gonna hafta kill you.' That's when I really got scared. I knew I couldn't just try to run, that he'd shoot me. So I decided the only thing I could do would be, like, just the opposite. I moved towards him instead of away."

"Hooo, brave girl," Caine whistled approvingly. Scott dropped himself into a chair along the wall. Face in his hands, elbows on the arms of the chair, he massaged his temples, trying to take the edge off the rage building within him.

"I talked to him real quietly. He listened at first. I said he had to believe me, that I didn't know who he was and that he couldn't blame me for something I didn't know anything about. But that whoever he thought I was must have done something really painful to him. He fell for it for a minute. At least, he stopped pointing the gun at me. I got to within a couple of feet of him.

"But then he snapped. He said, 'But you do know me, you lying bitch. You *are* Jenna.' And then he went crazy. He grabbed me and pinned me up against the side of the pool house. He was all over me, trying to kiss me, everything. I did manage to kick him once – I think that was when he slammed the gun into my face. Then I really started to fight. I just used everything I had. I like launched myself at him. I was totally off balance, but so was he. I managed to knock him down and he dropped the gun. He – Oh, my God…I shot him, Matthew, didn't I."

Jenna wrapped her arms around herself as she began to shake again. Scott jumped up and hurried to her side. "It's okay. Hold it together, baby," he whispered, his arms around her once again. Caine put a steadying hand on her shoulder.

"It's okay, Jenna. It sounds like a clear case of self-defense. We'll get all the pieces put together. This time I think we should be able to put him away for keeps. I'll be back a little later. In the meantime, you get some rest. You let Scott help you," he said, winking at Scott. Scott gave him a thin smile.

"Let me just have a couple of words with the Lieutenant," Scott said. Jenna nodded, suddenly overcome with fatigue. "I'll be right back, hon.'

Out in the hallway, Scott turned to Caine. "She isn't gonna be charged with anything, is she, Detective?" he asked anxiously.

"Really, call me Matthew," Caine insisted. "And, no, not if I can help it, Scott. As far as I'm concerned she was defending herself from a monster who was attacking her and threatening to kill her. I'm just concerned the DA may try to use what happened to her when she was a kid as a motive for why she shot him. *That* I'm not gonna let happen."

Looking up, Scott saw Jim, Kristin and Linda approaching. They stopped, conferred and then Jim came on down the hall to join them.

Caine repeated what he'd just said to Scott for Jim's benefit. "My concern isn't so much the sealed records," he continued. "It's what got into the press, regardless of what it took your father to keep it from getting out. The press has one hell of a long memory. Your dad couldn't hypnotize the media into forgetting what happened – he could only buy them off. And he couldn't buy a guarantee they'd stay bought off, any more than he could guarantee Jenna would stay hypnotized."

"How much got out?" Scott asked.

"There were leaks. The information exists out there. It's just a matter of what the DA might choose to do with it, if he did get his hands on it." Caine looked down. "I'm gonna make sure he doesn't do anything with it, if he does stumble on anything," he said quietly. "But I never said that." Scott locked eyes with Jim.

"Thanks," Jim said just as quietly, "for nothing, like you said," he hastened to add. "It's very much appreciated."

Sensing a suitable break, Kristin and Linda joined the three men. "Can I go have just a couple of words with Jenna?" Kristin asked Scott. "I'll be quick."

"Sure, Kristin," he said quickly. "Of course."

"Just nothing about the pregnancy," Jim insisted quietly. "Right?"

"I won't. Please, don't worry, Jim. I understand."

KRISTIN TIPTOED INTO Jenna's room. Jenna appeared to be asleep.

Quietly stepping over to her side, Kristin put her hand over Jenna's. Jenna opened her eyes and smiled up at her. "I was hoping you'd come to see me," Jenna said, wincing with the growing pain of speaking. "I guess you've heard all about it now, what happened to me when I was a kid." Kristin nodded. Jenna hooked a thumb over Kristin's hand.

"Something tells me there's more to it," Jenna went on sadly. "I'm still afraid to go to sleep. I don't want to know any more. I'm not sure I can take it."

Kristin squeezed her hand softly but said nothing. Finally, after what she knew was too long a hesitation, she just said the first thing that popped into her mind. "You've like been through hell, sis. We just have to thank God that this time didn't end up a rerun of the other time."

Jenna managed a small smile. "Thanks, hon," she said, then groaned. "God, I just hope Scott isn't wondering what the fuck he got himself into, when he decided he wanted *me* in his life – sheesh. He's gotta be kickin' himself black and blue. I mean, he hasn't said anything to make me think that – but, oh God, he's gotta be." Jenna burst into tears of exhaustion.

"Jenn, honey, no way!" Kristin didn't have to falter on this thought. "Scott's *so* in love with you. Oh, man, I just hope some day I like find someone who can love me the way that guy loves you. You just have to relax and let him, sis, that's all you've got to do. He's there for you, like so totally."

SCOTT, JIM AND Linda were talking with a woman at the nurse's station when Kristin left Jenna.

"This is Kristin, Dr. Albert, Jenna's half sister," Linda said as Kristin joined them. Kristin couldn't help but smile at Linda. She so appreciated being referred to this way. "Dr. Albert has time to see us right now."

The doctor put a hand out to Kristin. "Hi, Kristin. I'm Audrey. I'm a rape crisis counselor."

"Thank goodness," Kristin said. "The sooner the better. That was hard."

"It can be just as hard for the family as it is for the survivor herself. Come on with me and we'll see what I can do to help you all."

Taking them down a hall, Audrey ushered them into a small conference room. As they all settled into chairs, she moved a finger down the cover page of Jenna's chart, quickly scanning the material as she went. The finger, which has been moving swiftly and methodically, came to a halt halfway down, then proceeded very slowly indeed as Audrey absorbed the numerous complications behind Jenna's case.

"My goodness," she said gravely. "This *is* hard, for all involved."

"We need guidance," Linda said, "and we need it fast. Jenna's remembered almost all of what happened to her. It's just a matter of time before she's hit with the worst of it. What I'm not sure is in there is the fact that she was in a very bad automobile accident two months ago. She was almost six months pregnant. She lost the baby."

Audrey closed her eyes. Clearly this fact hadn't made it onto the cover sheet. She took a moment to absorb it. "Is there anything else I should know?" she asked. As the family augmented the summary with several other critical missing, details, Audrey jotted notes in the margins. Scott pulled Jenna's sealed letter from her father out of his pocket, explained about it and laid it on the table in front of him. Finally, when they were done, Audrey set her pen down, sat forward and looked around the table at each of them.

"You can't protect Jenna from the truth. Why her father thought he could, we can never know, obviously," she said. "The greatest mistake a caring family can make – and for all the right reasons, please don't misunderstand me – is to try and protect the survivor of sexual assault from the painful, unavoidable realities of life, and in trying to do so, becoming *over*protective. It's the most natural – and *destructive* – instinct there is." Audrey paused to allow them to contemplate that thought.

"Sexual assault leaves its victims feeling profoundly helpless in the face of brute force. And by victims, I don't mean just the person who was physically attacked. It means those who love her, too. You, Jim," she said, "have clearly suffered every bit as much as Jenna has. Your suffering has spanned twenty years. Jenna has just started experiencing her suffering recently. Now that it's out in the open, it's going to take both of you months, maybe years, to assimilate what you've experienced and move beyond it. It's a process, like grieving, that cannot be rushed. It takes as long as it has to take. That's just a fact of life." Jim sat nodding grimly.

"What you have to constantly remind yourselves is that the more you try to take on *for* Jenna, the more you unintentionally reinforce her underlying sense of helplessness. Which is precisely what her father did. What he did was the most extreme example of overprotection. Unfortunately, it isn't all that unusual – someone in the public eye, a man of means, as he was, needing to protect himself, his career and his family from a predatory press and the public it serves. As for the therapists involved, you're right, Jim, in your take on the state of the art in the 1980s. End results and expediency were all that mattered. The decade of the quick, residential fix. 28-day programs for whatever ailed you. Can't manage 28 days? No problem – reach for the prescription pad. There's still plenty of the latter still going on today, I'm sorry to say."

"So how do we break the worst of it to her?" Scott asked.

"Directly," Audrey said with no hesitation. "She's asking to be told. She knows there's something."

"All of us? One of us?" Jim asked.

"As a family?" Linda said, almost on top of Jim's thought.

Audrey nodded to Linda. "I'd suggest as a family," she said. "For one thing, it saves her having to acknowledge it over and over with each of you individually. Everyone knows what everyone else is saying and has said. It's never the same from one set of circumstances to the next, but you strike me as a close-knit, loving, supportive family. In your case, I'd definitely say talk to her together. And Kristin's right. Right away. If it seems right, give her the letter. Forget the instructions on the front. Her father cannot be allowed to continue his tyranny from the grave "

Kristin was on her feet before any of the others had finished pushing back from the table.

"I HOPE SHE'S not asleep," Linda said as they trooped down the hall to Jenna's room. She wasn't. To the contrary, she was sitting up, slumped over and in tears. Scott gathered her up again. "Tell me what's the matter," he whispered in her ear as he planted a kiss on her hair. "Man, we do have to get you a shampoo, my sweet."

Jenna, looking up at him, eked out a meager smile.

"What's wrong," he repeated. "Tell me."

"More memories," Jenna said miserably, "but these are different." She looked off into a distance only she could see.

"Being sent to another hospital...a lot of strange people. *Really* strange people. I was so afraid. Lt. Caine – Matthew – showed up one day. He – he could tell how afraid I was. He told me he'd try help make things better. A few days later my father came and took me home. But I couldn't figure out why I was there in the first place. Do *you* know?" she asked Jim, watching him closely. "Do any of you?" she asked her mother, Scott and Kristin by turns.

"Jenna, we do now," Scott answered her, looking her square in the eye. "I'm gonna tell you, but baby, it's gonna hurt. There's no way it can't." She dropped her head to his chest, held on to him for a few moments, then whispered that he should go ahead, that she was ready.

"Baby," he said as gently as he knew how, "you had a lot to recover from, after you were raped, emotionally as well as physically. Your dad was afraid to have you come straight home – he was so afraid the press would get wind of it and hound you if they did. You were sent to a place called Lakewood Hospital for a few months."

Jenna interrupted him. "In Thousand Oaks? The hospital for the mentally ill?"

"That's right. The strange people you saw were mentally ill. They frightened you. Hell, you were thirteen, for crying out loud," he said when she started looking guilty. "You can't blame yourself for that.

"Anyway, Lt. Caine told me he came to visit you. He knew the place. He was deeply concerned about you being there. When he saw how scared you were, he went to see your father and talked with him. You came home shortly after that.

"But something else happened before you went home." Scott hesitated, gave her a small kiss, then continued. "You'd been sick for about a week, honey. You were tired, nauseated, losing weight because you weren't eating, so they sent you to the doctor. You were examined, they did tests. Jenna –" He tightened his grip on her. "Jenna, you were pregnant."

"From the rape? Oh, my God, when I was thirteen? What – what happened?" Her eyes were as big as proverbial saucers.

Scott looked over at Jim. "You can explain this better than I can," Scott said.

Jim took over. "Dad consulted with the doctors, trying to decide what would be best for you. He couldn't allow you to go through anymore trauma then you had already. Everyone agreed an abortion was necessary." Jenna recoiled as if slapped.

"The doctors came up with the idea of hypnosis and drugs," Jim carried on. "As I understood it, it was a fairly new treatment for people who had undergone severe emotional trauma. You never knew a thing, for all these years. Scott has the letter Dad left you – my guess is, that's what it's all about. He was probably concerned that, if you got pregnant again, you'd need to know it wasn't your first pregnancy."

Scott let go of her momentarily and pulled the letter out of his back pocket. "I brought it with me, figuring it was at the bottom of everything. I think it maybe time for you to read it – but that's completely up to you, baby." He offered her the letter. She hesitated, then reached for it. Her hands trembled as she took it from him, and stared at the envelope for a long time before she could open it. Her mother settled on the opposite side of the bed and laid a comforting hand on her shoulder.

They all watched her as she skimmed the two-page letter, then went back to the beginning and read it, word for word, with tears streaming silently down her face. When she finished reading it, she let it drop from her hands and burst into sobs. Scott took her in his arms and held her close to him while she cried. To learn of the loss of not one but two babies in a matter of weeks was nothing short of crushing.

Chapter 27

IT WAS SEVERAL minutes before Jenna could utter an entire sentence without falling apart all over again, and when she finally could, none of those sentences came out as statements – they were all questions.

"Oh, my God, somebody tell me: how many different ways can one father betray one daughter? I can't believe he would have done that, and then not tell me for all these years?" Jenna expelled what sounded like it very well could be the last breath in her body. "I was pregnant? At thirteen? By a rapist? And he didn't think at some point in my life I might need to know that? Okay, he wanted to protect me – but not to have told me at all, ever? Did he really think reading that when I was pregnant was going to be doing me some kind of favor? I mean, good God, if I had read that when I was pregnant a few months ago…and known all that when I lost that baby…" She stopped and just stared at Scott, not knowing what else to say.

"Jenna, I can only imagine how you feel right now. I wish I could take your pain on as my own and spare you every bit of it. God, I know this has to be so much to absorb and understand and come to terms with. But, honey, at least now everything is out in the open and you can *know* what you have to deal with. Knowing has to be godawful, but knowing that there are things you *don't* know – that's has to be even worse."

Pushing the hair out of her eyes, he gently planted a kiss on her lips. "I know you have a million questions. Hopefully you'll be able to get some answers. But you have to realize that you may never get all of them."

"Oh, God. I don't know, Scott. I don't know, but I'll try my best." He kissed her forehead and looked at her.

"That's all anyone can ever do," he whispered. "I'm here, I love you, and I'll be with you to help in whatever way I can, every inch of the way, I promise you. You gotta know that by now."

Jenna looked over at her mother. Linda's hand still rested on her shoulder. Jenna took it in hers. "Mom, this has to be just terrible for you, too, in so many other ways. We both –"

She stopped and looked up at Jim and Kristin. "We *all* have so much to come to terms with, each one of us." And looking back up at Scott, she included him. "Welcome to the family, baby," she said with the most disillusioned smile Scott had ever seen.

IT WAS LATE. After long, poignant hugs, Linda, Kristin and Jim left a completely exhausted Jenna in Scott's care. An orderly arrived with a cot and set it up in an out-of-the-way corner so he could stay the night. As soon as he left, Scott moved the cot up against the lesser business side of Jenna's bed. Jenna fell asleep with her hand in his.

Sleep was harder to come by for Scott. The normal daylight hours din of the hospital took on the relatively quieter, hushed, true-emergencies-only quality of night in a 900-bed, big city melting pot of a medical facility. Even with the door shut, silence was not to be had.

Scott found himself counting ceiling tiles illuminated by the ambient light, counting helicopters criss-crossing the night skies of Los Angeles, counting the ticks of his watch when he set it by his ear on the pillow. Finally he started quietly humming the tune of the song he'd been writing for Jenna and, through the surreal, elongated hours of darkness, found the words of another verse.

> *The road she has traveled, the road now revealed.*
>> *My poor woman*
> *Lies sleeping. Her past lies unsealed.*
>> *My dear woman.*
> *Nightmares defanged, secrets laid bare,*
> *The things Daddy did to you – beyond unfair.*
> *Know this my dear, this my only prayer:*
>> *That you know you're my woman.*

He was sleeping soundly when a night nurse came stealing in at five a.m. to check Jenna's vital signs. He never stirred. Jenna woke him at seven.

JENNA WAS HIDING behind a cascade of hair as she picked at her breakfast of scrambled eggs, apple sauce and bagels when Linda and Kristin walked in bearing a cheerful arrangement of flowers. The little floral creation provided a welcome oasis of natural color in an otherwise lackluster, purely functional room whose only framed print had long since surrendered all but a trace of its original vibrance. Linda found a spot for the flowers where Jenna could see them easily, then turned to survey the damage by the light of day.

"Now sit up and let me see you," she suggested as only a mother can and will.

"You don't want to. It ain't pretty," Jenna said quietly.

"I don't think I could handle pretty this morning. I'm primed for ghastly," Linda said, reaching for the sweep of hair and pushing it behind Jenna's ear, revealing a fearful sight. Linda took it in stride – she'd been preparing herself for just this since sunrise. She harrumphed dismissively. "I know makeup artists that could do a better job. In fact – I know a makeup artist who can have you looking pretty darn *good* as soon as the swelling goes down."

Jenna smiled meekly. "Thanks, Mom, but I couldn't hurt Yumi's feelings – she'll want to do her thing."

"Yumi's excellent at stage makeup, but she's no Sonya Jacoby. Hell, if she can still make Eileen Hardwick look good, she can make anyone – in any shape – look good. With Sonya and the right agent, Frankenstein's monster might actually have a crack at playing the heartthrob. Where's Scott?"

"He just went in search of a decent cup of coffee. This may be *the* hospital in L.A., but the food seriously sucks." She paused. "Or maybe I'm just in no condition to judge."

"I'd say that's about the least of your worries," Linda said pragmatically. "How's your cheek, baby?"

"Oh, man, it hurts, Mom."

Linda put a finger under Jenna's chin and turned her face this way and that. "I'll tell you, hon, it's not half as bad as I was braced for. What do you think, Kristin?"

Kristin smiled broadly. "You look fabulous, Jenn," she said. "You're one of the most beautiful people I know – which puts you in pretty select company, with people like Linda Bradford, Jim Bradford, Scott Tenny… I'm sure I could name a few more if I had to, but you get my drift."

Jenna smiled gratefully. "You're a doll, kid. You really are. Come here and let me give you a hug." Kristin leaned across the bed and hugged her back.

"I can't stay. I have to get to class. But I'll be back later this afternoon. Can I bring you anything?" Kristin asked.

"Just your sweet self," Jenna smiled. "I have no idea how long they intend to keep me. I'm hoping for less rather than more. I can ache at home just as well as here."

"And maybe get a full night's sleep," said Scott, coming through the door in sunglasses with a tray of four tall coffees. "This place reminds me of Vegas at three in the morning. Café au laits, anyone? Had to go to the Beverly Center for them. I knew you'd be here," he said to Linda and Kristin. Kristin thanked him for hers, then dashed.

After giving Linda and Jenna coffees, Scott shoved the cot back into the corner and brought his coffee back to that side of the bed. "Shove over, gorgeous," he told Jenna, then hopped up on the bed next to her and gave her a kiss.

"To the most messed up beautiful woman in the world," he toasted her with his paper cup. "May this all be only one extremely bad memory among thousands of enormously wonderful ones for you and me, babe." His sincerity was palpable.

"Here here," Linda chimed in as Scott sealed his wish with the most tender of kisses on Jenna's swollen and bruised lips.

With his fingertips, Scott touched the lips he'd just been kissing. "You look a bit like me today, Baby Blue."

DR. MICHAELS PUT in a brief appearance. Linda and Scott stepped out in the hall while he checked Jenna over thoroughly. "Hmmm. Good. Yes, very good," he said as he moved from one area of concern to another. "It's all looking very good indeed. Vision's still okay this morning?"

Jenna nodded.

"We know your tear ducts are in tact," he said, giving her a sympathetic smile. Returning it caused her to flinch.

"Right. The cheek bone is going to require a good six to eight weeks to heal, but you were lucky. I'm pretty confident you aren't going to require surgery. I'll want to get another set of X-rays when the swelling goes down, just to be on the safe side, and I do want you to be seen by a dental surgeon as well. I had some conversation with Dr. Albert last night. We're both in complete agreement that you are a very strong young woman, my dear, and that you have what it takes to come to grips with all you've been through. I can only wish you the best."

"Does that mean I can go home?" Jenna asked hopefully.

"Sorry, Jenna, not quite so fast. I do still want Dr. Herrera to come in and talk with you. He's a psychiatrist on staff. I'd feel better if you would at least explore the possibility of inpatient treatment for post traumatic stress. Working through the kind of misfortune you've experienced, both recently and in the past, will be quite difficult indeed. The fact that you live in the public eye as you do can make the kind of adjustment you need to get through just that much more difficult."

"Another Lakeview? No way, my friend. That's so not gonna happen," Jenna stated flatly. "I'll see a therapist daily, if that's what I have to do, for as long as necessary, but no residential treatment program, no way, no how."

"Hmm…you don't sound exactly open-minded on the subject. Just give it a hearing, would you? Humor an old man?" he said with an ingratiating smile. "Or at the very least, discuss an outpatient approach with him. I just need to know you've explored your options."

"I'm sorry, Dr. Michaels," Jenna said. "I will. I promise you."

"Thatta girl," Dr. Michaels said approvingly, as he made a note on her chart. "You can go as soon as he's been by to see you."

"OKAY, MY PETS, I'll see you when you get home. I'm so glad you don't have to spend another night in this place," Linda said, gathering up her purse and some magazines she'd brought. "Call if –"

"No so fast, Mrs. Bradford," sang a rich Yankee baritone coming in the door.

"Dad!" Scott exclaimed.

"As you live and breath, my son," Joe Tenny grinned as he wrapped one arm around Scott while giving Jenna's toes a squeeze with the other hand. "Well, my goodness, ain't she a pretty sight," he said as if he were appraising a classic wooden boat coming up the lake, not the bruised and battered love of his son's life.

"Say, Mrs. Bradford, that guest room you mentioned still available for an itinerant ol' pain in the butt?" Joe asked Linda.

"Of course it is, for you, Joe," Linda said, her smile both bemused and sincere. "Until I move, I've still got my endless supply of guest rooms. You come with me. They'll be letting Jenna out for good behavior very shortly now."

Joe took the arm Linda offered him. Turning back to Scott and Jenna, he gave them a little wave over his shoulder that clearly said, 'well, if this don't beat all.'

SCOTT AND JENNA had plenty of time to explore the subject of inpatient versus outpatient treatment in the hour they sat waiting for Dr. Herrera to appear. "I don't care what anyone says, Scott. I'm coming home with you. Boston's got hospitals and doctors on every street corner. There must be more doctors per capita in the city of Boston than anywhere else on the planet."

"I'm all for it, babe, but *only* if you've got a note from your doctor. Okay, I'm exaggerating –"

"As usual," Jenna interjected.

"Guilty as charged," he allowed. "But no way am I taking responsibility for the state of your health, physical *or* mental. You talk them into it and I'll be fine with it. Just no going out on some risky limb."

"Pretty conservative talk coming from the King of Risk."

"Wait a second, name one risky thing I've done since we've been together," he protested.

"Other than fall in love with me in the first place, you mean?"

"Got me there," he chuckled. "Talk about the ultimate risk." He pulled her to him. "But you know what? If this is taking risks, then I'm ready to take a whole bunch more and to hell with the consequences, babe." He was just about to kiss her when there was a knock at the door.

"Hi. I sure hope I'm interrupting something wonderful," said a cheerful young man in full beard and moustache. "I'm Jimmy Herrera, you're Jenna and you're Scott. I wish we were meeting under happier circumstances. I'm quite a fan of both of you."

"Thanks," Jenna said. Scott nodded.

"I've gone over your records. You're one lucky, traumatized lady, to put it mildly," he said. "Dr. Michaels has told me that you'd prefer to discuss outpatient treatment. It's pretty clear why."

"And I'd prefer to go back home to Boston to do so," Jenna said decisively. "I don't want to start with a doctor here, then have to start all over back there."

"Makes sense. So, you're making Boston your home, then?"

Jenna smiled almost shyly at Scott, who took her hand. "She is if I have anything to say about it, Doc," Scott said.

"Boston represents new beginnings for me. It always has. I love Boston. I'll always feel at home in L.A., and of course my family's here, and we've gotten tremendously closer in the last twenty-four hours – dear God, has it only been twenty-four hours?" Jenna marveled. "It doesn't seem possible. But anyway, what I was saying?" She had to stop and think. "Boston's different," she finally said, "in so many ways. I feel like I can be myself there, in ways I've never been able to be in L.A. Does that make any sense?"

"Reinvention is a healthy undertaking, Jenna. As long as it doesn't represent running away from you problems. If you're willing to tackle your problems head on, with the help of a trusted professional, I have no problem with the thought of you undertaking that job in Boston. I have several very good people in Boston I can recommend. I just hope you'll follow through. I can't say this strongly enough, Jenna: you need to accept the *depth* of what's happened to you. If you are willing to commit to the hard work of healing yourself, you'll be able to go on and live the full life you want and deserve. If you don't, what's happened to you could cripple you for the rest of your days."

A few minutes later, Dr. Herrera scrawled his signature on the bottom of the release form and Jenna was free to go.

Chapter 28

JENNA HADN'T BEEN home a half hour when Adella appeared at the study door to announce a visitor. "Policia to see you again, Jenna," she said with a smile. Adella had taken a liking to the dour Lt. Caine. Jenna was resting comfortably on the couch, a few extra pillows behind her head.

"Come in, Lieutenant," Jenna said, welcoming the interruption. Her thoughts had been growing morbid, in spite of everyone's best efforts to keep things light, upbeat and amusing. Scott was sitting at the piano – her baby grand from childhood – picking out snatches of favorite tunes. First he'd offer one of his favorites, then she'd request one of hers. He knew them all. The few times she tried joining in, she quickly discovered the painful limitations of a fractured cheekbone when it came to singing. All she could do was sit and listen, far from her usual style.

"Good afternoon, Jenna. I was headed over to the hospital to see you when I got the word you'd already gone home. Afternoon, Scott," Caine said. Scott greeted him with a nod and kept noodling around on the piano. It took Caine a couple of tunes to notice he was spinning off a medley of T.V. cop shows themes. Caine smiled blandly when Dragnet finally caught his attention.

"I have two pieces of news for you, both good in my book. First, the DA's not going to be pressing any charges. You're free to go back to Boston as soon as you're able."

"Sing hallelujah," exclaimed Linda from the doorway. Adella had let her know Caine was here.

"I'll second that," Scott said, moving seamlessly from the theme for CHIPS into a double-time rendition of "When the Saints Go Marching In."

"Lt. Caine, thank you *so* much," Jenna said reaching for his hand to squeeze.

"*Please*, call me Matthew," Caine said with a note of frustration. "You don't think I got into plain-clothes for the pay, did you? I like people to see me as more than a rank and a badge."

"Matthew," Jenna said. "Matthew it is and Matthew it will be. I will never address you with respect again, I promise."

"Deal." He solemnly put his free hand gently over Jenna's bandaged hand and the one of his she was still holding and gave all three an official shake.

"Okay, now that's settled –" His tone shifted from light to somber. "There is something else you need to know. Peter Malone is dead."

Multiple gasps came out as one.

"Heart attack, apparently. I don't have all the details yet, but don't worry, it's not gonna affect the DA's decision."

Jenna was stunned. "But – if I hadn't shot him, he'd still be alive. Doesn't that mean that I – killed him?" she murmured, completely bewildered.

"I haven't spoken with the medical examiner, but from what the DA himself told me, the s.o.b. was way overdue for a heart attack. It was just a matter of time, and not much from what Abe told me. You shot him, in self-defense. End of story. *Then* he died."

Jenna was at a loss for words. Even Scott, tastefully resisting a few bars of "Pray for the Dead," was at a loss for tunes.

"Jenna, you've got more than enough to grieve over. Do not – I repeat, do *not* waste one ounce of energy grieving over this bastard's death. Ten to one, what he did to you, he probably did to others or would have. You've avenged them as well as yourself, and perhaps spared others the ordeal you've survived – which they might *not* have survived. Please, comfort yourself with those thoughts."

Jenna nodded quietly. "Okay. Thank you, Matthew. That does help."

"Now, I'll tell you again, you just call me if there's anything I can ever do, I mean that. You get help dealing with all this and go on and live a very happy life. That's my wish for you." He bent down, kissed her on the forehead.

"Hmph. Where did that come from? Never did that before," the detective mused gruffly. "I must be going soft." He smiled at Scott and Linda. "Bye, folks."

"Soft enough to come see us sing?" Jenna said.

"Never know. Stranger things have happened…"

"If you're ever where we're performing, call and let me know. Be our guest, front row seats. It's the least I can do for you, Matthew. You've done so much for me."

"Will do, little lady," Caine said with wink and a two-fingered salute, and exited the room.

Scott came over to Jenna and perched on the arm of the couch behind her. "Little lady," he whispered in her ear. "That guy's got a crush on you."

Jenna looked up, the picture of innocence. "Cut that out. He's just a nice guy who cares. Cut him some slack."

"Slack, my grandmother's unmentionables. Call-Me-Matthew's got a little crush on you, 'little lady.'" He bent down and planted a big kiss right on top of Caine's little one.

KRISTIN CAME IN and offered Jenna an air kiss in the vicinity of her injured cheek. "How you doin', big sis?" she whispered. Scott was asleep sprawled across a lounge chair, his feet up on an ottoman. Jenna, a magazine open in her lap, had been looking off into space.

"I'm okay," she said wearily. "I'd love to sleep, but I'm hyper as hell. I can't get my fuckin' brain to shut down. If I close my eyes, it's like I'm nailed to a seat in a screening room and some sadist's running the projector."

"Want me to fill the prescription for whatever it was they gave you to help you sleep?" Kristin offered.

"Guess it *would* be a good idea," Jenna admitted. She'd assured Scott she could do without pills as they drove home.

"Guess you're human," Kristin said.

"Guess you're right," Jenna smiled sadly.

"It's okay, you know."

"I know. Doesn't mean I have to like it."

"There's a lot about life not to like," Kristin said quietly, sounding wise beyond her twenty-three years.

Jenna looked at her sister. "You've had a rough life, haven't you."

"Guess I've been around the block, a couple times – on foot," Kristin acknowledged.

"Deviant behavior in L.A.," Jenna pointed out.

"Precisely," said Kristin with a laugh. "Only way to go, though. What are you gonna learn from a car? Especially if you're the one drivin'?"

Jenna smiled. "So what words of advise do you have for a sad lady?"

"Want to talk about it?"

"I guess." Jenna looked over at Scott who, breathing heavily, was clearly sound asleep. "I've been thinking that I'd have a child almost your age, if they'd let nature take its course. What that'd be like. What it would have been like to be pregnant as a kid – that's a big one."

"Wow. Yeah," Kristin agreed. "I can't even imagine. Who would you be today?"

"Somebody totally else. It's exhausting to think about. It's so huge. What if it had been a girl. What if it had been a boy. What if it had been born with problems. What if it hadn't survived, for whatever reasons, but that I'd had to grow up knowing that. Or had been born and died. Oh, God, the possibilities are endless."

"You could make yourself crazy..." Kristin whispered.

"I know." She stopped, then sighed. "I've given it a name," she said ruefully. "I can't help it. A lot of names actually. Bradley James Christopher Scott if it had been a boy."

"Because…"

"James, Christopher and Scott you know. Bradley for Brad Pitt," Jenna said matter-of-factly with a smirk. "And Kristin Elizabeth McKenzie Fiona if it had been a girl. My grandmother's maiden name was Elizabeth McKenzie. I've just always loved the name Fiona."

"And what would Brad have been doing today?" Kristin asked.

"Premed."

"And Fiona?"

"Dancing. Ballet. Or maybe tap. Yeah, tap, but with a solid base in ballet. And she'd sing, and act. She's auditioning for a Broadway show tomorrow," she said, smiling poignantly. "It's a harmless daydream. It keeps my mind from going darker places."

"Did you name the baby you lost?" Kristin asked.

"Yes," Jenna said. "Tess." She shrugged her shoulders. "No reason. I just love the name." Tears started to seep from her eyes. "Damn," she whispered.

THE NEXT MORNING, after a much-needed deep and dreamless sleep, Jenna felt reasonably ready to contemplate the future. Over coffee in the study by themselves, Scott brought up the fact that he'd been talking with Jeremy about schedules.

"He's wicked concerned about finishing up the album, babe. Ben's been working with Dan and Jeremy on a couple of new songs, but they can only take them so far without me. Mark's got all the footage he needs from our last show but he still needs studio footage for those videos, so we need to schedule that, plus we have to work up the new songs strictly in-studio. We gotta get the album and the videos out before we hit the road. He's ridin' my ass. The timing's getting' tight."

"I know you need to get back. How about we go tomorrow? I want to get started on my therapy, get back to work and get on with our lives. What do you say?"

Scott wrapped his arms around her and gave her a kiss. "Baby Blue, you are one fuckin' incredible woman," he marveled. Sitting back, he dove into practicalities. "Which one of us is going to tell your family? You know they're expecting you to stay on for a while, and I gotta say, I'm not sure that's such a bad thing. Emotions are running high. They're – you're *all* still reeling from way more information about your dad and the things that happened to you than anyone should ever have to cope with, and it affects each and every one of you in such different ways. Maybe you should stay and try to help the rest of them, which could help you at the same time?"

Jenna frowned. "I thought you wanted me to go back with you. Are you saying you don't think I should come back now after all?"

"I'm just saying it might be for the best if you stayed on a little longer, that's all I'm sayin', babe."

Jenna went silent, then turned and eyed him closely. "You sure that's all, Scott?" she asked skeptically. She paused, then plunged on, her voice growing decidedly harsher. "You sure this isn't step one of letting Jenna down gently? Because if it is, please, let's get it out right now."

As Scott reached out for her hands, she pulled back from him. "Don't," she said sharply. "If you're going to tell me you don't want me back, just say it and get it over with, now. I'll just add it to the growing laundry list of issues I need to face and deal with it."

Scott was thunderstruck. "Damn it, Jenna, what on earth are you talking about? Of *course* I want you to come back with me. That hasn't changed one bit, and you of all people should know that. But see, that's what I'm talking about: the emotional end of all this. You've gotta be on one hell of an emotional rollercoaster right now. If you can say something as asinine as what you just said, then you're just not thinking clearly."

"You don't go tellin' me how I'm thinking, Scott Tenny," Jenna said heatedly. "You don't do my thinking for me."

"Honey, that's the last thing I want to do," Scott said, flailing in his attempt to understand the sudden turn in Jenna's mood. "All I'm saying is that if you were to stay out here a while, you and your family might be able to deal with some of the issues you all have in common, that you all might be the better for it. Just take a little time together and see how it goes. Calm down, please. Think."

Jenna went to speak again, then suddenly stopped, angrily pressed her lips tightly closed and sat shaking. She stared out to the patio, avoiding looking at Scott, but said nothing.

"Just think about it for a while," Scott said, more quietly now. "If you still want to come back now, we'll tell your family we're leaving tomorrow."

Jenna got to her feet gingerly. It would still be several days before she'd stop limping from the beating she'd received. Arms crossed angrily, she started a painful pacing of the room.

"Babe," Scott said gently, "I just don't think it's a good idea to be making any hasty decisions. Not when your moods are swingin' like a cage full of monkeys on meth. Don't you go thinkin' you're gonna lose me – lady, that ain't gonna happen. I've told you before and I'll tell you again: I love you, Jenna. You gotta believe that, babe, or else we're in big trouble."

Scott got to his feet. Without approaching her, he said, "I'm gonna go for a walk, maybe find my dad if he isn't holed up somewhere private with your mom, and get him to take a walk with me. You spend some time alone thinking. Okay?"

Jenna nodded sulkily.

"I'm here for you. Got that?" Jenna's nod in response was measurably less hostile. As satisfied as he could be under the circumstances, Scott left.

Jenna lay back down on the couch, covered her face with shaky hands and sighed deeply. Then she permitted herself to burst into tears.

SCOTT FOUND HIS father in the kitchen educating Adella.

"In New Hampshire, we'd simply call you 'one of them people from away.' Either you're from New Hampshire or you're not. People from Massachusetts, Maine *or* Mexico, them's just 'folks from away.' People whose families don't go back five generations: 'folks from away.' We're a little more discriminating about folks from southern New Hampshire – they're 'flatlandahs,' which is a whole 'nuther breed. We've got mountains where I'm from. Not big like the Rockies, but big enough for New Hampshire."

"You get lots of snow in New Hampshire, Meester Joe?"

"Let's just say I've got more miles on my snowblowah than on my cah, Miss Adella," Joe said cheerfully. "Why, last wintuh, I had to call Triple A when I got my snowblowah stuck on the roof."

"Goodness. You must get a lot of snow in New Hampshire!" Adella exclaimed.

Scott refilled his coffee cup and found a chair. Joe was clearly on a roll.

"Well, let's just say, the four seasons in New Hampshire are known as 'Almost Wintah,' 'Wintah,' 'Wintah Still' and 'Bad Sleddin'.' Summah takes place the second week of July."

"He's just pullin' your leg, Adella," Scott said, chuckling. Adella crossed her arms and gave Joe a cantankerous look.

"Nobody pulls Adella's leg," she said sternly. "Now, really, how much snow? Tell Adella the truth." Joe looked to Scott. He'd get no support from that quarter.

"Got more than two feet in one day, last March," Joe said honestly. "The wet and heavy kind. No fun shovelin', I can tell ya that."

"That's more like it," Scott affirmed with a grin. "Gotta watch my dad. He likes to overstate the case a little bit. Don't get me wrong. He doesn't lie. He just exaggerates."

"Mornin', son," Joe said.

"Mornin', Dad," Scott said. "Feel like a walk? Spare this poor woman more of your Yankee humor?"

"People used to pay good money to hear that Yankee humah."

"I know, Dad," Scott chuckled. "I could use a dose of it myself. Actually, what I'm after is a little Yankee wisdom."

"Ah, it's Yankee wisdom you want, is it? Now that's gonna cost ya. I give the humah away for free. Wisdom goes by the ounce."

"How much per," Scott said, indulging his old man.

"More than you can afford, son – but your credit's good."

"Well, ain't that a relief," Scott said, wiping a dry brow. "Grab a cup to go."

Joe filled his cup, then bowing, said, "We'll continue your Yankee tutorial latah, Miss Adella. Without the censor," he added, indicating Scott with his thumb.

13

"SO, WHAT MANNAH of wisdom are you lookin' for, son," Joe said as they hiked down the driveway out towards the access to trails that criss-crossed the steep hills between Coldwater Canyon and Mulholland Drive.

"Woman wisdom, Dad. Got any tips that might fit what Jenna's going through? I can't tell her what to do – she's make *that* clear, but that doesn't stop me from wanting to. How's her mom doing with it all?"

"She's not one to be shy about tellin' ya what she thinks, that's for sure," Joe said. "She's furious. She started takin' it out on me last night, as a matter of fact. Men in general. Can't blame her, of course. Didn't let her get away with it, though. All you can do is state your case. Clearly. How's Jenna doing?"

"She's fragile today. I thought with a good night's sleep, she'd be in better shape. It's like walking on eggs this morning. I can't say anything right."

"That's women for ya. Volatile as hell. They should come with those hazmat warning signs: 'contents under pressure.' But ya just gotta accept that. Love of a good woman's more than worth it, my boy. Ya loved many good women?"

"Thought I had, Dad. Turned out I never had, not till I met Jenna."

"Then ya just gotta grow another layer of armor, son. If the mother's any example, you're gonna need it."

"She wants to go back to Boston."

"Why shouldn't she?"

"I mean, tomorrow."

"That might not be a bad idea," Joe said after considering the angles. "Let her deal with her own problems. It's gonna be wicked confusing around here for a bit. Let the rest sort their own stuff out. Her's is different."

"Didn't think of it that way," Scott admitted. "You've got a point, old man."

"Ha! Hoped I'd live long enough to hear you say that. The 'you've got a point' part. Who you callin' an 'old man'?" Just to prove his point, Joe raced Scott to the top of the next promontory, and won.

Chapter 29

LYING ON THE couch, Jenna fell asleep, but had only been napping briefly when she was awakened yet again by another nightmare. Laying there shaking, she moaned, wrapped her arms around herself and moaned again.

This was the first time she'd found herself alone waking from a nightmare, which frightened her even more than ever. Trying to calm herself, she realized how much she'd come to count on Scott to steady her and help her back from the brink of darkness. The thought of him leaving her here terrified her. Tears flowed yet again, but this time for an entirely new reason.

A few minutes later, Scott came back in the study, came over and sat down on the edge of the couch by her. He pushed a lock of hair out of her eyes and looked down at her gravely.

"It happened again," he said, simply.

"How did you know?" Jenna asked.

"I heard you from the patio. Dad and your mom and I were sitting out there talking. I – I felt like I needed to know how you'd deal with it."

Jenna exploded. "Oh, good Christ. Now I'm your psychology experiment? You know damn well how I'd be without you. Was that entertaining? Did you enjoy that?"

"Baby, baby, no. No! I just wanted to make sure I was doing the right thing. I was actually in the middle of a conversation with Dad and Linda about whether you should stay on or head back."

"Oh, great, now a whole committee's making my plans for me?"

"What, I can't consult with experts?" Scott said, half teasing. "Look, your mom's pretty amazing – she'd love to have you stay, but she knows you'll be better off coming back with me, getting started with your therapy and not having to worry about them so much." Jenna seemed somewhat mollified by this information. "But her biggest concern was what just happened – how you'd react if you were alone when one of these things hit, and she's right. Look, just forgive me and we go home tomorrow. What do you say?"

Jenna ran her hands through her hair. "I'm sorry, hon. I'm really sorry. I guess I *am* a nervous wreck. Forgive *me*?"

She threw her arms around him and buried her head in his chest. He hugged her close. "Forgiveness all around," he whispered in her hair.

"Do you think we can get reservations on a flight tomorrow?" she asked, sitting back and drying her tears on the sleeve of his t-shirt.

"We've got 'em, babe. We were originally scheduled to fly back tomorrow. Other than the fact that your entire world's turned upside down since we got here, nothing's changed."

SCOTT AND JENNA went out to the patio to find Linda and Joe.

"So, what have you decided?" Linda asked Jenna.

"We're going back tomorrow, Mom," Jenna said. "I'd stay longer but –"

"Honey, you don't have to say another word. I understand. You're going to need someone sturdy to lean on for a while. Scott's more than qualified for the job," she said, smiling over at Scott. "These Tennys have broad shoulders. Hell, I've engaged a Tenny to perform the same service for me." Pointing to himself with his thumb like a proud school kid, Joe beamed. "Joe's going to stay on for a few days."

"For however long ya need me," Joe said solicitously.

"Do you feel up to a family supper?" Linda asked Jenna. "Shall I try to corral Chris?"

"That'd be great," Jenna said with genuine enthusiasm. "And Jim too." Scott, behind her, wrapped his arms around her.

"Jim and Sue both, right?" her mother asked, lifting her eyebrows pointedly.

"Sue," Jenna said, rolling her sister-in-law's name around on her tongue as if cautiously testing for tartness or, worse yet, mold or outright decay.

"Hey, maybe the new Jim will come complete with a new Sue. Stranger things have happened..." Linda suggested.

"I'll give her the benefit of the doubt," Jenna conceded. "I'm game."

Scott hugged Jenna close and bent to kiss her, which kept him busy as his father took Linda's hand for a quick, surreptitious squeeze and a wink.

"Dinner at seven," Linda said brusquely.

EVERYONE WAS ASSEMBLED in the library at before the clock could finish striking seven times.

Jim, the last to arrive, poured himself an inch of Scotch and made a big show of filling the rest of the tall glass with ice and soda. Sue, who'd come separately, smiled approvingly. "I'll have the same," she said pleasantly. Jenna shot her mother a look that carried with it a message of 'okay, maybe you're right.'

Linda smiled back. She was sitting in the chair that had sat vacant since Bob's death. Joe had taken a seat in the matching chair across from her, the one that had always been considered hers.

Chris was sitting on the couch on one side of Jenna with his arm around her. Scott sat on the other side, entirely pleased. Jenna, finally out of pajamas, was wearing a sleek purple silk lounging outfit Kristin had brought her.

Kristin, standing across the room, surveyed Jenna's outfit. "Not bad, big sis. Matches some of your bruises to a T," she said, nodding with approval.

"You've got a good eye," Jenna said with a smile. "I may have to put you to work on wardrobe."

"Sorry – too busy on my career," Kristin said with refreshing confidence. "I just found out I got a part in *Streetcar* at the Westwood Theatre." She tried to pass the remark off casually, but there was no question she was popping with excitement. "It's not Stella or Blanche, but it's all the rest of the females. It's a start."

"A start?" Linda exclaimed. "It's history in the making. Here, here for the beginning of a tremendous career! Another generation takes to the boards!" All toasted the vision of potential at its purest.

BY DINNER'S END, everyone was waxing philosophical. Linda got up, went over to stand behind Jenna and wrapped her in her arms. "A lot's happened here in the past few days that's changed all of our lives, but nobody's been more affected than Jenna," she said, hugging her daughter. "You've got the hardest row to hoe, honey, but you'll make it. You are easily the strongest woman I have ever had the pleasure of knowing." Linda reached down and gave her daughter a kiss. Jenna closed her eyes against fresh tears.

Reopening them, she looked up at her mother and then at the rest around the table. "I just have to say that I'm so grateful to you all. The past few days have been very difficult, for every one of us. I want to thank all of you for your help, your support and your love. I know with the help of one family here and a whole 'nuther one in Boston, I'm going to be okay." Looking across the table specifically at her older brother, she continued, "And, Jim, I just want to say to you in particular, that I am so looking forward to rebuilding our relationship. That means more to me than you can know." Smiling, she nodded at him. He returned her smile in kind.

Linda moved to stand behind her youngest in the next chair. "Chris," she said, giving him a hug, "you've always been labeled 'the baby of the family.' That doesn't begin to do justice to the role you play. You're the golden child, the pot at the end of the rainbow. You represent unconditional love. You provide solace to us all, especially Jenna." Jenna, nodding in appreciation and agreement, dropped her head on his shoulder where she left a small kiss.

Linda moved to stand behind Jim. "You, son, only have to heal from twenty years of guilt. If you can do everything else you do, you can do that, especially with a good woman at your side." Jim kissed his mother's hand and Sue smiled.

Hugging Kristin, she said, "Honey, you only have a few, selective memories of your father. Some of them are positive. I hope you can hang on to those. With everything that's happened, your feelings have to be quite confused. You must have a lot of thinking to do. Don't let it slow you down from your studies. You have a lifetime to come to terms with the man who was your father." Kristin smiled up at her gratefully.

Moving behind Scott, Linda squeezed both his shoulders, then massaged them as she spoke. "Scott Tenny. The day you showed up here, on the heels of – what was it, four dozen roses? – I knew you were something special. How special I hardly had a clue. You have broken down the walls of Jericho, my friend – you've brought Jenna out of a now entirely understandable self-exile, even before she knew where she was coming from. That's no mean feat! You've given her rock-solid love, a foundation on which she can now start building a sound, healthy life. And you've given her an extended East Coast family as well – and that means the world, too. You've brought so much into her life, and our lives as well, Scott."

"Not bad for a kid who was known far and wide as pretty much of a fuck-up," Joe said with a broad smile and a wink. "I think Scott knows how much I admire the man's he's grown up to be."

"Thanks, Dad," Scott said with a grimace that quickly morphed into a full on, shit-eating grin.

"And you, Joe Tenny," Linda continued her journey around the table. "You. Where would I be without you today?" she asked rhetorically. "I'll tell you where I'd be. I'd be hanging off the chandelier. I'd be hanging off something, and it scares me to think what that something might have been. You showed up just when I needed you most. How did you know?"

"Us Tennys have a long history of showin' up just at the right moment," Joe said, as much for his son's benefit as for his own, a remark that wasn't lost on Scott.

"The thought of what my daughter and son have had to go through," Linda said plainly, "the fact that my husband didn't tell me anything about it, the fact that I wasn't here. Each and every one of these things is hard to live with. But live with them I will, in the knowledge that you are all living with your individual part of the whole. I will take courage from your courage, strength from the strength you share with one another. We'll all be okay." Joe crossed his arms, reached up and took both her hands in his.

"And this is a woman of her word," Joe said, smiling up at her. "Where I come from, I'm known as a pretty fair judge of character. Or I'm known as a pretty good character – I can't remember which. Doesn't matter. I know a good woman when I see one, and this woman's good as they come. If I can help her in any way, I intend to. And if that helps any or all of you, well, I'm more than ready to take the credit."

LONG AFTER DINNER was over, after sitting out on the patio by themselves and talking quietly for the better part of a late hour, Jenna stood up. "I've gotta take a little walk, hon. Don't worry about me, okay?"

"Okay," Scott said.

"I'll be right back."

"Right back. Great, babe. I'll be in our room." No way she was getting out of his sight. Once she was far enough along the path down to the pool, Scott got up and followed her silently.

Jenna stepped from the overgrown vegetation onto the field of flagstone that surrounded the pool. Standing still, she took time to let the quiet of the night sort itself out into its many constituent parts. There was no such thing as silence within the city limits of Los Angeles. Palm fronds rustled high above. Yips of domestic dogs met yips of canyon coyotes, both equally restless under an almost full moon. The abrasive hum of the motors of hill-climbing cars met the pulsing hum of the motors of sky-climbing helicopters. The occasional screech of a barn owl riding the hot summer night winds in search of a midnight snack stood out in sharp contrast to the muted thrum of crickets in the underbrush and air conditioners in the house above.

Jenna took it all in as she stood there, the aural and the visual: fifty-foot palms swaying high above a dense understory of acacia and bougainvillea, ever-flowering hibiscus and gardenia. The opulent perfume of the jasmine vines growing up the trellised side of the pool house reached her nose.

She stood there, alone but not alone. Ghostly images arranged and rearranged themselves in the moonlight into momentarily frozen tableaus of memory. Learning to dog paddle with Hero, the family's big golden retriever, paddling faithfully beside her. She, Chris and Jim and a full complement of childhood friends staging comic swim competitions for an audience of appreciative and amused parents. Her father, practically falling backwards into the pool as he photographed her and her patient date the night of her senior prom.

But new old memories came barreling in to shove the old ones she'd always enjoyed off the stage of her mind's eye. Jenna was practically blinded by the klieg-light intensity with which these new memories now burned into her imagination's retina, and every tableau featured Peter Malone. Peter Malone approaching her, Peter Malone abusing her, Peter Malone forcing her to do repulsive, revolting things. Peter Malone afloat in a pool of his own blood, all but dead on the flagstone, soon to be dead in a hospital bed.

Scott watched from the shadows as Jenna finally walked over to the pool house, opened the door, hesitated for a long moment, then entered, pulling the door closed behind her.

Inside, Jenna waited for her eyes to adjust to the half-light. Finding her way to the bar along one side of the lounging area, she fished in a cubby for the box of matches that had always been kept there. Scott watched her light the stub of a candle on the bar. By the flickering light of the candle she turned and looked about her.

Two cushioned lounges, a pair of rattan swivel-rocker armchairs and a footstool, a few end tables and some bar stools pushed under the bar filled the most used part of the pool house. Flimsy rattan blinds covered the windows across the back of the room; French doors, which could be folded back to leave the entire facade open to the elements, formed the front wall.

How many wonderful minutes of how many wonderful days had she spent in this room? How many days and months – perhaps years, even – did all those minutes add up to? And how could the memories of one man's relatively few minutes in here ruin it all so easily?

It was the nature of those minutes, she knew, that made all the difference – those terrible, violent, invasive few minutes which had wreaked havoc on a childhood of trust and innocence, had sent her running into her teenage years angry, driven and fiercely autonomous.

Who would she have been had none of this ever happened? she wondered. A hand on her fractured cheek, she stood there shaking her head with the enormity of that line of speculation. How she yearned to know that alternate Jenna Bradford. How she hoped she could still meet up with her, somewhere down the road. Would she even recognize her, if she did? Would they have anything in common? Would the Jenna who'd been cheated of a calm and normal existence even speak to her? Would the Jenna-that-never-was hate her?

Almost unconsciously, Jenna turned back to the bar, opened a drawer and reached for the paring knife she knew she would find there. Catching the glint of it in the candlelight, Scott almost bolted from the shadows until he saw what she had in mind. Jenna raised the knife high above her, then brought it plunging down into the cushion of the nearer of the two lounges. Again and again, she repeated the motion, sending kapok filling flying in all directions. A brief, high-pitched wail escaped the closed room as Jenna attacked the cushion for the last time. Scott watched as, just as half-consciously as she had found the knife, Jenna returned it to its appointed place and destiny of cutting up nothing more than a few dozen lemons and limes a year. Then she turned and carefully blew out the candle, left the building and quietly closed the door behind her.

Scott pulled back behind the base of a tall palm. Jenna moved to stand over the blotches of Peter Malone's dried blood, dimly wondering if they could ever be eradicated from the flagstone on which they'd pooled.

How distinct, how separate are blood stains from the man, she thought. How amazing to think he'd left this behind here, blood his diseased heart would no longer be required to pump. It would have been replaced, of course, perhaps even as he traveled the same few miles she'd traveled, but for a brief while, had his heart had been grateful for a lightened load?

She thought of him at Cedars-Sinai, just down the hall from her, most probably, hooked up to an IV of fresh blood, blood that might one day have stained yet another floor, sidewalk or patio. No, he never would have walked free, even if he had recovered; Matthew Caine had assured her of that. He would never have bled again, unless someone had attacked him in prison – a pleasing thought to contemplate, indeed, which set Jenna's head nodding now, accompanied by the smallest of smiles. But of course, Peter Malone's days of leaving blood stains anywhere had come to an end that night, just two short nights before. Just two long nights before.

Then the thought of all she'd learned during the intervening days came crashing back down on her, as surely as her hand had brought the paring knife plunging down into the cushion in the pool house. The crushing weight of babies never born and fathers who never should have been trusted dropped her to her knees, atop the blood stains so black in the moonlight. Recoiling in horror, she skidded away from them into the side of a patio chair, which she threw herself against, then clung to as sobs overcame her and wracked her fragile frame.

Scott could no longer leave her to her grief. Emerging from the dark, he called her name as if he were just coming down the path, so as not to alarm her. She made no attempt to disguise her anguished state. He hunkered down and wrapped her gently, carefully in his arms. To his relief, she pulled his arms even tighter around herself and molded her body into his in search of comfort.

"Oh, God, Scott. I lost a baby. My own father ordered that baby be destroyed. I killed a man. I know it was in self-defense, but that doesn't change the fact that I shot a man. How am I going to live that? Not only did I do it but I know that I could do it again."

"Jenna, precious. Every one of us has the potential to kill. It's only a matter of circumstances and, honey, you had the circumstance. Come on. Let's get you out of here." He helped her up, helped her dry her tears and put his arm around her as they walked back up to the house. Very few lights showed in the windows, all the find-your-way-in-the-dark lights that Jenna knew from childhood, the lights you could always count on to be lit.

Quietly, they tried the French door into the study. The door opened. Obviously who ever had closed up for the night had assumed that the fact the room was in darkness meant that the door was locked as well.

"Come here, babe," Scott whispered, sitting down on and stretching out the length of the big leather couch. He reached an inviting hand up to her. She managed a smile and accepted his offer, snuggling into the sanctuary of his arms. Slowly she turned her aching body to meet his. His hands carefully explored her face, her lips, her hair, and his lips soon followed his hands. A sudden surge of unexpected, unbearable passion pushed all discomfort out of her mind as she arched her back and offered herself to both their needs.

JENNA, UP EARLY to pack, was interrupted by a knock at the door. At her invitation, Kristin poked her head in the door.

"No, no, come in," Jenna insisted.

"Scott told me you were packing. I've gotta run – class in an hour. But I wanted to say goodbye and tell you that I love you," Kristin said simply. "I know you'll be fine, with Scott and all them to help you in Boston."

"You've gotta come out and visit me, little sis," Jenna said warmly. "I mean it, the sooner the better. Maybe your next break?"

"I'll try. That'd be so cool."

"You can let me know," Jenna said, opening her arms to give Kristin a hug. "I want to show you Boston."

"I will. Take care. I love you," Kristin said, gave her a kiss, then dashed out the door.

Two minutes later, it was Linda at the door. "I don't know what's going on here!" she exclaimed. "The groundskeeper just came to tell me the pool house has been trashed! I'm going to have to call the police. Twice in the same week. What on earth is this world coming to?"

"Whoa, Mom. I'm sorry. That – was me," Jenna said, chagrinned.

Linda stopped, shocked. "What in the –"

"Sorry. I guess I let off a little steam last night. I went a little crazy. I owe you for a cushion. Can you forgive me?"

Linda came over and took Jenna's face in her hands. "Did it help, sweetheart?" she asked laughing.

"Probably not. I – I don't know where it came from and I don't know where it went when I stopped. It's still inside me, that much I do know," Jenna said, shaking her head.

"Maybe it's a good starting place for therapy. I'm just lucky you didn't take a shovel to the place and really destroy it. I very well might have." She looked Jenna in the eye, then wrapped her in her arms. Jenna returned the embrace.

"I'm gonna miss you, Mom," Jenna started.

"Hush. We'll talk every day, like you promised."

"I'll call. I will, I mean it."

"No, you'll get busy and there will be days you won't always be able to. I don't want you to worry about the days you can't. I just want you to know I'm here any time you need me."

"I know, Mom. Thanks. Thank you *so* much."

Just then Adella called from down the hall. "Jenna, telephone!"

"Be right there, Adella," Jenna called and went out in the hall to pick up an extension.

"So I have to hear it from Harvey who heard it from Esther? You get to town, you don't call now?" came the perennially cranky voice of Jenna's manager.

"And I gotta read it in the *paper*?" came the abrasive tones of her publicist, Bella Sutton, yelling over Brian's shoulder into a speaker phone. "I should be *puttin'* it in the paper, not readin' it there."

"Uh, it wasn't meant to be a photo op, guys," Jenna said evasively, not knowing how much they knew. "We just came out for a few days of like peace and quiet."

"You fly in for a quick weekend, kill a guy and think we don't need to be kept in the loop, honey?" Bella grated on. "Do I still work for you?"

"I was gonna call you from Boston, both of you," Jenna fibbed. Truth be told, neither her manager nor her publicist had entered her mind all weekend. "I – I didn't know it had gotten into the papers."

"Not page one, thank you, God," brayed Bella. "But wouldja mind tellin' me just what it is you'd like me to tell all the reporters I got on hold right now? The phone's lit up like friggin' Times Square."

"Tell them anything you want, Bella. You're good – that's what I pay you for. Make up whatever works, then call me in Boston and tell me what you said. Just don't tell them we're getting on a plane in an hour and a half."

"Oh, honey, don't be childish. They know *that*."

SCOTT AND JENNA wandered hand-in-hand down beyond the pool to the secluded little grotto at the furthest end of the property.

"The first time we came here, after my dad died, I was feeling sad, confused and upset. Here we are again, and I'm still feeling just as sad, confused and upset, for a whole different set of reasons, of course, but they're the same emotions, just multiplied by who knows what. It's just as well Mom's selling the place. Somehow the good memories don't outweigh the bad. I won't miss it."

Jenna sought comfort in Scott's arms for a few minutes. Then looking at her watch, she looked up at him. "Well, I guess as all the well-meaning therapists say, it's time to move on. Or in this case, time to run the gauntlet at LAX."

Scott chuckled. "Funny you should say that. There's something I forgot to tell you," he said with a secret smile.

"What?" Jenna demanded.

"Oh, just that Jeremy and I decided to name the tour the 'Movin' On Tour.'"

She took his hand in hers and they walked back to the house.

Chapter 30

THE L.A.-TO-BOSTON flight got in just before one a.m., Scott's long-proven approach to avoiding reporters. Georgie was there to meet them at the luggage carousel.

"Evenin', folks. Hope you had a pleasant weekend," he said with a finger to the peak of his chauffeur's cap. Jenna gave him a tired smile in response.

Georgie was old-school. He took his professional duties as seriously as any butler back in the balmiest days of the British Empire. Summer or winter, his three-piece uniform was never less than impeccably pressed. He reached for the first of Scott's aluminum Halliburton suitcases as it approached.

"And there's mine," Jenna said pointing to the Vuitton garment bag just falling onto the conveyor belt, easily distinguished by a band of day-glo yellow leather strapped to the handle. "Just the one, Georgie. Thanks."

BY THE TIME they'd walked in the door at Scott's, Jenna was wide awake.

"This is great," she groused. "Two in the morning. Now I'll never get to sleep."

"Come out on the patio. We can decompress out there," Scott suggested.

The chill in the night air sent Jenna back in for a sweater. When she returned, Scott was sitting on the porch swing, patting the empty spot beside him. "Just the cure for insomnia and jet-lag, babe," he said. She curled up next to him and his arm snaked around her. After a few moments, she dropped down into his lap and he rubbed her back as the swing glided back and forth, its chains in their eye-bolts emitting little rhythmic squeaks as it went.

"So – first order of business, call the therapist, I guess," Jenna said a bit grimly, resisting abandoning herself completely to the comfort of Scott's arms.

"The sooner the better," Scott said casually.

"That's easy for you to say," Jenna grumbled.

"The sooner you get it behind you, the better. I never said it was easy."

"I've been dragged to therapists all my life," Jenna graoned, "for one reason or another. I think they kept one on retainer. Of course, now I know a lot more about why…"

"Hell, me too. You ever been to one on your own volition, though?"

"No," Jenna sighed.

"It's different. Trust me. It couldn't be more different."

"I'll try and keep an open mind," was the best Jenna could offer.

"Start there. It's as good a place as any. Start with your history."

"Well, there goes eight weeks, right off the bat."

"You might want to do what I did with the last guy I saw. Start daily, to get the doc up to speed faster. It really helped."

"The whole thing makes me – nervous," Jenna admitted. "What a joke – I can sing for twenty thousand people. The idea of talking to one makes me nervous," she laughed, but her laugh had an edge to it.

"So sing your troubles to the shrink," Scott suggested in mock helpfulness, then tickled her till she begged for mercy. "Oh, it's mercy, you want?" he said with a sparkle of lust in his eye. "I'll give you a mercy and then some, baby. I'll take your mind off shrinks."

Scooping her up in his arms, he carried her up to the bedroom and dropped her unceremoniously on the bed. Clothing flew.

THE NEXT MORNING, Scott turned on the coffee, then flipped on the TV.

"… then, last but not least, Clinton met with Egyptian President Hosni Mubarak before slipping back into Washington quietly in the early morning hours today," the newscaster was saying. "And now to Kelli, who's covering the entertainment desk today. A couple of folks in the news were doing the same thing here, quietly slipping into Boston well after midnight last night, isn't that right, Kelli?"

"It certainly is, Kurt, and it was *late* last night. Arriving on a 12:45 a.m. flight from L.A., Boston's Scott Tenny and paramour Jenna Bradford managed to avoid the cameras, but not the eagle eyes of fans." The camera cut from the reporter to a stock photo of Jenna and Scott singing at the Garden. Moments later that image was replaced by a photo of Scott helping Jenna out of a wheelchair and into the Bradford limousine. "This is singer Jenna Bradford," the reporter continued as the camera zoomed in on the image, "two days ago, leaving Cedars-Sinai Hospital in Los Angeles after she reportedly killed a man."

Scott jabbed at the off button on the remote. "Oh for chrissakes, this is all we need," he moaned. He spun around and slammed the remote on the top of the television set. "Fuck!" he exploded. Both Jenna and Serena dropped what they were doing and came running to see what was the matter.

The phone rang and Serena answered it. Covering the receiver, she turned to Jenna. "It's someone named Bella, for you."

"Bella? Okay, I'll take it," Jenna said, surprised. "Damn. I told her I'd call her."

"No, *I'll* take it," Scott interrupted and reached for the phone, leaving Jenna looking perplexed. "Bella? Scott here. Is it on the air in L.A. too?"

"Sure is, babycakes, with a vengeance. Can I talk to your guy there?"

"Stanley? Sure. I'll clear it for you. You guys coordinate this mess, okay?"

"Got it, baby. You two just put it out of your heads. Stay in and stay away from the T.V. We'll keep the press from your door, best we can. You give Jenna a big fat smooch for me, hear?"

"Will do, Bella."

"And don't answer any phones till we tell you you can. Or at least have somebody screening your calls for you. I'll get back to you with whatever we cook up for the official story."

"Fine by me, hon. Hey, thanks," Scott said sincerely.

"Gotcha covered," replied Bella. "That's what I do."

Scott broke the connection, then speed-dialed his publicist. "Stan?"

"Expected your call," Stanley Havlik answered briskly.

"You heard, too?"

"Me and every entertainment harpy out there, my friend."

"Look, you and Bella just take care of this. I told her I'd tell you."

"You take care of yourselves. We'll take care of the rest," Stan said with a sigh. "Good thing we got ten days between this and the next show. People got such short attention spans, bless 'em, that even something like this'll be ancient history by next Saturday. I'll get back to you."

"Thanks, man," Scott said. "Later." He hung the phone up.

"Is anyone gonna tell me what in the *hell* is going on?" Jenna asked, slamming her fist on the counter in exasperation.

"Word on the street: you killed a guy."

Jenna closed her eyes, then sank to a stool by the counter. "It's in the news?" she asked quietly.

"I just saw it on TV," Scott said, coming over to rub her shoulders.

"Will this nightmare *ever* end, Scott?" Jenna moaned. "Tell me I'm still dreaming – hallucinating flashbacks, even. Anything'd have to be better than this."

Serena left the room and returned with the morning paper. "Guess you better see this too," she said. Scott took the front section she held out to him, glanced at the headline and hurled it across the room. Jenna got up to retrieve it.

"Oh, my God, that was taken just afterwards," she gasped, looking at the photo that accompanied the article. "That's gotta be one of the L.A.P.D. photos. Nobody else was around with a camera. I don't believe it." She held the page up to Scott.

The stark photo caught everything: Malone's body on the ground, plenty of blood and an entirely recognizable Jenna slumped over on the end of a chaise lounge, the pistol lying at her feet where she'd dropped it.

"How the fuck did they get that?" Scott roared. "Somebody handed that to the press. Or sold it, more likely."

Jenna fished a card out of the mini wallet she kept in her back pocket. "Give me the phone," she demanded. Scott handed it over to her. Furiously, her forefinger pounded the keypad ten times. She gritted her teeth while waiting for the phone to pick up on the other end, then punched three more digits as soon as the computerized answering system went into its exasperating spiel.

"Balerio," a man answered tersely.

"Lt. Caine," she spat at him. "Quick."

"And who shall I say is calling Lt. Caine?" asked the irritable Balerio.

"Jenna Bradford. I want to speak to him, and I want to speak to him *now*."

"Whoa up there, hon. He just came through the door. Give the man time to put down his coffee and his bag of–"

"Don't you 'hon' me, mister. Just put Caine on the phone."

The phone went silent for a moment, then Caine's voice came on. "Hey, Jenna. Calm down. What's got you going this morning?"

"Excuse me, you haven't seen the papers?" Jenna said.

"Somebody hand me the *Times*," she could hear him saying, followed by the rustle of the paper as Caine rifled through it. "Oh. Holy shit. I see why you're up in arms. How the hell did that happen?"

"That's what *I* want to know, Lt. Caine," Jenna said acidly. "Matthew," she added, her voice dripping sarcasm. "My good old friend who's gonna take care of everything. Right. Looks like you really took care of this, didn't you."

"Jenna, you better believe I'm gonna take care of whoever *did* this," he said in fury equally matched to hers. "They'll be lookin' for a job before lunch. I can promise you that." He slammed the phone down before she could even respond.

Mollified, Jenna placed the receiver back in its cradle, then turned back to Scott with a sigh. "Well, I guess there's nothing else we can do till Bella and Stan get back to us." She took a deep breath, held it as long as she could, then exhaled through pursed lips. Then she got up, rolled her head left to right and back again a couple of times to unknot the tension that had taken her hostage. Scott resumed his shoulder massage.

"Mornin', Baby Blue," he said, planting a kiss on the back of her neck.

"Mornin', hon," she echoed hollowly.

"Okay," he said, taking control. "Today's gonna be a totally down day. No phones, no visitors, no interruptions."

"I'm calling the therapist the Cedars guy gave me," Jenna said. "That's all I'm doin' today."

"Right, that call's allowed." Scott slid his lips to her ear and continued in a whisper for her benefit only. "But that's not all you're doin' today, babe. Not by one fuck hell of a long shot. Just you wait and see what Scott's got in mind for your day of R&R."

BY THE NEXT morning, Jenna was about as relaxed as anyone could possibly be – who'd been through what she'd been through, still had a throbbing fractured cheekbone, but had been treated like a princess for the better part of twenty-four hours. Bella and Stan had placated the press with the promise of a brief 5 p.m. end-of-the driveway press conference. "Just a three-line statement, hon," Bella had told Jenna. "Just 'I did it. It was self-defense. I wanna thank all my fans for their concern and support in this difficult yada yada yada' – you know what to say. You'll do just fine, Jenn. Here's a three-thousand-mile mwahh from the coast, sweetie." The phone resounded with the sound of one of Bella's boisterous kisses.

THE BAND ARRIVED by ten for a day of rehearsal. Carrie, who'd come along with Jeremy, headed for the house as the rest straggled over to the studio. Serena opened the back door. "Oh, hi, Carrie. Let me go get Jenna," she said.

"Tell her to meet me around back on the porch," Carrie suggested.

"Would you like some coffee?" Serena suggested.

"Sure, hon. Thanks," Carrie said.

Jenna found Carrie sitting on the edge of the porch, kicking at the tops of a stand of daylilies with her dangling feet. "Hi, sweetie. How are you?" she said. Carrie turned around. Jumping to her feet, she tried not to let her mouth drop.

"Kiddo. Oh, jeez, that has *gotta* hurt," she said, pulling Jenna to her in a sisterly hug. Jenna gingerly touched her cheek.

"Doctor said it'll take a couple weeks just for the swelling to go down completely."

"Guess you won't be able to sing for a while," Carrie sympathized.

"Well, not the next show, but I still have hopes for Albany. They said that's 'not entirely unrealistic.' Those were the doctor's words, for crying out loud. I love his positive take on things," Jenna groused. "I'm gonna sing Albany if it kills me. Let's go rehearse being brilliant members of the audience," she suggested with a nod of her head towards the studio. "I've never been very good at that."

"You're good at anything you do," Carrie disagreed. "You'll be just fine as a screaming fan."

Jenna got herself a cup of coffee and the two headed over to the barn. They walked into the cool of the studio, dropped themselves on the couch and put their feet up on a couple of sound monitors in front of them. A few bars into the second verse of "On the Floor," Tim, Jeff, Dan and Jeremy all acknowledged Jenna's appearance with nods and smiles as they sang and played. Scott blew her a kiss between verses. A moment later he blew a gasket.

"No! That sounds like fuckin' horse shit, Jeff," he screamed, ripping his earphones off and heaving them as far as their short cord would allow, a rather pathetic exercise in Jenna's eyes. "Absolute total fuckin' crap."

"It sounds fine," Jeremy countered, calmly. "You're the one who sounds like crap, my brother." Carrie braced herself for what she knew would come next.

"I know the fuck what I sound like, and I know the fuck what Aquino sounds like. You cut the bullshit and get honest here. Or do you need to have Mommy wash out your ears, my friend? May I suggest with battery acid, perhaps?"

"Go tell it to your sponsor," Jeremy suggested.

"Go tell it to *your* fuckin' sponsor," Scott retorted.

"Oh, Christ. Here they go again," Carrie moaned to Jenna. "You gotta wonder what they'd be like if they didn't fight all the time."

"God, it's so childish," Jenna agreed, closing her eyes and rubbing her temples. She might be rested, but not for this kind of baloney. "I've seen enough prima donnas in my day, but this is fuckin' ridiculous."

"It's all a pose, that's the joke. Same old shit, over and over and over. Guys. They're enough to fuckin' wear you out."

"Got that right," Jenna said, shaking her head as the noise escalated.

Scott suddenly flung a maraca at the wall and Carrie broke up in laughter. "Hell, gotta give him credit. That's reasonably original, at least."

Jenna started to laugh, but winced with the attendant pain. "Hey, cool sound," she yelled over Scott's din. "Maybe you could work it into the arrangement. Flying maracas. A little tricky on stage, but great in the studio." She and Carrie giggled like a pair of cheeky schoolgirls taunting a surly batch of guys at recess.

"Laugh all you want," Scott hissed. "This is serious."

"Oh, come on, kiddies, grow up," Jenna said with a motherly smile she found herself using more and more to defuse situations just like this one. "You're just wasting your energy," she scolded them. "Put it to work, you turkeys. You're the lucky ones – you can sing." Scott scowled back at her, but turned around and signaled Jeremy to take it from the top.

As they started back in singing, Jenna found herself nodding with the beat. Pretty soon her entire body was keeping time. A few notes escaped her as she experimented with singing with her cheek in the condition it was in.

"It's gotta be driving you nuts, not being able to sing," Carrie said quietly to Jenna as the guys settled back into work.

"A couple of sounds aren't too painful – oo's are okay, sounds that don't open the mouth. Not many songs written with just oo sounds, unfortunately."

"Guess you'll have to write your own," Carrie laughed.

"'*When you screwed a few new true blue stews from Peru, I knew the crew would sue.*' How's that?"

"A bit limiting."

"Just a little. Look, ya know what I really want to do with this time till I can work again? Can you keep a secret?"

Carrie nodded. "Of course. What?"

"Well, I started fiddling around with a song for Scott a while back. He's so been there for me, through this entire godawful mess. I recorded it a couple of weeks ago. It won't be released until my next album's finished – we're still a few songs away from being done with that, which is actually fine by me. I want a chance to surprise him and sing it for him at a concert before it's released. But I need to work it up with the guys. I can rehearse it without having to sing full-bore. I just don't know how to get Scott out of the way so we can get in a full rehearsal."

"Maybe suggest he go up to the lake and take care of the things he was saying he wanted to get finished up before the end of the season?"

"He already got someone to do that work."

"Too bad. Talk to Jer when they take a break. He'll think of something. He'll love it. I'll distract Scott for you," Carrie suggested.

"Great idea," Jenna said with a wink and a crooked half grin that was already becoming a habit. Carrie shook her head empathetically.

"You poor, poor thing," she said and gave her a hug.

Chapter 31

"So, Scott," Carrie said, falling behind to talk to him as they all headed back to the house for lunch. "You okay with everything? Jenna sure seems to be all right. God, she's one tough lady, man."

"You got that absolutely right, hon," Scott agreed. "I'm in constant awe of how tough she can be."

Carrie kept him preoccupied. He never got a chance to notice that Jeremy had stayed behind in the barn where Jenna had separated him from the rest of the band with the finesse of an old hand on a seasoned cutting horse.

"Jer, I need to talk to you," she said.

"Sure, babe. Shoot."

"I wrote a song for Scott," she explained.

"Cool. Nothin' like a kiss-and-tell-all love song, I always say," he said with a wink. "I assume it's X-rated?"

"You guys in the gutter," Jenna laughed. "It's sweet and touching and sensitive. You know, a waltz, a girl song." Jeremy groaned.

"So you want us to help you work it up?" he surmised.

"The real work's done. I laid down tracks for it last month, over at Red Light. The guys in L.A. did their thing out there. The whole thing came together really nice. We're using it on our next album. Grant Martin – you know Grant?" Jeremy nodded. "Grant did the mix. Philly and Brian are talking about releasing by early October." Philly Argo, Jenna's record producer, hailed from Philadelphia. His given name, he assured anyone who asked, was not worth knowing. His services were. He was the kind of guy who complained about dusting his full shelf of Grammys.

"So where do we fit in?" Jeremy asked.

"I really want to sing it for Scott, like publicly, before it's released. Which means the show at Great Woods – that's, of course, if you guys like it and want to do it," she hastened to add.

"You need to ask? You know we will. I don't have to poll the guys on that, Jenn," Jeremy assured her. Jenna smiled her appreciation.

"But first things first. We'd need to rehearse the damned thing. How the hell do I get Scott outta Dodge between now and then? The schedule's pretty crazy."

"Hmm…" Jeremy muttered, mulling the question. His face lit up as he snapped his fingers. "Oh, wait, this is too easy. Has he said anything to you about the fashion show that Laurel wanted him to go down to New York for on Friday?"

"No."

"I didn't think he'd tell you. He wasn't sure about leaving you. Last I heard, he hadn't given her an answer yet."

"She's modeling in it?"

"Yeah, and it's like a major coup for her or something. She's wicked excited about being in it."

"Jeez, he should go anyway. But if I don't know about it, how am I supposed to bring it up?" Jenna said with frustration.

"Just go along with me. I'll make it happen. Come on. We'll catch him before he finishes cooking. Get him when he's mellow." Jenna had to smile. Jeremy certainly had a handle on the many moods of his double-edged friend.

WHEN THEY WALKED in the kitchen, Scott was busily sautéing a huge skillet of onions and peppers to pile on the veal parm subs that were already lined up, assembled and waiting. Jeremy planted himself on a nearby stool.

"Hey, man, I gotta talk to you. I may have gotten you into trouble." Scott looked up sharply.

"Yeah? What now?"

"Well, like how come you haven't mentioned Laurel's fashion show to Jenna?" Jeremy asked. "I thought she knew about it. I'd say she's a little upset you didn't tell her. I'm really sorry, man."

"Aw, shit," Scott muttered.

"It's okay," Jenna said, stepping from behind Jeremy. "I'm cool with the idea, baby." Scott stopped what he was doing and smiled ruefully.

"Lemme take care of those. You go talk with your woman," Jeremy counseled.

"You be careful with them peppers, bro," Scott said, handing over the wooden spatula like a nervous master chef turning responsibility for the specialty of the house over to a new sous chef, "or you'll have me to answer to."

"Like I'm shakin'…" Jeremy laughed. "And if it helps you make up your mind, hell, go to New York on Friday and give the rest of us a fuckin' day without you. So we can get some work done for a change." Jeremy smirked, then took over at the stove.

"So, *why* didn't you tell me about Laurel's fashion show?" Jenna asked, taking him by the hand and leading him out to the little kitchen porch. "You don't have to be with me all the time, you know. I *can* manage by myself for a day or two." She perched herself on the porch railing, pulled him between her legs and slipped her arms around his waist.

"I know you can manage, babe," Scott said, coupling his hands behind her neck. "I just wasn't sure how much pain you'd still be in. I didn't want to leave you if it was too bad."

"The only real pain I have is when I laugh or eat. Or try to sing. I'd tell you if it were more than that, promise. Hell, if we can make love like we did last night…" She let the thought trail off seductively, then pulled him to her for quick kiss.

"I just wasn't sure yet, that's all," Scott said, reaching up and running his fingers through her silky hair. Then he returned her little kiss with long, slow, wet one. "You come first right now," he said finally, coming up for air. "I can't help it. That's just how it is, baby."

Jenna smiled. "I'd be crazy to argue with logic like that, hon – but we can discuss these things, decide stuff together. Right?"

"You're right. I didn't want to upset you by bringing it up yet, that's all."

"Call Laurel and tell her you'll be there. It'll give you time with Luka too."

LATER THAT AFTERNOON, Jenna sat nervously in the waiting room of the Cambridge therapist, looking out the window across the Charles River to the Back Bay skyline. Scott held her hand.

A few minutes later, Melanie Campbell appeared at the door to the inner office. "You must be Jenna," she said with a small smile. An attractive, physically fit woman in her forties, she put out a hand in welcome.

"Come in and make yourself comfortable." A love seat and several armchairs offered a number of possibilities. Jenna chose a comfy, overstuffed chair covered in corduroy. Melanie, black-haired and dressed head to toe in black, settled herself in a black suede club chair across from them. Jenna felt a little like Alice in Wonderland confronting the Cheshire cat.

"Let me tell you a little about myself, and then we'll talk about you," Melanie began. "I just want you to know a bit about my background. I have an M.S. in psychology and an M.S.W. – a Masters in Social Work – as well. I come to my work from both a clinical and a social perspective – I am equally interested in the diagnosis and treatment of psychological disorders and in an organizational, community-based approach to helping my clients function in the world. Call me Pollyanna with way too much education." She smiled self-effacingly.

"I've been in practice for fifteen years. My specialty is physical and sexual abuse. I was the victim of sexual abuse myself – it's what sent me in this direction. A really good therapist helped me put my life back together. I decided that's what I wanted to do with the life she gave back to me, to be able to help others. I also do volunteer work in women's shelters and sponsor events to raise money for them." She stopped, then smiled. "So – that's me. What brings you to see me, Jenna?"

"I was sexually abused and raped as a child, became pregnant, had an abortion and didn't know about it or begin to remember any of it till a few weeks ago," Jenna said matter-of-factly.

"Phew. That's a lot to process," Melanie said. "Any idea what triggered the memories?"

"It started as momentary flashbacks, bits and pieces of nightmares. I'm not sure why. Then we went out to California, to my Mom's, to see if there was anything in my past that might explain any of it. We found out everything I just told you. And then –" Jenna stopped and gulped. "And then I was attacked by the same man, the man who did it to me in the first place," Jenna explained and burst into tears.

Melanie passed her a box of Kleenex. "Is that how you got all those bruises?"

"Yeah. And – well, there's more. I shot the son of a bitch. I didn't kill him. But then he died, in the hospital, from a heart attack. They said it was overdue, that I didn't actually kill him. I – I hate thinking about it."

Melanie gave Jenna a few moments to calm down. "We have a lot of ground to cover," she said finally, nodding compassionately. "What I ask of you, Jenna, is that you be honest and open with me. Otherwise I can't help you. A man was with you out in the waiting room. Is he an important part of your life?"

"He certainly is. I love him more than anyone else in the world and I know he loves me. If it weren't for him, I don't know if I would be here right now."

"That's excellent, having someone in your life you can trust."

"Funny you should bring that up. Trust is a big issue with me. I rarely let myself get into situations where I have to trust others, count on others," Jenna said reflectively.

"No, trust is always a big issue for anyone who's suffered abuse. But you feel you can trust him…"

"He's different. He's special. He's just the best damned thing that's ever happened to me," Jenna responded without hesitation.

"And how old is the relationship?" Melanie asked.

"We've been together since last spring," Jenna answered.

"And has it all been smooth sailing, or have there been any problems, any major stressors, crises?"

Jenna grimaced, then started ticking events off on her hand. "Well, let's see. My dad died. I was pregnant by another man when Scott and I got together. I was in a bad auto accident in June and lost the baby. Then the flashbacks started." She moved on to her second hand. "Then I found out all that stuff about my childhood, was attacked and for all intents and purposes killed a man. You mean crises like those?"

"My God, dear," Melanie said, "You're off the charts for life stressors. We've got some serious work to do."

"Scott suggested doing what he did with a therapist a while back, coming daily till the background work was done. Would you be able to do that with me?" Jenna asked.

"Would you be willing?"

"Absolutely," Jenna said with conviction. "I feel like I'm treading water here. Scott's doing the best he can to help keep me afloat, but that shouldn't have to be his job. I just want to get on with my life. An hour a week's not going to get us very far."

"Well, once we get into the heavy lifting, an hour will provide you with a week's worth of work to do, but for now…"

She reached for an appointment book and ran a finger across the page. "Could you make it at 4:15 every day? I could make that work for a couple of weeks."

"That'd be excellent," Jenna said. "I gotta tell you, I was nervous as hell coming to see you. I can't believe how comfortable I'm feeling with you already. I really appreciate your help."

"This is enough for today. Go home and do something to pamper yourself. You've taken a big step just in coming," Melanie said, standing up. "Here's my card. I want you to know that I'm here if you need me. Call me if you're having problems. I can make myself available if you need to talk."

"Thank you," Jenna said simply. "Thank you *so* much." The two shook hands warmly.

Melanie walked Jenna out to the waiting room. Scott jumped to his feet and took Jenna's hand. "Melanie, I want you to meet Scott," Jenna said with a smile. "Scott Tenny, Melanie Campbell." The two shook hands.

"I'm very pleased to meet you," Scott said. "And I'm really pleased that Jenna will be getting the help she needs. I gotta tell you, it's been scary as hell. I was calling *my* therapist for advice," he said, rolling his eyes and shaking his head at the thought of what they been through in the last month "I was in *way* over my head. But we've gotten to the bottom of it, at least, and I want to do whatever I can to help Jenna get past it now. Thank you so much for your help."

"Scott, at some point I'll probably want to talk with you, too. Would you be agreeable to that?"

"Most definitely. Please, just ask."

Melanie turned to Jenna and nodded approvingly. "I can see why you love him."

IN THE CAR, Jenna was quiet. Scott turned to her as they waited for a light.

"It's a lot to think about, isn't it," Scott said. "Let's stop for coffee. I know a neat little place right around the corner. You'll love it."

"Yeah. That'd be nice," Jenna said with a long sigh. "I guess I'm feeling sorta whipped."

The light changed and he made a turn into a quiet side street. "Well, will you look at that? Parking right in front. Good omen. And it's late enough that the lunch crowd's gone. This is excellent." He pulled into the open space and came around to open her door. "Madam," he said, reaching for her hand and ushering her into the tiny bistro with a sign above the door that simply said just that – "Bistro."

"They do things with coffees here that'll make your head swim," he promised her, "and the pastries – the best, nothing short of it." He kissed his fingertips to illustrate his point. "You know sfogliatelles?" Jenna shook her head. "To die for."

"Inside or outside?" the hostess asked them.

"Inside," Scott said. "Away from the window, if you could."

The hostess sat them at a little table in a quiet alcove near the back.

"Perfect privacy. That's what I love about this place," Scott said. Taking her hand in his, he bent over, kissed it and smiled at her. "My little sfogliatelle."

"I'm going to have to try one of these whatever you call 'ems," Jenna said with a laugh.

"You won't regret it, babe. Trust me," Scott said confidently.

Jenna went serious. "We got into trust. Melanie said how important it is to have someone in your life you can trust. I told her I trust you. It got me thinking…" She went quiet again.

"You still here?" Scott finally said.

"Yeah, Oh, sorry. My thoughts keep straying."

"Don't worry. I don't take it personally," he said with a smile.

She smiled back. "I think everything's finally hitting me. Up till now I've had so much going on it's kept me distracted from thinking about it. I gotta tell you, dealing with the reality – well, it pretty much scares me like hell."

He took her hands again, put them together between his and kissed them.

"The first time's the roughest, babe. I still remember the first time I went to my therapist. Shit, I was shakin' in my boots – you shoulda seen me." He laughed ruefully. "I was a wreck. And this was *after* detox – you'd think that woulda been the worst." He shook his head at the memory. "Not like I'm the voice of reason or anything, but can I make a suggestion?"

"Sure. You *are* the voice of reason, Scott." He chuckled.

"I can pull off a passable impersonation once in a while. Other times…well, we just won't go there. What I wanted to say, though, seriously, is please just remember that I'm here for you when you do get scared. And I don't want you to think I'll get tired of you coming to me, either," he said in earnest. "I did that with Jeremy, thinking he didn't want to hear any more about it. In the end, all I did was make it worse for myself. Just know that I want to help. Don't make the mistake I did by shutting down because you think you're becoming a bore or, worse yet, a burden."

Jenna, listening intently, started nodding and ended up with a smile on her face. As the waitress set their cappuccinos and sfogliatelles in front of them, Jenna looked Scott in the eye. "I'm the luckiest woman in the world. I promise I won't stop talking and I won't stop loving you." She looked down, then looked back at him and took his hand. "Thank you. For being you and for loving me."

Chapter 32

"YOU HAVE A great time with Laurel and give her my love," Jenna said. "Call me when you get there and let me know if you decide to stay overnight. Now, kiss me quick and get out of here."

Scott chose to totally ignored her. Taking her in his arms, he allowed himself to sink to the depths of her soul before releasing her. "Tootle-oo, Baby Blue," he said with a wink and a loopy smile, picked up his small suitcase, then sauntered out the door to leave for the airport.

JENNA WAS ALREADY in the studio when the guys arrived to start rehearsal. Jeremy had filled them in on what Jenna had in mind.

"I've got an idea on how we can pull it off without Scott figuring out what's comin' down until the last minute," Jeremy said with a smirk.

"Lay it on," Tim said, reaching for his Thermos of coffee.

"I second the motion," Jeff chimed in.

"Okay. Second set. Scott sings the first song. When he's done, Dan makes sure he's as far on the other side of the stage from Scott as he can be without going off stage altogether and then he goes something like, 'whoa, guys, something's missing' – but sorta the way Scott would if he was starting to get pissed. He asks the rest of us if we agree. We all jump in, getting pissy too. Then he asks the crowd and we get Bruce to throw a giant 'YES' up on the screen and they all start screeching. Dan keeps baiting Scott, so of course, by this time Scott's ready to kill him –"

"Uh, Jeremy, does it *have* to be me?" Dan asked.

"Won't work without you, bro. Stay with me here – this works. Okay, you're keeping three paces ahead of him – whatever it takes to stay outta his way until Jenna's in position. You say something to him like, 'uh, bro…' and point to her. Bruce hits her with a spot. The audience goes nuts. Scott's totally dumbstruck. You get to live another day. Jenna sings her song. Bada bing bada boom. Whaddya think?"

"You fuckin' *nailed* it, man," Jeff said with a wicked grin. "Poor Dan. We better spend as much time rehearsing the set up as we do the song. Talk about playing matador to Scott's mad bull."

"I'll play decoy if we need it – we'll watch your back, Dan," Jeremy assured him. Raising his right hand, he said solemnly, "I hereby swear that no guitar players will be hurt in the pulling off of this little stunt."

JENNA'S CHEEK WAS throbbing by the end of two hours of work. Jeremy called a break.

"You sure this is a good idea?" he asked her as she threw herself on the couch and covered half her face with an ice pack.

"Don't you worry about me, hon. A little crack in the skull ain't gonna slow ol' Jenna down," she said with a half grin. "We just have to make the most of today. I gotta tell you, I'm lovin' what you guys are doing with it. You're all just so damned great to work with. I'll have a week to nurse my damned cheek. It'll be fine."

Tim wandered over and straddled the arm of the couch. "That song's like optimo – no, optissimo – in my book, Jenn. It's not totally there yet, but we'll pull it off. It's the best. Scott's gonna be blown off the fuckin' map."

"And considering that you were barely singing your part," Jeff added, "God, when you get to work beltin' this thing the way you do, man, it'll be off the charts."

Dan agreed. "I love the rollercoaster feel to the chord progressions, up to the top and then droppin' the way it does. Reminds me a little of something Golden Earring did – I can't think which. I just know I was feeling like Cesar Zuiderwijk for a moment there."

"I thought Jeremy was bullshittin' when he said it was a waltz," Tim laughed, shaking his head. "They're gonna have to come up with a whole new genre for this thing – hard rock waltz? Heavy waltz?"

"Balls waltz," Dan volunteered.

"Back to work, guys," Jenna ordered and started to get up. Just then her cell phone rang. She checked who was calling, put a finger to her lips for silence, then answered it.

"Hi, sweetie," she said cheerfully. "You there?"

"I'm at Laurel's," Scott said, "and I miss you something fierce, woman."

"Good," Jenna purred. "I miss you too."

"You okay?"

"Oh, yeah. I'm just stretched out on the couch. Watching soap operas and eating bonbons. Taking it easy, just like you told me to, hon." She threw a wink at Jeremy.

"Did the guys come over to rehearse some more today?"

"I – haven't been over there. Let's see – oh, yeah, I see cars. Yeah, they must be working."

"Go over and tell them I changed my mind about the last verse of "On the Floor" – I want it back the way we played it at the Garden. Tell Jeff –"

"No, you tell Jeff yourself, when you get back. You aren't dragging me into any of your little games."

"Okay, okay. I get the message. You about ready to drive into Cambridge?"

"In a bit. Have to finish all the bonbons first."

"I love you, babe."

"I love you too. You have fun. Give everyone my love." She gave him a telephonic smooch and rang off. As she clicked her cell phone shut, everyone cracked up.

JENNA GOT BACK home from Cambridge and some shopping to find a note on the counter from Serena. "Supper's in the fridge," it read. Pouring herself a glass of wine, she took her meal out onto the porch to eat.

A brisk wind had kicked up a chop across the surface of the Atlantic stretching out before her. The low rays of the early evening sun caught the topmost curl of each tiny wavelet, causing the sea to glitter brilliantly. "Sea bling," she whispered to herself with delight, marveling at the sheer beauty of the moment. She soaked in the solitude and silence, then realized that there was no silence. A quiet medley of natural background music filled the air. The distant sound of surf underscored the late summer hum of crickets warming up for a night of chirping syncopation. Birds competed with one another for her attention. A dog barked in the distance. Another dog answered his call. A high steady hissing of cicadas rose above all. Regardless of all her troubles and pain, Jenna could still register the commonplace, everyday magnificence about her.

AFTER SUPPER, JENNA called her mother.

"Hi, doll," Linda said with genuine pleasure. "So you're home alone?"

"And loving it, Mom," Jenna assured her. "It's a beautiful night. I'm out on the porch. It couldn't be more beautiful."

"You sound good," Linda said.

"I am. I saw the therapist again today. I really like her. It feels good walking in. It feels good walking out. That's all I can tell you so far."

"Jim's talking about seeing someone. That's a big step for him."

"Good," Jenna said. "I hope he does."

"And Kristin's started with someone. She asked me if I'd be willing to go in with her after a while."

"That's excellent, Mom. You and she are developing such a nice relationship. It's so amazing," Jenna said.

"It sure is," Linda agreed. "She's got so much of her own baggage, not to mention everything she suddenly inherited from all of us. Actually, she was sounding a bit confused about school yesterday. She's not sure U.S.C.'s really for her, that maybe she jumped in without doing enough research first. I told her nothing's set in stone here. She seemed quite relieved that I wasn't critical of her questioning what she was doing."

"I respect her for taking a second look," Jenna said, nodding. "To suddenly have the world open up for her like it did – that's gotta be wicked confusing, especially at such a young age."

"She's here. Do you want to talk to her?" Linda asked.

"Sure. Put her on," Jenna said. In a moment, Kristin's voice came through the phone.

"How are you, big sis?" she asked, putting an immediate smile on Jenna's lips.

"I'm doing good, little sis. Mom says you're not sure about school after all?" Jenna believed in getting straight to the point.

"I've got second thoughts," Kristin said simply.

"All I can suggest is to keep an open mind. Hey, look, Mom's coming out here early next month. Why don't you come with her?"

"Not a bad idea," Kristin said noncommittally.

"I wanted to show you the place. Maybe you should be taking a serious look at Boston. There's *so* much going on here."

"You with the Chamber of Commerce or something?" Kristin laughed.

"I'm serious."

"I know you are, and I appreciate it. Maybe I will."

"Do. Come," Jenna insisted. "Even if it's just for a weekend. Plan it"

"I'll let you know."

JENNA SAT MESMERIZED by the moon as it rose before her, golden from the sea. Nocturnal noises seemed to increase with every hour, as did the wind. Trees were whipping in earnest now, as luminescent clouds tore across the starry night sky. Laying back on the lounge, she breathed deeply of the sea air. Allowing shadows and solitude to envelop her in their warm, dark cloak, her eyelids fluttered and she found herself dozing for a few moments, startled awake briefly, sighed and then fell into a deep and peaceful sleep.

THE NEXT THING Jenna knew, the moon was high overhead. Something – a noise – had disturbed her slumber. It came again, footsteps on the gravel drive. A security light flashed on. Jenna's heart jumped, and so did she.

The night had turned silent – except for the relentless crunch of approaching footsteps. Her heart pounded; her palms turned clammy. The sound continued to draw nearer. Then it stopped.

Frozen with fear, Jenna heard a door open, then saw the glow from the mudroom light stream out across the lawn, beyond the reach of the security light. Silently, she turned towards the kitchen in time to see a light go on in there as well. Then Scott moved into her field of vision.

She ran in from the porch. "Oh, my God, Scott! You scared the fuckin' hell out of me," she said furiously. "You said you weren't coming home till tomorrow."

Scott grabbed her and held her tight. "Oh, baby. I'm so sorry. I parked down on the street. I thought you'd be upstairs sound asleep – I just didn't want to wake you. I got to talking with Laurel about how this was the first time you'd be here alone at night, and I guess I worked myself up into a state. I ended up calling a buddy of mine who's got a plane and asked him if he'd fly up here so I could be with you, you know, just in case…"

The thought trailed off as he realized just how badly he'd frightened the woman he loved. "Shit. Look what I've done to you. Baby, can you forgive me?"

"Honestly, I don't know whether I should thank you or kill you," Jenna growled.

"Personally, I'd prefer the thanks," Scott said, "but you feel free to take all night making me make it up to you, babe."

Chapter 33

SCOTT AND JENNA slept in the next morning, waking late and rising luxuriously slowly, complete with breakfast in bed.

"This could be habit forming," Jenna sighed.

"Don't tell anyone, especially that Jenna person, but it'd drive me fuckin'nuts," Scott confided with a chuckle. "Okay, once in a blue moon, but man, I'm waaay to hyper to do indolence on a regular basis – idleness ain't in my vocabulary, sorry."

Jenna laughed. "No, you're right. It'd get old, fast." She turned and snuggled into his open arms. "Especially the sex…"

Scott ran his hands down her spectacular body and his lips over the curve of her bounteous breast.

"It's okay, honey. I understand …" Jenna went on, her voice slowing to a hypnotic crawl that matched the pace of her hands as they traveled up his legs. "… that'd bore you to tears … the repetition of it all … the monotony … the same ol' same ol'…"

Her voice caught as his tongue circled about a nipple, slowly, maddeningly making its way to the apex.

"… business the fuck as usual… nothing new under the –" She never got to finish the thought.

SCOTT WAS LAZILY telling Jenna about his day in New York as the clock struck ten.

"You shoulda seen her. What a vision that daughter of mine is," he marveled. "The runway was fuckin' *invented* for her. They can hang anything on her and it looks like it was made for her and her alone. It's absolutely amazing."

"Proud papa," Jenna smiled, running her finger in and out of the little dents and crags that formed the rugged typography of his face.

"And that Luka – oh my God, he's more of a character every time I get to see him," he went on, reinforcing every thought with a gesture. "He's talking a blue streak – well not as blue as his grampa. But verbal – cripes, he can talk circles around me. He's got something to say about everything. You can't make half of it out, but that's okay. He's gonna be one hell of a talker … sales, a front man, the guy who's out there. Damn, I love that kid."

The look on his face made Jenna laugh, but the laugh was cut short as a sharp twinge of pain coursed through her cheek. Her hand flew up to sooth it reflexively.

"Ow, that hurts. No more laughing for me today," Jenna said, forcing her mouth into a frown.

"Lemme kiss it and make it all better," Scott said, offering pursed lips.

"Mmmm … that *does* make it all better," Jenna murmured.

"How do you put up with me?" he asked, seemingly out of the blue. Jenna looked up at him, puzzled, needing to read his expression to decide if he was kidding or serious. His face said the latter.

"You mean that, don't you," she stated quietly.

"Yeah. No. I guess what I'm saying is that you don't have a clue how much more there is to put up with – and will you want to? That's what I'm really asking. But you can't know so you can't say, either. Damn, I love you, babe. So much it scares me shitless. "

"And I love you, and I'm just as scared," Jenna said softly. "Scott – tell me about your wives," she said tentatively. "I mean, if you want to…"

"No, that's okay. I loved them. I can say that. Actually, I can say I've loved every woman I've ever been involved with, on a certain level. I've been totally committed to each and every one of them."

Jenna smothered a laugh, then had to cradle her cheek again. "Come on, I told you, this thing really hurts. No fair!"

"I'm not trying to be funny – hey, I'm barin' my soul here, woman. How about a little respect?"

Jenna struggled to recompose her amused face into a look as sober as a judge. The effect was comical in itself. Now Scott was laughing.

"No, really," he insisted. "I'm a totally monogamous. Okay, I'm a serial monogamist. One woman at a time only, no cheating. The next one may be waiting in the wings, I'll admit to that, but that's as much because of the lifestyle, you know what I mean. They're always waitin' in the wings. I only act on it when I'm not involved. When I'm involved, I'm totally involved."

He rolled over on his back, folding his arms behind his head, and looked at the ceiling. "But I can be such a shit, Jenn. God, I hate doing it, but I do. I try to control it – I've invested a fortune in trying to learn how to control it. I beg and bargain with the ol' Higher Power to control it." He rolled back to face her.

"You know why I'm such a shit with the guys?"

"Why?"

"To get it out of my fucked up system. So, with luck, I don't have any left to take home with me. Cuz it's screwed up every relationship I've ever had, sooner or later. And, God, Jenna, I do *not* want that to happen with you." She reached up and touched his cheek. He slid his lips over to kiss her fingertips.

"Both of my wives put up with it till they couldn't take anymore. My first wife – well, if you must know – I finally found her in bed with another man." He went silent, his jaw clenching and unclenching beneath Jenna's fingertips. "Never saw that coming. I'd thought that marriage was fuckin' forever."

"How long were you married?" Jenna asked quietly.

"Twelve years. Missy was the glue that held us together for seven or more of those years."

"But it ended because you found her in bed with another guy?"

"No. She was in bed with another guy because of the drugs and my raging temper. It ended because of – the drugs and my fuckin' temper. It's taken a long time to be able to accept that. I was responsible for her screwin' around. It was my fault. That was no home." He blew out a lungful of air.

"Number two?" he continued, "Well, I don't know. It wasn't drugs anymore, at least, but the temper was still there. But, under it all, something was missing. I finally just gave up trying to make it work. She's sorta in the same place. It just sputtered to an end."

He took her face in his hands. "And then I found you. And now I know what was missing. And now I have to dread fucking it up, like every single minute of every single day."

SCOTT WAS BUSY exercising his famous temper as Jenna threaded her way through the Albany Pepsi Arena's tight backstage security in search of his dress-ing room, flashing her pass numerous times before arriving at the right door. Just as she reached for it, Jeremy came out, the echo of Scott's "...go fuck yourself!" trailing behind him.

"I'd be wicked careful goin' in there if I were you, my friend," he warned her, putting a hand on her forearm. "Our boy's in the middle of a Category 5 meltdown in there."

"Because...?"

"Because something wasn't on the tray in the fuckin' green room. Don't ask me what – I couldn't understand more than ten percent of the noise hewas spewing. Who the fuck gives a shit. Green room food's fuckin' green room food, and that's just how it is, for chrissakes. I'm sure they tried. His list gets fuckin' ridiculous. In Kalamazoo or somewhere the hell 'n back, he went ballistic because they didn't have any Napoli salami – they got some other kinda salami – and it was good, nothin' wrong with it at all. But, no, I had to hear about that friggin' *Napoli* salami for a the next two thousand miles, for the love of God. In San Francisco, he wants Cincinnati chili. In Cincinnati, it's gotta be beignets. Beignets, as I'm sure you know, you only find in New Orleans. "

Jenna grimaced. One of Scott's rants suddenly rang to the rafters. They could hear him just fine in the hallway.

"Thanks for the warning," she said with a feeble smile, then turned, squared her shoulders, knocked and walked in.

"No! I could care the fuck less," Scott was screaming. "I told you. Read my –"

He stopped short when he saw Jenna at the door. She did not look amused. "Uh – hi, babe," he choked. "Um ... hell, sorry."

As she stood there looking at him, her hands moved unconsciously to her hips. "Fuck, if looks could kill I'd be six feet under right now," he said meekly.

"Scott, I'm getting tired of people warning me to watch out, that you're on the warpath. For some reason, you seem to pride yourself on being such a spoiled, arrogant pain in the ass," Jenna said acidly. "Just because some insignificant little thing you had your heart set on wasn't available, you have to throw a tantrum, and go ruin everyone else's day in the process. Where on the planet do you get off, anyway?"

Jenna stopped and stared at him. She thought about what she really needed to say, choosing her words carefully. "Look, Scott, the last thing I want to do is tell you what to do. I'm not your mommy and I don't want to *be* your mommy. This is simply a suggestion: get over whatever it is that's eatin' you, and then go and apologize to each and every person who's gotten a dose of tonight's bullshit. I'll see you later."

She turned without waiting for an answer and slammed out of the room.

JENNA WENT INTO the audience and took the front-row seat that Carrie had saved her. Dan's Jill gave her a hug hello; Denise and Paula both reached over and gave her warm squeezes as well. This was the first she'd seen any of them since her trip to California and all the troubles that had pursued her back east.

Just as Blacklace was about to take the stage, one of the roadies came out, pressed a folded-up piece of paper into Jenna's hand, then dashed backstage again. Jenna was just unfolding it as Tim, Jeff and Dan came loping onstage to a cheer of approval from their impatient fans

"Forgive me, Baby Blue," it read. "I found every last person I pissed off tonight and apologized to them. I told the opening band to throw in an extra song so I'd have time to get to the last 27. I love you. S." A penciled heart encircled the entire sentiment.

She'd read it by the time he and Jeremy came striding out together. Scott had an arm around Jeremy's shoulders and a grin on his face. Both waved at the audience, but Scott's eyes went straight to Jenna's. She smiled back at him, and mouthed the words, "I love you." He blew her a kiss, then went to work. The house went wild. He certainly didn't let anyone in the audience know, but he played the entire show to her and her alone.

THE CONCERT WAS roaring right up to the arena's 11:00 p.m. union-enforced curfew. Just as Scott was about to introduce the band's last encore, he growled into the mike, "Hey, before we go, people, let's everyone put it together for my beautiful lady – Jenna B."

The place exploded as a spotlight pinpointed her for 17,000 fans to see. Jenna was completely taken by surprise; Carrie had to push her to her feet. With the most genuine of grins, she waved all around her as Scott continued, "I know I speak for Jenna when I tell you she sure wishes she coulda performed for you tonight. I knows she's just glad as hell she could be here in Albany at all." The crowd joined as one in roaring their appreciation and understanding as she nodded at each of his words and blew them all kisses.

After the show, Scott begged off the usual quick dinner out for the entire band and its extended family. "Jenna's tired," he told them and she couldn't deny it. "I'm having someone call over to the hotel and have room service send something up for us by the time we get there." It had been a long, emotional day. The recuperative powers of the human body amazed her, but her usually bottomless reserve of energy still had a way to go before it had completely replenished itself.

After a midnight snack. Scott and Jenna stood at the window of their 15th floor suite overlooking all of Albany. Scott held her in his arms.

"I really am sorry about earlier," he said to her. "I feel like such an ass. I know I lose my temper some times – but, damn it, they could have tried harder to find what I wanted."

Jenna sagged, then turned to face him. "Oh, Christ. Scott, do you even hear yourself? You're still acting like a brat. Please, explain it to me – maybe it's me. Maybe I'm just stupid. What precisely is the big deal about not being able to have everything you want, when you want it? It happens – that's life. Did you grow up with such deprivation that your entire childhood comes crashing down on your or something?"

"No," he said, hanging his head.

"Then what in the hell is it?"

"I – I don't know, Jenna. Honest to God, I just don't know. I come fuckin' unglued."

"So 'I come fuckin' unglued' gives you license to treat people like dirt? What are you, some kind of spoiled nobleman's brat who gets his every whim or off with their heads? Where *do* you get off?"

"Hell, baby, I wish I knew. It just – happens."

"You act like you're some innocent bystander standing on the sidewalk watching your own life's parade go sailing by. It doesn't 'just happen.' You *let* it happen. But you have no *right* to let it happen. Nobody does. God, listen to me. No – scratch that. Here I am again, trying to tell you what to do, not that you'd listen anyway. What am I thinking? I'm going to bed. It's been along day. I'm tired."

"Baby, you're absolutely right. I *am* spoiled. I never said I was perfect. I'll try not to lose my temper next time. I –"

"And whatever you do, don't think an eleventh hour apology's gonna earn you any action in the sack tonight, brother." Jenna went into the bathroom and slammed the door.

IN THE MORNING Scott tried not to wake her, but the sound of the shower woke her up, regardless. Scott came back into the bedroom.

"Morning, babe," he said with seemingly offhand nonchalance. "Sleep okay?"

"Mmm," she said, stretching. She laid back on her pillow watching him step into a tiny pair of shiny black briefs. "Man, you're in great shape for a guy of forty-five," she said with a sleepy smile.

"You think so?" he replied. Making faces, he went through a series of cartoon-like body builder poses, one sillier looking than the next. She started to giggle, but it was true what she'd said. He kept himself hard, trim and muscular, working out religiously. He looked far younger than his years.

"It's no wonder the girls drool when they see you on stage without your shirt," she said. He came over and sat next to her on the bed.

"Yeah? Do I make you drool, baby?"

She ran her hands up his chest and down his arms. "You sure do," she said. "Me and a million screaming fans. It gets a bit messy actually."

"I do have a pretty sizeable fan base, don't I," he said, teasing her.

"That's not your fault. They can't help it. You're – well, I might as well tell you this. You're incredibly sexy."

"I am?!" he said, his eyes going wide in mock surprise. "No! Sexy? You gotta be shittin' me."

"No, I mean it. Yeah, I mean, hell, I've been around the block a time or two. I don't like to admit that, but I have, actually," she said, "and I've gotta say, I do know sexy when I see it, and – well, yeah, you are. You're one sexy dude," she said nodding sagely. "It's actually entirely understandable why all those girls act the way they do, especially when you take off your shirt." Her fingertips traced along the valleys that helped define the mountain ranges of his muscles.

He was grinning now. "Babycakes, they may be drooling, but you're the only one I want." He bent down and kissed her. "Hold that thought," he said suddenly. He jumped up and went to his suitcase. Fishing around the side pockets, he retrieved an envelope and brought it over to her. "A little present for my girl."

"What is this?"

He shook his head. "You gotta open it to find out."

She sat up and opened the envelope as he looked on. Drawing out the document inside, she gasped.

"Oh my God, you're divorced? It came through?" She started to throw her arms around him, then stopped.

"I don't quite know what the proper response is when someone's divorce becomes final. I mean, it feels like it should be a celebration, but at the same time, it's – it's a sad thing, the end of a marriage. Any marriage. It's gotta hurt."

He demurred. "Well, yes and no. I can't say I'm hurt. It was over a long time ago. But, your right – it *is* sad. I mean, you love and share things with someone for a long time. Then –" He snapped his fingers. "– it's over. It's emotional, no matter what. But – I have you now. You, my dear lady, are what I want. And I want so much to get it right this time. I mean that, babe. Please, please have patience with me. Don't give up on me. Keep giving me hell. I mean it, I know I deserve every bit of it. Help me make it work for us, babe."

Chapter 34

"GREAT, HON. TOMORROW, the corner of Newbury and Clarendon at eleven," Jenna told Carrie. "That gives us time to do a couple of shops before lunch. See you there, kiddo. And seriously, thanks for your help."

"Help, schmelp. It'll be fun," Carrie said enthusiastically.

"Looking at myself in mirrors doesn't feel like fun right now, to tell you the truth," Jenna confided.

"You're looking better every day, sweetie," Carrie said honestly. "But I know it's gotta be hard."

"I can't wait till there are no more visible reminders. God knows I've got more than enough invisible ones. Every time I catch a glimpse of my big fat purple cheek, I feel that gun connecting with it and my brain's off and running and won't rest till I've rerun the whole damned thing to the point where somebody put a blanket, or whatever it was, around me. So I don't look. But – I want something new to wear and new to wear means trying on stuff, and trying on stuff means mirrors. I'll deal with it," she sighed.

"You'll deal with it just fine," Carrie assured her. "You know what? If you can't, then we can just get them to let you take a bunch of stuff home to try on there. You know they will."

"I hadn't thought of that. Not a bad idea. Well, we can just play it by ear."

"You can," Carrie laughed. "I couldn't carry a tune if they offered me the Hope diamond to pull it off. Thank God Jeremy didn't marry me for my musical abilities."

THEIR FIRST STOP was Thalonoki, a wildly colorful boutique featuring the work of the hottest designers currently working in Greece. The owner of the shop, a tiny blond whose hair hung halfway to her waist in myriad ropes of braid, was a whirling dervish of efficiency.

"Make yourselves comfortable, please, ladies," she insisted in heavily accented English, gesturing to a long white leather couch. "You let me do the work. I am Thalia," she added with a smile. Another saleswoman appeared with demitasse cups of strong, sweet Greek coffee to sip while they shopped.

Both Jenna and Carrie were quickly overwhelmed with the opulence of offerings and Thalia's infectious passion for the designers she worked with. "We may not have to look any further," Jenna told Carrie after only a few minutes.

"Not that we won't," Carrie laughed. "But you're going to find what you came for here. The Oracle has spoken."

"And the Oracle speaks only the truth, you may be sure," Thalia agreed, arriving with another armful of choices for Jenna to consider. "It is has been so for centuries and will be for centuries to come." Carrie nodded sagely, then winked at Jenna.

A pair of twenty-somethings came in and headed straight for the racks. The first, a tall, anorexic-looking redhead pulled a strappy little green jumpsuit out and held it up to her for her friend's approval. "Oh, pu-leeze, Lucille, that's like so 20th century," her friend intoned.

She in turn reached for a simple, sleeveless, floor-length white satin, with décolletage to the waist, both front and back. "Only if you lost like twenty pounds," Redhead said cattily, "and, really, you'd have to spend a month at a tanning salon, sweetie. Twenty-four/seven. You'd die of cancer before you ever got to wear it." It was clear from the way both Thalia and her saleswoman ignored the pair that they were known browsers upon whom any personal attention would be wasted. Thalia kept an eye on them a moment longer, then returned her attention to Jenna.

"Now, then, if you can tell me, would this be for a special occasion or for a particular use, my dear?" Thalia asked Jenna.

"I'm a singer," Jenna answered simply. "It's actually for a performance tomorrow night, in quite a large venue. I need something that'll look great from a distance, ,and *really* look great from close up. Something pretty bold. Spangly, bright. Something really eye-catching?" Thalia vanished into the stockroom.

The redheaded browser looked over at Jenna and Carrie, recognized Jenna, then elbowed her companion, indicating where to direct her attention with a tiny nod of her head in Jenna's direction. They started whispering to each other.

Thalia emerged from the back with a number of outfits piled one on top of another in her arms. She hung them all on a display hook, then selected the first, a glittering, low-cut silver lamé mini toga which she held up for Jenna and Carrie to consider.

"Now this might be just the thing. You certainly do have the legs for it," Thalia enthused, bringing the outfit within Jenna's reach. Fingering the silky material, Jenna found herself murmuring, "Oh, my, yes…" It went on a separate hook.

"Or…" Thalia took an electric blue spandex jumpsuit from the hook. "All the zippers. This one is fun!" Again Jenna was invited to get a feel for the fabric.

"I'm not sure. I've never been crazy about that shade of blue," Jenna said, playing with a zipper that ran all the way up the outer leg from hem to waist. "But the zippers do add interesting possibilities," she observed with a grin.

"It could be wicked hot under the lights," Carrie pointed out.

"Mmm, right. I'm gonna say that one's a pass, Thalia."

"And this?" Thalia asked, holding up a filmy confection of crocheted red lace. "It is made of an alpaca/silk blend. With a flesh-colored bodystocking under, very seductive. Feel this – it is luscious."

"Oh my, it certainly is," Jenna had to agree in amazement. "This is a keeper!"

None of them noticed Redhead step outside to make a call on her cell phone.

IN ALL, THALIA packed up six outfits for Jenna to take home to try.

"You double-park in front and we will bring them out to your car for you, later, after you eat your lunch," she offered.

"I can't tell you how much I appreciate this," Jenna said sincerely. "You've been so helpful, really."

"You take your time, dear. No rush. You make me happy taking them home," Thalia insisted. "Now you two go and have a wonderful lunch. You will love Estrellita's. Try the espetada. To die for."

As Jenna signed the credit card receipt, Carrie turned to look out the window. "Oh, shit," she whispered under her breath. Out on the sidewalk were a tiny knot of people, including a photographer and a TV cameraman. Redhead and her friend were monopolizing one reporter's microphone. Another was holding her mike out to someone who was clearly just a passer-by.

Carrie turned to Jenna just as she slid her credit card back in her wallet. "Don't turn around, Jenn. There's press on the sidewalk. With cameras."

Returning her wallet to her bag, Jenna threw her head back and groaned.

"This place has to have a back door. We could ditch them," Carrie suggested.

"They'd know that just as well as we would. They're back there too, I guarantee you," Jenna said, realistically. "No, I might as well just deal with it."

"You poor thing," Thalia sympathized. "You deserve your privacy."

"Don't worry, hon," Jenna told her. "It's just part of the job." She sighed, squared her shoulders and headed for the door.

Stepping out onto the sidewalk smiling graciously, Jenna was grateful to have Carrie right behind her. A CBS cameraman worked his way around the growing crowd to get a clear shot the two of them. The reporter who'd been interviewing Redhead and her friend spun around and advanced on Jenna aggressively, her microphone outstretched.

"Jenna! Tori Landry, KLFM 101.9. Jenna, how are you feeling?"

Before Jenna could say a word, the second reporter shouldered KLFM 101.9 aside, shoving her mike a few inches closer to Jenna. This reporter, a big, beefy woman, was dressed head to toe in motorcycle leather. It wasn't hard to imagine her gunning a high performance Harley around town in response to some reader's phoned-in tip. She spoke only in questions.

"Andrea Battersby? Boston Blurb? Jenna, did you really kill that guy? You haven't been charged with anything, but are you afraid they still might?" Jenna chose to ignore Andrea in favor of Tori's more polite approach.

"I'm on the mend. Pretty much, I've just been resting at home since I got back. Other than to see my therapist and a quick trip to Albany, this is really the first time I've been out. My cheek bone is fractured, which is why my face is so swollen, and I do have to admit that it's painful. But what I really want to say is how much I appreciate that you folks haven't hounded me" she said, flashing a big smile directly at the second reporter, "and I do thank you so much for your support. You'll have to forgive me – that's all I can say, because my face really does hurt."

"Well done," Carrie whispered as they maneuvered their way through the throng that had quickly enlarged as people had been attracted to the commotion and cameras. Jenna shook a few hands and acknowledged well-wishers with gratitude. For the most part, her smile remained genuine throughout the entire ordeal.

"You handled that beautifully," Carrie said as they finally got clear of the crowd.

"Beauty is as beauty does. Let's see how it comes out on the news and in the papers," Jenna said.

"Yeah," Carrie said, "especially in the Boston Blurb."

IT TOOK JENNA and Carrie another hour after they got back to Scott's to settle on what Jenna would wear for her one song the following night. "God, I've never put so much time into anything," Jenna laughed. "I feel like I'm picking out my dress for the senior prom."

"They'd never let you into a senior prom wearing *that*," Carrie giggled. Jenna was practically falling out of an amazing construction of odd bits and pieces of black satin, strapped together with countless bands of shiny black leather. "I've seen strippers wearing more. You wear that and you won't be able to let Scott see you in it till you appear on the stage, or the two of you'll end up spending the night in his dressing room and miss the show completely."

"We'd have to let security in on it and cue them when I came on," Jenna agreed as she checked out the back view in the mirror. "He'd need some wicked serious restraining. The real problem is that he'd wreck it trying to get me back out of it," she laughed. It had taken her ten minutes just to figure out how to put the thing on. "Bad investment," she decided finally after she checked the price tag.

With Carrie's help Jenna was able to whittle her choices down to two. She decided to keep them both.

THE FILM THAT accompanied the CBS report that night wasn't as bad as Jenna had dreaded. She lay on the couch and watched the six o'clock news in the living room. Scott caught it in the kitchen as he fixed their supper.

Speaking and in motion, her face didn't look at all like the one she'd been meeting in her mirror for so many days now, Jenna thought. It actually helped her to put some perspective on her appearance.

A few minutes later the phone rang. Scott picked it up in the kitchen.

"It's for you, babe," he called to her. "It's Carrie."

She picked up the phone. "Got it," she yelled back to Scott. She heard him hang up before Jeremy's voice had a chance to greet her.

"Hi, kiddo. I had Carrie phone so Scott wouldn't wonder why it'd be me calling you. I just wanted to let you know that everything's worked out for tomorrow night. I just finished with Bruce and their lighting people. How's your cheek doing? Carrie said it was still really giving you trouble this morning. You looked good on T.V."

"You saw it too? No, the pain – that was mostly just to get the press off my back," Jenna assured him. "I'm singing tomorrow night, come hell, high water or both. Better bring your ear plugs – I'm plannin' on blowin' the amps, baby."

"That's our girl," Jeremy chuckled.

THE LIGHTS WENT down and a roar went up as twenty thousand fans welcomed Blacklace to the stage of the outdoor amphitheater at Great Woods. The audience cheered as the five musicians took their places, both on the stage in real life and on giant screens positioned up the sides of the lawn which afforded everyone an equally intimate view. Jenna sat, as she had the week before, with the band's ladies, in a relatively demur midnight blue jumpsuit studded with matte black nail heads up and down the seam lines, the runner up of the outfits she'd brought home from Thalonoki. Scott had been appropriately complimentary when she'd put it on earlier in the evening.

"Oh man, babe," he'd said with a whistle. "I'm gonna have to keep you in view at all times. You look *wicked* hot tonight!"

"I got it to match my bruises," Jenna said only half-jokingly.

"Honey, on you even bruises look like a fashion statement," Scott assured her with a kiss. "You gonna be okay tonight?" he asked with genuine concern.

"I'll be fine," she assured him, "but if I get too tired, I'm gonna just duck out and lay down in your dressing room. That's okay with you, right?"

"God, sure, hon. You do whatever you have to do."

"Just so you're not worrying about me," Jenna insisted. "If I go lie down, it doesn't mean I oughta be headed for the hospital or anything. If you see an empty seat, it just means I'm being sensible."

"No problem, babe. I won't worry about you, promise."

"You just get out there and knock 'em dead," Jenna said. "Make me prouder than proud." She pulled him to her and gave him a soulful kiss.

So Scott only had to remind himself not to be concerned when he noticed the vacant seat between Carrie and Jill as the band launched into the second set.

Jenna hurried back to the dressing room and scrambled into the skimpy knit she'd rolled up and secreted in the bottom of the tiny tote bag she was carrying, along with a pair of stiletto heels to match. The designer had used far less than a yard of iridescent emerald green cashmere to create the shimmering suggestion of a dress she slipped herself into. The floor-length scarf of the same fabric she wrapped around her neck only accentuated the gulf between itself and the dress's plunging neckline, a neckline that went so far as to fully reveal her navel. Quickly removing a few pins, she let her hair fall to her shoulders, threw it back and forth a few times to let it really go wild, then raced to the wings.

From the darkness, she found herself grinning at the sight of Scott strutting along a catwalk through the first twenty rows of audience, reaching down occasionally to grab one of the hundreds of hands straining to reach him or catch his eye. The grin was a test and she was relieved to find it didn't pain her as much as she'd feared. She had dosed herself after dinner with some of the pain relievers she'd been given when she'd left the hospital two weeks earlier. She would need them to pull off what she had in mind for tonight.

As the cheering that followed the first song died down, Scott started to raise the mike to his mouth for a little banter with the band and the audience, but before he could say anything, Dan shouted out, "Guys, we're missing something tonight. Anybody else feel it?"

Scott turned to him, puzzled. "Uh…" was all he was able to get into his mike before Jeremy chimed in. "You're right, Dan, only I think we're missing some*one*, not some*thing*. Wouldn't you agree?"

Scott started going red in the face, never a good sign. Dan took over again, backing away from Scott as he spoke.

"Hey, fans, what do what do *you* think? *Are* we missing someone tonight?"

The fans weren't blind. "Yes!!!" they yelled as one, right on cue.

"Any idea who it could be?"

Without prompting, a male voice called out, "Jenna!" Immediately, the name was picked up and repeated until it became a rhythmic chant. "Jenna! Jenna! Jenna!!!"

The stage went dark for several beats, during which Scott's voice could clearly be heard saying, "What the – fuck?"

A single spotlight came up on Jenna standing with her arms hanging limply at her sides, a microphone in one hand. Flash photography, strictly forbidden by the venue, flared through the darkness like an explosion of shooting stars.

Scott made a beeline for the vision of the woman he loved standing before him bathed in white light. The spot widened to include him as he pulled her to him and gave her a long and passionate kiss. The crowd, the band included, screamed and whistled its approval.

Then Jenna stepped away from him, brought the mike to her mouth and looked to Jeremy for his introductory chord. Cuing the band with a nod of his head, he launched into a night-rending riff that took Jenna by surprise. He'd clearly spent time with Jeff and Dan improving on the already kick-ass arrangement they'd worked up the week before.

After the opening eight bars, they dropped the volume in half, allowing Jenna to step into the gap. She reached for Scott's hand and held it while she sang, quietly at first.

Please take my heart, dear – it's already yours.
Please take my heart, love, cuz I am yours,
Take me in your arms, I am ready to go.

The audience held its collective breath, entirely aware that they were hearing a new song sung for the first time, a moment of authentic, raw emotion the likes of which they knew they might never be witness to again. With each verse, Jenna's voice ramped up another decibel. By the final verse her voice could have reached the back of the audience without amplification.

Take my hand, take my heart. Ready to go.
Gratitude, thankfulness. I'm ready to go.
Take care, my lover. I do love you so.

Here is my hand – I can give it to you,
Cuz here is the heart I have given to you.
Hand and heart, mine to give – take them in yours.

Take me in your heart. I am ready to go.
Take me to heaven. I'm ready to go.
Take me right now. I am ready to go.

Jeremy echoed the final line twice. By the time his last chord died away into the night, it was a whisper. The crowd, jumping to its feet, shrieked, stomped and whistled insanely.

After a huge ovation, the house went silent again as Jenna brought the mike back to her mouth. She waited a beat and then spoke.

"I wish I could sing you another song tonight, but I'm afraid I can't. Scott just got all I had," she said with a huge grin. The cheering resumed as Scott bent her back in a kiss worthy of any ever committed to film in Hollywood.

Chapter 35

AFTER RUNNING A gantlet of particularly eager reporters after the show, Scott ushered Jenna into the waiting limousine. As used to grand gestures as Scott was, even he was taken by surprise by the full stretch limo's worth of roses of every hue awaiting them inside.

"Georgie, what *is* this?" he asked their driver, who produced a small envelope and handed it in to Jenna.

"I was told to put this in your hands only, ma'am," Georgie told her, a wide grin on his broad face.

"Who…? Oh my goodness," she gasped, extracting the small card from inside the envelope. "It says, 'Congratulations, Jenna B, on your great new song and the incredible performance tonight. And thanks for including us – getting to watch Scott's face from start to finish was priceless! We all love you and we're so glad you're back on your feet. Jeremy, Dan, Tim and Jeff.' Oh, Scott!"

Jenna blinked back tears as Scott wrapped her in his arms for the ride home.

THE BAND AND the ladies, who'd been lounging around the driveway awaiting their arrival, swarmed the car like paparazzi when Georgie pulled up. Doors were yanked opened and every vase was quickly extracted and hurried in to make bowers of both the living room and their bedroom

"You guys!" Jenna beamed as they walked into more of the heady fragrance they'd just left behind in the limo. "Thank you so much for all the roses. They're just beautiful – and so are all of you. You pulled it all off, the surprise, the timing – and man, the stuff you did with the music! I loved it! I wish we'd recorded it that way, but that doesn't matter. It'll be a special treat for concerts. You guys are so fuckin' wonderful. I love you all."

Jeremy folded her in a tremendous hug. "That's from everyone of us. We just want you to know how special you are to all of us, not just Scott, and how totally cool it was that you wanted our help on your little surprise for the bro here."

Conversation quickly moved from the great show just finished to the schedule for the rest of the fall. Late September and early October would include a swing through the west, including this year's World Without Abuse benefit in LA. Jenna was particularly relishing the thought of performing with them on that stage this year. Her performance for the benefit the previous year had been a form of support in the abstract. This year it was personal.

"What a way to celebrate an anniversary," Scott chuckled. "What a difference a year makes. Somebody pinch me," he said quietly.

SCOTT AND JENNA stood on the front steps with an arm around each other after waving everyone off, breathing deep of the late summer night air under the spotlight of an almost full moon. "What a special night," Jenna sighed quietly.

"Honey, I just have to say one more time, what you did for me tonight was just so damned fantastic," Scott smiled, shaking his head for the nineteenth time since they'd gotten home, still in wonder. "I hereby predict that "Ready to Go" will go to number one and you get, at the *very* least, a nomination and probably a Grammy for it."

"Oh, you're just saying that," Jenna said modestly.

"Excuse me? You're questioning the opinion of a seasoned pro? I never get this stuff wrong. I know winners when I hear them. Ask anyone. They'll tell you: do *not* question the word of Scott Tenny."

"Yeah, but I think that's for another reason..." Jenna let the thought trail off with a giggle.

"Oh, you do, do you? Well, people can agree with me for whatever reason – that's their own damned business. I just know my track record, and it's pretty friggin' accurate. Time will prove me right, you just watch," he said and kissed her as if to seal some unspoken deal.

"And now, my love, I'm going to demonstrate my gratitude … and appreciation … and admiration … and respect … and awe of you in the best way I know how… all night long." Each item Scott intended to demonstrate inspired yet another kiss, each strategically placed and administered with one end goal in mind: to take Jenna's breath away.

THE PHONE RANG at 7:35 the next morning. Scott groped for it, finding Jeremy on the other end. "Hey man, quick, check out Channel 4. And catch the papers." Scott reached for the remote as Jenna struggled awake to find an image of herself filling the screen, standing in the spotlight on a black stage. Amazingly, the clip showed the entire scene, from spotlight to Scott's final kiss. The reporter spoke only in superlatives.

Jenna pulled on a robe to retrieve the morning papers while Scott continued his conversation with Jeremy.

"The reviews of the show were great, but Jenna's performance was clearly the highlight," Jeremy went on.

"All I can say, man, is your timing was fuckin' perfect," Scott laughed. "You don't know how close I came to throwing things. If the stage hadn't gone dark when it did, somebody woulda gotten a mike shoved somewhere fuckin' uncomfortable, you know that. You all get bragging rights on this one – bravo, bro. Man, I was absolutely ready to kill somebody."

"We anticipated and planned for your every move, my friend," Jeremy chuckled. "I'm sure you like to think you're a total original, but you know what? You can be entirely predictable in certain circumstances. We had your every reaction pegged to the hundredth of a second."

"Yeah, sure. Well, do you have this one predicted? I'm taking my lady and we're headin' north for a couple of days and we're not answering the phone, if you get my drift."

Jenna, returning with the paper, looked sleepily pleased with the idea of Scott's impromptu travel plans.

"10-4, my brother. Have a good one – or ten or twenty," Jeremy said and hung up.

Jenna climbed back into bed with the paper. "Holy cow. Look at this, Scott!" She spread the entertainment section out in front of both of them. The entire front page was a photo montage and review on the previous night's show, and in the center of it all, the largest photo was a close-up of Jenna, her eyes glistening with tears as she clearly sang her heart out. The accompanying article detailed the concert, Jenna's role in it and her remarkable come-back in such a short period of time from what the reviewer referred to as "significant physical and psychological trauma."

"We're gonna be the talk of the town for a few days. I don't know – maybe we should stick around and enjoy it. Whaddya think?"

"You're joking, right?" Jenna said, not at all sure he was.

"Of course I'm joking," Scott laughed. "I only have one thing I have to do before we go," he told her, reaching for the belt of her robe.

"Wait," she said and picked up the CD player remote. She already had "Ready to Go" cued up to play.

> *Please take my heart, dear – it's already yours.*
> *Please take my heart, love, because I am yours,*
> *Take me in your arms, cuz I'm ready to go.*

MELANIE WAS ABLE to take Jenna early. Scott busied himself in the waiting room, then they headed north with the rest of the off-early Friday afternoon traffic. As soon as they could, they abandoned the highways and wound the rest of the way to the lake house on back roads. It was one of those bittersweet, perfect, slightly crisp blue-sky days, the kind that make it hard to accept the tinges of red, gold and yellow that were beginning to nudge aside the greens of summer.

"One more blow-out, then time to close her up for the winter," Scott said with a sigh, as the big, rambling, rustic camp finally came into view. "Never enough time…"

"Let's just treasure the time we've got, then," Jenna said.

"I know where to start doing that," Scott smiled.

"I hope you're thinkin' what I'm thinkin'," Jenna laughed and, grabbing bags from the back of the car, raced him to the front door.

THE PHONE NEVER rang till late the following afternoon.

"Hi. Just me," said Jeremy. "No emergency, but I though you'd both like to know that Jenn's song is the number one requested song in Boston today."

"No shit!" Scott said. "Hey, honey – that song about me, it's number one in Boston today," he yelled to Jenna over his shoulder.

"Number one *requested*, ya fuckin' egomaniac," Jeremy said. "But I called because the people in L.A. for the abuse charity thing want to know if Jenna will be there. They called me when they couldn't reach you guys. Somebody named Carol Atkinson wants to talk to her. Sounds like they want to make her the poster child for this year."

"Her call," Scott said. "I'll tell her." Jeremy gave him a number for Jenna to contact.

SCOTT AND JENNA climbed out of the car after a brief foray out into the world for dinner.

"Let's go for a walk," Jenna suggested. "It's just too beautiful a night." Holding hands, the two descended the path to the lake shore.

"Better yet, how about a canoe ride, my lady?" Scott offered gallantly.

"Perfect," Jenna enthused.

Scott opened the padlock on one of the boathouse doors, reached inside the door for a light switch and they both went in. Pulling one of the canoes down from its resting spot, he slid it easily into the water. Handing Jenna the thin bowline, he turned back and grabbed a couple of paddles and life jackets. Jenna shrugged into the smaller of the two, running its zipper up several inches.

"Man, you can even make one of those things look like designer clothes," Scott marveled. "I swear, woman, a Kevlar vest'd look sexy on you."

As they paddled across the lake, the moon emerged from behind a cloud just as a loon broke into its mournful cry. Jenna set her paddle down in front of her, across the gunnels of the canoe, and dropped a hand into the water as they drifted quietly. After a few minutes, she swiveled around carefully and turned to sit facing Scott.

"I've been thinking," she said, hesitating a bit. "I want to get out and tour a bit with my band through the fall. The album's going to be released in a couple of weeks. Would you be okay with that?"

"Well, of course, hon. We've said that all along. You do your thing, we do our thing, you join us whenever you want to and can. You're timing's impeccable. Ride that little ditty you wrote for me!" They both laughed, then she smiled at him appreciatively.

"I just feel like I've left them hanging way too long. Long distance recording gigs don't make for a tight band. We need to work together. I want to talk to them about it when we're out in LA."

"Did you think I'd be upset or something?" Scott asked.

"It crossed my mind."

"Then erase it from your mind, babe. Hell, nobody understands careers better than I do. The one thing I'd say though, take it easy. Don't schedule too much. You're really just getting started with the therapy – you need to focus on that first and foremost. If you go out on the road, you're gonna add the stress of trying to manage both."

"Don't worry, I'm not going to let anything interfere with that," Jenna stated firmly. "And as for singing with you guys, we'll work things out."

Scott nodded. "The tricky part will be coordinating our tour schedules. I just don't want us coming and going and never getting to see one another, be together."

"That's what we pay those guys the big bucks for," Jenna said. "I'll feed them your schedule and give them my parameters. I'll have them work something up – but I get the final say."

"You need to do this for yourself," Scott said, reinforcing what she'd been thinking for several days. "I know how hard you've worked to get where you are today, babe. You need to get back to the work you love. If you can control the craziness factor, it can only help you regain that sense of the you that's you." Scott laughed at how that had come out. "Pretty profound, huh…"

Slipping down into the bottom of the boat, Jenna put her head back against the seat she'd just vacated, played 'toesies' with Scott and marveled at the firmament of stars arrayed above them.

Scott paddled them back to shore while she started humming "Ready to Go." After a few bars, he fell in with her, in close harmony. Anyone sitting out on a porch on the lake that night got a very special earful.

"WE'VE JUST GOT to come up more often," Jenna insisted the next day as they started down the road that would eventually take them back to Boston and home.

Conversation ranged all over the place, but by the time they finally merged onto Route 16 heading south, they were back to talking about the L.A. benefit.

"Well, without having actually talked to her about it, I don't know, but I think coming forward and adding my face to this kind of thing makes a whole lot of sense," Jenna was saying.

"I've had the craziest idea," Scott said.

"Bet it's the same crazy idea I've been having," Jenna said confidently. "About putting together an abuse benefit here in Boston?"

"You read my mind!" Scott said, slamming the wheel.

"Nope, you read mine first," Jenna said. They both laughed. "But in all seriousness," Jenna continued, "I would love to do it. Put a group together. Make it happen here."

"You certainly know enough good people you can tap around here," Scott said, "and, gee, I *think* I just happen to know a famous rock band that would sign on as your number one supporters for a big shindig, if you felt like putting one together. Really, your name couldn't be more timely."

"Just the idea of doing something positive with all the shit that's gone down – God, it'd be great. It's perfect," Jenna murmured.

"You can work through the L.A. branch – I know they'd be there for you completely. Hey, maybe they already have a branch out here – who knows. I'm sure somebody's doing this kind of work. You know, you could probably get half of L.A. to come out for it, with your pull," Scott said. "And we – the rest of the guys and me – we could deliver a heck of a lot of Boston you've never even met."

"Maybe some of the 'ladies' would like to get in on it, too. I'm sure Carrie would," Jenna said, speculatively. "Man, I do love this idea. Now, if I just had some idea of what band this is you think you could get..."

Scott reached over and messed her hair up even more than the wind had already done. Jenna threw her head back against the leather seat, turned to face him and yelled loud enough for everyone speeding south with them to hear, "Scott Tenny, I love you so much."

PULLING INTO THE driveway, Scott was surprised to see Jeremy coming from the studio.

"Hey, guys, glad to see you back. Let me help you with your things," Jeremy volunteered, opening the trunk as Scott released the latch. "The guys just left. We've been working on an idea Jeff had. Wait'll you hear it – it's fuckin' wild." Reaching in, he grabbed out the two larger bags and headed for the door with them. Jenna and Scott followed with armloads of smaller totes and bags.

Inside, Jenna grabbed her bag and a few other things and headed upstairs.

"Good weekend?" Jeremy asked.

"The best," Scott confirmed, nodding enthusiastically. "Hey, bro, I've gotta finish that song I started for Jenna months ago. Really, this weekend was just incredible. It was just so mellow – and so hot. What a combination. Damn, I love her so much."

"The hot part I get. Mellow? What's 'mellow?' Rationalization for not gettin' as much as you were hoping for?"

"You're funny, you know that? We had plenty of time for it and we didn't waste a minute, you can trust me on that, bro. Why the fuck am I tellin' you, anyway? It's not like it's any of your damn business." Jeremy laughed, until he noticed Scott wasn't.

"Hey, don't tell me you you've reformed? Your best friend doesn't get to hear about your fucking experiences anymore? If that's true, all I have to say is that you really *have* changed, and for the better, I might add."

Scott just stood there shaking his head. "I don't know if I've reformed, as you put it so diplomatically. Okay, let's see if you can understand this. It's just that with Jenna there's more to it then just fucking. I can't explain it to myself, let alone try to make an animal like you understand. Sure we just fuck sometimes – everybody does sometimes. But most of the time, we're making *love* – the real thing, and all I can say is, that's a whole 'nother ballgame, brother. And the distinction's important to me. Does any of this make sense?"

Jeremy put his hand on Scott's shoulder. "My friend, it makes perfect sense. You've finally found what every man searches for: a woman you can truly love, who can truly love you. Look, Scott, we've known each other for a very long time, bro. I can honestly say I never thought I'd see the day when you could finally settle with yourself – sorry, I don't even know how to put it into words. My only hope for you is that you just don't go do anything to fuck it up."

Jenna had just about walked in on the conversation but catching its drift, pulled back and listened from the shadows of the hall. Her first opportunity to comprehend the greater depths of Scott and Jeremy's friendship, she was humbled by the intimacy these two men shared; she never knew that two men could. She found herself wondering if she'd ever have a girlfriend with whom she could be so candid, so close, someone with whom she could share the most intimate details of her own life.

"Hey, you two. What's going on?" she said, finally walking in, acting like she'd just come down. "You both look so serious. Is something the matter?"

"Hell, no, honey. How could anything be the matter?" Scott asked rhetorically, corralling her from behind and wrapping his big arms around her. "Nothing's wrong. As a matter of fact, everything's just about as right as right can be," he said, planting a kiss as far down into her cleavage as he could reach from this vantage point.

Jeremy nodded in agreement, then grabbed his things to head out. "Night, guys. Pleasant dreams."

"He should know how pleasant they can be," Scott murmured in her ear.

JENNA WAS JUST headed for her car to go into Cambridge for her therapy appointment the next day when Jeremy roared up the driveway on his Harley and killed the motor. He stepped off and removed his helmet all in one smooth motion.

"Afternoon, Mr. S," Jenna said brightly.

"Afternoon, Ms. B," Jeremy responded in kind and gave her a warm hug. "Actually, I'm glad we ran into each other out here. Got a minute?"

"A couple, actually."

"Did you intend to tell Scott you overheard our conversation last night?" Jenna was caught off guard.

"I – you knew I was there?" she stammered.

"I saw you. Actually, I'm glad you heard us. You women need to know how we guys all kiss and tell. It's – it's our history, hon. You live in the same room with five guys for years before you've got enough bread to get two rooms and you're gonna know every intimate detail of every single one of those guys' lives, trust me." Jeremy rolled his eyes. "By the time we did start to hit it big, started renting suites with plenty of bedrooms, we still all ended up in the living room with that night's crop of groupies. Let's just say we've got a communal kinda bond, all of us, especially Scott and me."

"So – so why are you telling me this?" Jenna asked.

"Look, I just wanted to say that sex has always a big issue with Scott, ever since I've known him. He's told me stories that, believe me, I wish I never heard. So for him to say his feelings for you were more about making love than just fucking all the time, I knew that things have finally changed in that area. He's changed because of you. I only hope you can keep him from falling backwards. I, for one, way prefer the new Scott to the old one, big time."

"Jeremy, do you know *why* he's changed?" Jenna asked him. "Listen, he and I both have issues with sex. You probably know ten times as much about his as I ever will, and that's fine. Mine are from the abuse. Maybe helping me with mine has helped him deal with his own. That's one thing love is suppose to be about: helping each other through things and being there for one another. I never intended to tell him I heard you two talking – that was between the two of you. I know he needs to confide in you when he feels it's necessary. That's what best friends are for."

"All I can say is, he's one lucky bastard, that guy," Jeremy said vehemently. Jenna gave him a wink and went on out to her car.

Chapter 36

JENNA AND SCOTT'S flight descended through the late afternoon L.A. smog. Looking down on the familiar rooftops of Inglewood as the plane lined up for touchdown, Jenna squeezed Scott's hand. "I love coming home with you," she whispered.

"One year tomorrow night, babe," he said appreciatively, then kissed her gently. "Welcome home."

IT FELT ODD pulling into the driveway of Jim and Sue's old house to come spend a few days with her mother and Kristin, both of whom were home to greet them. It may have been Jim and Sue's old house, but Linda's touch was apparent from the moment they stepped in the front door.

"Oh my gosh, it's such a change from the old place, isn't it?" Jenna exclaimed, gazing about her. "It looks great, Mom." Jenna felt a rush of comfort. This house, she knew, held no secrets waiting to trip her up or pin her down. And that was only one way among many in which it differed from the house she'd grown up in.

The new house was as starkly modern as the old house had been opulently old-world Mediterranean. Sleek, clean lines and gallery-like open space provided a dramatic backdrop to display memorabilia and art collected over a lifetime. Linda's things seemed to take on new life in this space – and so did her mother, Jenna suddenly realized.

"I'm glad you like what I've done with it, sweetie," Linda was saying. "Kristin was such a big help with everything, too – I couldn't have done it without her. She's got a heck of an eye for decorating, this girl." Kristin clearly enjoyed the praise. "Kris, honey, show Jenna around and help her decide which room to use. There are certainly enough of them! Scott, you look like you could use a cup of coffee."

Following Kristin down the hall, Jenna found herself surprised to run into old pieces of furniture she knew as well as she knew her own face in the mirror, reborn in new settings, some with new functions as well. A drop-leaf table at which she'd eaten breakfast across from Jim and Chris through her entire childhood now stood, its leaves at its side, behind a small sofa, holding the lamp from the desk in the study, an African mask she didn't recognize and a stack of magazines.

Scott straddled a stool while Linda poured him some coffee and set cream and sugar in front of him. She tried not to gape as he spooned what seemed to her an obscene amount of sugar into his cup. "You're not going to get away with that all your life, young man," she started to say, then eyeing his scrawny frame, reconsidered. "Or maybe you just will."

"Nothing sticks to me," Scott said. "Trust me on that."

"I do, Scott. I'm also trusting you with my daughter. Tell me, how is she doing? And tell me the truth. She tells me a lot, but I can't help but get the feeling that she tries to spare me some of it."

"She's doing well," Scott said candidly. "She's in therapy – that I know you know. The nightmares have decreased considerably. She'll have one most nights after she's had a therapy session, which is understandable, but not every time. We took a weekend up at the lake house in New Hampshire last weekend. We had a great time, and she didn't have any nightmares at all. Has she told you she's planning on taking up with her own band again real soon?"

"Great," Linda said. "That's excellent."

"And you know she sang one song with us last week at a show," Scott went on.

"The whole *world* knows she sang one song with you last week at a show," Linda laughed. "It was all over the news here, and it's getting plenty of air time out here. It's beautiful. I was really proud of her, getting up and facing a crowd so soon like that, after everything that's happened. She's amazing, if I do say so myself." Linda smiled.

"She sure is," Scott had to agree.

"And that's everything?"

"Everything. Scott's honor," he said holding up backhanded devil's horns in parody of the traditional Boy Scout salute. Linda grimaced.

"Well, I'm just glad to hear she is doing well. So…how's your father?"

JENNA AND KRISTIN joined them in the kitchen.

"Wow, Kristin really has a talent for decorating," Jenna raved.

"Kristin's got all sorts of talents. Have you told Jenna what you want to do, Kris?"

"I would if I had half a clue," Kristin groaned. "Turns out I'm sorta good at all sorts of things. Everything, actually, at least that's what my professors have been telling me. It's so confusing."

"You should hear her sing," Linda said. "And her acting is just wonderful. She only had a small part in Streetcar, but she got mentioned by name in the *Times* review."

"You're kidding! You should have sent it to me," Jenna protested.

"I just don't know what I want to pursue," Kristin said.

"Neat problem to have," Jenna laughed. "Let me just say, though, whatever you choose, I'll support and help you in any way that I can."

"I don't want to get any special treatment because I'm your sister or because of who our father was," Kristin objected.

Scott knew what Kristin meant. "Being your father's daughter and your sister's sister can get you opportunities you may never get otherwise, Kris. But if you want to make it on your own, then I've gotta say, this ain't the place to try. Everyone knows who your dad was and, out of respect for him, they're gonna give you preferential treatment."

Jenna put a hand on Kristin's shoulder. "Scott's right, sis. That's what happened to me when I decided to try acting. Dad pulled strings and I got my so-called 'big break.' However, in my case, I hated it and I wasn't very good at it, either. I'd always known that what I really wanted to do was sing. He tried to use his influence in that arena too. That's why I left. I'd never know if I had it or if he'd arranged it. I had to achieve success on my own. When I said I'd help you, I didn't mean by pulling strings – I don't consider that help. What I should have said was I'd happily help you with schools or to get hooked up with private teachers or whatever."

"I've got a suggestion," Scott offered. "You were planning on coming out to Boston in the next few weeks, weren't you?" Kristin nodded. "Why don't you just come back with us now. Let us show you around, introduce you to some people, in both the acting and singing business. You can check things out for yourself. Maybe it'll help you decide what you want to do. Getting started would be strictly on your own, but at least you'd have a head start with contacts. What do you think?"

"That's very kind of you," Kristin said, genuinely touched. "Thank you – thank you both. I'll think about it. Really. "

JENNA MET EARLY the next morning with Carol Atkinson and several board members of the Southern California chapter of World Without Abuse. Carol sipped from a glass of Perier, ignoring the spread of pastries and muffins she'd provided for her guests. You didn't stay as thin as Carol Atkinson any other way.

"We know it's last minute, but we so appreciate your willingness to speak tonight, dear," Carol said, coming right to the point of the meeting. "I think you can get our message out to an entirely new audience, in an entirely new way, Jenna."

"Talk about a challenge," Jenna said, smiling. "I don't know about that. All I can do is tell my story and hope it reaches others."

"It will, dear, it certainly will," said an elegantly dressed, silver-haired dowager over her teacup. "Abuse happens across the board. You – and I – represent parts of the spectrum that rarely get heard from." Jenna felt a rush of empathy, a sudden sense of connection with this total stranger. The small smile creasing the old woman's face suggested that she was experiencing the same feelings.

STAR AFTER STAR took to the stage, entertaining while also focusing attention on the fight to end abuse in all its malignant forms, but the entire house went silent when Jenna strode to the podium. Scott, sitting in the fifth row with Linda and Kristen, all but burst with pride, respect, awe and love.

As they'd dressed two hours earlier, she'd stopped him dead in his tracks when she turned and asked him how she looked. Instead of the spandex, leather and metal of kick-ass rock 'n roll, she'd opted tonight for a sophisticated full-length gown of deep Chinese red, with a strapless bodice that clung to every curve until it exploded into a sweeping skirt of a million impossibly small pleats. A man rarely at a loss for words, Scott found himself stumbling as he tried to find terminology adequate to express the vision of perfection and grace she embodied. "You look absolutely stunning," was the best he could manage.

Jenna looked around the packed auditorium. "Good evening," she began, simply. "I am here tonight, as I have been for the past several years, in support of a cause I deeply believe in. But I am here tonight in a new capacity as well. I am here tonight as one of the abused we have all joined hands all these years to help."

The entire house rose to its feet as one.

Jenna spoke quietly and from the heart. Hushing the audience, she continued, "A month ago, I shot a man, a man who subsequently died. A man who molested me when I was thirteen. A man who impregnated me when I was thirteen." The audience gasped. This information hadn't made it into the gossip columns, nor had what Jenna would tell them next.

"When I was thirteen, my father, who I am sure thought he was acting from the best of intentions, had that fetus aborted without my knowledge and had me hypnotized so I would remember *none* of what happened to me when I was thirteen." Jenna stopped and let the enormity of all that sink in.

"When I was thirty-three, I remembered some of what had happened to me and found out the rest." Again, Jenna paused. "And now a lot of good people are helping me come to terms with it all and helping me move forward.

"First and foremost, I want to acknowledge Scott Tenny, who's been at my side through this entire ordeal." Scott smiled up at her and responded to the audience's applause with a half wave. "And my mother and sister, who are also here tonight – Linda Bradford and Kristin Yates. Thank you so much for your love and your support, both of you," Jenna said, her voice ringing with sincerity. Linda and Kristin smiled and nodded their acknowledgement. Linda blew her daughter a kiss.

"With the support of good people like this, and the support of good people like all of you, every victim of abuse can find help. Friends, we in the entertainment business are in a unique position. We can help in ways that many cannot. We can bring the spotlights that shine on us to bear on problems that have stayed hidden in the dark for far, far too long. I for one intend to use my spotlight to expand the work of World Without Abuse to Boston, my new home town. This morning I met with the board of the Southern California chapter – our hosts tonight – who are willing to help me make this happen. I can't think of any better form of therapy – but don't tell my therapist I said that!" Laughter rippled around the room.

"Before long, I plan to assemble a group of like-minded, dedicated individuals and get to work, and you all will be getting invitations to *my* First Steps benefit. And I expect to see you all there – Boston's great and so are you!"

Jenna left the stage to a standing ovation.

AT THE DINNER afterward, Jenna found herself the center of attention. She wasn't prepared for the candor which some of the guests felt free to address her revelations. She'd met kinder tabloid reporters.

"What you said tonight, all that, that's nothing, ducky," the worst of them, a total stranger, said to her as if they'd been drinking buddies for half a lifetime. "Why, I have a friend who's brother's wife was…"

Jenna fled to the balcony for a few minutes of cool if not entirely fresh air. Leaning on the railing looking across the nightscape of downtown LA, she found herself humming a few bars of "Ready to Go."

"Catchy tune," said a familiar voice. "Evening, Jenna." Jenna turned.

"Well, my goodness. Matthew Caine, as I live and breathe. I didn't know you did the benefit circuit. Or do cops refer to as the benefit beat?" She smiled and held out a hand, which he took, then reeled her in by it and planted a kiss on her cheek.

"Hey, don't turn Boston Puritan on us, lady. This is Hollywood. We kiss here, remember?" he said with a wink. "No, I heard you'd be here and thought you might need some support from an old friend. I forgot that all of Hollywood are your old friends," he said with a self-deprecating grin. "You had them eattin' outta your hand up there. Good job, kid."

"Thanks. How have you been?" Jenna asked, leaning back on the railing and enjoying the chat.

"Okay. A well-rounded life like mine, how could I complain? A little homicide here, a little drug dealing there, kidnapping, some white collar bullshit. Toss in the occasional bank robbery. The new stuff: identity theft and all the other kinds of digital larceny I can't begin to understand. Shit, I have enough problems just filing reports these days. I hate computers. Whatever happened to carbon paper, anyway? So, where's Scott?"

"He's inside, probably talking deals with somebody. I just had to get a few minutes away from every abused person's Aunt Mildred."

"Ah, the 'I know *exactly* what you're going through but I know a much worse version' syndrome. I hear it all day long. Somebody gets run over by a truck, somebody's at their ear whispering how her Great Uncle Wilbur got run over by a steamroller." They were both laughing when Scott put his head out the door, ostensibly looking for Jenna. Seeing them, he came over and joined them, shaking Matthew's proffered hand.

"How are you, my friend," Matthew asked heartily. "Taking good care of our girl?"

"You bet, my man," Scott responded in kind, slipping a proprietary arm around Jenna and giving her a kiss. The fact that it landed right where Matthew's had wasn't lost on either Jenna or Matthew.

"I noticed Jenna out here by herself and just wanted to be sure no homicidal maniac tossed her off the balcony," Matthew said lightly. "But she's in good hands now, so I'll say goodnight and leave you two to enjoy the view. Jenna, you take care now. Scott, good to see you again."

JENNA WATCHED SCOTT watch Matthew walk back inside. It didn't take a PhD to read Scott's expression.

"You're jealous," she said, "and it's not becoming."

"Sure I'm jealous," Scott said plainly. "You'd be too, if someone looked at me the way that guy looks at you."

"Which they do, but you don't see me turning green, do you?" Jenna said calmly.

"Yeah, but you don't find the same one turning up over and over, either, do you?" Scott pointed out.

"You've got plenty of professional women making repeat appearances in your life. This guy's no different. I'd be much happier if I'd never met the man, believe me – *much* happier. And trust me, the reason *why* I know the guy is never far from the front of my mind."

"I tell you, and I told you before, I think his interest in you is more than what he lets on," Scott insisted.

"I don't know where you get that harebrained idea, but it totally doesn't matter. Listen carefully: I love you, Scott Tenny, and nobody else. So would you do you and me a favor and try to remember that? As far as Lt. Matthew Caine is concerned, he's just a well-meaning professional, no different from my doctor or my mailman. He's my cop, my friendly neighborhood cop."

"So, then, are you like in the habit of letting your doctor and your mailman kiss you hello?" he finally asked.

"Ah, so that's the problem," Jenna said, rolling her eyes. "Well, we're making progress – at least, I guess you can call it progress. He kissed me. So does just about half of Hollywood."

"The other half, not this half," Scott said sullenly.

"Excuse me, and this behavior differs from all the women who kiss you – how?" Jenna was beginning to get irritated with Scott's attitude. "Look, before we need to bring more L.A. policemen into our lives, something tells me we should just take ourselves back inside. If we're not careful, my mother's gonna send the National Guard out looking for us, and you'll end up jealous of all of them, too."

Chapter 37

JENNA WOKE FROM a deep and dreamless sleep to caresses so tender and gentle she thought perhaps she *was* just dreaming. Then she knew she was feeling hands, hands that knew her well. "Mornin', beautiful," Scott whispered as her eyelids fluttered open. "Happy anniversary."

She started to get up. "And just where do you think you're going?" Scott protested, grabbing her and pulling her back to him. "I want a foul-mouthed, disgusting, first-thing-in-the-morning kiss before you go." Rolling her eyes, she indulged his bizarre mood.

When she slipped back into bed and into his arms, it became readily apparent that he was very much in a silly, playful mood. Before they knew it they were laughing so hard neither one heard the knocking at the door. Kristin was reduced to yelling.

"You guys! I can only imagine what you're doing in there. Keep the racket down so some of us – well, all right, so *I* can sleep." Jenna got up, pulled on a long t-shirt and was opening the door as Scott headed for the shower.

"What do you mean sleep?" Jenna said, the picture of innocence. "We were just playing alarm clock for you. It's time to get up, little sis. We've got a lot to do today. You need to get dressed." Kristin giggled as Jenna turned the tables on her. "Come on in. Scott's in the shower."

"So what do we have in mind for today," Kristin asked, dropping in a chair.

"Got time for some shopping?" Jenna asked.

"Always," Kristin grinned.

"Then Scott wants to take you and Mom out for lunch. I'm doing lunch with my manager. We've got special plans for tonight, and then we leave tomorrow at ten. You're coming with us, right?"

"Yep," Kristin said. "I've decided. I'm coming."

"Great!" Jenna grinned, then gave her a big hug. "So you've got packing to do."

"Right," Kristin agreed. "Good thing you got me up early."

ADELLA GREETED JENNA in the kitchen with a huge, motherly hug. "My leetle girl. How are you, baby?" she crooned as the two rocked back and forth. "I wanted to be here yesterday, when you arrive, but it was my granddaughter Luisa's first birthday – beeeg party!"

"I'm fine, Adella. I'm good," Jenna said, knowing full well that the woman who'd practically raised her would decide that for herself. Adella took Jenna by the shoulders and looked her up and down before finally nodding.

"Yes. You are," Adella agreed, then gave her "leetle girl" another big hug.

Jenna and Kristin got themselves cups of coffee, then went to join Linda in the dining room. Jenna gave her mother a kiss on the cheek, then grabbed the entertainment section of the *L.A. Times*.

"Thought you'd want to see that," Linda said. "There's a nice spread on the benefit last night. There's a picture of you and Scott on page three. I'm surprised they didn't have one of you speaking. You should talk to Brian or Bella about that."

"Mom always did like to manage my managers," Jenna explained to Kristin, as they both poured over the article. Linda read the editorial page.

"You're awfully quiet this morning, Mom," Jenna finally observed. "You okay?"

"I'm fine. I'm just trying to decide if I should go with you when you all leave tomorrow."

"That's a great idea," Jenna said. Kristin agreed.

"Actually, I'm thinking I'll wait and go later. I don't want to intrude on your sisterly time together."

"You wouldn't be intruding," Kristin protested. "The three of us could have a blast."

"No, I've got a lot of legal matters to get finished up, the houses and everything. I'd enjoy myself more if I knew that was all done and behind me. I promise I'll be out soon."

"As long as you promise to come when you're finished," Jenna said, getting up to deliver a hug to her mother.

"Don't you worry. I promise, sweetie," Linda smiled.

THE END OF the afternoon, Jim and Sue pulled into their old driveway and let themselves in the kitchen door. "Anybody home," Jim yelled.

"Out here," Jenna called from the back deck where she, Scott, Linda and Kristin were lounging by the pool. Linda had had enough of the labor-intensive tropical landscaping of the Beverly Hills house. Nor was she content with the overgrown rose garden that had come with this house. Jim and Sue had rarely spent much time at home, much less relaxing outdoors, so they'd barely ever even noticed the landscaping, beyond noting that the gardeners had come through with their leaf blowers, leaving everything in their wake neat and trim. Jim had used the pool as part of a crack-of-dawn fitness regimen, nothing more.

All that had changed. Decks had been built to accommodate and compliment the freeform shape of the pool and a landscape designer had brought a coherence and Zen-like calm to the rest of the space with contrasting swaths of river rock and washed gravel amidst a minimalist xeriscape of drought-tolerant dessert plantings. The effect was tranquil and serene. Linda felt profoundly at peace in this garden.

Jim came bounding out to greet them, with Sue not far behind. Jenna jumped up. The way her brother hugged her, then hugged her some more, brought immediate tears to her eyes.

"Hey, don't you go getting all emotional on me," Jim laughed. "Don't worry – I'm still the S.O.B. we all know and love. Okay, with a soft side now. Just let's keep it within these four walls, okay?"

Jenna wiped her eyes, then gave him a sisterly punch on the arm. "You always were a softy," she joshed.

"Well, that softy's back, where you're concerned, little sis," Jim said, dropping the shuck and jive. "I want to pick up where we left off twenty years ago. I want to erase the last twenty years between us the way Dad erased them for you. I want to show you that I love you again."

Jenna couldn't speak for a moment. Finally, she tipped her head to one side and looked her brother in the eye. "I have my big brother back," she marveled. "Man, this is so great. I love *you*, Jim."

After a quick half hour of catching up, Jim got to his feet. "I hate to have to run, but we're due downtown before seven. Next time you're out, let's plan a real visit. Scott, it was good seeing you again." The two shook hands. "One thing, Scott," he said, looking entirely serious. "You ever decide to make an honest woman outta my sister, forget anything you heard here about me being a softy You better be prepared to make one hellova case, young man." The two grinned at each other.

"You had me worried there for a minute, bro," Scott laughed.

"Stay that way," Jim said. "You're gonna have to *beg* me for my sister's hand."

SCOTT WAS IN the study with Linda when Jenna came down, dressed and ready for their dinner and celebration. Scott jumped to his feet, stunned and whistled in appreciation. The tiniest of halter tops, spangled with rhinestones, plunged to meet a suggestion of a skirt made up of diaphanous strips of chiffon. At rest, the dress provided plenty of coverage. In motion it presented an entirely different picture. The evening's plans called for going dancing.

"My God, I thought you looked incredible last night, but this is – outstanding," he said in the measured tones of a knowledgeable connoisseur. Taking her by one hand, he spun her around for the full view. "Last night was wholesome, demure, ripe. This – oh, my – far sexier. Provocative, alluring, tempting. Maybe we should order in. I don't know if I can handle all those men staring at you." She laughed at him and kissed him on the nose.

"I can change if you think you'll get too jealous," she teased him. "I mean, if being jealous of one man makes you crazy, what's going to happen when it's a roomful? That'd be hard on you, poor baby, wouldn't it?"

"You think you're so funny, don't you?" Scott played at sulking. "I may be jealous of one man in particular," he whispered in her ear, then pulled back to share the rest of his thoughts with Linda as well, "but every man who looks at you tonight will be the jealous ones, not me. I'll be the envy of them all, and I'll love every minute of it."

"You two better get going before I have to call the vice squad," Linda laughed. "Scott, you better keep an eye on her tonight."

OVER A GLASS of champagne for Jenna and a cranberry juice and sparkling water for himself, Scott toasted the woman of his dreams. "To us! A year tonight since we met, and look at how far we've come. I knew I loved you that night, but God, I love you even so much more tonight."

Jenna raised her glass with a quiet nod. "To us. It's been a tough year, but you've been there for me through it all and showed me how to love, and for that I'm grateful. You told me that night that one day I'd be in your life, and I thank God you were right. I love you more then I ever thought possible."

They enjoyed a sumptuous meal, danced their feet off at not one but two dance clubs, then finished the night up at a little Santa Monica jazz spot Scott had stumbled on a few years earlier. Curled up in the back of the family limo on their way home, Jenna finally fell asleep in Scott's arms. Scott played with the amazingly silly strips of her skirt and smiled.

When they pulled up to Linda's, Scott put a finger to his lips as Randy opened the door for them. Disengaging himself from her, he stepped out of the car, then reached back in, took her in his arms and managed to carry her into the house without waking her. He got her all the way to their room, set her on the bed and reached for the light before she opened an eye. Her grin told him she'd been awake the entire time.

"You weren't going to let this night end without kissing me, were you?" she whispered. "After all, you got that far last year." He touched her lips with one finger, then brought his lips to hers.

"Let me go further this year?" She didn't resist.

THE NEXT MORNING, Kristin was packed, ready and eager to leave with Scott and Jenna.

Jenna sought out Adella and hugged her goodbye. "You take good care of Mom, okay?"

"Don't worry. I take good care of everything and everybody," Adella said. "You take good care of yourself."

"I will, Adella," Jenna assured her. "I'll miss you."

"You are too busy already. Don't you waste any time missing Adella," she said dismissively, stepping back and crossing her arms over her broad chest. She gave Jenna one more parting visual inspection. "I never think you can be all healed so soon You look good. You will be okay," she said, satisfied with what she saw.

Jenna found her mother by the front door and slipped an arm around her. "You get your business taken care of and then we expect you in Boston."

Linda wrapped Jenna in an all-encompassing embrace. "I will. You take care, sweetie. I love you," Linda whispered in her daughter's ear, then repeated the same hugs and sentiments with Scott and Kristin. For Kristin, she added, "Honey, I'm going to miss you, more than I can say."

Kristin gave her an extra hug. "Me, too."

Then they all hurried out to the waiting car. Randy helped load bags into the trunk and they pulled away. Linda and Adella stood on the step waving them off.

Adella went bustling back to her work. Linda drifted out to the deck. Cupping the palms of her hands into the flow of a small wall-mounted fountain, she carried the contents over to a miniature rose she'd brought from the old house and watered it. It had been a Mother's Day gift from Chris – when? She remembered. It was the Mother's Day after he'd finally decided he wanted a place of his own, her fiscally conservative son who knew he had a good thing going, living at home and socking away his paychecks towards a down payment on a luxury condo on the beach. She'd nursed that little rose for six years now. Suddenly, for the first time, her nest felt empty.

Linda sat down and allowed herself to examine that feeling, prying and prodding at its many mysterious facets, tentatively, cautiously, like a wary farmer who's just discovered a glowing, pulsating little UFO in the lower forty. The feeling for her, she discovered after sufficient introspection, held as many charms as fears, as much promise as pain. She found herself anticipating her trip to Boston, not only for the pleasure of spending time with her girls, as she'd taken to referring to Jenna and Kristin, but also at the anticipation of spending time with Jenna's new extended family – a family that extended to that cantankerous Joe Tenny.

She went inside and placed a call to her attorney.

THE SUN WAS setting as the limo pulled through the gates and up Scott's gravel driveway. It had taken them an hour to make the drive from Boston's Logan Airport. Kristin gaped at the beauty and age of the old place, at the broad lawn and towering trees, at the ocean in the distance. The three of them climbed out of the car, Jenna and Scott with tired sighs, Kristin in a hurry to see it all. Scott and Georgie unloaded the trunk and brought all their bags around to the kitchen. Jeremy and Carrie emerged from the studio at the sound of their arrival.

Kristin was everywhere at once. "Oh, this place is just so wonderful. No wonder you love it here," she said to Jenna. "It's so different from California."

"And this is just the tip of the iceberg. The differences are endless," Jenna assured her. "I can't wait to show you."

"I didn't get to see anything but the hospital and the hotel, the last time we were here," Kristin realized.

"Don't worry, there's a heck of a lot more to Boston, and New England, than that," Jenna laughed. "Wait'll you see."

"Welcome home," Carrie called to them as she and Jeremy made their way across the path from the barn.

"You remember Kristin," Jenna said as Carrie reached them.

"Hi, Kristin. It's great that you've decided to come east for a while," Carrie welcomed her. "I know Jenna's really happy you're here."

Scott came out and rejoined them on the grass. The sound of crickets filled the warm night air.

"Hey, man," he said to Jeremy. "What's up, bro?"

"Plenty," Jeremy assured him. "You gotta hear what Tim came up with for that song Jeff and I wrote, the Harley guy thing. It really kicks butt now. I also spent some time on that other thing…"

"Let me hear," Scott said, taking Jeremy by the arm and heading with him back out to the studio.

"We'll hang here, show Kristin around and get her settled," Jenna said called after them.

"Fine, hon," Scott said. "We won't be long. I know everyone's hungry."

"So how was the trip?" Jeremy asked as they headed over.

"Categorically unfuckingbelievable, bro," Scott said. "Now I really have to get that song finished for her."

"That's what I was referring to," Jeremy told him. They entered the barn and stepped into the sound-proofed inner studio space.

"Mmmm, it always feels so good comin' home," Scott said, feeling mellow. His mood lasted for less than twelve bars of what Jeremy wanted him to hear.

"You're shittin' me, right?" Scott said, trying to hold his temper in check. "You – like that?"

"No, as a matter of fact," Jeremy said vehemently. "I *love* that."

"It's – grotesque," Scott said. "Loose it."

"The fuck I will," Jeremy said, starting again at the top. "Give it half a fuckin' chance, will ya?" Scott wouldn't. At bar ten, he went and unplugged Jeremy's amp. Then he grabbed a Porto Real panatela, lit it up, blew smoke in Jeremy's general direction and stormed back out of the studio.

Jeremy was right on his heels. "So when the fuck do you plan on finishing the damned thing so we can record it? It's been months since we started working on it. So much for your idea of collaboration. Collaborating with you's like trying to collaborate with some kinda lunatic squid, all attitude and squirting ink."

"Very colorful," Scott snapped, puffing away.

"Only the squidd'd have the goddamn song done by now."

"If it had somebody with some semblance of talent to work with, it would," Scott said. "I can't explain to you why something's not working. I just know when it ain't. And that definitely ain't, my friend."

The two came storming into the house. "Come on," Jeremy called to Carrie. "We're outta here. It's time to go home."

Carrie came hustling into the kitchen. "Whaddya mean? I thought we were all going out for dinner?" she questioned, confused.

"Come on," Jeremy said and ushered her out the door without a further word.

Jenna, who'd followed Carrie in from the porch, turned to Scott, who was still furiously puffing on his cigar. "Now what?"

"What?" Scott tried to bluff his way around his latest outburst. "I can smoke in my own house if I want to."

"This isn't about smoking and you know it. You guys are fighting again."

"And if we are?"

"Oh, for cryin' out loud," Jenna said angrily. "Do we have to do this again?"

"No, we don't," Scott said adamantly. "It's really none of your business. Just go and find Kristin and let's get some dinner."

Jenna looked at him. He held her gaze, then stubbed out the cigar. "Come on, baby," he said, quieter now. "Let's not get bent outta shape. We're tired. We're hungry. Let's just kiss and make up and go eat."

Jenna sighed, thought about it and decided this wasn't a fight worth fighting tonight. She could take him on another day, that she knew. And there'd be another day, that she also knew. Scott provided opportunities. She took his hand and kissed it.

"I love you," she said. "Even when you act like a child."

"Think of it as on-the-job training for motherhood," Scott suggested.

Chapter 38

THE NEXT FEW weeks flew in a creative hash of writing, rehearsing and recording, and in Scott's case, arguing, exploding and apologizing.

Jenna brought her band out to Boston, subletting a condo nearby for them for a month. Three weeks later, Brian flew out to hear the results. The net effect of their prolonged hiatus was a slingshot delivery of energy and drive: their output was electric. The following day they went into the studio and laid down the final four tracks for an album that would hit the stores well in time for Christmas.

Blacklace had a pair of huge shows coming up in early November at Madison Square Garden in New York. Jenna would sing with them on both of those. And for the first time, she would record two songs with them. They too had an album scheduled for release in November. They also had another new voice singing with them.

"You gotta hear this kid," Jeremy told Scott. "You gotta let me bring him down. He's phenomenal, absolutely unique. Here's this delicate little guy who looks like he'd get blown away in a breeze, for chrissakes, who barely moves his fuckin' mouth when he sings. You get like absolutely zero sense he's working to produce the sound that comes out of him."

"So what does he sing?" Dan asked. "Bass? Baritone?"

"Yeah, and tenor and then some. This freak's got a full fuckin' two-octave range, and what he does with a falsetto should be illegal. You get him, you get the whole friggin' package."

"Get him in," Scott said. "This I gotta hear." Ryan Ellis signed on as back-up vocals. A week later, they discovered the kid played a mean ocarina as well. A week after that, Scott started calling him Wonder Boy. It'd be six months before Ryan would be old enough to order a beer in Boston.

Kristin, a fast study, was all over Boston, taking to the city like Boston's Duck tour buses took to water. A few introductions and she was off and running, both professionally and socially. Jenna invited her to sit in with her band, though Kristin has no desire to play little sister backup to her famous big sister, nor did she take seriously Scott's invitation for her to sit in with Blacklace. It was fun, but she knew she was too sensitive to deal with all the underlying tension, the twenty-plus-year residue of long unresolved anger his band seemed to thrive on. She got to watch Scott and the rest in action, on more than one occasion, amazed by the way they could get over whatever the fracas of the moment was about and move on. She watched Scott oscillate from an almost childlike delight to towering rage in a flash, then careen off into a creative frenzy the likes of which she'd never seen. She wondered at Jenna's ability to tolerate – and love – a man of such volatility

JENNA HADN'T SEEN much of Carrie with all she was squeezing into her schedule. The two finally found time for to meet for lunch in Boston a week before the band would go to New York. Kristin joined them. Jenna and Kristin were already perusing menus when Carrie came hustling in.

"I'm so sorry I'm late," she said. "Fuckin' construction." Carrie took her seat, quickly skimmed the menu and was ready when a waiter approached the table. She ordered, then settled back, sighed and prepared to forget the demands of the world and enjoy Jenna and Kristin's company for the next hour or two. She found herself studying Jenna's face as Kristin finished ordering. When the waiter left them, she sat forward.

"Jenna, are you feeling okay? I've gotta tell you, girlfriend, you look tired," Carrie said with concern. "You getting enough sleep?"

"I'm tired, all right," Jenna agreed, "between working with two bands and keeping up with Scott. And you're right, I haven't been getting anywhere near enough sleep. I'll be fine once New York's over and the albums have been released. I feel like I'm suddenly being pulled in twenty directions. I used to handle stress like this without even noticing. I guess I'm just out of practice."

"She isn't eating right, either," Kristin said.

"Tattle tale," Jenna chided her. Kristin stuck her tongue out in response.

"My, my. Aren't you getting good at this little sister business," Jenna complimented her.

"No, really. She says she isn't eating because it makes her sick," Kristin told Carrie. "I think it's nerves. You're trying to do too much," she said to Jenna.

"You're too young to know what you're talkin' about," Jenna retorted.

After taking another critical look, Carrie sat back and crossed her arms. "You're pregnant," she stated flatly. "Don't bother wasting money on a home pregnancy test. I'm never wrong."

Both Jenna and Kristin's mouths dropped.

"Oh, Carrie, don't be ridiculous," Jenna said, once she'd regained her equilibrium. "You know I'm on the patch."

"Yeah, and I know you've told me twice how you've forgotten to put a new patch on when you should and had to start over because of it."

"What do you mean?" Kristin asked.

"You change them weekly," Jenna said. "I'm in a hurry, I remember to take it off, I take a shower – okay, maybe I forgot to put a new one back on, once or twice."

"And maybe one of those once or twices was critical," Carrie persisted.

"But I remembered within a day of –"

Jenna stopped mid-sentence with a realization. "No, wait – I know what happened," she said, finally remembering. "Labor Day weekend. I didn't start on time. Scott surprised me with a quick trip up to the lake. I got up there and realized I should have started but I didn't have one with me. I didn't figure it'd be a problem. I got home, but then I didn't remember till the day after that. It must have been like three, maybe even four days. I totally screwed up."

"And, let's see, in three or four days, knowing you guys, you probably did it, what, a dozen times?" Carrie said somewhat sarcastically. Kristin's eyes went wide.

"You're kidding, right?" she said to Carrie.

"She doesn't know?" Carrie said to Jenna.

"No, she doesn't know," Jenna said defensively, "at least, not until now she didn't know."

"Know what?" Kristin asked, now thoroughly confused.

"That Scott and I practically qualify as sex addicts, by some people's definitions of what's normal," Jenna said. "Let's just say that he's always been pretty compulsive about sex, and that ever since I've been with him, I'm right there along for the ride."

"Scott and Jenna make rabbits look like lazy-ass slackers, sweetie," was how Carrie summed it all up.

"Oh," Kristin said. "Ooookay. So – if you *were* pregnant, how do you think Scott'd feel about it? How would *you* feel about it."

Carrie laughed. "I can tell you how Scott'd feel. He'd be thrilled. He's an awesome father. God, you should see him with babies."

Jenna smiled at the thought.

"And you?" Kristin persisted.

"I know I'd be wicked happy," Jenna said, feeling herself flush with pleasure at the thought.

Carrie reached into her handbag and withdrew a cell phone. "Call your doctor and make an appointment. The call's on me – consider it an early baby shower present."

Jenna was offered an appointment a week hence, or if she could get there in twenty-five minutes, a time slot had freed up because of a last minute cancellation.

"Forget dessert," she told Carrie and Kristin. "You guys are coming with me."

DR. WILLIAMS GREETED Jenna warmly as she entered her office.

"I trust everything's well since I last saw you?" she asked, glancing quickly through Jenna's records. "No problems, I hope?"

"No, I got through all that all right, Julie."

"What can I do for you today, then, Jenn?" the doctor asked.

"Well…I haven't been feeling well, generally speaking. I'm tired all the time. I get nauseated and can't eat. I – think I may be pregnant," Jenna said a bit sheepishly.

"You were on…" Julie looked back at Jenna's cover page for birth control information, "the patch, I think?"

"I may have messed up, so to speak. Labor Day weekend. An unexpected trip. I was several days late starting a new month…" she finished lamely. "I feel like an idiot. But – I'll be a happy idiot if I am."

"Well, let's just find out. I'll have the nurse get you ready."

JENNA REJOINED THE doctor in her office after a complete physical. "Well, you *are* a happy idiot, my dear," Julie said with a smile. "You're about six weeks pregnant. This should be a Memorial Day baby. Holiday to holiday – how auspicious!"

Jenna strolled back out to the waiting room attempting to look as nonchalant as she could manage.

"So?" Kristin said, jumping up.

"Yeah? So?" echoed Carrie. "What did she say?"

"She said – yes!" Jenna smiled ear to ear. "I'm pregnant!"

"Did I tell you?" Carrie said proudly. "Can I call them or can I call them? Oh my God, Jenna, Scott is going to be so damned happy. You just wait and see. He'll go absolutely berserk with joy."

"God, he was so wonderful when I was pregnant with Derek's baby – he was totally cool with stepping in like it was his," Jenna said. "This time it really *is* his baby. Oh, Carrie, I just couldn't be happier."

Kristin put her arm around Jenna and gave her a sisterly kiss. "Congratulations!" she said. "Okay, let's see if I can figure this out. I'm gonna be a, what, half-auntie? Is there such a thing?"

"Hey, let's not worry about the half stuff any more," Jenna said, giving Kristin a loving squeeze as they left the doctor's office. "You're gonna be the best auntie ever. And this is going to be one lucky child." Her hand instinctively moved to rest on her still washboard-flat belly.

"So, when are you going to tell Scott?" Kristin asked, already bursting with excitement at the thought. "Tonight would be good, don't you think? I'm going to be out. You can fix him a romantic dinner, then like pop the news."

"I think I'd rather wait till next weekend when Mom's here. We're planning an end-of-the-season bash at the lake – all of you guys'll be up there, of course, and Scott's trying to get Missy and Alex and Laurel and her family to all come. His sister's even trying to come – I've yet to meet her. It'd be perfect, telling him where it all began."

"I can't say anything for a whole week and a half?" Kristin cried. "Oh my God, I can't!"

"Oh, yes you can," Jenna assured her. "You spill the beans and you can hitchhike your sorry butt back to L.A., baby sis. Not one word."

GETTING READY FOR the end-of-summer weekend proved far more demanding than Jenna had ever expected; she couldn't have pulled it off without Kristin's help. Between trying to hide the early symptoms of her pregnancy and maintaining dual rehearsal schedules, she was exhausted beyond anything she'd ever experienced. She didn't want it to show. She was delighted when her mother announced she was coming a few days earlier than she'd originally said she would.

"Oh, Mom, am I ever glad to see you!" Jenna exclaimed to her surprised mother when she arrived.

"I know you love me, dear," Linda said, "but I have to say, I've never had such an enthusiastic welcome!" She gave her daughter a bemused hug.

"I need help!" Jenna said, honestly. "There's so much to do and I'm flat running outta time!"

"Then put me to work, my dear. You know I love feeling useful," Linda said. "Where do I start?"

"No, no. I didn't mean right this second. Relax! You just got here."

"She means grab a cup of coffee and start takin' ordahs," growled a familiar voice from the kitchen. Scott's father came strolling out.

"Well, Joe Tenny, as I live and breathe," Linda said with evident pleasure. "They roped you into working, too?"

"Just another galley slave, at your service. I take ordahs from anyone, ma'am," Joe said affably. "I should think, between me and you, we can whip this little shindig into shape in no time. May I take your bags to your room, madam?"

"That would be most kind," Linda responded demurely.

Jenna couldn't wait until they were up at the lake, everything was going smoothly, the news had been announced and she could just kick back with Scott and relax. Her biggest problem now would be disguising her condition not only from Scott, but from her mother's sharp eyes as well.

DINNER THAT EVENING was a catch-as-catch-can affair. Joe threw a couple of huge steaks on the grill. Missy and Alex pulled in just as he flipped them. Laurel had called to say that she, Rick and Luka wouldn't be able to get there till the following afternoon. In the hands of a temperamental photographer, a three-day photo shoot she was working had turned into a four-day nightmare; she promised to keep everyone well entertained with stories from those horrific four days.

Scott's sister Annie had cancelled at the last minute. "Typical," had been Scott's one-word reaction.

Dinner was laid out buffet style in the kitchen, which fit Jenna's needs just fine. She served herself small portions, carefully cantilevered to appear larger than they actually were, and hoped she could force herself to choke down enough of her dinner to avoid notice. She was prepared should her mother comment. She'd never expected Scott to notice, but he did.

Coming around with a platter of seconds, he tried to encourage her to take more. "Come on, babe," he wheedled, "you haven't been eating half enough lately. I know you love looking fabulous – and you do, don't get me wrong – but you've hardly eaten anything today. You're gonna make yourself sick."

"I've been snacking all day, like a world-class couch potato, honest," she assured him with her mental fingers crossed. "Grazing. Eating on the fly. Don't you go worrying about me, Mr. Skin and Bones."

Scott shrugged, accepted what she said and moved on, but Kristin caught her eye as she said it and the look that telegraphed between the two sisters lasted just long enough to catch Linda's attention. Like the phone company putting a trace on a call, she'd had just enough time to register and interpret this look's possible implications. After dinner she cornered Jenna in the laundry room.

"Okay, my sweet, tell Mother what's wrong," she said. She'd never been one to beat around the bush.

"What do you mean, what's wrong?" Jenna said, pulling a small load out of the dryer. "Nothing's wrong, Mom. Everything's fine. The weekend's gonna be great, once we get everything done and get up there."

"You're pregnant, aren't you." She wasn't asking a question.

Jenna suddenly found herself wishing she'd followed her father's dreams and become the actress/daughter he'd so hoped for. She could use some training in method acting to fall back on right about now.

"Good grief, Mom. Where would you get an idea like that?" she tossed off casually, she hoped, buying time. She didn't want to have to lie, but she was prepared to if given no other choice. She started folding a sheet. Linda took the other end to help.

"Mothers know," Linda said.

"Mothers *think* they know," Jenna countered.

"You're clearly bone tired, you're as white as this sheet, you aren't eating. You're pregnant," Linda summed up her case.

"Hell, Mom. I've been working like a horse, I don't live at the beach like I did when I was a teenager and I'm eating just fine, thank you very much. Please, enough of this nonsense," Jenna said.

Scrambling to get control of the conversation, she tried introducing a new topic. "Wait'll you see the lake house, Mom. You're going to absolutely love it. I don't know what it is about the place, but I can like totally relax up there like nowhere else. It's heaven."

"You're changing the subject," Linda observed correctly.

"What subject?" Jenna said, completing the last fold and taking the sheet from her mother's hands.

"You know what –"

Linda's thought was cut short by a rapping on the open laundry room door. "Ain't interruptin' anything, am I?" Joe asked, putting his head in.

"Not at all," Jenna said, breathing a silent sigh of relief. Saved by the bell – or in this case, the knock. "We're just gabbin'."

"Can I steal your mom for a bit? She seems to think them California beaches are the last word. I keep tellin' her, it ain't a beach if it don't have dunes. Might as well be a lake beach with trucked-in sand. She needs showin'."

"You got a problem with beaches with sidewalks, Joe?" Jenna laughed. "I never knew there was any other kind till I was twenty."

"Well, your mom still don't. Gotta get her set straight."

"Good luck. When Mom thinks she knows something, it's hard work to change her mind," Jenna observed with a wink to her mother.

JENNA FINISHED PACKING for herself and went in search of Scott, but the only person she found in the house was Kristin.

"Where is everybody?" she asked.

"Missy and Alex went into Boston looking for entertainment. I though about going with them but decided not to – there's more than enough entertainment here, watching you trying to keep your dinner down." She giggled.

"Thanks," Jenna said wryly. "You seen Scott?"

"He said he was going over to the studio."

Jenna looked out the window. The studio lights were on. "I'll go find him," she said. "As for you, Ms. I've-Got-a-Secret, don't you *dare* blow my cover, you hear?"

"Just as long as you don't blow your dinner, sis," Kristin vowed.

"Gee, thanks," Jenna said, almost ready to head to the bathroom at the thought.

JENNA FOUND SCOTT hunched over the piano with a notepad in his lap.

"Am I interrupting?" she asked him.

"Yep, but feel free," he responded, casually tossing the notepad to the floor beside him. Face down.

"Come. Sit," he said, moving over on the piano bench to make room for her to sit down beside him. He started playing "Heart and Soul."

"What are you up to?" she asked.

"Just trying to lure the Muse," he answered. "Snarky dame, my Muse. She can give me the hardest damn time." He started to sing, "*Heart and soul, I fell in love with you, heart and soul, the way a fool would do...*"

"*Madly...*" Jenna joined in harmonizing, "*because you hold me tight...*" She picked out the accompaniment, three octaves lower than Scott's melody line.

Jenna stopped singing. "Your Muse – you do treat her right, I hope," she teased. "Or do you try controlling her the way you try to control everybody else in your life?"

"Damn straight. What's the expression – you train them or they train you, right? I don't let her get away with shit." Scott started in on the next verse. *"Heart and soul, I begged to be adored, lost control and tumbled overboard..."*

"Gladly..." Jenna joined in again, for just the one word. She stopped plunking the bass line, swung a leg over the bench and turned to face him. "No, Scott, you have to woo the Muse. You gotta buy her jewels, send her flowers, make passionate love to her all night long," she said with a seductive smile. "Honey, you gotta treat her at *least* as good as you treat me."

Scott stopped playing, jumped up and grabbed his head, miming agony. "Oh, man, you mean I gotta go all out for *two* dames? I'm just one fuckin' guy here. Women!" he groaned dramatically.

Abruptly, he reached down, grabbed her and swung her up in his arms. "Like this?" he asked and kissed her hard on the mouth. Then he carried her over to the couch and dropped her unceremoniously along its length.

"Like this?" he asked again, reaching down to brusquely unzip her jeans.

"Like this?" he asked, grabbing the hems of both legs and yanking them off of her in one swift motion.

"Like this?" he asked, running a hand up her leg and reaching for her undies...

Chapter 39

IT DIDN'T HELP that morning sickness kicked in the following morning. Fortunately, Scott had woken early and, in a rush of first light energy, had gone over to the studio in a sunrise tryst with that finicky Muse of his, to finish up the lyrics that had eluded him the night before.

Jenna didn't appear in the kitchen until her stomach had completely settled, and even then could barely tolerate the smell of coffee. Scott offered to pour her a cup, not once but twice. The second time, she decided to deal with what she knew would be a continual problem if she didn't. "Actually, I'm thinking about giving up coffee for a while. It's making me too jumpy – I'm switching to tea just to see if it helps." That satisfied both Scott and her mother, who'd bemoaned her daughter's heavy caffeine intake for years.

"Okay, listen up, fellow travelers," Scott said, pushing back in his chair as breakfast wound down. "As soon as we douse the campfire, we menfolk'll finish packing up the wagons for the expedition to the North Country. And as soon as the womenfolk have finished primpin' and puttin' on their bonnets and stowed the rest of their gear, we'll get Ozzie the ox hitched up and hit the trail."

Jenna, who'd been pulling perishables from the refrigerator to go into a cooler, came over and wrapped her arms around Scott. "Oh, Mr. Tenny, sir," Jenna purred with a backwoods accent, "You really know how to get to a woman. I just go all to mush when you get all manly like that. Why, you stir my very soul, Mr. Tenny."

"I'm hopin' you'll want to park your pretty behind on my front seat when it's time for the wagons to roll, little lady," Scott drawled. "An' Miss Kristin, I'd be perfectly honored if you'd be wantin' to join us."

Not one to miss a thematic opportunity, Joe caught Linda by the wrist as she passed by him. "And would you, pretty lady, be innerested in hitchin' a ride with an ol' – I mean, a seasoned codger? I got me a pert little pair of mules to pull my rig. You could do worse," he said with an exaggerated wink.

"I would entertain such an offer, sir" Linda answered loftily.

"Looks like you're stuck with me, ma'am," Alex managed a drawl with distinctly Liverpudlian overtones, doffing an imaginary cap to Missy.

Missy gave her boyfriend, in his favorite old Liverpool soccer shirt and cutoffs, the once-over. "If your buggy's as fashionably turned out as you are, why, I'd be honored, Mr. Calby," she decided.

The wagon train, composed of two 4x4s and Alex's perfectly restored, pale yellow 1965 Jaguar XKE, pulled up in front of the lake house a few hours later.

"THIS IS GORGEOUS!" Linda announced taking in the scope and scale of what Scott had described to her as his little summer getaway. "This isn't a lake house. This is a lake estate."

"Compound is actually the technical term," Scott said in a feeble attempt at modesty.

"Oh, man," Kristin breathed in agreement. "The smell of the woods and the breeze and the autumn colors and the – oh my God, is that a moose?" she said, excitedly pointing down towards the shore below. "I've never seen a moose!"

"Oh, wow, she's right! Look, Mom," Jenna said, now pointing as well and equally excited. "It's my first, too!"

None of the women saw Scott and Joe elbow each other. Scott finally had to laugh. "It's a sculpture. It's actually just a flat piece of steel, a silhouette. I came across it last month. Dad brought it up and installed it for me. I knew it'd get the city slickers."

"Seems to work pretty good, too," Joe agreed with a grin.

"I'M POOPED," JENNA said, following Scott into the master bedroom. She dropped her bags on the floor and threw herself face down on the king-sized four-poster. She loved this room, with its wraparound windows, giant fireplace and treetop view.

Shivering, she told Scott, "Build me a fire, mountain man." He went over to the fireplace, picked up a remote control and turned on the flames.

"You sure you're okay, Baby Blue?" Scott asked, coming over and joining her on the bed, curling up beside her and rubbing her back. "You were quiet all the way up. You look so tired."

"I'm sorry, hon. I *am* tired. Now that we're finally here, I'll be able to unwind and get some rest. I feel like I could sleep for the next twenty-four hours. No – now that we're here, I want to get out and do things, too. This place brings out the explorer in me. What am I going to do?" she groaned.

"Do both," he suggested. "Come for a walk, some warm-up exploring, then take a serious nap, why don't you? People won't start getting here till later in the afternoon. You can clock some serious Z's before then."

Rolling over, Jenna snuggled into his arms. "How's about we start the explorations in here…?"

JEREMY AND CARRIE arrived first, with a seemingly reluctant Aiden in tow but he cheered up when Travis came bounding in, Jeff and Denise not far behind.

"I've got a new tent," Travis announced. "It's huge. Want to bunk out there with me?" he asked Aiden.

"Wicked cool," the normally sullen fifteen-year-old decided, nodding shrewdly. "Okay by you, Mom?" he asked Carrie.

"Oh yeah, that'd be wicked okay by me," Carrie agreed without hesitation. "In fact, do me a favor and camp a couple counties over." What had started on the way up as a light-hearted conversation on school-night curfews had turned into a fifty-mile sulk. A little breathing space between the two of them would be a good thing. Aiden was out the door in a shot, Travis right on his heels.

Tim and Paula came tramping in just in time to hear Carrie mutter a less than motherly, "Teenagers. They should be flash-frozen and stored till the hormones settle and they're fit to live with again."

Ten minutes later, Laurel and Rick descended with Luka and all the requisite pre-toddler paraphernalia it would take to contain and amuse the ten-month-old. It took Rick four trips in from the car to unload everything they'd brought.

"Phew," said Joe. "It that everybody for tonight?"

"I do believe the gang's all here," Scott said cheerfully. "Let's party!"

"Laissez les bons temps roulez!" Joe offered.

"What's that mean?" Scott asked his father.

"Let's party!"

CARRIE TOOK JENNA aside as soon as she could without attracting unwanted attention. "How are you doing?" she asked with genuine concern.

"I'm hanging in there," Jenna answered. "Man, I can't wait for this rollercoaster to settle down though. I'm so queasy, and not just in the morning. Plus I keep getting lightheaded, and of course only when I can least deal with it, natch. I'm going to tell Scott tonight, no matter what. I don't think I could cover it up another day if I had to. It's not fair – I know people who breeze through pregnancy symptom-free."

"Sure you do," Carrie scoffed. "Anyone who says they're symptom free's just damned good at denial. Carrots and crackers, trail mix, and plenty of liquids. That's how I got through the worst of it."

"And what's with the weird taste in my mouth?"

"Just another variation on the theme," Carrie assured her. "It'll settle down again. Keeping it a secret can't help, though. The sooner you go public the better."

LATE AFTERNOON CHORES settled out along the usual gender lines: the women in the kitchen readying supper, the men, Luka included, hauling firewood and building their fire in the cavernous indoor fireplace, all under Joe's close supervision, then huddling around the grill on the deck while Joe held forth on the finer points of Yankee grilling technique. The minute the meager October sun dipped below the horizon, the temperature took an unmistakable nosedive. Winter was in the air.

In the kitchen, pots of water were on the boil and cutting boards covered practically every surface. Jenna was decimating a head of cabbage for cole slaw when a wave of dizziness forced her to find a stool on which to sit down until it passed. This time, Linda saw her and came right over.

"Jenna, what is *wrong* with you?" she demanded. "You haven't been yourself since I arrived – and for who knows how long before that, if I know you. If you're not pregnant, then something's very much the matter and we have to find out what it is," she insisted.

"Mom, please," Jenna said, rolling her eyes in exasperation. "I know you mean well but having you hovering over me doesn't help. I'll be all right. Please, don't worry so much about me. Do me a favor: go find Joe and keep him company. I have a feeling he's driving Scott equally crazy. "

Before long, platters of meat were being handed out to the men to start their grilling. Late season corn went into pots to boil and bowls of salads and chips, pitchers of lemonade and fixings all began to materialize on the long dining room table that could easily accommodate twenty. Scott never enjoyed these weekends more than when seeing this table ringed round with friends and family.

Most everyone was seated when Jenna took her place at one end of the table.

"You gonna make it, sis?" Kristin whispered to her.

Jenna was opening her mouth to respond in the affirmative when Scott swooped in dramatically with a large platter of sizzling baby back ribs, the last off the grill, and passed it under her nose to tantalize her – at least that had been his intention. "Baby backs for my Baby Blue," he said to tempt her. "Sloppy, yummy ribs – these you'll want to eat!"

Before he could even set them down, the pungent aroma of vinegar wafting from the barbecue sauce sent Jenna's stomach reeling. Jumping up from the table, she knocked her chair over backward with a crash that brought half the table to their feet as well, then rushed from the room, both hands clapped to her mouth, gagging wretchedly. Scott dropped the platter to the table and hurried off after her.

"What in God's name is going on? Jenna!" gasped Linda, starting to go after her daughter and Scott.

Kristin and Carrie's eyes met immediately. Carrie, who was closest, jumped up and caught Linda by the elbow to stop her. Kristin quickly joined her to put a restraining hand on Linda's shoulder.

"It's okay, dear," Carrie said. "Let them have a little time alone. I know it doesn't look it, but it's okay, really it is."

UPSTAIRS, SCOTT FOUND Jenna laying across the bed, as white as a ghost and gasping with nausea.

"Honey, oh God. I am so worried about you. You can't tell me this is just being tired. There's something wicked wrong. The minute you get back, you've got to see a doctor. I'm getting scared shitless here – do it for me, will you, babe? We've got to find out what the hell is going on with you."

Jenna pulled herself up, then slumped back against the pillows. "Hon, come here," she said weakly, patting the bedspread beside her. "Come hold me." Scott quickly kneeled next to her and pulled her to him. The fact that she was shaking set his heart racing with fear.

"Baby, baby," he murmured. "My poor baby."

"Well, yeah, actually," Jenna said quietly. "That *is* what's the problem. I've been to the doctor. Last week."

She pulled back to watch the effect of her words on him. So far, he was only registering fear, but bewilderment was beginning to make inroads.

"And...?"

"And, well, I just wanted to wait till we were all together up here to tell you."

"Tell me – what?" Scott asked, but the meaning of her words started to filter through the veils of confusion. He pulled back and looked at her – closely. "Jenna...?"

"Well, you remember Labor Day weekend, when we came up by ourselves? And had such a wild time? Well, we got me pregnant, my love, and that's what's going on. I've just been trying to cover it up so I could surprise you with the news, up here."

"We...you...oh, Jenna. Oh, my God! You're – pregnant? You're going to have a baby? My baby? We're – pregnant?" She nodded her head sweetly in response to each question.

"I'm – I – oh, God, this is fuckin' incredible. Wait a second – you're on birth control – aren't you?"

"I goofed," she said, meekly. "Turns out I'm a fool and it's not foolproof. I screwed up the timing. I'm – are you –?" Suddenly she wasn't quite sure what to say. "Are you – okay about this?"

"Am I okay about this? Does getting pregnant make you crazy as well as nauseous? Hell, I couldn't be happier. Yeah, like wow! I can't believe it! You're going to have a baby – our baby! I love you so much!"

Scott's voice had risen with each sentiment until he was shouting loud enough for everyone downstairs to hear that something was going on upstairs.

Carrie and Kristin looked at each other. "Finally!" Kristin said, laughing, which sent Carrie into hysterics, which rendered Kristin helpless with matching hysteria. The entire room fell abuzz with speculation.

"Will somebody *please* tell me what the *hell* is going on here?" Linda exclaimed in total exasperation. The whole room fell silent at the unexpected profanity from her oh-so-proper lips.

"Relax, deah," said Joe, dryly. "The parents are always the last to know..."

"No, what do you mean, finally?" Linda demanded of Kristin. "You *know* something, young lady – both of you do. Now you just tell me what's going on, you two, right now." Linda all but stamped her feet in frustration.

Scott appeared in the door of the dining room, with Jenna in his arms.

"Don't grill them, Mom," Jenna cried. "It's all my fault." Linda wheeled around. "I'm sorry – I didn't mean to go scaring anyone. I hate to say it, Mom, but – you were right. You guessed."

"We're going to have a baby!" Scott shouted. "Jenna's pregnant. She's gonna have our baby. I can't fucking believe it – we're pregnant! I'm going to be a father again, and this time, I swear on the souls of my two fabulous daughters who are fabulous entirely in spite of me, I'm gonna get it right."

Scott set Jenna down in front of her mother and went and threw his arms around Missy and Laurel. "Sorry, Dad. I'll listen to you about pretty much anything, but no way, 'in spite of you,'" Missy contradicted him, giving him a big kiss. "That's just plain ridiculous. I love you. Congratulations, Daddy!"

"Same goes for me, Dad. We couldn't be happier for you. And this means Luka's going to have a – what? – an uncle, I guess, almost his age for a playmate. Cool!" Rick joined her with Luka in his arms and all three gave Scott an all-inclusive family hug.

"Luka wants to say, 'Way to go, Grampa,' and so do I," Rick said, laughing. "My hat's off to you, old man."

"Watch the old man shit," Scott growled. "I'm young and virile and studly, and there's gonna be no livin' with me now!"

"Oh, if only you were jokin', my brother," Jeremy called from the far end of the table. "You have my heartfelt congratulations, regardless, and may God have mercy on all our sorry souls."

"How far along are you, Jenn?" Paula called across the table to Jenna.

Carrie intercepted the question. "About two months now."

"Your due date?" Denise wanted to know.

Kristin yelled, "Memorial Day."

"Excuse me, but you guys have been in on this for, like, *how* long?" Jeremy wanted to know.

"Just last week," Carrie told him.

"And you didn't tell me?" Jeremy said, miffed.

"Sorry darling, but it wasn't my secret to tell. It was Jenna's and Jenna's alone. Friends keep friends' secrets."

Jenna came over, put her arms around Carrie and planted a big kiss on her cheek. "Sweetie, since I met and fell in love with Scott," she said, flashing him a loving smile, "I've had a lot of amazing things happen to me. Amazing good and amazing bad. But one of the best amazing things has been you coming into my life, Carrie. I've never had a friend like you. Thank you for everything. You have become one of my favorite people in the universe, and that's no exaggeration."

Carrie held her close and whispered in her ear, "And you are mine, Jenn. I love you, so much." Scott came over and threw arms around both Carrie and Jenna, as if blessing a sacred union.

"Come on, now's our chance," Joe said in a stage whisper to Linda. The two quickly moved in Scott and Jenna's path.

"Ahem," Joe said, clearing his throat dramatically. "Son, I've told you before how happy I am to see you with this great woman. And now you're going to be parents together – goodness me. I just want to know when you plan on making an honest woman of her." Scott smiled, rolled his eyes and nodded. "Well, let me know so I can get it on my calendar," Joe said with a grin.

Linda all but pushed Joe aside. "Those sentiments go double for me. Jenn knows how happy I am to see this man in her life, this man who's loved her and been at her side through the most incredibly difficult year. I know you two will be wonderful parents."

Jenna found herself in tears as her mother embraced first her and then Scott. Joe took her mind off it with a bear hug, complete with a "congratulations, deah," and a peck on the cheek. Then he embraced his son.

Scott turned to all his friends, one arm around Jenna. "I want to thank all of you. I know this has been a rough year, not only for Jenna but for all of us, because we're family, and what happens to one member of a family happens to all. I have to say, this is the one of the best days I've had all year. What more could I ask for? I have at my side this wonderful family, the woman I love most in the world, and now we're going to have a baby. It doesn't get any better." He turned and planted a tremendous kiss on Jenna's lips.

"Yuck," could clearly be heard in the momentary silence.

"Travis, shut up," Jeff laughed.

Right on cue, Luka broke into a burbling infantile giggle, which brought the whole house down.

Jenna caught her breath after Scott's kiss, then turned to their assembled friends. "Guys, what Scott said about family is true, but I didn't have a clue how true until I had you in my corner this past year. When I got involved with Scott, I had no idea how you'd feel about me, but it didn't take long to find out. Now I have this wonderful extended family, the love of my life, and I'm carrying our child. I couldn't ask for more to celebrate."

"Are we *ever* gonna get to eat?" asked Aiden, peevishly.

"Yeah," said Travis. "We're starving to death."

Joe turned to the two boys. "Betcha didn't know it takes a month to starve to death, provided you've got watah."

Chapter 40

JEREMY, CARRIE, SCOTT and Jenna outlasted everyone else that night. Jeremy and Carrie were curled up in front of the smoldering remains of the fire. Scott and Jenna were stretched out on the couch, Jenna with her back to Scott, his arms wrapped around her, resting on what he no longer thought of as her flat belly. He was holding the woman he loved and their baby.

"So – inquiring minds hafta know: just how did Carrie and Kristin get roped into this little secret of yours?" Jeremy asked Jenna with a tired, loopy grin.

"We were having lunch and decided to take a pass on dessert and find out."

"You're making that up, right?" Scott said.

"Am I making it up?" Jenna asked Carrie, laughing.

"That's precisely how it came down," Carrie concurred. "I had it pegged. The minute she walked in, I knew."

"Then I swore them to secrecy," Jenna said. "It was going to be the great Columbus Day Surprise – guess I didn't quite make it to that. Mother Nature had other plans." Scott kissed the top of her head.

"You really had me goin', babe," he admitted ruefully. "I was ready to fly you out to the Mayo Clinic. All I can say is, it was the best damn surprise I've had in a very long time."

Climbing wearily into bed a while later, Scott pulled her to him, kissed her and held her tight. "You get some sleep, babe, and remember I love you." She slept all night, barely moving from his side.

Waking with the morning's first light, Scott lay gazing at the miracle in his arms. Quietly, with all the impact of a butterfly landing on a gossamer thread of milkweed fluff, he set a hand upon her belly, then brought his lips hovering to within mere millimeters from the surface of her skin. Her unconscious self was awake to him, however; she stirred, then opened her eyes to find his. She closed her eyes again and relaxed into a smile of absolute contentment. "You *are* happy about this, aren't you," she murmured.

"You know what? I'm thinking I can't wait till you're showing," he said sweetly, trailing a forefinger along the perimeter of her stomach. "I just can't wait to show you off – you'll be even more beautiful then you are now, which seems utterly impossible, but you will be. What do you think? Do I sound happy or what?"

Jenna grinned sleepily. "Just give a girl a kiss. That's all I want." He complied. The kiss, however, took on a life of its own, a life as vibrant as the seed of life in her womb. They made love making until they heard the rest of the household stirring.

JENNA TRIED TO join in with the breakfast making and socializing, but had to retreat to the deck for fresh air almost immediately. Linda and Joe were coming up the path from the lake shore. Jenna waved. Linda continued on up to join her as Joe took the path through a stand of brilliant red maples to the garage beyond.

"Honey, how come you're out here when everyone else is inside?"

"Couldn't take the smells," Jenna said with a grimace.

"It won't last forever, honey. God, I wish I could make it better for you, but it should stop soon."

"I know I just wish it didn't have to start this weekend, of all times. I feel so bad that I can't join in or help. It's the last weekend everyone's gonna have up here this summer, and I have to go and spoil it."

Carrie, standing just inside the screen door, overheard Jenna's words. Gathering up Laurel and Denise, the three quickly came out.

"Excuse, me, Jenn," Carrie said sternly, "but having appointed myself chairman of the Jenna Bradford Intervention Committee, I know I speak for all us 'mothas' when I assure you that you haven't spoiled anything for anybody – you've *made* our weekend, you dodo." She gave Jenna a warm, sisterly hug.

"God, Jenna," Laurel jumped in. "We know what you're going through. Don't feel bad! Enjoy what you can and you'll get through the rest."

"And ditto from me," Denise said. "And we expect you to let us help you any way we can, sweetie. Lean on us. We all leaned on others. That's what women do."

"I have to tell you all, you've just made *my* day," Linda said with sincerity. "I can go back to California knowing Jenna's in good hands. Bless you all for being her friends."

"Beat you to the fuckin' lake," shouted Travis, bursting through the screen door in a bathing suit with Aiden only a few steps behind him.

"Like hell you will, dipshit," Aiden hollered.

"Language!" Carrie and Denise yelled in unison.

"I have no doubt that the very first word out of Luka's mouth, I'm gonna be hollerin' the same thing," Laurel said.

"Jenn, honey, you're gonna just love motherhood," Carrie laughed.

SUNDAY AFTERNOON WARMED up to a perfect crystal clear, breezy seventy-five degrees, a day to treasure any time of year, but of particularly poignancy in the pivot month of October.

Everyone was out, some on the local golf course, others taking boats to explore the far reaches of Lake Sunapee in pursuit of elusive trout, bass and perch. Joe was paddling Luka and Linda in a canoe.

The less ambitious just lazed in the brilliant sun or played in the water, down at the lake's edge. Aiden and Travis were relentless in trying to recruit competitors in what they were billing as The First Annual Columbus Day Blacklace Invitational Diving Championships. Dan signed on when they gave in and added a Cannonball Division.

Scott, Jenna and Kristin were about to head down to join the group at the shore as they heard a car pull into the graveled parking area out front. "That's gotta be Ryan," Scott said, heading for the door. Jenna noticed Kristin give a quick glance at herself in the hallway mirror and make some minor adjustments to her hair.

"Yo, man, come on in," Scott said heartily. "Glad you could make it."

Ryan stepped inside awkwardly, holding a small duffle in one hand and a bunch of daisies clutched in the other. "Um, hi. These are for you," he said to Jenna, who'd joined Scott at the door. "I really want to thank you for inviting me."

"Thank you, Ryan – that's so sweet!" Jenna said, smiling broadly. "I'll go put these in water. Um, Scott, could you help me with something in the kitchen?"

"Be right back, man. You know Kristin, right?" Scott said as he turned to follow Jenna down the hall.

"Oh, yeah, sure," Ryan said, practically blushing. "We've met a couple times. How're you doin', Kristin?"

"Okay. You found the place okay?" Kristin said. Normally comfortable in social situations, there was something about Ryan she found disconcerting, something about him that threw her off her game. "Well, of course you did – you're here, duh." She stopped, giggled, hated herself for it, then pulled herself together and said, "I gotta tell you, Ryan, I'm really glad you're here. There's nobody else our age."

Ryan smiled shyly. "Good," he said, looking at the toe of his boot.

Out in the kitchen, Jenna was laughing as quietly as she could. "Trying our hand at a little matchmaking, are we?" she whispered to Scott, who was reaching to the top shelf of a cupboard for a vase for her. He turned around and smirked. Jenna laughed out loud.

"You should see your face. You crack me up. You could be the poster child for kids caught with their hands in cookie jars."

"Who, me? You think I'd go and do something like that?"

Kristin put her head in the kitchen door. "I'm gonna give Ryan the tour. We'll see you down at the beach after a while." She was grinning ear to ear.

"We'll be out in the Chris Craft, as soon as Dan and Jill get back with it. Feel free to grab a boat and play if you guys want."

"We will," Kristin said, throwing a wink to Jenna.

OUT IN THE middle of the lake, Scott cut the motor and tossed the anchor overboard. Pulling his shirt off, he dove over the transom where "Blacklace Bad Buoy," the 1956 vintage runabout's contemporary name, had been rendered in black and silver, matching the distinctive script lettering style of the band's logo.

"Weee-ooo! Come on in!" he yelled, laughing, as he surfaced alongside the boat and shook his shaggy head of hair like a water dog. "It's cold but, man, it's great!"

Jenna didn't need a second invitation. Pulling off her shoes, she dove fully dressed into the lake, coming up within arm's reach of Scott. "Oh! Oh, my!" she burbled. "Oh, God, it's cold. Oh my God, I love you!" She gave him a very fast kiss, laughing and already shivering. "Meet you at the beach," she gasped. "I'm swimming! I'll freeze to death if I don't!" Jenna took off back across the water towards the distant raft and dock by the most direct route possible.

Scott clambered back into the boat and was waiting for Jenna on the boat house dock with a huge, fluffy towel to wrap her up in. Laying out on a lounge chair on the beach, Jenna let the sun dry her clothes and restore her body temperature to something a lot more like normal, and before long, the warmth of the sun and the indolence of the holiday weekend afternoon conspired to lull her into a deep and restorative sleep. Scott got up and with a finger to his lips to the others, left her in the company of the ladies while he and several of the guys invested a couple of hours in playing pool and listening to music in the big basement playroom of the old house.

DINNER THAT EVENING was a bittersweet affair, as it always was this time of year, marking as it did the last official night of the summer season. As everyone gathered, Scott tapped his glass, pushed back in his chair and addressed them all.

"Before we dig in, I just want to say that I'm as glad as ever that we've all been able to get together again this year, all us old-timers. And the family's gained a few very welcome new additions this year. *And*, if all goes well we'll have another new addition next year, too. Thank you for all for making this an especially great weekend, particularly for Jenna. Now, time to chow down!"

After dinner, everyone either helped do dishes or found themselves milling about restlessly, trying to decide what to do with this last night. The evening had held the afternoon's warmth, so Dan and Tim went down to the beach and built a bonfire in the fire pit which was visible from above in the main house, throwing an eerie backlight on the intervening pines. Before long, the sound system in the boathouse was cranked up and everyone was down there, casting long, wild shadows dancing across the white sand of the shore.

Couples formed and reformed as the entire group danced one with another in what might sonstitute a dancing master's fevered nightmare, a drawing room's formal figures transformed into hysterical, writhing chaos, to music of their own creation.

Scott danced with every woman there, but when he returned to Jenna, he reached for her, encircled her, ran his hands up and down and around every inch of her, then pulled her close and reprised every bit of the sensual ecstasy of their first night performing on a stage together, which tonight seemed very long ago indeed. The world fell away and it was just the two of them, gyrating up through myriad levels of physical passion, just as Jenna's beautiful secret had carried them to far higher realms of love this wonderful weekend. If it weren't for the sight of Jenna's mother and his father dancing nearby, he might have taken her right then and there. He had to chuckle to himself at the sobering realization that perhaps, after all these licentious years, there *were* limits to what he had always liked to think of as his absolute lack of inhibition. He groaned at the thought.

Out of the corner of her eye, Jenna glimpsed a vision of Kristin and Ryan groping through the darkness to find their way into each other's hearts, just as she and Scott had once found each other. Both danced with their hands to their sides, their not touching a conscious choice, perhaps more arousing even than if they had. She saw Kristin reach up as she danced before him to gently push the hair out of Ryan's face. Her fingers trailed down his cheek to trace the line of his sensitive full lips, then she ran her hand through his long hair and on down his chest. The sight was mesmerizing.

Scott looked across through the darkness to see his father twirl Linda out from him and back into his arms, push her away and pull her back, again and again, and there was no question in Scott's mind that Linda was loving every minute of it. Each time, Joe pulled her closer until he finally folded her in his arms. Scott had no trouble imagining what happened next: ignoring the wanton beat of Blacklace, his father had clearly begun humming a ballad in Linda's ear. They started moving to Joe's beat, not the one echoing through the night across Lake Sunapee. He slow-danced Linda across the sand the way a woman this fine ought to be handled, Joe would be thinking to himself. Both Joe and Linda's eyes were closed. Both wore matching beatific smiles on their faces.

Scott looked down at Jenna just as her eyes rose to his. Their lips met in a kiss that spoke of love and pain, despair and hope, and life. Of a love that was beyond beautiful.

TO BE CONTINUED….